The Line Between

Enemies with Benefits
Book 1

Love, Fey

Dedication

To all the book girlies out there who want a Demon
Daddy. Case can get the job done. 😊

To all readers interested in an enemies-with-benefits
story. I got the idea for *The Line Between* because I
wanted to create a story with *true* enemies who end up
having sex. And lots of it. But they stay enemies.
Paisley and Case had their own ideas, as strong,
stubborn, independent characters tend to do. I can't get
enough of them and their story, and I hope you won't
be able to get enough, either.

Content Warning

The Line Between is a paranormal/monster/demon erotic romance. All of the sex scenes involve a demon (male main character) and a vampire-fairy hybrid (female main character), and those scenes are with the door thrown happily wide open on these two. (You're welcome.) There are detailed descriptions of all the acts involved. (You're welcome again.)

Below is a more thorough list of what you will encounter between the pages of this novel. Keep in mind that these are the main content warnings and may not cover smaller warnings that are specific from reader-to-reader. Take care, dear reader.

Explicit Language
Graphic Sexual Content
Alcohol Consumption
Masturbation (MMC)
Dry Humping
Fellatio
Cunnilingus
Vaginal Sex
Anal Sex
Spanking
Bullet Wounds
Blood
Vampire Feeding (blood bag and body)
Self-Harm (past, discussed)
Molotov Cocktail

Burn Injury
Menstrual Cup
Oral Sex During Period
Kidnapping of FMC (not done by MMC)
Torture of FMC (not done by MMC)
Characters are Unalived (not main characters)

If these are okay with you, please proceed.

Happy reading!

1

Long Live the Queen

Paisley

uck all of them.

Sitting on a throne, wearing a purple satin and black lace gown, Paisley peered out at a sea of creatures—vampires, fairies, elves, centaurs, demons, and more. Lined up in front of her were the eleven faction leaders who ruled over those creatures. In a matter of moments, Paisley would be joining their ranks as the vampyre-faye queen. A dual throne. The first in history.

She didn't have to hear their opinions on the matter. Most of them thought it would rip the threads of the Enchanted Hierarchy apart. One ruler for the vampires *and* the fairies? Unheard of! But she was the heir to both, whether they liked it or not. And she didn't give a damn if they thought she didn't deserve it. She didn't give a damn if they objected. They'd objected to her existence her whole life.

As the first-ever hybrid, she'd experienced it all— bullying, harassment, stalking, threats. She was no stranger to being an outsider, even among her own kind. Being half-vampire, half-fairy, she claimed some of the traits and weaknesses of both. Even her wings were different. They weren't large, leather-like wings of a vampire or the dainty, shimmering wings of a fairy. Her wings—currently tucked into her body—were a blend of the two and a clear sign that she wasn't one or the other. She was a mixed-breed freak, as she'd heard whispered from the mouths of all creatures in the Enchanted Hierarchy, like the ones before her now.

Zara May, the head of the Enchanted Hierarchy Cabinet, stood to her left, reciting all the necessary statements that needed to be said during a faction leader's coronation.

Paisley wasn't paying attention, though, because this wasn't how Paisley had ever wanted to become queen. Not on the heels of her parents' murders, not without their guidance, not so soon, and not alone.

She glanced at the fairy lingering off to the side, holding a black velvet cushion with a crown atop. No, she wasn't entirely alone, and for that she'd forever be thankful. Aster was Paisley's best friend and lady-in-waiting, and she was giving Paisley an encouraging smile. Her periwinkle blue wings were fluttering on her back with excitement, her sparkling lavender eyes shone beneath the glowing lights, and her violet hair flowed down her back. Aster would make a lovely faye queen, but she wasn't the heir to Queen Primrose.

Paisley was.

Her gaze shifted to a tall, muscular vampire with red wavy hair—Uncle Silas. Her dad and her uncle hadn't actually been related. Not many vampires were, but they had been best friends as mortals and were turned together by the vampire king. Centuries of brotherhood later, someone had killed the vampire king and her father occupied the throne as his successor. Uncle Silas would've been next in line before her dad fell in love with a certain fairy and had a daughter. Two weeks ago, her dad had officially named Paisley as the one who'd take the throne in his place. Now he was dead. Anyone who didn't agree with his decision was suspect.

Even though he wasn't next in line, Uncle Silas was nodding, encouraging her as well. He would be a strong ruler for the vampires, but he wasn't King Evanger's heir.

Paisley was.

Beside Uncle Silas stood Phoenix, who grinned and gave Paisley a thumbs-up. She was the heir to the Fier faction, and unlike Queen Enya, Phoenix's mother, she actually liked Paisley. Also unlike her mother, Phoenix was in her human form, not her dragon shifter form. Her dark auburn hair was piled atop her head, and she wore a red dress that showed off sun-kissed skin.

Just behind Phoenix, Paisley met the eye of Jude Ironwood, the Centaur King and her godfather. He'd been best friends with her father and had always doted on Paisley. Now, he was smiling as if he were a proud father.

Her chest tightened. She hoped to make him proud. She hoped to honor the memory of her parents, because it was all up to her. The fate of two factions was her responsibility now.

Aster stepped forward, and Zara picked up the sterling silver crown embedded with diamonds and pearls. The crown had belonged to Paisley's mother.

Zara stepped to the side of Paisley's throne. "Enchanted Hierarchy, I hereby present unto you, Paisley Nightingale, the undoubted queen of the vampyre and faye factions." She lowered the crown slowly while enunciating, "Long. Live. The. Queen."

The crown settled atop Paisley's head, and a smirk tugged her lips. While everyone uttered the words back, she had one thought. *Look at the mixed-breed freak now*.

As she eyed her peers, her gaze connected with a pair of golden eyes. Those eyes belonged to a gray demon with thick, white horns that curled behind his head. Dark, silver hair skimmed vast shoulders. He wore a maroon suit complete with a tie that matched the color of his hair. That suit appeared stitched onto his body, and he looked damn good.

The demon was Lord Case, her enemy.

She'd heard about Lord Case. He was rumored to be sexy and insatiable. She'd never met him before, but she could confirm the sexy part. No one, not even her, could deny that rumor. His face was chiseled, his body packed with muscles, his legs long, and his shoulders wide.

As for the insatiable part, the way he was staring— holy shit. His stare was pure heat, and it ignited her in a way that no single look had ever done before. She resisted the urge to squirm on her throne from the blatant desire zeroing in on her from his golden stare. Still, she met his eye steadily.

Beneath his suit jacket, his chest expanded.

Along his jaw, his muscles popped.

She didn't break eye contact.

Suddenly, Case about-faced and parted the crowd as he left.

A demon with violet skin and large buffalo horns followed close behind.

She arched a brow. *What in the world was that about*? She supposed she shouldn't be surprised by his quick departure. The vamprye and daemon factions were eternal rivals. Her coronation meant a new problem for Lord Case, especially following the murders of her parents. She'd find out who was responsible for that, and it it was him, he'd pay for it. With war.

Zara announced it was time to pay homage to the new queen. Hoping her nerves were disguised by a blank mask, Paisley stood. One by one she endured high-profile vampires and fairies in attendance kissing her right hand, pledging allegiance to her in front of the other faction leaders. She held herself stiff to keep at bay the cringe that wanted to take over her face and body with each press of strange lips to her hand. After the final kiss, she stole away to scrub her hand and compose herself. She didn't have long before Aster slipped into the lavatory.

"Paisley, the American President would like a quick word with you."

"Of course." She checked that her mother's crown was straight before stepping into the hall. The American President, the only human representative among a room full of paranormal creatures, wore a stylish pink pantsuit, and she waited for Paisley.

"Madam President." Paisley bowed her head out of respect.

President Summerfield returned the gesture. "Queen Paisley. I am deeply sorry about your parents."

"Thank you."

"Are there any leads?"

Aside from the fact that dragon fire had reduced her father to ashes?

"None."

"I'm sorry to hear that."

"Me, too. How can I help you, President Summerfield?"

"Your father was a remarkable man and king. Every president before me only had wonderful things to say about him."

Paisley nodded. Many had admired her father.

"The vampires followed his rule because of the exemplary king he was. I assume you will keep the vampires in line."

Paisley smiled.

In line?

Made them sound like a pack of dogs that Paisley had on leashes. Her smile didn't falter, even as she desperately wanted to sneer at the president, giving the politician a little flash of Paisley's fangs. She didn't doubt that President Summerfield thought she had Paisley "in line."

"I will follow my father's footsteps and keep the vampires in line. You have my word."

"That's good to hear. My condolences and best wishes. Long may you reign."

Paisley bowed her head again. *Oh, I'll reign, and I'll reign long.*

No amount of bullying, harassment, stalking, or threats would stop her.

Once the final guest left, she slipped out of her gown and dressed in a royal blue corset with shimmering peacock feathers, a mini velvet skater skirt, and over-the-knee suede boots with chunky heels. At least in this, she could feel a little normal.

Aster joined her outside, and the two of them strolled back to Paisley's home, the house her parents had built for their life together. The two-story building, understated for royalty but exactly what her parents had wanted, was tucked into the woods that separated their factions. To one side wild gardens grew around cottages—the faye faction. To the other side, homes sat on cobblestone, surrounded by iron gates—the vampyre faction. She'd always lived smackdab between them, never fully welcomed in one or the other. And now she ruled over both.

Paisley held her garment bag and stared at the ground. Atop her head, her mother's crown still sat, feeling oddly heavy. She didn't say anything as they walked. There wasn't anything to say. Someone had murdered her parents a week ago. The culprits were still out there. She wasn't naïve to think that she wasn't their next target. Maybe she'd been the goal all along. After all, she was the hybrid who shouldn't exist, and now she had two factions at her disposal. Their killers had inadvertently made her the most powerful being in the Enchanted Hierarchy.

Not too smart.

She followed the tree-lined path toward her home.

Aster jolted to a stop with a gasp.

Paisley glanced up to see a mountain of dead bats on her front lawn. "What. The. Fuck." She dropped the garment bag and marched up to the horrid display. A ring of blood soaked the ground around the towering pile of slaughtered nocturnal creatures.

They hadn't just been killed; they'd been beheaded.

Off with her head?

It was a clear threat to her life.

"Paisley. Come here. Quick."

She found Aster on the other side of the dead bats, pointing at arched horns burned into the grass—the daemon faction's brand. Was that why Lord Case had left her coronation so abruptly? He had a plan to execute? A threat to deliver? Well, the demons had another thing coming if they thought she was a pushover just because she was half fairy.

She removed the crown from her head and passed it to Aster. "I want you to go inside and lock the door."

Aster's wings shivered. "What are you going to do?"

Paisley plucked the bobby pins from her hair and discarded them into the grass without a thought. "I'm going to properly introduce myself to Lord Case." She picked up a bat from the bottom of the pile. "And make a few things perfectly clear to him."

"You can't go there by yourself. It's not safe."

"I'm not putting you in danger or telling anyone about this. Stay here." She glanced around. Once she was sure no one was there to see, her wings popped out of her back. With strong beats, she lifted into the air.

"Paisley!"

She ignored Aster's shout and flew toward the castle, passed down from demon lord to demon lord. The sight of the towers and tiers sent her teeth on edge.

Lord Case was in for a rude awakening.

2

Little Bat Diva

Case

ase had to get the hell away from the coronation, otherwise everyone would've seen his boner big enough to hold up that crown on Paisley's head. Diablo, she was gorgeous. He'd never seen her in person and hadn't been prepared for the stunning creature she was. Her parents had kept her under lock and key for safety reasons. At least, they hadn't allowed her near the other factions, but Case wondered if her father had hidden her away to keep horny demons like him from coming anywhere near his beautiful daughter.

Paisley's purple-black hair intrigued him. Her glittering black irises, thanks to her fairy blood, lured him in. Her pale skin made his mouth water. She was a treat that he wanted to taste. Every inch. The spot beneath her ear. The nape of her neck. The inside of her wrists. The crease of her elbows. And what he couldn't see because the purple and black dress hid them—the crevice between her breasts, the smooth skin of her stomach, the flesh of her thighs…her pussy.

Diablo, he shouldn't have thought of that.

His cock thickened as he flew. The swiftness of it had him wobbling in the air. He touched down quickly in front of his door.

Thatch, his right hand, landed beside him.

Case led the way inside to the parlor. He plucked off the crystal topper to a decanter of whiskey and poured himself two generous fingers.

"Are you okay?"

"Why wouldn't I be?"

"Well, to state the obvious, you have a boner the size of a redwood, and we left the coronation earlier than would've been acceptable."

"I had to leave because of said redwood boner."

"And you got it because…?"

Case knocked back whiskey and faced his best friend. "Did you not see that delicious hybrid of a woman sitting in that throne?"

"I did. I wouldn't call her delicious, but I did."

Case lifted a fresh glass of whiskey to his lips and muttered, "I would."

"So, you full saluted the moment she was crowned."

Case smirked. Thatch was averse to cursing, but the visual was spot on. "I certainly did."

Thatch lifted a brow. "Why?"

"The hell if I know. She looked right at me once that crown was in place, and it was like a jolt of lust through my system. If I could've managed it, I would've eye-fucked her right there." He left the parlor. Link, a young demon with long horns, waited near the door for an order. "Get the council here. Now. We have something to discuss."

"Are you going to discuss your hard-on for the vampyre-faye queen, too?"

Case sent a glare in Thatch's direction. "Stop talking about it. It can hear us, and it's excited with all this talk. At this rate, it'll never go down." He shoved open the door to the conference room and sat at the head of the table. Thatch filled the seat to his right.

His council showed up immediately and filed into the room. Discussion got underway immediately for the issue at hand—Paisley.

"What kind of trouble could one little girl be?" one of his men asked.

"She's not a little girl anymore," Case said while studying his empty glass. "She's a woman, and I wouldn't underestimate her."

"I agree," Thatch said. "She was raised by leaders of two vastly different factions. She received the kind of training and insight her whole life that none of us did."

"Certainly not me." Case had been tossed aside from birth and raised in an orphanage. He hadn't gotten the advice from parents in preparation for the day he'd rule. He became demon lord the hard way—a bunch of dead demons who'd opposed him, lying in blood, and all the rest of the demons kneeling in that blood, vowing their allegiance.

"Girl, woman…she's half-vampire, half-fairy. Who can take that seriously?"

Case's gaze cut over to the demon to his left. "I used to think the same thing. Our greatest enemy and the fruitiest creature in our hierarchy came together and procreated? Fucking repulsive." His council, all except for Thatch, roared with laughter. "But." They fell silent. "What I saw today…there's a strength there that we shouldn't underestimate. We definitely shouldn't underestimate the fact that I want to fuck her in every imaginable way."

"That could create a problem," Wren said.

Wren was one of his most loyal friends and warriors, an ice demon he'd known since Wren was a tiny squawk who hadn't yet mastered how to conjure snow. Now, he was a tall, slender demon with white-blue skin and silver hair. And he was wise beyond his years, with a grace earned through hardship.

Case nodded. "But a potentially fun one. I'd give anything for her to burst through that door and offer herself to me."

Right then, the door opened, and Paisley stomped in wearing the sexiest over-the-knee boots, the shortest velvet skirt, and a corset of peacock feathers that showed off her bare shoulders. The sight of her made him jerk.

Her hair was down. All that purple-blackness to sink his fingers into.

Thatch leaned forward. "Quick. Make another wish."

Case glared at him before turning to Paisley as she stopped before the table directly across from him. "What are you doing here," he asked. "And what did you do to my apprentice?"

"Him?" She jabbed a thumb at Link, standing behind her. "I hypnotized him." She snapped her fingers in front of his face.

The young demon shook himself and peered around, startled. "I'm sorry, sire. She caught me by surprise."

Paisley snorted. "Sire? You make them call you 'sire'?"

"I don't make them do anything." He rose to his feet. "I'll ask again. What are you doing here, unwelcomed, unannounced, with the nerve to hypnotize my apprentice?"

"I'm unwelcomed, really? Didn't you just say you'd give anything for me to burst through that door?"

"You heard that?"

"I did. You all talk really loudly. I even heard the part where you think I'm repulsive. Fairies think demons are disgusting, so the feeling is mutual."

Feisty. He could say that she'd missed the part when he said he'd *used* to think that, but the way she was glaring was turning him on.

Case smirked. "What are you doing here, Paisley?"

"Where'd you go during my coronation?"

"Did I hurt your feelings when I left early?"

"Hardly. You made me suspicious."

"This is you being suspicious?"

14

"This is me grieving and being pissed off."

That one word—grieving—put things into perspective. She'd just lost her parents. He may not have had any, but that didn't mean he couldn't recognize the pain that'd cause.

"I'm sorry about your parents' deaths. You have my condolences."

"Fuck your condolences," she spat. "They didn't die. They were *murdered*. A *demon* slaughtered my mother and then burned my father alive. Was it you? Or did you order another demon to do it for you?" She tossed a dead bat onto the table. It slid across the surface and halted right at his place.

He peered at it.

"After the coronation, I found over a thousand beheaded bats on my front lawn, next to *your* brand burned into the grass. I don't take kindly to innocent bats being killed in an attempt to threaten me."

His gaze lifted.

"And after the murder of my parents, that display solidified what I planned to do regardless. You want a war with the vampyre and faye factions? Well, congratulations, because you fucking got one."

The other demons around the table shoved back their chairs.

He lifted a hand, staying them.

Showing a fearlessness that he had to admire, she eyed each member of his council one at a time. "Don't think that because I look cute that I'm weak. I haven't lived this long without killing my fair share of enemies." Her glare landed on him. "Demons included."

The demons around the table growled, but she didn't take her gaze off him. He had two reactions to that. One, it excited him. She had a fierceness that he hadn't encountered before. Two, it called to his anger. Threats didn't sit well with him. Not even when issued from a pretty set of lips in the most curious shade of purple.

He didn't shift his stare away when he said, "Everyone. Out."

Two words, and his council scattered, leaving them alone in the vast room.

He stalked toward her and enjoyed the fact that she didn't shrink or shift or step back so much as an inch. "I didn't kill your parents."

"Fucking liar."

His hands balled into fists. His chest heaved. "I. Did. Not. Kill. Your. Parents. It would've been stupid of me to do so. One being in charge of two factions? Giving my greatest enemy more numbers? Don't you see how dumb that would've been? As it is, I have no interest in the fairies, and vampires, while an enemy, I prefer to ignore. And killing thousands of innocent bats certainly doesn't benefit me in anyway."

"Well, if you didn't, then someone in your faction did, and to me, that's the same fucking thing. A demon declared war, and I'm answering. I don't give a damn if you weren't behind it. What kind of leader can't keep his minions in line? Not a very good one, I'll tell you that."

He stopped in front of her.

Paisley was tall, taking the vampire's height gene rather than the petite fairy form. With her four-inch heels, that brought her to about six-foot-two, but he still towered over her by a good six inches. So, when she tipped her head back to glare at him, he was awarded with the view of her long neck. He had to resist the urge to trace his thumb down her throat.

He clenched his hand to stay it from doing just that. And to help contain his anger. "I'll tell *you* something," he growled. "My *minions*, as you call them, would never do anything without my permission. We're not behind your parents' murders. Don't believe it if you must, but someone is framing me and my faction. I will find out who, and when I do, I expect an apology from that pretty mouth of yours."

"Dream on."

"I think I will." His gaze settled on her mouth. "What color is that anyway?"

She shook her head. "What?"

"Your lipstick. What color is it?"

"It's a matte plum, and why do you care?"

"It's a fascinating color, and I like watching your lips move, even while you're threatening me with war."

"Seriously? I just lost my parents and now I'm facing a death threat. My lips moving, while declaring war, is not for your sick enjoyment. You're never going to get an apology from me, no matter what color my lipstick is. Someone is framing you? I'll believe that when I see it, but you're not getting anything from me."

"You so sure about that?"

"Yes," she hissed. "My parents were murdered and demons are a part of it in some way. *You* are responsible."

"How do you figure?"

"If you *are* being framed, there's a chance that my parents would still be alive, but *you* did something to make their killer want to do that. *You* made them plot. *You* pushed them. *You* angered someone enough to commit murder. But instead of killing you outright, which I would've preferred, they decided that they wanted me and the factions I would unite more than ever before to do it for them, and I am fucking tempted."

"Relax," he ordered.

"Don't tell me to relax! You don't know what I've been through."

Burgundy rings appeared around her sparkling, black irises.

"What's happening with your eyes?"

As he peered into them, her pupils gradually transitioned from black to red.

Then she bared her teeth and hissed the legendary "you're dead" vampire hiss.

"Paisley—"

Mouth wide, she hissed again. Then her hand lashed out and clamped around his throat. "For my mother. For my father. For *me*. I'll kill you, your entire council, whoever framed you, and whatever demons come after me."

He grabbed her shoulders with a steely vise. "Calm. Down."

"Fuck you."

His grip tightened, and he bore down on her. In response, her fingers dug into his neck, threatening to pierce him. "You're talking about wanting to kill me and my faction in my own home, with my council right outside. You're making a big mistake. Calm down or you'll regret it. Look into my eyes."

He could feel her resisting him, but she met his eye. "There you go. Breathe."

She was seething, but her breathing slowed and her hand loosened.

"That's it." He peered at her graceful neck and the thin chain that adorned it. "Is that a paisley necklace?"

"What?" He heard the confusion in her voice. Even when her voice came out softly.

"Your necklace. Is that a paisley symbol?" It was gold and diamond encrusted, and it rested against her chest.

"Yes, it was a gift from my mother."

His gaze lowered even more. One of his hands left her shoulder, and he swept a finger across the feathers on the top of her corset.

"Don't touch me." She lowered her hand from his neck to slap his fingers.

"I wasn't touching you. I was touching feathers." He tilted his head. "Is that a tattoo?"

The feathers hid a rose tattoo. The stem emerged from the crevice between her breasts and followed the curve of her right breast with green leaves. At the top of the swell was a crimson bloom. Four loose petals floated up toward her right shoulder.

How far down did that stem go? He wanted to find out.

"You have a short attention span."

He laughed. "Yeah, and my short attention span snapped you out of your vampire fight mode."

"Whatever the purpose of this conversation is, whether distraction or something else, it's not going to help you. I can hold a grudge like no other, and I'm never going to forget that you may be the reason why I don't have a family. If one more thing happens that points at you, I will take action, and you don't wanna fuck with a fairy who has vampire blood coursing through her veins."

"What if I *wanna* fuck a fairy who has vampire blood coursing through her veins?"

"I said 'fuck *with*.'"

"Well, I say 'fuck.'" His voice rumbled as his gaze feasted on her.

When she inhaled, he knew instantly that she was tempted by his claim. Her lips parted, and damn. She shouldn't have done that. She shouldn't have reacted at all because it was clear she wanted him, no matter how much she'd try to hide it.

"There's something wrong with you. I'm beginning to see why someone would want to frame you or flat-out want to kill you." She spun on her heel and stormed toward the door. "You've been warned."

He watched her leave. The sound of her heels on the tile, the way her skirt swished back and forth with the movement of her hips…Diablo. He wanted his head beneath that skirt. He wanted those thighs to clamp around his skull.

Lust aside, her words came back, and with it a flash of anger.

"Did the little bat diva just say I've been warned?"

He laughed.

Well, he just may have to test out exactly what she'd do when pushed.

Because he intended to push.

3

Thigh Holsters

Paisley

*a*ster rushed over as soon as Paisley entered her home. "What happened? Are you okay? Tell me everything."

"I'm fine. Their leader, Case, is a real piece of work, though."

"What did you expect? He's a demon."

"I didn't expect him to say he wants to fuck me."

Aster gasped. Both from the word choice and from the statement. "He did not."

"He did."

She'd keep to herself how that idea had intrigued her pussy. *That's what I get for not getting laid in a long time. My pussy is desperate enough to accept an offer from a demon.* She'd have to remedy that, and fast.

"But why would he say that?" Aster asked.

"Because he's a man." Paisley headed for a curio cabinet and opened the doors to an array of weapons. She strapped a thigh holster around her legs and shoved daggers into them. "You need to arm yourself, too."

"Me? I can't."

"Yes, you can." Paisley caught Aster's hand and tugged her closer. "I'm not letting anyone kill my bestie. You need a weapon. Choose."

With a sigh, Aster picked up a blow dart and a bag of sharp spikes, a typical fairy weapon, but it was better than nothing. Paisley selected a belt, looped it around Aster's waist, and tied the bag to it. Then she slipped the blow dart beneath the strap of leather. "Keep these with you at all times."

Aster nodded. "I will."

A knock had them turning toward the door. Fingers around the hilt of a dagger, Paisley indicated for Aster to stay back.

In response, Aster removed the blow dart, poured spikes into her hand, and nodded.

Paisley yanked the door open.

Case stood there, leaning against the doorframe, hands in his pockets. His golden eyes were burning with clear anger. "I've been warned?"

She tugged free the dagger, twirled it in her hand, and shoved it beneath his chin. The sharp point dug into

23

his skin, and the flat side of the blade pressed into his Adam's apple. "Yes," she spat. "You've been fucking warned."

He didn't flinch but continued to lean his shoulder into the doorframe. He didn't even remove his hands from his pockets to lift them in surrender. "Easy, Pais." The glow of Case's eyes faded. "Now that I see what happened here, I want to help."

Pais? Her hand lowered a fraction. No one had ever called her that before, so why did she like it? "I don't need your help."

"You have a mountain of dead bats on your lawn. What do you plan to do with them?"

"I have people who can help me with that. I don't need you."

"I hope you don't intend to make that cute little thing shovel dead bats."

Paisley glanced over her shoulder at Aster, who stepped back, startled. "Leave her alone."

"She's safe. You? Not so much."

Paisley poked the tip of the blade to the underside of his chin. "Is that a threat?"

"A different kind of physical threat, and one you'd enjoy." For the first time since she'd opened the door, he moved and wrapped his hand around her wrist. "If you don't lower this dagger, I'll get physical in a less fun way." His fingers tightened when she didn't budge. "I came to help, because, as I said, I had nothing to do with this, despite what you think and the evidence against me. This isn't my style. If I want someone dead, I don't taunt. I don't play cat-and-mouse games. I let them know point blank, and I don't hesitate in killing them. You're lucky I don't want you dead, no matter how much you infuriate me. Now, put your dagger away."

Gritting her teeth, she inched the dagger from his chin before yanking her wrist free. She didn't holster it, though, but kept it gripped in her hand.

He swiped a finger under his chin. It came back streaked with blood. She caught the scent of it, and her hand became a white-knuckled fist around the hilt of the dagger. He licked the blood from his finger. *That* was meant to be a taunt at her vampire genes. The way he eyed her while he did it, and the curve of his smirk, told her as much. He couldn't know how much of a taunt, though, and she didn't intend to let him know.

"Do you need a bandage?" she leered.

"You wanna be my nurse?"

She clenched her jaw. She could heal the cut using her fairy magick, but the way her healing magick had twined with her vampire being was Mother Nature's sick way of toying with her, and she sure as hell wasn't going to do to him what would be required to heal that cut.

His smirk grew. "As I was saying, someone did this to point a finger at me, and that pisses me off. And because these bats are here because of me, I feel obligated to help." He indicated the front yard. "How did you plan to get rid of them?"

"I'll have them hauled to the back field and set aflame."

He nodded. "Probably the best course of action. Do you have a shovel?"

Sighing, she glanced back at Aster. "I'll be right back. Go to the balcony. If Case tries anything, take out his eyes."

Aster nodded and spun toward the stairs.

When Paisley faced Case, he was grinning. "If I try anything?" He leaned closer. "What if I touched you intimately?"

"That would count as anything." She flattened a hand to his chest and shoved, but he didn't budge.

He peered at her hand, flat against him. Beneath her palm, his chest rose as he inhaled deeply. His golden gaze pierced her. Then his hand grasped her jaw. "That wasn't a smart move if you don't want me to touch you." In the next second, his other arm came around her, and he tugged her to him, pelvis to pelvis.

Her eyes widened. Their foreheads were nearly touching.

A whistling sound zipped past her ears.

Just as quickly, Case released her. "What the hell?"

A thin cut in the bridge of his nose leaked blood.

He tilted his head to the side.

A metal spike stuck out of the wall.

They shifted toward the balcony and Aster as she lowered the blow dart from her lips.

"She shot a spike past our eyes."

"Yes, she did." Paisley rotated, pretending to close the door, but licked the tip of her finger at the same time. When she faced him again, she slicked a thin layer of saliva over the cut on his nose, healing it instantly. "That was a warning shot."

He touched his nose. "You healed me. How?"

"Fairy magick." And Mother Nature's twisted sense of humor. "Follow me." She led him to the back of the property where a gardening shed stood.

"Fuck," Case said.

She shot a look over her shoulder. "What?"

He was staring at her thighs. "You're even sexier with weapons."

She faced forward. "I didn't strap these on to be sexy."

"Still…paired with those boots and that skirt…you made your thighs even more inviting."

She swallowed. "Stop saying things like that."

"Why? Do you want my head between your thighs?"

Her pussy throbbed at his words. *Yes*, it shouted. *Yes! Fuck me with your tongue, with your mouth. Give me your saliva.*

She stopped at the shed, opened it. "Take whatever you need." When she turned, she found he'd braced his hands on either side of the doorway.

"Take whatever I need? Does that include you?"

She tugged the dagger from its holster and laid it against his thigh. Staring into his eyes, she dragged the dagger up to his crotch. He didn't tear his heated stare from her hard one.

"You won't want to do that," he said, all deep voiced.

"Yeah? And why not?"

"Because then you'd never know what's like to have my dick inside you."

A wet heat burst from her vaginal opening and streamed deliciously over her vulva.

Annoyed that her body was reacting to him, she twisted the blade, making a clear statement that she'd separate him of his dick without a second thought. "Back. Off."

He lowered his arms and stepped back.

She shifted out of his way. "There's gardening shovels, snow shovels, and a wheelbarrow."

He selected a snow shovel and laid it in a wheelbarrow. This time, she followed him to the front yard and watched the fabric of his pants stretch over *his* muscular thighs as he walked. She bit her bottom lip.

Beside the mountain of bats, he lowered the wheelbarrow handles.

"I'll change," she said. "And get a shovel to help."

He caught her arm, halting her. "No. You're going to keep that sexy little number on, and you're not going to lift a finger. I'm doing this." He released her arm and removed his maroon jacket, which he tossed toward the stone path, but she caught it.

"I'll hang it up inside," she said.

He drew the tie from the collar of his shirt, and she held out a hand for it. He didn't stop there, though. She stood in front of him as he pulled his shirt from the band of his pants and then worked his fingers down the buttons, undoing them one at a time.

Don't stare, don't stare, don't stare. Hell, she was staring. With each button he loosened, more of his chest became visible. His skin was smooth like gray marble, and damn his pecs and abs appeared to be carved in stone. He had so many abs that they disappeared beneath his belt and pants that perfectly hugged his hips.

"Like what you see?"

Yes.

Her gaze snapped to his.

He passed her his shirt. When she tried to take it, he held fast. "Be honest, Paisley. I've admitted that I like what I see." His lust raked over her. "I like it a lot. Do you like what you see?"

"Do I like the body of a demon I can't stand? Who I am restraining myself from hurting because he may be responsible for the murder of my parents? I'd be demented if I did."

"None of that has anything to do with attraction. You vex me, but you also drive me mad with desire. You're half-vampire, half-fairy, and I want to fuck you so bad that it's laughable."

"It *is* funny." She yanked his shirt from his hand and spun away. "So go ahead and laugh," she called over her shoulder.

Inside her house, after hanging up his shirt and jacket, she joined Aster on the balcony. They stood at the rail. Below, Case shoveled dead bats into the wheelbarrow.

"You know...for a demon...he's kinda hot," Aster said. "Except, hold the kinda."

Paisley nodded. "Thanks for that warning shot."

"You're welcome." Aster paused. "But I debated over whether or not to do it."

Paisley frowned. "Why?"

"Because I sensed something from you."

"What?"

"Desire."

Crap.

Paisley studied Case as he worked. "He's a demon." Still, she couldn't take her eyes off him no matter how much she tried. "He could have something to do with what happened to my parents. Even if he didn't do it himself, even if he didn't order it, they may be dead because of him. It'd be sick of me to bang the demon responsible for their murder."

"Not if he's innocent. He can't help what someone does out of revenge."

That was true. Still, Paisley couldn't justify having sex with a demon who claimed her very existence was repulsive.

"Keep an eye on him."

Aster nodded. "I will."

Paisley made herself scarce. She wrote correspondence to Zara, who needed to know about the threat on the heels of Paisley's crowning. The deaths of her parents had shaken the cabinet. Paisley taking dual thrones further shook it. Now, this threat jeopardized the entire cabinet. If she died, two factions would be without a leader because she didn't have an heir. Vampires and fairies would be thrown into upheaval and fall prey to their enemies, like the demons. So much was at stake.

She finished the correspondence and asked Aster to deliver it. Aster flew off immediately, and Paisley took her post on the balcony to keep an eye on Case.

Why the hell did he have to look so good while shoveling dead bats into a wheelbarrow?

The sky opened, and it poured, but Case didn't stop. He filled the wheelbarrow again and again. Seeing him soaked from head to foot, his hair dripping, his wet pants clinging to his legs, rain trickling down his horns, aroused her in a way that she didn't think possible. He was a demon, for Goddess' sake. The leader of the daemon faction. Possibly the reason she no longer had parents. She could not want him. But she did. And that pissed her off. She was pissed off at herself, and at him.

Gradually the rain became a trickle before stopping altogether. A quick spring shower.

When Aster returned, Paisley was itching for a fight. To keep herself from doing
something she'd regret, she hurried to the opposite side of the house from the shed. A target was nailed to a tree there. She worked out her aggression on that target by throwing the six daggers around her thighs at it, one after the other. Once all six daggers were impaling the target, she retrieved them and did it all over again. Gradually, the repetition relaxed her. She tugged a dagger free, aimed, and threw it. The tip of the blade struck the middle of the target. She wrapped her hand around the hilt of the next dagger.

A twig snapped.

She spun and sent the dagger flying.

Case jerked his head to the side as his hand came up and caught the dagger inches from his temple. He studied the blade. "Lose something?"

She marched up, snatched the dagger, and continued to the front yard.

"Was that supposed to be a demonstration of what you can do?"

"That was me venting my anger, and it was working, until you ruined it."

"Sorry."

She rolled her eyes. "You sound real sorry."

"I *am* sorry, but at the same time, you're sexy when you're mad."

She whirled and let the dagger soar, flipping hilt over blade.

He shifted to the side and caught the dagger from the air that would've hit him in the shoulder if he hadn't dodged it. "Do that again," he challenged.

Her fingers fluttered over the hilts of the remaining daggers around her right thigh.

His gaze lowered to the holster, watched her fingers.

She purposefully removed another dagger.

Without a word, she whipped around and marched back into her house. In her bedroom, she snatched up a pillow, buried her face in the purple satin, and screamed until she fell to her knees. She stayed in her room, clutching her pillow, battling rage and grief over the events of the past two weeks, rage aimed at her parents' killers, rage aimed at Case, and rage aimed at herself for the way Case had awakened her desires.

A knock on her door sometime later startled her.

"Case is at the front door for you," Aster said.

Sighing, Paisley climbed off the floor and opened the door.

Concern drifted over Aster's face. "Are you okay?"

Paisley didn't answer.

Case stood in the doorway, still shirtless. "I haven't started the bonfire yet, but I fin—"

He stopped and tilted his head to the side. "Your eyes are red, and not in a fun way."

She ignored him. From the coat closet, she retrieved his shirt, jacket, and tie. "Here." She held them out.

He didn't say anything as he accepted his clothes.

She laid a hand on the door. "Thank you for taking care of the bats. I'll light the fire." She attempted to close the door, but he halted it with his hand.

"I'll be back first thing tomorrow to fix the lawn."

"You don't—"

"I'll be back tomorrow. You can't keep that brand there. I'll fix it."

"Fine," she huffed.

He peered behind her. "Have a good evening, cutie pie."

Paisley peered over her shoulder to see Aster waving a small hand. She shut the door and gave Aster an amused smile. "He seems to like you."

Aster's cheeks flushed. "We talked while he was working. He's nice."

"Nice?"

"Yeah, nice. You may like him, too, if you gave him a chance."

Paisley scoffed. "Not in a million years."

4

Horny Son of a Bitch

Case

ase slipped on his shirt and jacket, left both unbuttoned, and stuffed the tie into his pocket. He flew home and met Thatch on the way to the kitchen.

"How'd it go?" Thatch asked.

"She held a dagger to my throat, my cock, and threw two daggers at my head."

"She *what*?"

Case retrieved a glass from a cabinet and filled it from the tap. He downed the water in a few gulps.

"She didn't give you anything to drink that entire time?"

"She didn't, no, but her sweet lady-in-waiting did. Aster. She gave me three glasses of water, as a matter of fact."

"Where was the queen?"

"Paisley disappeared. When I finished, sweet Aster fetched her, and she…she looked as though she'd been crying. It was oddly unsettling."

Thatch lifted a brow. "You were unsettled?"

"I was."

"You were unsettled that she might've been crying?"

"Apparently."

They stared at each other.

"Interesting," Thatch said.

"Very."

Thatch nodded slowly. "I suppose I'd be unsettled seeing a woman as fierce as Paisley cry, or looking as though she had been."

"It was oddly unsettling."

"We've established that."

"I'm going to shower." He set his empty glass on the counter. "And masturbate for the next hour."

"Are you serious?"

"I'm always serious when it comes to masturbating. You'd want to go blind, too, if you saw the thigh holsters paired with those boots and that skirt."

"Wait. Thigh holsters were involved?"

"One on each thigh."

"Shit. Take as long as you need."

In the shower, Case braced his left hand on the tiled wall while water beat down on his head. He wrapped his right hand around his dick. There was no need to coax it to a full erection. His cock was already there. It had been there before he climbed into the shower, before he stepped into his bedroom, before he reached the staircase. He'd been at full erection as soon as he passed through the kitchen entrance. Now, visualizing Paisley's pale thighs, those holsters with the daggers she'd threatened him with, that sexy velvet skirt, and those suede knee-high boots, he stroked his hand up and down his shaft.

With the warm water beneath his palm and the tightness of his fist, he could almost believe he was inside her. Almost. What was missing were her hips that he'd grip, her legs twined around him, her scent filling the air, her moans.

Diablo, he wanted to hear her moan from his cock filling her, pounding her, hitting her in just the right way. He worked his hand up and down his length faster.

From the moment Paisley had looked his way during her coronation, his desire stirred. She'd created something inside him that he'd never felt before, something that he couldn't explain but was undeniable. It wasn't as if he'd never had sex with an enemy before. He'd fucked many vampires. In fact, he'd had every creature in the Enchanted Hierarchy, but he'd never fucked a hybrid, because only one existed. Paisley. Now that he'd seen her face-to-face, he wanted to taste that forbidden fruit. Taste it, devour it, get sated off it.

He'd said the thought of vampires and fairies procreating was repulsive, and a part of him still believed that. Have sex all you want, but don't have children. Everyone knew it as an unspoken rule. But, damn, a vampire and a fairy fucking sure created a delectable treat of a spawn. Paisley was a feast for the eyes, and she'd be a feast for his hand, mouth, tongue, and cock, too. If only he could get close enough and knock down those walls.

A groan rumbled in his throat.

He'd accomplish it. He'd knock down those damn walls and show her how good sex with a demon could be. So good that she'd want him again and again. That was the goal. He wanted to be the one she came to for pleasure. All the pleasure. Anything and everything she could ever desire. Flashes of him going down on her, taking her from behind, railing her against the wall, and her riding him into a frenzy made his lust surge.

Forehead against the wet tile, his hand motion became frantic.

The fact that she was stubborn and tough and, yes, his enemy made him want her more. And how she hated him only encouraged him to go for it. To go hard.

His hand fucked his cock harder. He needed to come. He needed to come now. Faster.

Tighter. Harder. Stroke, stroke, stroke.

A groan rattled his vocal cords and grew louder.

Finally, Diablo, *finally* the exquisite sensation of his balls tensing. A surge of ecstasy right up his cock to his stomach. Then it erupted out of the head of his shaft like a geyser while his penis spasmed. The moment of ejaculation was sublime, and he roared as a stream of semen gushed forth. That rush of semen surged on and on, longer than he'd ever expelled from masturbating before. Damn, it was more than he'd spent with any single partner. It spurted out in bursts again and again. He didn't want it to end. When it did, he collapsed into the tile. Weak, heart racing, breathless, and amazed.

It was Paisley. All of that semen had collected for her. The orgasm that hadn't wanted to end was because of her. Who knew how much he'd have when he finally could sink his cock inside her sweet pussy? He badly wanted to know.

Satisfied, for now, and clean, he headed back downstairs to the parlor.

"How'd it go?" Thatch lounged on a couch, smirking.

Case poured himself a stiff drink. "Phenomenal, but the real thing would be better." He tossed back the whiskey.

"What are you doing, Case?"

"Hell if I know. All I know is I want her."

"It's not my business who you have sexual relations with, but it is my business if you're about to do something that could be a mistake."

"I'll deal with the mistake after I have her."

Even after masturbating a second time that evening, Case couldn't get Paisley out of his head. He yearned for her so deeply that his balls ached for a release despite the fact he'd purged his semen twice. His cock wanted her. Not his hand. *He* wanted her. Her flesh. Her heat. Her juices. He couldn't sleep because she was there, burdening his mind with her sexiness.

Downstairs he sought a bottle of whiskey to lull him to a sound sleep. He stepped into the parlor. The room was pitch dark. With a flick, he activated the light switch, and a golden glow filled the space, revealing five vampires in all black.

He growled. "You're trespassing."

"We don't care," a tall, burly vampire said.

Case eyed him. "You *should* care. I kill trespassers."

"We're here to tell you to stay away from our queen."

Case sneered. "That's not going to happen, and it's none of your business if I go near Paisley or not."

"She's our queen," another vampire spat. "It *is* our business." This vampire was young, like a damn puppy.

"She sent you here to tell me to stay away? I don't buy that. If she wants me to stay away, she can tell me that herself. She's a big girl."

A third vampire surged toward him. "Do not talk about our queen like that!"

Case's sneer became more menacing. "You don't like me calling your queen a big girl?

Okay. What if I call her a beautiful cunt that I want to fuck?"

All five vampires attacked.

He snatched the young pup-vamp by the throat and snapped his neck without effort. The vampire fell limp in his grasp. Case dropped him unceremoniously at his feet in time to duck as another flew at him. The vampire sailed over his head and crashed into the bar, shattering the glass shelves and bottles of spirits.

All that good alcohol. Wasted. Fucking assholes.

Case rammed his fist into a third vampire's sternum. Bone snapped and impaled the vampire in the heart. The vampire dropped to the floor.

The less tall and burly vampire came at him, fangs bared.

Case swung a fist into the bastard's face. A long, curved fang shot out of the vampire's mouth with a spurt of blood. An uppercut to the chin disconnected the vampire's skull from his spine.

Three down. Two remaining.

The vampire who'd smashed into the bar came back for more, drenched with alcohol and smelling of whiskey. Case caught the vampire, lifted him high, and then drove him onto a piece of wood that stuck up from the demolished bar. The wood pierced the vampire through the chest. Case left him impaled—back bowed, arms and legs dangling—to face off with the last vampire, the burly bastard. He wedged his foot beneath a piece of wood from the bar, kicked it into the air, and grabbed it. "Let's get this over with."

Burly Fucker rained fists at him, but none of the blows struck.

Case dodged each attempt. Not even the vampire's speed could help the bastard land a hit. Case may not have a vampire's agility, but he knew how to move, how to fight, how to survive, and no vampire had proven to be a match yet. Burly Fucker wasn't, either. Case shoved the makeshift stake into the vampire's chest with a thud and a crunch of bone.

The stake stabbed the vampire's heart, killing him on his feet.

He released his grip on the chunk of wood, and the vampire fell backward.

"They ruined the bar."

Case turned to see Thatch in the entryway. "They did. Where were you?"

"Eh. You had it handled. If you didn't, I would've lent a hand."

Case snorted.

"You think Paisley sent them?"

"They said she did, and if she did, she made the biggest mistake of her life."

He considered the dead vampires, chose the young one, and dragged the limp body to the front door by the shirt. His wings unfurled from his body. Then he launched into the air, towing the dead vampire. In no time, he arrived at Paisley's. Hand in a fist, he pounded on the door.

Moments later, the door opened to Paisley, clearly pulled out of bed. She wore a short, silk black nightgown with spaghetti straps. Her purple-black hair was in a loose mass atop her head. Tendrils fell down to frame her face. She was barefoot. Her toes were painted royal purple. He couldn't stop from appraising her, even while his anger boiled.

"What are you—"

He lifted the dead vampire by the shirt to give Paisley a good view of him. Without a word, he let the vampire fall behind him. "There's four more at my place. Dead."

Her eyes did that thing again. Burgundy rings circled her black, glittering irises and speared their centers. She let out a low hiss of breath while baring her fangs.

"Aster," she said, her glare unwavering. "Find somewhere safe. Do not come out until I come and get you."

Aster scampered away.

"There's no need for—"

Paisley grabbed his horns and jerked his head down. Her knee bashed into his face. Blood gushed from his nose.

"Fuck." He pinched the brim of his nose. "I didn't come to fight."

"No, you came to parade a dead vampire in front of the vampire queen." She jabbed a fist into his gut with a force that stole his breath.

He'd fought countless vampires before, but none of them had exhibited such strength. Hell, she hit harder than most demons he knew.

When he dropped to his knees, she grasped his wrist, stomped her foot into his shoulder, and yanked. Bone popped. He roared with the flash of pain that zapped down to his fingertips and momentarily blinded him.

"He was a fledgling vampire! Recently turned to spare him from a cancer that was killing him. He was nineteen in human years."

Case shoved to his feet. He rammed his shoulder into the doorframe to pop it back into place. Another flash of pain stole his breath before it faded. "That is regrettable, but he came to my mansion, looking for a fight. Fledgling vampire or not, he attacked me. I defended myself, as was my right."

"Fuck your right! He wouldn't have been able to kill you."

Case slammed the door at his back, hiding the corpse from sight. "He tried. Or at the very least his companions did. What did you expect me to do when faced with five blood-thirsty vampires?"

"Well, now you're faced with one." She caught his horns again, tugged him down until he was bent at the waist, and then forced him around so he arched backward. His spine protested the position. Her elbow came down on his chest, striking his ribs. Not once, not twice, but three times before she let him drop to the floor.

He rolled onto all fours. Hand to his side, he searched for Paisley. She sprang onto him from behind, hooked his shoulders with her legs, and fastened her arms around his neck with a hold that would knock him unconscious in five seconds flat if he let her stay there.

Reaching behind him, he grabbed her shoulders and wrenched her off. She hit the floor, and he caught her arm to whip her around. Then he yanked her over the tile so that her legs were on either side of him, and Diablo help him, but her nightgown had risen, exposing her black underwear.

His mouth watered. Actually watered.

Before he could make another move, she slid her right foot up his chest until her leg curved over his shoulder. She did the same thing with her left foot and then clamped her thighs around his neck, hitting the pressure points that'd have his vision going black and his muscles falling lax. Darkness crept along the edges of his vision. If he fell unconscious, he didn't have any doubt that Paisley would kill him. He reared up and then dove to the floor, slamming her back against the tile. She gasped, and her legs loosened.

Shaking off the darkness that swallowed him, he placed his hands on her knees, hoping she wouldn't try that again while he was disoriented. Looking down at her, though, she appeared shaken, unable to catch her breath.

Her hand sought the back of her head, and she winced. He hadn't seen her head knock against the tile, but the possibility that that had happened was high, and he stilled. The glare she pinned on him, though, was still burgundy. She couldn't be that injured then—unless she really was that insanely strong—to continue fighting even with the back of her head cracked open.

She lowered her hand from her head. No blood on her fingers.

Some relief at that.

He scanned her as she breathed hard. Now he could see the full crotch of her panties. Needs like he'd never felt before clawed at him. They were too intense to ignore. If he died from this, so be it. Write on his gravestone that he was a brave, horny son of a bitch.

He pushed her knees to the floor, opening her legs like a butterfly. Then he dropped down and buried his head between them. He inhaled, taking in her scent. So good. No, it was phenomenal. He drew in another whiff, this one deeper as he sniffed her thoroughly. His nose rubbed up the length of her crotch. A vicious, ravenous growl rumbled up his throat. He had one instinct and one instinct only; he wanted that pussy, and if something or someone stopped him from getting it, he'd commit murder.

He trailed his nose up her body, between her breasts. With his body now planting her legs wide, he shifted his hands to either side of her and rose up to meet her eyes. They were no longer burgundy. And no longer was she shaken from the hit. Now she trembled, but no fear reflected in her eyes or across her face. She was biting her bottom lip so hard that the delicate skin of her lips whitened around the pressure of her teeth.

He brushed her mouth with his thumb. "Don't do that. Don't make them bleed."

She released her lip. Indents marked the tender flesh. He bent his neck and slicked the tip of his tongue over her bottom lip.

Wrong move.

She wrenched his head back by his horns. The moment enough space formed between their bodies, she rolled backward into a headstand and then flipped to the floor. One leg bent, and one leg stretched out behind her, she glared. The burgundy was back.

She hissed, and he smirked.

On his knees, he held out his arms. "Come and get me."

She sprinted toward him and performed a flip that sent her springing clear over his head. Midair, she caught his horns with her hands. He jerked backward so harshly that his head whiplashed, and the base of his horns ached. His back hit the floor.

When he blinked, he found her crotch right above his head. He grabbed her hips so she couldn't move. "You're making this way too easy for me."

And he licked her cotton panties.

With the grip she had on his horns, she slammed his head against the tile. A second later, though, she was tugging his head toward her crotch. He understood the demand immediately.

"You want it."

Her eyes flared, but staring at her as he probed his tongue over the cotton again, he

witnessed what she would rather hide from him— desire. The burgundy dimmed. With the tip of his tongue, he rubbed the damp cotton. Feeling his way, he located the bud of her clit.

The burgundy in her eyes faded completely.

"Do you want me to make you come?"

She nodded.

His fingertips dug into the fleshiness of her hips. "Say it," he ground out. "I want to hear you say it."

She squeezed his chin. Her fingers dug into his jaw. "Make me come. Now."

"It'll be my pleasure." And he attacked her pussy through the cotton.

She hunched over, inadvertently pushing his head back because of the hold she still had on his horns. He yanked her down so that she was fully seated on his face.

"Oh my—" Her words dissolved, replaced with a sigh of pleasure.

Soon, the cotton became wet from his mouth, and he was able to suck on it to taste her flavor through the fibers. The salty sweetness with a hint of fragrance from the cotton teased his tastebuds. He was tempted to rip a hole through the panties with his teeth to feel her flesh with his tongue, but he didn't. If she felt his tongue, she could either snap out of this carnal trance and attack him or fall deeper into that carnal trance. While he'd enjoy the latter, he also didn't want to risk it. Besides, she was liking the feel of the wet cotton's friction, and the way she rolled her hips told him he could make her come without direct contact.

He sucked her hard through the cotton.

She let go over his horns to flatten her hands to the tile. Without her hold keeping his head in place, he was able to get closer. His tongue probed at the yielding opening of her vagina.

If her panties weren't there, he'd plunge into the wet, hot depths and fully taste her.

A moan echoed.

He paid attention to her clit, the source that would make her unravel. After a few strokes, her body quaked. Another moan ricocheted. He attacked her clit with his tongue relentlessly. She cried out again and again as she convulsed.

Finally, a peal broke from her. Her pelvis rolled slowly forward, so her clit pressed firmer to his tongue. She bent so far over him that her forehead touched the tile.

Before her cries could fully diminish and her spasms could calm, he switched their positions, putting her beneath him. "Now that you're out of commission for a while, you're going to listen to me."

Her eyelids drifted open, heavy with the aftermath of orgasm.

"Sending vampires after me was the worst decision you could've made, but not as bad as letting me make you come. One, I will kill any vampire who gets in my way. Two, I'm not annoyed anymore. I'm pissed. Three, I'm not going to leave you alone, because now I want your pussy more than ever." He slid a hand down her center and cupped her between her legs.

She gasped.

"And she wants me, too. Just because you and I are sworn enemies doesn't mean she needs to be denied what she wants. The next time she wants oral, tell me, and my tongue and mouth are hers. I will lick her and kiss her and make out with her to her little heart's content. I could have her for breakfast, lunch, dinner, and snack on her day and night. And if she ever wants my cock, tell me that, too, and she can have it. All of it. I'll do things to her that she's never experienced before and that she'll be begging for, but she won't need to beg. *You*, she may have to beg, but not me. Say the word. Take off your panties in front of me. Open your legs. You won't have to do much, and I'll come to her aid. Tell me what she wants. Mouth or cock. She'll get it, whatever it is. Every time. I can guarantee that. I haven't even laid eyes on her yet, but I adore her. I've gotten a little taste of her. I've smelled her. I know how she feels like this." He stroked his thumb over her swollen flesh through the damp cotton. "And I'm already crazed for her. I want more of her. In every way. I'll have her, too."

He grasped her dark purple hair with his other hand. "As for you, Paisley. You better be careful. I'll leave the dead vampires outside my gate so your people can collect their dead, but the next time you send vampires my way, I will show up at the vamprye faction with torches, silver, and hundreds of demons at my back. It won't be a war. It won't even be a battle. It'll be a slaughter. Remember that."

He stood, fingers tingling, and resisted the urge to smell them until he was outside, with the door at his back.

5

A Fairy's Wet Dream

Paisley

*P*aisley lay on the floor, stunned from the orgasm he'd given her. Staring up at the ceiling, she muttered, "Asshole." She lifted her head. "And you," she said to her pussy, "*you* are a traitor." She didn't even have the energy to get up, so she lowered her head back to the tile.

Fuck, Case. Fuck his exquisite mouth that could drive her mad through cotton. Fuck his thumb that knew how to stroke so wonderfully. Fuck his "I want to get to know every inch of your body" gaze. Fuck his sexy face. Fuck his ripped body. And fuck the universe for making her want to fuck a demon.

"Are you okay?" Aster stood to the side.

Paisley hoped her underwear wasn't showing, but she didn't have it in her to check. "Fine. What was the last thing you saw?"

"You smashing Case's face with your knee."

That was good.

"And what did you hear?"

"Well, it sounded like…it sounded like you were having sex."

Paisley couldn't even muster the energy to feel mortified. "How do you know what sex sounds like?"

Aster's face reflected mortification for Paisley. "I've heard fairies having sex before. I'm not that sheltered, you know."

Paisley smiled. "No, you're not. I'm sorry." And living with Paisley, the poor fairy was bound to get corrupted.

"Did the two of you…?"

"No!"

Aster raised a brow.

"Sort of. Not entirely. A little. Ugh!" She stamped her hands over her eyes. "I can't believe this! Why do I want him?!"

"Because he looks at you as if he could melt your panties off."

Paisley groaned. Way too accurate.

Aster sat on the floor. "What could go wrong if you gave over to your desires?"

"A lot. Two factions are my responsibility. They depend on me. All vampires' and fairies' lives could be at stake. If the demons are behind these threats and the death of my parents, if Case is behind everything, I would've fallen into a trap. I'll be dead. You'll be dead. And vampires and fairies will cease to exist."

"I get that sex has been used as a trap before, but…I don't think Case would do that. And why would he clean up the bats if he was behind it?"

"To fool me."

"Do you think a demon would go through that much effort?"

She had a point.

"If not him, then who? I think I'm more scared of that than if it is Case, because then who could be?"

"I don't know, but maybe he could help you find out. It seems that he's a target, too. Enemies can come together for a common cause. It's happened all throughout human and creature history."

Staring up at the ceiling, Paisley sighed. "This is why you're my lady-in-waiting."

Aster was the wisest fairy she knew.

"What are we going to do about the dead vampire out there?"

"Crap." She still had to deal with that. Not to mention the fact that Case claimed five vampires had shown up at his mansion to threaten him. She certainly hadn't given that order, and she would find out who did. "I need to go to the vampyre faction. They have some explaining to do."

The vampyre faction was lit with light posts and torches and bursting with activity in the middle of the night. She dodged the glow of the lights and landed in front of the home in the center of the sprawling town. She knocked, and the door opened to Uncle Silas.

"Hey, kiddo, this is a surprise." He embraced her in a hug that smelled like cigars and blood. "I thought you'd be too busy to visit after your coronation."

"Well, I'm here on official queen business. Can I come in?"

"Of course."

In a parlor of maroon velvet, highbacked chairs and leather couches, she sat across from him. A sea of flickering candles made shadows in the corners. Smoke streamed up from the lit end of her uncle's cigar, resting in an amber dish.

"How are my cousins?"

Her uncle did not have biological children, but a handful of the dozens he'd changed over the centuries had stayed close. One of her cousins was a woman, Cinda, and four were men.

"Cinda visits periodically. She's off doing her own thing." Which usually meant she was off doing *someone*. "As for the boys, I don't keep close tabs on them anymore. I stopped trying long ago."

She chuckled. "I don't blame you." They tended to cause havoc wherever they went.

"I know your queenly business isn't to check in on your family. What's going on?"

She exhaled. "Lord Case came by tonight to tell me that five vampires broke into his home and attacked him. He killed them all."

53

"He what?"

"In self-defense."

Her uncle huffed. "Right."

"They went in unprovoked. Breaking into a faction leader's home is cause for death upon sight. No questions asked."

"Why would they do that?"

"You tell me. Lord Case said they claimed to be there on business from their queen. I didn't send them. I didn't give the order. Someone did, though. I need to know who. Did *you* do it?"

He leaned back, brow arched. "You really think I'd go behind your back?"

"You were running things after my father's death, before my coronation. If any of them would take an order, it'd be from you."

"I gave no such order."

"Have you heard any whispers about attacking the daemon faction?"

"No."

"Do you know of anyone who would want us at war?"

"That'd be about half the faction."

She studied him. He was acting a little too cool for her liking. "Which half would you be in? The side who wants war or the side who doesn't?"

"I'm undecided."

The dangerous side. You could never trust the undecided.

Her uncle picked up his cigar and drew a long drag. "Which vampires broke into Case's home? You didn't say."

"I don't know who four of them were, but one was Georgy."

"He killed Georgy?! He was a fledgling."

"A fledgling who attacked him inside his home. I'm pissed over Georgy's death, too, but Lord Case had every right to defend himself. Georgy's body is outside my home, by the front door. The other four he said he'd leave outside his gate so we can collect our dead. Can you send a small group out to get them? With the explicit order not to engage, not to say a word, not to step a fucking toe onto Case's property?"

"I can."

"Thank you. And make sure the entire faction knows not to do anything against Lord

Case or the daemon faction unless they hear it from my mouth. If another vampire does something I did not order, I'll kill them myself."

Her uncle bowed his head. "Consider the faction informed."

Early the next morning, the knock didn't surprise her, but it did annoy her. She stomped to the door, prepared to tell Case to get lost, but when she opened it, the scent of blood nearly knocked her back a step. She gripped the doorhandle and fought down the punch of nausea.

Once again, Case leaned against the doorframe with a sexy smirk on his face. "If you think putting blood on your doors and windows is going to keep me away, think again."

The door was coated with blood.

"Damn it," she hissed.

"I take it you didn't vandalize your own house with buckets of blood then."

"I did not."

Her stomach revolted at the sight of the blood streaming down the door. The scent of it jabbed her in the gut. Pig's blood. She swallowed down the urge to vomit.

That shouldn't happen. Vampires would grow hungry at the sight and smell of blood. Even an animal's blood. But Paisley's fairy half complicated matters. She didn't enjoy drinking blood because she struggled to get past the death that preceded or followed her feedings, which was why she relied on blood bags, but even that wasn't problem-free. People needed those bags. Fortunately, she didn't need blood as much or as often as other vampires. One bag a week was enough to sustain her. Sometimes, she could extend it to two weeks. She was going on ten days, but the odor of the pig's blood was making her lightheaded. If she'd had blood fairly recently, she wouldn't be feeling so weak or nauseas.

Case shifted closer. "Are you okay?"

"Why do you care?"

"I care if you keel over before I ever get to taste your pussy with my tongue."

Two reactions. The first was rage at his audacity. Followed by a surge of lust.

"You're not coming near my pussy ever again."

His teeth showed in a rabid grin. "How much you wanna bet?"

Infuriating, cocky son of a bitch.

"Look, I have blood drying on my door and windows. I'll deal with that if you deal with the lawn. As soon as you're finished, you're going to leave and the next time you come onto my property without my permission, I will draw *your* blood. Got it?"

"Whatever you say, My Queen."

"I'm not your queen."

"Maybe not…" His gaze scanned her body and left behind a steamy trail of desire. "But I'd bend the knee." He turned.

Yet there was something she had to tell him, something he had to know, despite the fact that he grated on her every nerve. "Case."

He paused but didn't turn.

"I didn't send those vampires last night."

He faced her.

"After you left, I went to the vampyre faction. My uncle, who is basically in charge when I'm not there, had no idea what I was talking about. He didn't send vampires after you. He didn't know who did. If you hadn't killed them, we could've tortured the truth out of them."

"Next time," he said.

"There won't be a next time. I told them that if anyone sends vampires after you again, I'll kill them myself."

He tilted his head. "You would kill your own?"

"For going against my orders? Yes."

"Why does that turn me on?"

"Because you're a demon."

"Probably, or it could be the memory of those daggers around your thighs and the way you fought me last night."

"Stop thinking about my thighs."

"Your thighs are the least of what occupies my thoughts."

"Stop thinking about my pussy."

"Never." He sauntered off to the shed.

Her pussy tingled from his stare and his words. "Will you stop that," she muttered. "You don't need to react to him every time."

Her sex throbbed, as if to say, "Yes, I do."

She spun about to change out of her pleather pants and crop top and into something that could get filthy. In dark jeans and a black tank top, she collected a bucket of water and a rag. When she opened the door, she found Case kneeling in the front yard, using a trowel to remove chunks of scorched lawn. She set the bucket on the stoop, shut the door, and dunked the rag into the cold water.

While scrubbing away the pig's blood, she forced herself to think of it as paint. It was paint from a gallon, splashed onto the door. It wasn't from an animal's arteries. The scent was chemical, not nickel. Still, she breathed through her mouth so she couldn't catch a nauseating whiff. Red-tainted water streamed down her arms to her elbows as she worked. She ignored it. Every time she wrung out the rag, the water in the bucket became redder, darker. She tried not to notice that, either, but it was impossible not to.

She cleaned the door of every last speck of red and dumped the dirty water into the bushes. Then she got up to refill the bucket. Aster opened the front door right then, carrying a tray with a pitcher of water and two glasses.

"Hey," Aster said. "I have water for the two of you."

"That's nice of you. I'm going to refill my bucket." She paused. "Be careful with him."

Aster frowned. "He's not going to hurt me."

"You're sure about that?"

"Yes, I am. I told you, he's nice."

"Nice to you, maybe." Paisley nodded. "Give him all the water he needs. I'll be right out."

She refilled the bucket using a water spigot at the side of the house and carried it back to the front door. Aster was holding the tray in front of Case while he guzzled a glass of water. The pitcher on the tray was half-empty.

The demon was thirsty.

He wiped his mouth with the back of his hand and set the glass on the tray.

Her abdomen clenched with urges simply from seeing him wipe his mouth.

"Thank you, cutie pie."

Now Paisley's jaw clenched.

Aster came over to Paisley with fluttering wings and a smile on her face. A fairy charmed by a demon. Who would've thought?

"Here, you have to be thirsty, too."

Paisley poured water into the other glass and sipped on it slowly, testing her stomach. If she threw up in front of Case, forget embarrassment. Her weakness would be out there, and she couldn't allow that.

"Are you sure you can do this?" Aster whispered. "I can help. You don't have to do it alone."

Paisley lowered her glass. "Fairies shouldn't have to deal with blood."

"And neither should you. You're the queen. You can get anyone to do this."

"I don't want anyone to see this. It's fine. I'll be fine."

"And if you're not, tell me. I don't care if fairies shouldn't have to deal with blood. You're my best friend. I will do whatever you need."

"Thank you, but I've got this."

Aster sighed before going inside with the tray.

Paisley glanced toward Case. He plunged the shovel into the earth, pried out a chunk of grass, and heaved it into the wheelbarrow. Seeing him with dirt smudges on his hands and arms and across his white T-shirt aroused her. Why did he look sexier like that than in the beautifully tailored suit he'd worn yesterday?

She stepped up behind him. "Why do you call her cutie pie?"

He impaled the ground with the shovel. "Because she's fucking adorable." He stood and dusted off his hands. "Minus the fucking part." When he faced her, his stare penetrated. "You're the only one I want to fuck, Paisley."

Lust. Scorching, exhilarating lust.

"Get back to work."

His lips twitched. "Oh, I will."

"Not on me. On the lawn."

"Lawn first, and then you."

"No."

"Yes." His voice was a hiss of longing.

She stepped back.

"Paisley." His voice rumbled. "You can't deny it. Every time you become aroused, I can smell it, and you become aroused every time you're around me. It's the same for me. Every time

I'm around you, I want you. More than breath."

"That doesn't sound very good for survival."

"Fucking you is becoming a need for survival."

"Then you're not going to survive."

"We'll see." He twisted around and lowered to his knees to resume his work.

She followed his cue and went to the first window dripping with blood. Swiping the glass clean was easier and quicker than the door. Once the window gleamed, she dumped the contents and retrieved more water.

Six windows, six trips.

Lots of bloody water.

Near the end of washing the sixth window, she felt weaker. She poured out the dirty water, emptying the bucket for the final time. The wet, filthy rag plopped onto the bottom of the bucket when she dropped it.

Glad she was done with the task, she checked to see what Case was doing and found him placing the last squares of grass. From the shade by the front door, she studied him. His fingernails were caked with dirt. His hands covered with it. His arms streaked. His shirt stained. And holy Mother Earth Goddess, he was a fairy's wet dream.

"I can smell that."

6

Straining, Pulsing, Ravenous

Case

The second she became aroused—again—his nose picked up on the mouthwatering scent. Hunger jabbed him in the gut with a steel fist. Diablo, the scent of her arousal was the most intoxicating thing he'd ever had the pleasure of sniffing. No other woman's scent—human or creature—had ever caused such a desire in him or smelled so fucking good. He licked his lips, starving for her pussy.

He rose to his feet. Despite the glorious scent teasing him relentlessly and the way her chest rose and fell, her cheeks weren't flushed with arousal, and her eyes weren't gleaming with lust. Her skin was paler. Even the sparkles in her eyes weren't glittering as strongly as they had.

"Not used to work, princess?"

"Fuck you. I'm queen, and you have no idea what I'm used to."

He stalked after her. Her scent wouldn't allow him to do anything else but follow like a fish on a hook. "Is it the fairy in you that makes you horny, seeing me covered in dirt?" He caught her arm on the stoop and whipped her about. "Because as a demon, I'm horny for you, seeing you covered in blood."

"You're *always* horny for me."

"Right you are." He inhaled deeply. "And it seems…you're always horny for me, too."

Her jaw clenched.

They stared at each other. The more eye contact they held, the harder it was to restrain himself from ramming her against the door and taking her while she cried out louder, and louder, and louder. He wanted to rattle the door beneath their bodies. Shake it right off its hinges. Diablo, he desired to rail her so much that she'd be begging him not to stop, pleading for him to fuck her. Harder. Harder. Harder.

"Screw it," she said and launched herself at him.

Her mouth on his surprised him.

Kissing wasn't something he engaged in. Pleasing his dick was all he cared about, all that mattered. Kissing was too personal, too intimate. After growing up without an ounce of affection, avoiding any type of passion became a necessity, but here Paisley's lips were. On his. Her lips were warm, soft, yielding. And they left him stunned.

When he didn't engage, she stiffened. "I'm sorry. I shouldn't have done that. Sorry." She turned away, but his hands caught her shoulders.

"Wait. Just wait." He'd never wanted it, but Paisley's lips against his had ignited a new longing in him. His heart pounded with the desire to take her mouth, plunge his tongue into its depths, feel her tongue against his, taste its flavor. Unable to resist, he whirled her around, molded a hand to the back of her head, and stamped his mouth to hers. He closed his lips around her top lip, testing the sensation, examining the reaction inside him. To his dismay, his inner beast liked it. No, that was too tame of a word. His inner beast was licking its chomps.

She responded to the pressure of his lips, applying pressure in return.

That. That contact broke a barrier inside him.

He switched his lips to her bottom lip. Sucked.

Urges clawed up. Urges he'd never had before.

His tongue slipped into her mouth, glided with hers.

A groan rumbled in his throat. He didn't understand how that—simply the touch of their tongues—could illicit a groan of pleasure. But it did.

He broke off the kiss to peer into her eyes. Some of their sparkle had returned. "I don't kiss," he admitted. "I never have." He rubbed her bottom lip with the pad of his thumb. "That's why I reacted the way I did."

"I'm sorry. I should've asked permission."

"No." He stroked his thumb back the other way over her sweet lips. "Don't apologize. You didn't know, you did nothing wrong. As it turns out, I want your lips as much as the rest of you." This time when he devoured her lips. His tongue sank into her mouth and stroked against her tongue again and again, in exactly the same way he yearned to sink his cock into her.

She moaned.

Her hands were suddenly under his shirt, exploring his abs.

The touch of her hands, so close to the top of his pants and his belt sent blood rushing to his penis. His cock filled, expanded, lifted. He grunted as he came to full erection. Grasping her hips, he lifted her up and flattened her to the door.

A gasp rushed from her.

She locked her legs around his waist in a purely sexual move that spoke to his instincts. Spoke fucking volumes. He ground his erection against the crotch of her jeans. The friction of his pants and her jeans rubbing, rubbing, rubbing was exquisite.

He groaned into her mouth as their tongues twisted, and he drove his hips forward in time with his plunging tongue. Beneath his hands, he could feel her own hips rolling. That motion granted him a sneak peek of how she would be in bed, riding him with those glorious hips rocking, her abdomen like a wave.

The kiss ended when they both moaned at the same time.

"Paisley." Neither of them stopped gyrating. "Fuck."

Her legs contracted, and she tugged him closer.

A grunt burst from his vocal cords. He was so close to climaxing.

"We have to stop or I'll come in my pants."

"Then unzip them," came her breathless response.

"Only if you lose your pants."

"Then take them off."

She didn't have to tell him twice.

He pried her legs off him and set her on her feet. Kneeling before her, he tugged off her shoes one at a time, chucking them behind him. Then he took her jeans in his hands. His fingers popped the button. All the while, he stared, waiting to see if she'd snap to her senses and tell him to stop. Or do it more physically with a knee to his face. He lowered the zipper.

Still, she didn't stop him.

Hands back on her hips, he drew her jeans down her legs.

Black boy shorts appeared, magnifying his hunger.

Pale thighs.

Smooth skin.

Long shins.

Legs for fucking days.

He deposited her jeans in a heap on the concrete.

Then he grasped her hips and stuck his nose in the apex of her legs. Inhaling deeply, he drew in the smell of her sweat and arousal. "Diablo, that's good."

He could strip off her panties, drape her legs over his shoulders, pick her up, and go down on her like how he'd dreamed, but then his raging cock wouldn't get the action it craved. Although his cock wanted to be buried in her, he wasn't about to push his luck. On his feet, he yanked her back up.

Her legs came around him without hesitation. Between their bodies, he unzipped his own pants, unleashing his straining, pulsing, ravenous cock from its confines. With his erection snug against her crotch, he pumped his hips, on a mission to dry hump them to orgasm.

Paisley wrapped her arms around his shoulders, clutching him with all of her limbs, and buried her face in his neck. Her moans urged him to hammer his hips faster.

"Yes," she panted in his ear. "Yes, harder. Harder."

Exactly as he had hoped.

He answered her plea by striking her sensitive clit harder. Each thrust had his penis stroking her entire clothed pussy.

"Fuck me," she said. "Fuck me."

It took everything in him not to rip her panties to shreds and plow his cock into her. "I'm not fucking you, yet, Paisley. If you truly want that, we can do that another time. But now, now it's too late."

She shook.

The door behind her banged inside its frame with each forward motion of his hips. Her moans morphed into cries that called to his demonic ways, bringing forth growls that vibrated his entire body.

She tightened around him. Her nails dug into his back. Then the sexiest wail he'd ever heard filled the air.

He didn't stop pumping his hips, rubbing his cock against her damp crotch. And that alone had her orgasm stretching on. She squeezed him with her legs while she cried out again and again from the continued sensations.

Cum surged out of his penis with the greatest pleasure he'd ever felt. The veins in his neck bulged as he roared. For a split second, he feared he'd shatter his vocal cords when his cock finally emptied and fell limp. Even so, he didn't move.

Nor did she. Paisley, too, had gone limp. He supported her with his arms, thankful they hadn't lost their strength.

"Paisley." He glided his nose up the side of her neck. "Imagine how good it would be if we did that for real."

"I don't need to, because it's not going to happen. We're never going to see each other again."

He leaned back to cast his glare on her. "Yes, we will."

"No, we won't."

He gave her a smirk that even he knew was dangerous. "The Enchanted Hierarchy Council Meeting is tomorrow."

"Shit." It was barely a whisper, but it was loud enough.

His smirk grew. "As queen, it is a requirement that you attend each meeting. Every month. And guess where I'll be."

She exhaled.

"Exactly." He backed off the stoop, taking her with him. "I came all over your door." He set her on her feet and rezipped his pants. Then he picked up her jeans. "I'll clean it."

She accepted her jeans. "You don't have to do that."

"It's my cum, Paisley, and there's a lot of it. Stay here." He picked up the bucket. "Where can I get water?"

She pointed. "Around the corner."

He filled the bucket and returned to find Paisley inspecting the lawn.

"It looks good," she said.

"I'm glad you think so. Even demons can be gardeners." He rung out the rag.

"You really don't have to do that. I'll take care of it."

"You're not a maid. I'll clean my own mess."

He cleaned every last drop of creamy cum from the door and mopped up the puddle that had collected like an erotic welcome mat. When he finished, he hefted the bucket. Paisley wasn't behind him. He carted the bucket off to the woods, dumped the water at the base of a tree, and headed back, but Paisley was nowhere in sight. Was she throwing daggers again? If those holsters were on her legs, there'd be no stopping his lust.

On the porch, he laid the bucket on the concrete and rapped on the door. A moment later, it opened to the sweetest fairy he'd ever met. "Hey there, cutie pie."

Aster's cheeks blazed fuchsia.

"Is Paisley inside?"

"No, she hasn't come in yet."

"Do you know where she'd go?"

"Actually, yeah, check the wisteria tree." She indicated at a tree bursting with vibrant lilac-colored flowers that trickled to the ground.

"Thanks, cutie pie. I'm heading home. If I don't see you for a while, I'm compelled to tell you to be careful. Something sinister is going on, and this house and Paisley are targets for it.

I don't want my favorite little fairy to get caught up in all that."

Her gaze lowered as that flush rose to her temples.

"If something happens, get word to me. Do you have one of those human cell phones?"

"I do."

"I'll give you my number."

She removed a cell phone from a pouch tied at her waist.

He borrowed it a moment to program his number. "You can contact me. Day or night. With any sign of danger. Don't hesitate, okay? Even if you think it's nothing, call me."

She nodded while tucking the phone back into the pouch. "I will. I promise."

"You're precious. I'll see you soon."

Smiling, he headed off to the wisteria tree. He brushed aside a rope of wisteria and ducked beneath the heavy branches.

Paisley sat with her back to the trunk and her eyelids closed.

A few feet from her, he knelt. "Paisley?"

She jolted. Her eyelids sprang apart.

"I didn't mean to scare you."

"You don't scare me, Case."

"I imagine I do a little."

"You think too highly of yourself as a demon."

He chuckled. "I don't mean as a demon. I mean sexually."

"It's not you who frightens me in that regard. It's myself."

"Because you're attracted to a demon?"

"Because I'm attracted to my enemy."

"A demon."

"Yes, a demon."

He nodded and rose to his feet. "See you tomorrow."

She nodded back. "I guess you will."

He pushed the flowery rope to the side again and stepped out into the sunshine. As he left, a desperate need filled him to not only be *a* demon, but to be *her* demon.

7

Enemies with Benefits

Paisley

*P*aisley considered her wardrobe. All throughout her childhood, her parents had attended the Enchanted Hierarchy Council Meetings dressed in their finest. Her father had worn tailored suede and silk suits with vests, ties, cufflinks, and pocket squares. Her mother had filled her with awe in dresses of satin that swished, shimmered, and sparkled. The two of them had made a gorgeous pair.

For Paisley's first meeting, as the queen of two factions, she needed to make a statement, stun, leave them speechless. She removed a black and red gown from her closet. "This is the one." She slipped it on and stood in front of the full-length mirror in her bedroom. The dress was sleeveless, with a bodice that molded to her curves. Black vines weaved up the length of her abdomen, swirling around her waist and ribs and breasts. Red roses, blooming full and wide, covered her breasts, concealing her nipples, but her rose tattoo and the rest of her curves were visible through the black vines. Sheer fabric wasn't sown beneath the bodice, just her pale skin, offering a sensual peek at her body beneath the dress. The dress expanded from her hips to a sweeping skirt with large red and black roses.

Satisfied with the dress, she set to work on her hair and makeup. She piled her purple-black locks atop her head to keep her neck and shoulders bare. Then she applied crimson to her lips and kohl to her eyelids. The look combined the vampyre faction's red with her fairy flower, a clever blend to declare her duo throne status to all in attendance. She finished with a pair of strappy red heels and a spritz of rose perfume at her neck and wrists.

She headed downstairs.

Aster gaped. "Holy rose petal! Is it your plan to cause everyone at the meeting to have heart attacks?"

"I want to make a statement."

"That's some statement." Aster tilted her head. "There's something missing, though."

Paisley peered down at herself. "What?"

"This." Aster revealed Paisley's mother's crown, but now silver twined around four garnet spears.

"Did you do this?" She held the crown.

"I did. I thought your mother's crown needed a bit

73

of your father."

"It's beautiful. Thank you." She placed it atop her head. "Is it straight?"

"It is. And it's where it belongs. You truly look like a queen."

Paisley smiled. "I hope so. This is my first time out in public after my crowning."

"You'll do great."

"Thanks. I better get going, or I'll be late."

"Good luck."

While she flew, she kept an eye out for other winged creatures so that she could duck into a canopy before they could see her. No one—absolutely *no one*—could see her wings. They weren't worthy enough to lay eyes on the wings of the first-ever hybrid. Especially not after those who had seen her wings had laughed, snickered, called her an abomination.

No one.

Absolutely no one.

She landed in the shade of the Enchanted Hierarchy Hall. A quick glance showed she was

alone, so she entered the building. At the very end of the entryway, Jude disappeared through a pair of opened double doors.

At the threshold, she paused to take a deep breath. Stepping through that door would change everything. Lifting her chin, pulling her shoulders back, she entered the hall. On the other side, all gazes landed on her. Whispers and murmurs filled the air.

She met the eye of Jude. Gold chains twined up his large antlers, like a crown. He crossed an arm over his chest and bowed low, bending one of his legs. She bent her neck in acknowledgement as she continued past him. Parallel to where he stood was a throne with her name etched onto the back. She sat and found Case sitting directly across from her.

Holy Earth Goddess, he looked sinisterly good in all black. Black pants, jacket, vest, shirt, tie, and boots. Silver accents sparkled along the vee of the black vest. The collar, pocket square, and cuffs of his jacket were textured, like black snake skin. He filled his throne with his large body that stretched the fabric of his clothes so temptingly that she couldn't help but stare at the lines of his pants. His legs were spread, and his lap appeared damn inviting. She desired to straddle that wide lap. Sit on it. Rub against it.

Goddess, he was a demonic snack in that chair. A sexy, gothic snack.

She crossed her legs as her loins throbbed.

He angled his head ever so slightly. His eyelids lowered, and his chest rose slowly as he filled his lungs. His chest expanded so fully that the buttons threatened to pop off his shirt. Around the edge of the armrests, his fingers gripped the black leather, turning his knuckles white. Then his eyelids sprang open. A glint of gold flashed in his eyes. Pinning her with that stunningly golden stare, his lips spread.

He knew. The bastard knew that he'd turned her on merely by sitting there and looking

the way he did. If that was all it could take to make her want him, she was screwed. More precisely, *they* were bound to screw. Resisting at this point was no doubt a waste of time. Why delay the inevitable? Why deny herself pleasure?

Zara gave her a much needed distracted when she entered the space next. Her voluminous golden hair cascaded to her hips in luscious waves, her eyes glowed a delicate yellow, and she wore a glamorous dress of rainbow colors and flowers. The enchantress radiated beauty and elegance. She sat at the head of the hall. "The Enchanted Hierarchy Council Meeting commences. We have a new member attending today. Welcome, Paisley Nightingale, queen to the faye and vampyre factions."

Around the room, the other creatures nodded and uttered a welcome.

Atlantica, Queen of Mermaids and all water creatures, perched on her throne. Her tail, which usually shimmered with scales of metallic purple, was now a pair of pale legs so she could walk on land. Beside her sat Julius, the Basilisk King. His long body tumbled from his chair and spiraled on the floor in blue and green scales. Next to Julius, Blair, the Banshee Queen, who represented all otherworldly spirits, faded in and out in shades of gray. Then there was Case. To his right stood Jude, king to all part human creatures. Finishing their row was Zeke, Orc King, with his jade-green skin and sharp tusks.

On the other side of the room, Langston, Giants King, dwarfed a throne built specifically for him. Enya Carnelian, the Dragon Shifter Queen and ruler of all fiery creatures draped over her throne in bright red and burgundy scales. Between Enya and Paisley lounged the alpha to the werewolves, currently in human form. Alarick Malone wore a blue suede jacket and had a scruffy beard. To her left, Lena Fox, the Elf Queen, was regal and eternal in greens and browns. Finally, there stood Philippa, a Pegasus and queen to all other winged creatures.

"Paisley."

She directed her attention to Zara.

"What happened to your parents is a tragedy and an unforgivable crime. We will not stop investigating until we know who murdered them. You have my word."

Paisley nodded. "Thank you, Your Majesty."

"Dear, don't thank me until we're successful. You're actually the topic I want to discuss today."

Paisley stiffened.

"It has come to my attention that the queen has been threatened."

The letter Paisley had written.

"Someone slaughtered thousands of bats—"

Lena gasped. As an elf, she honored animals as much as fairies did.

"—and they left those bats on the queen's lawn, a grotesque omen meant to intimidate and frighten, a statement of death to the queen. I will not tolerate threats to any of our members, especially not after what happened to her parents, two of our own. It is my understanding that the daemon faction's brand was burned into the grass beside the mountain of murdered bats."

The enchantress's yellow eyes sought out Case.

Paisley looked, too.

Case's jaw flexed. "Paisley came to me about that." His gaze flicked to her. "I told her what I am telling all of you. We had nothing to do with it. I don't care if any of you believe otherwise." He scanned the rest of them before settling back on her. "Whether she believes me or not, it's true." Now he addressed Zara. "I personally shoveled away every last bat and fixed the lawn. And I'll say this once and only once…" His eyes flared with an enraged gold, and he laid that glare on each of the members of the council. "When I find out who is framing me and my faction, I will make them sorry."

Paisley's eyes widened. *What are you doing?*

He didn't look at her, but spoke directly to Zara. "That *is* a threat, Your Majesty. After what happened to her parents, only that threat will do. Kick me out of the council. Sentence me if you must, but I will live up to my vow. I will hurt whoever is at fault, and I can't promise that they'll be alive when I'm through."

Paisley gaped. Why in the world would he make such a vow? For his reputation? For her? No, that was ridiculous. She didn't matter to him. Couldn't. His desire couldn't be that strong to risk banishment, or worse…execution.

Zara sighed. "I suppose I can't expect anything less from the demon lord. If it comes to that, we'll deal with it then, but I warn you, you will face the consequences."

"Understood."

Zara nodded. "Now, the threat to the queen's life is not something I will ignore. And if someone is, indeed, framing an innocent faction, the culprit will face punishment."

"If they're still alive after I'm through," Case said.

Zara eyed him.

He glared right back, unafraid of retribution.

"As I was saying," Zara continued. "The queen is one of us. None of us should be taking the threat to her life lightly. Although she's the queen of two factions, she's new in her role, and without family, alone. Until this matter is handled, and she is safe, she needs a protector."

Paisley clenched her hands into fists. Leader of the cabinet or not, the enchantress had no right to make such a declaration without Paisley's input. "With all due respect, Your Majesty, I don't need a protector. I am capable on my own. I have hundreds of vampires at my back and thousands of faye. And allies." She nodded at Jude, and then at Lena. "I am *not* alone. Nor am I weak. I've kept myself alive this long, after facing threats that none of you know about, that not even my parents were privy to."

"That may be so, but you're a queen now, not just a princess. The danger is tenfold. And being the ruler of two factions means anyone who desires to harm you, kill you, will try twice as hard. I fear the bats are the beginning."

"And I will deal with whatever comes my way, myself."

A growl touched her ears, and then, "I will protect her."

Silence.

Startling silence while everyone, including Paisley, turned to Case.

"No," she snapped.

"Yes."

"No!" She whipped her head toward Zara. "I refuse."

"Will anyone else step up?" Zara asked.

"I don't need anyone else," Paisley spat. "And I certainly don't need him."

"Well, you've got me," Case seethed.

"I don't *want* you."

His sneer was dangerous, and she was afraid he would spill the beans and announce to the entire cabinet that her scent revealed otherwise: she wanted him.

"Whatever you say, darlin'."

She clenched her jaw. "I refuse his help. I refuse the help of anyone."

Zara addressed her bold statement. "It is my right to make orders that not even you can refuse, and this is one. Case, do you vow to protect Paisley?"

Paisley stared wide-eyed.

"I will protect her, whatever means necessary. She has my faction at her disposal." He met Paisley's stare. "My word is hers. My body is hers."

His body. Goddess, why did he have to say that?

He'd done it on purpose. That was evident by his smirk.

"It is done," Zara announced.

"No, it's not," Paisley said.

"Yes, it is, dear. Do not go against one of my orders at your first meeting."

Paisley bit her tongue. She wouldn't go against Zara's orders, but she could make it crystal-fucking-clear that she didn't want Case's help.

She sat through the rest of the meeting, ignoring Case, even when it became clear that he was watching her and boiling.

Zara's voice cut through her anger when she said,

"That'll conclude our meeting. I will end it with this…it is our responsibility to keep our factions in line. If you find out one of your own is behind the threat to Paisley, it is your duty to bring them forward."

Everyone nodded in agreement.

Zara stood, dismissing the meeting.

Neither Case nor Paisley stood.

They merely glared each other.

A clomping of hooves and a throat clearing jarred her from their staring contest. She smiled up at Jude.

He held out his hand. "How have you been, sweetheart?"

She rose to her feet and laid her hand in his. "As well as could be expected."

"I would've offered my services to protect you, but I didn't want to get in between you and Case."

"There's nothing to get in between of."

"Mm. It seems there is. Or at least there is to him, and Case is not a demon to get in the way of." He lifted her hand and kissed her knuckles. "Excuse me. I need to have a word with

Zeke."

When he walked away, she found Case still sitting in his throne, still eyeing her. Exhaling through her nose, she marched up. "I don't care what Zara says, you're not my protector. I don't need you to protect me."

He rose slowly. "I made a vow."

"Break it."

"I can't do that."

"So, you're a demon of honor now?"

"I am a demon of many things. Honor is but one of

81

them." His gaze lowered. "That's a dangerous dress, Paisley."

She sucked in a breath when his fingers followed the hollowed-out lines of her bodice, touching her bare skin. Her hand flinched. She wanted to slap his fingers away so no one would see him touching her like that, but aside from that flinch, she couldn't make herself do it, because the way he traced her skin felt good.

"It's a distracting dress, too." He continued to trace her skin, getting higher and higher. "Do you like this? How I'm touching you?"

"No."

His teeth appeared in a smirk. "Then stop me." He slid his hand higher. The tip of his finger tickled the underside of her left breast.

Her lips trembled apart.

"Whether it's true or not, I'm going to believe you wore this dress for me."

Part of her had, although she wouldn't tell him so.

"And that you wanted me to do this." He stepped closer, blocking what he was doing from view as he dipped his fingers beneath the rose covering her breast. "And this." He pinched her nipple with his thumb and index finger.

She gasped.

He rolled her nipple between the pads of his fingers.

Arousal exploded throughout her body.

"Mm. It doesn't take much for me to turn you on. Earlier, I did nothing."

Nothing but sit there and look delectable.

He continued to tease her nipple, and she couldn't

look away.

Jude passed behind her. "You two need to fuck already and get it over with."

Case's lips lifted into a sexy smirk. "That's not a bad idea."

"Smartest thing I've heard today," she agreed.

They gazed into each other's eyes, breathing hard, as the room emptied.

"Don't tease me, Paisley. I've been telling you from minute one that I want to fuck you." He shook his head. "Don't tease me."

"You're my enemy. You annoy me to no end, and yet, for some unexplainable reason, you turn me on like I've never been turned on before. I think hate sex is the only thing that's going to get us through this dilemma."

"Agreed."

"Enemies with benefits then?"

"So many benefits." His hands swallowed her waist, and he yanked her to him. He crushed his mouth to hers.

She opened to him, and his tongue stroked hers. She slipped her arms under his, beneath his jacket, and gripped his back with her hands. His hard, muscular back. The desire to tear his shirt from him, to feel his skin, to lick her way up his spine and between his shoulder blades had her fingers curling in the soft fabric of his shirt.

"Hell, I want you so bad."

"Then take me," she gasped. "Take me like you're stealing something."

Groaning, he dragged the skirt of her dress to her thighs and lifted her into the air as if she weighed nothing. She locked her legs around him as his hands grasped her ass. Feeling the tips of his fingers digging into her flesh had her legs clasping him harder. His impossibly large erection was snug beneath her.

He carried her as their tongues tangled, twisted, twined. Then he set her on her throne. He knelt in front of her, hands braced on the armrests. "Spread your legs for me."

She parted her legs.

"Wider."

She widened them.

"Drape your legs over the armrests."

She lifted her legs one at a time, hooking them around his arms so that they hung over the armrests.

"Open your lips with your fingers."

She slid her hand down her middle. He watched her as she watched him. Biting her bottom lip, her fingers glided over her wet pussy. He inhaled when she used two fingers to spread her labia so he could see all of her.

"Fuck," he said. "You have the prettiest pussy I've ever seen."

She gripped her knees.

His gaze met hers. "Every time you're in this chair, I want you to remember me doing

this." He bent his neck. His tongue snaked up the inside of her right thigh, and then her left. Then his tongue lapped up her vulva in one possessive lick.

She knocked her head back on a moan. His tongue claimed complete dominance over her pussy, exhibiting ownership over every centimeter as he licked her, and she liked it. She'd told him to take her as if he were stealing something, and he understood the assignment. He wasn't merely stealing. He was claiming. Her pussy was now his—labia, urethra, vaginal opening, and clitoris. But he wasn't a thief. She was a willing giver, and so was her vulva. Her pussy wanted to be taken by him. Taken and tasted and treated like the goddess it was. The fact that he could make her feel that way after he'd once called her repulsive staggered her.

Needing to forget that word, she grasped his horns and rolled her hips, fucking his face as he went down on her.

He groaned. His tongue twiddled against her clit.

She cried out as pleasure bloomed. Eyelids closed, fingers gripping his horns, she focused on the sensations he was giving her. Stunning. Marvelous. She never knew oral could be this good, this complete, this mindboggling. And who would have guessed a *demon* would be capable of such outrageously good oral? Certainly not her, but it was happening, and it was undeniable.

Her eyelids flipped open when his tongue vibrated. Literally vibrated. "What...? Is your tongue...? Is it vibrating...?"

He didn't answer, because he was too busy using that miraculously vibrating tongue against her clit.

The pleasure intensified. All she could do was sit there, back arched, legs clenched around the armrests, hands threatening to crack his horns while he drove her to surrender and absolute madness. Soft cries left her mouth. When the sensations heightened, she couldn't control her hips as they elevated off the chair, as her pussy fought to be closer to the source giving it that outrageous pleasure.

He seized her hips with his hands and lifted them for her.

Heat surged through her core. She rolled her hips closer to his mouth as pleasure washed over her, leaving her drenched. She cried out her release. Once that cry faded, several more fled from her vocal cords in a frenzy to be heard, to proclaim the gratification rippling through her loins.

Case stopped. Without the stimulation driving her to the brink, her body became lax, and her hands fell from his horns. He sat back on his heels, panting. She gazed at him through the haze of her orgasm. He was sexy as hell kneeling between her legs, breathless from going down on her, his eyes glowing with lust, his penis straining against his pants.

"I've never had fairy pussy before. I've had vampire pussy, and it's meh at best, so I'm trying to figure out why yours tastes so good." He stared at her crotch. "Are all fairies this delicious? Or is it just you?"

"I don't know, but if you go on a tasting spree through the faye faction, I don't want to know about it."

"I'm sure you'd hear about it, being their queen and all. Lucky for you, I don't want to go on a tasting spree." He licked his lips. "I think yours is the only one I'm ever going to want."

"That's good for me, because I think…if I knew you were doing that to another fairy, I'd be tempted to kill you."

He arched a brow.

"Your tongue can vibrate?"

His laughter rumbled. "That's not all my body can do."

He lowered her legs from the armrests and picked her up. He carried her to his throne, where he sat with her on his lap. While gazing into her eyes, he rubbed the pad of his thumb over her lips. "I want this pretty mouth on my cock."

She licked the underside of his thumb.

"Oh, fuck."

She smiled. "I want you to come as undone as I did."

"I don't think you'll have a problem there."

She got up to lower onto her knees between his legs. Meeting his gaze, she opened his belt buckle and unzipped his pants. His penis sprang free. She looked at it, and stilled. Impossibly large was an understatement. His cock was so thick that if she tried to fit it into her mouth, she'd dislocate her jaw, but his dick was beautiful, though. Like the rest of his body, it resembled exquisite marble, with a pattern of darker gray lines. They were the veins in his shaft, but they made his dick look more like stone than ever. The head of his penis was a pale pink that resembled candy. Candy that she wanted to suck and lick and enjoy. One problem remained.

"You're too large for my mouth."

He stroked his thumb along her jaw. "Do what you can manage."

With that, she licked him from base to tip, watching him the entire time. His mouth parted. His hands clamped around the armrests. She sampled the tip again and again, as if it were the sweet, round top of a lollipop. The silkiness of the head of his penis was everything. She slathered her saliva over it, and Case hissed. Her saliva could heal when she wanted it to, but she wasn't quite sure what her saliva could do when she wanted to give someone insane pleasure. By the way Case seethed and whispered "diablo," and held onto the armrests for dear life, she had a feeling her saliva was doing far more than she understood.

She closed her lips around the very tip. Sucked.

Case growled. The sound was primal, feral, and it aroused her.

She reached between her legs, coated her fingers with her cum, and brushed her juices over his penis until he was slick. Then she wrapped her hand around him. Her cum made her hand slip easily up and down his length. She stroked him as she swirled her tongue around the tip. Around and around. Up, up, up, down, down, down. Slowly at first, and then faster as he became more and more unhinged.

His knuckles cracked when he bore down on the armrests. He panted harsh and fast. Veins in his neck pulsed.

She directed her tongue to the slit at the head of his penis. With the tip of her tongue, she traced the sexy crevice, and she didn't stop. A bead of cum squirted free, and Case growled. She licked up his cum as if it were cream.

His hand closed around hers, forcing her grip to tighten and the movement of her hand to increase tempo. He threw his head back as his hand continued to guide hers to the pressure and speed he needed. She flicked her tongue along the slit faster, too, wanting to get him there.

Suddenly, his hand clamped around hers and his hips tightened. She closed her lips around his head and sucked as his cum shot forth. She swallowed a few times as his cum continued to fill her mouth.

Finally, he relaxed, and she sat back.

Breathing hard, he rezipped his pants.

"Come here." He held out his hands. She laid her hands in his and allowed him to pull her back onto his lap. He curled a hand at the back of her neck, and his other hand settled on her hip. When he kissed her, it was slow but deep.

She broke the kiss to catch her breath.

"Damn." He laid his forehead against hers. "We may not like each other all that much, but how amazing that was says something."

"What does it say?" she asked.

"That enemies can fuck each other to oblivion, and that was just oral."

"So, you're serious about being enemies with benefits?"

His hands vised around her shoulders when he drew her back. His face was hard. "Dead serious. And you better have been serious about it, too, because after that, there's no way I'm going back to mere enemies. I'm not going to let you keep me from it again."

She arched a brow. "You won't let me keep you from *my body*?"

"No," he growled. "And if you try, you'll see how demonic I can get."

She gripped his wrists. "Let go."

His jaw clenched, but his hold loosened, and she wrenched his hands from her. She climbed off him, righted her dress, and made for the exit. Her entire body quaked from a mixture of anger and arousal at his claim.

"Paisley!"

She should've kept going but knew if she did, he would've seized her. To avoid being in his grasp again, she faced him. He stood a few yards away, hands stuffed into his pockets, his belt still undone.

"Don't deny me what I want." His gaze raked over her as he stepped toward her. "Which, I'll make plain, is you."

She didn't respond with words. Turning her back on him and walking out said it all.

8

Hiss for Me, Baby

Case

He shouldn't have said that. His demonic nature had reared its ugly head at the worst possible moment. Paisley's body was hers. To give or reject. He would never take what she didn't want to give. Would never claim her if she didn't want to be claimed.

Pissed off at himself, he returned home.

When he entered, Thatch was coming downstairs, likely from his room. As Case's right-hand, Thatch lived in the mansion, not only as part of the security, but also if Case ever needed him for counsel. "How was the meeting?" Thatch asked.

"It started with Paisley showing up in a dress like you've never seen before. Halfway through the meeting, I was vowing to protect her at all costs. It ended with me eating her out and her sucking my cock."

"I didn't have to know that last bit."

"You asked."

"You don't have to divulge everything."

"Yeah, well, I likely screwed myself over. I might've told her that she'll see how demonic I can really be if she attempts to keep me from her body again."

"You didn't."

"Unfortunately, I did."

Thatch closed his eyes with a groan. "You act as though that was the first time you've ever gotten…"

"Pussy? You can say it, Thatch."

"You know I don't like vulgar words."

Case chuckled. "I do know that. You're the only demon who doesn't."

"We're not talking about me. We're talking about you. You've had how many women and you have the gall—"

"Balls."

"—*gall* to say something like that to a woman? And not just any woman, but a queen? Are you out of your mind?"

"It appears so. She does that to me. I can't control it, and I don't think I'll ever get enough of her. You were saying it's as though I've never had a woman's pussy before, and I've never had pussy so good before. Until today. Until Paisley's. She's fucking ruined me for other women...I don't want other women. Human or creature. Just her."

"Damn, Case."

Case gave a bitter laugh. "Exactly. I'm going for a run to clear my head."

He changed out of his suit and ran for two good hours without breaking a sweat.

Thatch raised a brow when Case returned home and headed straight for the bottle of whiskey on an end table in the parlor. "Did your run help?"

"It did not." His thoughts were still stuck on Paisley.

He poured a generous glass of whiskey and downed it in one swallow.

"I doubt whiskey is going to help."

"Something has to."

"Maybe a cold shower."

"Maybe." He tossed back another glass.

"And maybe some food."

"Later. I think I'll take that cold shower first."

It'd have to be frigid. Frostbiting. He set the faucet to the coldest setting and stood beneath the spray, feeling the beads of water on his back like needles. Eventually, his body fell numb from the assault.

When he stepped out of the shower, his phone was ringing. Ignoring it, he towel-dried off and pulled on a pair of dark gray sweatpants. His phone rang again as he entered his bedroom. He picked it up from the nightstand. The number wasn't one he recognized, so he hit the red button to reject the call. Immediately, the same number called back.

Sighing, he answered. "Who is this?"

"It's Aster. I'm Paisley's lady-in-waiting. You told me to call you…" She trailed off.

"I remember you, cutie pie. Is everything okay?"

"Well…when I asked if Paisley would contact you, she said she'd handle it herself."

His free hand balled into a fist. "Handle *what* herself?"

"Paisley found something tonight on her property. It'd be best if you came and saw it for yourself. You might want to be quick about it."

He ended the call and tossed open the doors to his balcony. His wings sprang free from the confines of his body. With one massive stroke, he lifted into the air. Rage had him arriving at Paisley's home in under a minute. He landed hard on the walkway, surprised his bare feet didn't crack the concrete. The door rattled in its frame when he pounded on it.

Seconds later, it opened to Aster. "That is certainly being quick about it," she said.

"Where is Paisley?"

"Out back."

He spun on his heel and marched over the grass to the backyard.

Paisley was back there, wearing a sexy, black spaghetti strap nightgown with strips of lace between solid panels. Through the lace columns, he could see her legs from thigh to ankle. And the sight of her pale skin through that lace did something to him. Something that excited him even as his wrath burst free. "What the fuck are you doing out here alone?"

She jumped, whirled around. Her eyes were burgundy and glowing. Her mouth fell open instinctively, revealing her fangs. A deep hiss met his ears.

He held up a hand. "It's me."

"Damn it, Case. What are you doing here?"

"Your sweet lady-in-waiting called me. She said you found something and intend to handle it yourself. What'd you find?"

"That's none of your business. You're not welcome here. Leave."

"I'm not welcome? Aster asked me to come. She opened the door for me. She told me where to find you. And let's not forget that I vowed to be your protector. So, I'm not going anywhere. Now, what did you find?"

She stepped to the side.

His gaze lowered to the ground. A pair of severed fairy wings lay there. "Fuck. Do you know who these belong to?"

"No."

The hot venom of anger surged through him. "A fairy's wings were cut from their back. They could even be dead, their body somewhere on your property, and you were going to *handle this* yourself? I could throttle you, you stubborn little hybrid." He caught her hand and hauled her toward the house. "You're going back inside. From now on, you and Aster are going to be under the protection of me and my faction."

"The hell we are. And don't call me 'little hybrid.'" She struggled to free herself from his grip.

He rounded on her. "What is wrong with you? Someone is clearly threatening your life. They might've killed one of your own. Not to mention your parents. You need protection and I'm fucking giving it. Now get back into your house or I'll throw you over my shoulder and carry you in myself."

She didn't budge. "You wouldn't dare."

"Oh, I would." He snatched her up and tossed her over his shoulder.

"You son of a bitch! Put me down!" She kicked her legs. Her fists pounded his back. "I said 'put me down!'"

If she really wanted to hurt him, she could. Her fight felt half-assed, and for some reason, that angered him more. He carried her back into the house. The door slammed when he threw it behind him. The pictures and the windows rattled from the force of it.

Aster stood there with wide eyes and her jaw dropped.

He set Paisley on her feet. As soon as he did, she slapped him across the face. Okay, so that wasn't half-assed. He grabbed her shoulders and lifted her onto tiptoe. "Do that again, when all I'm doing is looking out for your ass, and you'll pay for it."

"I don't need you looking out for me!"

"You clearly do unless you want your adorable lady-in-waiting to have her wings sawed off her back. Or worse." He dropped Paisley onto her feet and faced Aster.

The sweet fairy was trembling. Her wings had flattened against each other to the point where he couldn't even see them anymore. The poor thing was frightened, as she should be, but he hadn't intended that; he had wanted to get through to her stubborn queen, not terrify her. "I won't let that happen," he told Aster. "I'm going to charge my right-hand to be your bodyguard. He'll keep you safe." He spoke to Paisley next. "And I'll be yours."

"The hell you will."

He saw red.

"Aster, cutie pie, can you give your queen and me some privacy?"

Aster appeared unsure of what to do.

Paisley was seething, not saying a word to keep her lady-in-waiting there. She didn't even meet Aster's eye but continued to shoot daggers at him.

He nodded at Aster, indicating it was okay. No, he wasn't going to hurt her queen, but he would make sure that she understood him. Whatever means necessary.

After a moment, Aster scurried away.

As soon as she was out of sight, he pinned Paisley with his glare. "You are being reckless with your life and the life of your lady-in-waiting, and I'm not going to allow that."

"Why do you care about protecting me?"

"The hell if I know, but I do." He didn't understand it one bit, but it was the truth. He wanted to protect her. "Do you have wings?"

"Yes, but you don't need to worry about them."

"I don't need to worry about them when severed wings were left outside?"

"You don't need to worry about them because no one sees them."

He tilted his head. "No one?"

"No one."

He smiled. "I will."

"That'll never happen."

"I like a challenge.

"Case, leave."

"No."

"I don't need you here, Case!"

"The fuck you don't. I'm going to take care of those wings outside, but first…I'm going to take care of you."

"I. Don't. Need. You."

He inched closer. "You're quivering."

"Anger."

"It's more than that." His gaze swept over her. "It's desire. You want me as much as I want you, but you're afraid to admit it."

She clenched her jaw and balled her hands into fists at her sides. Her chest rose and fell. Seeing her like that increased his lust to the point of exquisite erection. He didn't even try to stop it but let it expand to its fullness. She was staring right at his erection, and she couldn't hide how her body quivered now. Her lips were parted as she drew in shaky breaths.

"Tell me you don't want my cock inside you, and make it convincing."

Her heated glare met his. "I hate you."

"You don't have to like me to want to fuck me."

Her hands lowered to the skirt of her nightgown. Her fingers bunched up the silk into her palms. "You're right." She was breathless. "I do want your cock inside me. Stretching me. Filling me. Pounding me."

Her words made his penis ache.

"I want it so badly that I'm dripping. I can feel streams of cum slithering to my inner thighs. My clit is swollen. My opening is throbbing."

He swallowed, not expecting her to admit all that. "Fuck, Paisley."

"I want your penis so much that if I don't get it tonight, I'm going to have to find someone else to fulfill my needs."

Possessiveness overtook him. "No," he growled. "Me. And only me." He stepped closer. "Where's your room?"

She started to move past him.

He blocked her way with his arm and curled a hand around her hip. The feel of her hipbone beneath his palm had more blood rushing to his dick. He cocked his head toward her, inhaled, taking her scent into his lungs. She smelled like rose and sandalwood, but that wasn't all. He also caught a whiff of a salty sweetness that was her cum.

"Diablo," he muttered. "I want you now, Pais."

"Let go of me and you can have me."

With a groan, he released her.

She continued past him, and he followed her up the stairs and down the hall. At the end of the hallway, she opened a door. He couldn't make out much of what was on the other side. No lights were on in the room. He could make out the dark shape of furniture positioned around the space, black rectangles on the walls, and a four-poster bed in the middle of the floor. He picked her up and tossed her through the air.

She landed in the middle of the bed, without a yelp, without a squeal, without a gasp. Her legs were bent at the knees, opened. The skirt of the nightgown covered her sweet pussy, though. She leveled up onto her elbows. Her hair cascaded down her back, off her shoulders. The visual was breathtaking.

His penis twitched.

At the foot of the bed, he worked the band of his sweatpants over his erection and pushed them down his thighs. He lifted his feet out of them one at a time and kicked the sweatpants to the side. Her gaze settled on his penis, and she licked her lips. Seeing her tongue reminded him of what it'd felt like to have her mouth on his dick. Glorious. And something more.

"When you went down on me, I could swear that your spit tingled."

Her mouth quirked at the corners. "Well, that explains your reaction. I was wondering."

He rested his hands on the bedposts and bent his neck. "What was that?"

"I don't know. Never happened before. Are you complaining?"

"No. Definitely not." He glanced at his dick before meeting her eyes again. "I know I was too big for your mouth, but you don't have to worry. If I'm too big for your pussy at first, I can split it in two."

She blinked. "What?"

"Look again."

She peered down, and her eyes rounded.

Instead of one thick penis, he had two, one on top of the other.

"What in the world would you need two penises for?"

"I'll show you."

Her legs trembled.

He smiled. "Hiss for me, baby."

She frowned. "Why?"

"Because it turns me on. Give me a good vampire hiss."

"You'll have to piss me off if you want me to do that."

"That'll be easy."

She nodded. "If anyone could, it's you."

"I'm the reason someone wants you dead."

No reaction.

Interesting.

"I'm the reason thousands of bats were slaughtered."

Her jaw clenched.

"I'm the reason a fairy was murdered tonight."

Burgundy rings formed in her eyes and dominated her pupils.

"I will be the reason why sweet little Aster is killed."

She scrambled onto her knees, into a crouch.

"Viciously."

Her mouth opened to long fangs and a low hiss.

"I'm the reason your father was burned alive."

A deep, throaty hiss left her as her mouth fell wide.

"And I'm the reason your mother was butchered."

She let out a scream and launched at him.

He caught her.

Her arms and legs latched onto him.

"I fucking hate you," she growled in his ear.

He grabbed a fistful of her hair and tugged her head back to look into her eyes. "I know."

She licked his mouth. "And I hate how much I fucking want you."

"Same."

He lowered her nightgown's strap, exposing her right breast. His gaze feasted upon the rose tattoo. The green leaves extended over the gentle, fleshy swell, and the red bloom opened full and wide above her breast. The bottom of the stem pointed to her nipple. A nipple that was erect. She had the cutest, daintiest nipple he'd ever seen. So sweet, paired with such an adorable breast, on a woman who was a complete pain in the ass.

Groaning, he licked the tattoo from stem to bloom.

She sighed.

He planted kisses on the four petals.

She grabbed his face and dragged his mouth to hers.

The kiss was all heat, all passion, all tongue.

His hand slid up from her hip and cupped her breast. He pinched her nipple, and she gasped into his mouth.

"Fuck me, Case. Show me what you can do with two penises."

"Patience." He crawled onto the bed, with her wrapped about him, and covered her with his body. "I'm going to enjoy you first." He sealed his mouth around her breast and suckled hard, as if he could get her nipples to give him sweet nectar.

She bucked beneath him.

He massaged her other breast through the silk as his mouth worked on her. His fingers squeezed her nipple, and she cried out. His libido shot to the stratosphere, and his hands dove beneath her nightgown. Palms to her thighs, he stroked his hands to her hips. The nightgown lifted with the movement and bunched around his wrists. He drew the nightgown higher. His gaze raked over every inch of her that he uncovered.

When he pulled the nightgown from her head, her hair spread out over the bed. He studied her as she writhed under his scrutiny. "You're stunning." His voice came out on a rasp. "Who would've thought?"

"Thought what?"

"That a half-vampire, half-fairy mutt would look so damn sexy."

"Did you just call me a mutt?"

He closed his hands around her waist. "I did. I'm a mutt, too, Paisley." He bent down, licked the jut of her hipbone. "I don't even know who my parents are. I was an orphan, rose to become the leader of the daemon faction because I'm strong, smart, invoke loyalty, and I get whatever I want." He shifted lower, tweaked her clitoris with the tip of his tongue. "*Whatever* I want." He kissed his way from her pubic bone to her mouth. Holding her head in his hands, he studied her. "How is it that you're so damn beautiful?"

"Have you ever seen a female vampire?"

"Of course."

"Have you ever seen a female fairy?"

"Obviously."

"Take a sensual, bewitching vampire, and an elegant, enchanting fairy. Mix. And then you get me."

He nodded. "I certainly do."

"I didn't mean it like that."

He slipped a hand between her legs. "I did." He

eased a finger into her. She twisted beneath him as he stroked her soft insides. "You're tight."

"One of your fingers is two of mine," she gasped.

He petted the cushiony spot a couple of inches inside her vagina. "Diablo, you're so wet."

"I told you I was."

"Yes, you did."

Her thighs clamped around his hand. Her hips rolled, taking his finger deeper. She moaned. "Case, damn it, I don't want to come on your finger. I want to come on your cock." She grasped each of his penises. "Both of them. If you don't put one in my pussy and the other in my ass, right now, I am going to hurt you." Her nails briefly dug into him.

He hissed. Not from pain but from wanton desire. Desperate to be buried in her, he flipped her around. "On all fours."

She rose onto her hands and knees. He stroked a hand down the column of her back. Then he cupped her hips with his hands and sent a stream of spit from his lips. She shivered as the stream slithered over her parts, coating them, preparing them for penetration. He positioned his top penis at her anus, and his bottom penis at her vaginal opening. Without warning, he tugged her hips back while pumping his own hips forward, impaling her twice. She moaned, and he let out a roar of animalistic need. Being inside her felt like a dream. She was tight, but yielding. Soft but strong.

He pistoned his hips, plowing into her. At the same time, his hands yanked her back and forth so that he hit her harder, faster. Their bodies slammed into each other, smacking wetly. The squishing sounds, her cries—fuck!

He yanked her up. Her hair flipped over his shoulder, and her back met his chest. He glided a hand up the center of her body and closed his hand around her throat. His other hand journeyed from her hip to her mons pubis to seek her clit. She rocked against him as he drew circles on her clitoris and thrust his hips forward.

Whenever she breathed hard and cried out, he could feel it against the hand he had at her throat. He forced her head to turn to his, and he plunged his tongue into her mouth. With their tongues keeping pace with their hips, he slid his hand from her throat to her tattooed breast.

She stopped kissing him for the gasps that fluttered free. Their mouths stayed touching, though. "Case."

His name, on a strangled whisper, equally surprised and excited him.

His movements became even more vigorous, and so did hers.

In his arms, she vibrated. The vibrations became full-bodied convulsions.

"I'm coming," she gasped. "I'm—"

He sank into her with a violence to get himself to orgasm with her.

Suddenly, she drove her hips back, pressing her ass snug against him. Deep inside, her muscles spasmed around his penises. A cry broke from her. He pounded into her several more times as she let out moan after frantic moan from the pleasure of her orgasm and the continued stimulation of his penises caressing her erogenous zones and his fingers brushing her engorged, over-stimulated clit. Her cries and the rush of heat as she squirted and her body hugged his cocks was what he needed. He roared from the sheer bliss of his cum erupting from him.

Still buried inside her, holding her to him, he stretched out on his side. She was breathless and shaking. "I've got you," he whispered and kept his arms around her.

After several minutes, she finally stopped trembling.

He slipped out of her, and she let out a small gasp. Either from the residual pleasure in her body or from discomfort. It didn't matter which one caused the sound because the urge to comfort her came swift. "Ssh." Shifting away, he coaxed her onto her back and then onto her side to face him. He grasped her knee with his hand, hooked her leg over him, and scooted close again.

"We don't need to spoon, Case. You can let me go."

His hands cradled her head, and his fingers tangled with her hair. "Paisley?"

Her eyes were wide as she stared. "Yeah?"

"Shut up." His mouth closed around hers. He kissed her slowly, like sipping an expensive, decadent wine.

Another soft moan, this one of desire.

He eased back. "Was that your first time having sex with a demon?"

"Yes."

He brushed her hair from her face. "Well, it won't be the last."

"Does sex turn you into a softie, Case?"

"Darlin', I've always been a softie, but yes, sex turns me into a puppy."

She laughed. "Good to know."

He pinched her chin. "Don't ever use sex as a weapon against me, Pais. Once the puppy goes away, you'll have a beast."

"Yeah, I caught a little of that earlier before I left the meeting."

"That wasn't one of my proudest moments. You angered me, but I'll never force you to do something you don't want to do. I'll never force myself on you. I may be a demon, but I'm not like that."

She nodded. Without another word she climbed off him and strode to the end of the bed. He enjoyed seeing her naked, her hair swishing over her back, her thighs brushing each other. She slipped on her nightgown. The silk slithered over her curves in the most delicious way. Then she bent over, picked up his sweatpants, and threw them. They landed in a heap on his package.

"Get dressed, Case. It's time for you to go."

9

But What a Fun Line

Paisley

"No, it's not," Case said. "There's still a matter of those fairy wings. I'm not going to leave severed fairy wings on your property to rot or attract vermin." He climbed off the bed and pulled on his sweatpants. "Don't come outside. I'll take care of it myself."

"I'll come with you. It's my property."

Case about-faced, caught her shoulders in a strong grip, and propelled her back a full step. She instinctively shoved a hand to his chest, as if that could stop him from getting any closer if he tried.

"Will you ever do what you're told?" he demanded.

"Probably not."

A growl rumbled in his throat.

Beneath her hand, his chest vibrated.

Then the corner of his mouth tilted up in a lopsided grin.

He did take a step closer, and she was right, her hand there on his chest did nothing.

"One day, whether it's in your bed or mine, you will do everything that I ask you to do." The tip of his finger trailed up her throat. At her chin, it tipped her head back, forcing her to stare into his eyes. "Everything. Mark my words."

She arched a brow. "What happened to 'never force you to do something you don't want to do'?"

His hand closed around her throat, applying gentle pressure. "Stay inside or I will spank you."

"Spanking isn't one of my kinks."

"Mm. The way I'd do it, you'd enjoy it."

Curiosity made her pussy tighten. "I doubt that."

His eyes flared. "You get off on going against me, don't you?"

"And you get off when I go against you." She slid her hand down his chest and gripped his erect cock through his sweatpants. "Don't you?"

He wrapped a hand around hers and dragged her hand up his length. "Your disobedience is my aphrodisiac."

"Are you sure this isn't a permanent state for you?"

109

He chuckled. "It is when I'm around you." His other hand squeezed her throat slightly, enough that alarm flitted through her a millisecond before intrigue. "Stay inside, Paisley."

Without another word, he released her.

Heart racing, she stared after him. She'd never engaged in any sort of pain kink. No BDSM for her. Asking her partners to fuck her harder, Harder, HARDER was as far as she'd ever gone. Getting railed good and rough was one of her favorite ways to get off, but she'd always preferred to be in control. With Case, though, with this huge demon who had awakened her sexually in a way no other creature had ever done, she wouldn't mind handing over every last bit of control. While she didn't want to be choked, a hand around her throat, applying pressure on and off, could be exciting, because his hand around her throat right then had thrilled her. She also didn't want to be spanked with a paddle or leather, but his large hand on her ass...well, now, that was a different story. Merely thinking about it turned her on.

She ventured downstairs, knowing very well that she was tempting the beast. The severed fairy wings were out back, so she left through the front door and out across the lawn to the wisteria tree. Her heart raced with the adrenaline that disobeying him created. Yeah, she had always been the one to go against authority because it was dangerous and exciting. Case was *not* her authority, but his promises were equally as dangerous and exciting. More so, even.

About fifteen minutes later, the front door slammed shut. The bang echoed through the night. "Paisley, where the hell are you?" His shout gave her a little shiver of pleasure.

"Polo," she called out.

It didn't take him long to locate her.

He tossed aside the flowering wisteria branches. "You fucking pain in the ass."

He yanked her to her feet. With a growl, he whipped her around. One arm was braced across her middle, holding her up as she bent over it.

She didn't have a chance to do anything but blink.

Then his hand came down on her ass.

A yelp escaped her.

Where his palm had struck her, her skin stung. "That was for punishment," he hissed in her ear, "but the rest will be for pleasure. Get down on all fours."

"I was already on all fours for you," she panted, trying to ignore the sting.

His hand twined around her hair, and he tugged her head back gently. "On your hands and knees. Now."

She sank to her knees. When she flattened her hands to the earth, Case knelt beside her. His hand made circles over her backside. The cool silk of her nightgown felt good over her flaming skin.

"I only like to cause women pain when they want it, and only to a certain degree. You hadn't asked for that. I apologize."

His apology touched and confused her. She'd never expect that from a demon. "Case, what kind of demon are you?"

"Why do you ask?" His hand continued to draw lazy, intimate circles.

"Because I've never met a demon like you."

"What can I say? I'm one-of-a-kind." He lifted the back of her nightgown. The chilly night breeze made her skin break out in goosebumps. The shiver that coaxed out of her, though, was from his fingertips brushing over her cheeks. "No matter how much you make me want to throttle you, I don't want to hurt you. Do you want a safe word?"

The entire time he spoke, his fingertips swirled with the softest of touches.

"Daddy."

His fingers stilled. "What?"

She peered over her shoulder. "I would never call someone 'daddy,' so that's my safe word."

He smirked. "Alright. I gotta say, though, that's now my new favorite safe word. I may want to hear you say it now."

"The point of a safe word is that you *don't* want to hear it. If you do, you've crossed the line."

His finger traced her crack. "Mm. But what a fun line."

She shivered again.

Answering that, Case smacked her right cheek and then her left cheek. Right over the fleshiest parts. The slaps weren't hard, but they did make her jump and gasp. For the strangest reason, the slapping sounds filled her with desire, reminding her of how their bodies had slapped together moments ago.

He lifted her nightgown higher, exposing her back. His tongue slicked up her spine from her tailbone. Then he flicked the tip of his tongue here and there, where his hand had connected with her ass. The play of sensations from rough to gentle was arousing in a way she didn't think possible.

He paddled the top of her cheeks one at a time.

She bit her bottom lip. Her teeth sank deeper and deeper as he massaged her ass as if it were made of the most exquisite clay and he was molding something sensual, something erotic, something carnal. Suddenly, his fingers stroked over her sex and located her clit. They brushed the swollen gland in tantalizing circles.

His hand whacked the center of her ass, firm but not enough to hurt. The blow thrust her hips forward, right into his hand and his caressing fingers. When she gasped this time, it dripped with pleasure. His fingers didn't cease rotating over her clit, nor his hand tapping her ass.

Each slap increased her desire.

Each second filled her clitoris with sensation.

Electricity coursed up from her stimulated gland and throughout her pussy.

She moaned.

He spanked her again.

Another moan broke free.

Now, every intimate strike was equivalent to a thrust of his penis, hitting her in just the right way and coaxing cries out of her.

Thwack.

Moan.

Thwack.

Moan.

Thwack.

A detonation of orgasmic release bloomed in her core, and she cried out from the shockwaves that rippled up her abdomen and down to her knees. She bent her neck, panting from the startling conclusion.

Case lowered her nightgown and eased her onto his lap. He brushed her hair from the side of her neck and whispered, "That, darlin', is what's called a spanking orgasm."

She leaned against his vast chest. "I get the allure."

He chuckled. "I knew you would. Are you okay?"

"Yeah."

"Do you need an ice pack for your derrière?"

She tried to glare at him, but when she turned her head, his face was so close that her lips brushed his cheek. "Sorry," she muttered.

Case hooked her legs with his arm and maneuvered her sideways on his lap. His other hand cupped the back of her head, and his mouth closed around hers. Surprise gave way to passion. She snaked her arms around his neck. Kissing Case was like making out with the night. A dangerous, seductive, mysterious night full of possibilities and boundless pleasure. She sank into the kiss as if tumbling down a wormhole. He was a genius kisser. The way he sucked on her lips. The way he delved his tongue into her mouth to glide with hers in a sensual dance.

Holy Goddess.

She eased back, lightheaded. "For a demon who didn't used to kiss, you sure enjoy it."

His reply was gruff. "I enjoy kissing *you*."

Her eyelids fluttered open. "Careful, or I'll think you actually like me."

Smiling, he rubbed the pad of his thumb over her bottom lip. "I like certain things about you, I won't deny that. Will you try to deny it?"

Breaking his hold on her, she rose to her feet. "No, there's certain things I like about myself, too."

He stood. "You know that's not what I meant."

"There might be one"—she ogled his crotch—"or two things I like about you."

She went to duck beneath the wisteria branches.

With a handful of her hair, he tugged her to a halt.

"Okay, so maybe I like a few more things." Like the tingles that dominated her scalp from the hold he had on her hair.

That answer seemed to satisfy him, because he released her. "Come on. You should get back inside." He escorted her all the way to the door. She had a feeling that if he could, he'd bar her from leaving. "Come morning, I'll return with my right-hand. We'll search the property for a body and anything else that shouldn't be here."

"I can do that tonight."

He nudged her over the threshold. "You're not going to traipse around in the dark looking for a dead body with nothing but a flashlight. Your property is too vast, and it's dangerous."

"I have two factions who can search for me. One of which lives in the dark."

"There's that stubbornness again."

"There's that controlling jackass again."

He threw his head back in laughter. "Touché." His hand settled on the door handle. "Stay inside."

She rolled her eyes.

"I mean it, Pais. Stay inside. We'll search in the morning when it's safe."

"Fine."

"Goodnight, Paisley." He pulled the door shut.

"Sweet dreams, Case," she said and twisted the bolt.

Sure enough, a knock sounded on the door at first light. She opened it, unsurprised to find Case there in jeans and a black T-shirt. Another demon stood with him, the one with violet skin who'd accompanied Case to the coronation. He wore black slacks and a white shirt with the sleeves rolled to his elbows and the first several buttons undone. He wasn't as tall as Case, but his shoulders were wider and his chest broader to match the size of his huge buffalo horns. His chest tapered off into lean hips.

Paisley smiled. "The right-hand to the demon lord. It's nice to officially meet you."

"Likewise, and please call me Thatch."

"Thatch?" She tilted her head. "That's a fairy name."

"I was named after my father. Thatcher."

"Case wants you to be my best friend's bodyguard. I need to know if you will take that duty seriously, because if you don't, if something happens to her, I will filet you."

"I swear on my life that I will protect her."

"I hope so, because, as I said—"

"Filet. I know."

Nodding, she peered over her shoulder. "Aster,

come meet your bodyguard."

Aster had been hanging back, out of eyesight but within earshot. She stepped around the door and joined Paisley's side. Her head tipped back as she stared up at Thatch, who was twice her size. Her violet hair slipped off her shoulders and swished across her back. Right then Paisley realized that not only was Thatch a fairy name, but his skin was the same color as Aster's hair. Down to the exact shade.

Aster's eyes widened. "Oh my."

Thatch grinned. "Hi there, baby doll."

Paisley frowned. *Baby doll?*

Thatch knelt in front of Aster and laid a fist against his chest, over his heart. "I will lay my life down for you. You have my word."

Aster's wide eyes shifted to Paisley. She was speechless, and so was Paisley.

Damn, he's good.

"Th-thank you," Aster said.

Paisley studied Aster's flaming cheeks and diverted gaze, and Thatch, kneeling before her, promising to sacrifice himself to keep a fairy he just met safe, a fairy he'd called "baby doll" with a voice that dripped with affection. She cleared her throat. "Aster, why don't you show Thatch and Case into the parlor. I'll make us coffee."

Aster headed to the other room. After a few steps, she glanced behind her to see if Thatch was following, and indeed he was.

Case, however, was not.

"Cutie pie and baby doll?" Paisley said.

He quirked a brow. "Is that jealousy?"

"No. She's my best friend. We're like sisters. I'm looking out for her."

"You don't have to worry about Thatch. He's good. Honorable. He doesn't even curse. I trust him with my life. And you don't have to worry about her with me." He advanced. "I told you before, I have no interest in her." His voice lowered. "I only have a mind for you."

"A perverted mind."

He chuckled. "True enough."

Paisley peeked around him to check on Aster and Thatch. The two of them sat side by side on the love seat. A large demon and a petite fairy sharing a love seat. That should be a laughable sight, but it wasn't. Thatch appeared completely taken by Aster. He damn near had stars in his eyes.

"Apparently demons have a soft spot for adorable, petite fairies," Case said. "Or, at least, two demons have a soft spot for one specific fairy."

"She can have that effect on others. She's all heart and can make it into even the hardest of hearts." Paisley studied him now.

"I don't have a hard heart."

"Right, because your heart is a pile of mush." She spun toward the kitchen. At the white marble countertop, she set about making coffee.

Case slipped past her.

A stool's legs rubbed against tile.

Keeping her back to him, she felt his gaze on her. "We need to talk," she said, "and I need to make something perfectly clear." She opened a glass canister and scooped out fragrant coffee grounds with a wooden scoop.

"I'm listening."

"You came here to search my property with Thatch, right?"

"That's correct."

She snapped the lid to the canister closed. "I'll be coming with you."

"No, you won't."

She jabbed the button on the coffee maker. "Let's get something straight." She rounded on him. He lounged on the stool at the table, looking mouthwateringly good in tight jeans that hugged his thick thighs. "You. Do. Not. Order me around." She came closer. "You. Do. Not. Rule me." Another step. "You. Do. Not. Have a say in what I do on my own property." She stood a couple of feet away. "If someone is sneaking onto my property, killing my own, I will be a part of finding the son of a bitch. I will search my property, with or without you."

His jaw ticked.

"You. Do. Not. Get a say. You. Do. Not. Have any power over me." She erased the distance between them, grabbed the collar of his shirt into a fist, and tugged him by the hold she had on his shirt. When he jerked forward, coming within centimeters of her lips, his eyelids became heavy and hooded over his golden irises as he stared at her mouth, anticipating contact. "If you weren't a demon, I'd chew you up and spit you out." Her lips brushed his as she spoke. She inched back. "As a matter of fact, I think I still might"—she yanked him forward again—"chew you up and spit you out."

His lips were parted, waiting, ready. His eyes were

hooded once more while he stared into hers. She released his shirt and spun toward the counter to prep the coffee.

His long leg lifted, and his boot stomped onto the counter, blocking her way. "Get back over here." His voice rumbled gravellier than any romance hero in any romance book could accomplish.

Her body quivered from the pure desire leeching from his voice, his words.

She turned.

Case breathed hard. "I told you not to tease me."

"It turns out that I like teasing you."

"Then we compromise. Tease me as much as you want, but after you've had your fun, you give me whatever you've been teasing me with, whatever you've been holding out on me. And right now, that's a kiss. Your fun is over. Kiss me."

She breathed hard now, too. How could a demon wanting a kiss excite her so much? She laid her hand on his knee and glided it up his leg while stepping closer. With her hand on his upper thigh, she leaned in.

He grabbed her shoulders and yanked her to him, making her gasp. "Go on, darlin', chew me up and spit me out."

She flicked her tongue over the center of his mouth. Then she caught his bottom lip between her teeth. He seethed. She wasn't biting him hard enough to cause pain, and even if she did, she doubted she'd cause him an ounce of pain. When she stuck her tongue out again, she used the tip to trace the space between his lips.

Case's right arm hooked around her waist, and he

held her against his chest. She quickly jerked her head back, putting distance between their mouths.

He groaned.

"Ssh." She brushed her mouth over his, a sensual swipe back and forth, back and forth. His other hand cupped the back of her thigh and squeezed. The touch spoke directly to her pussy. Spoke luscious, lubricious words. She gave in and slid her tongue into his mouth.

His tongue met hers—smooth and slippery. A moan rattled in the back of his throat.

She'd had many kisses before, but none like the kisses she shared with Case, none that awakened her in such a way, none that made her dizzy with desire. Time stretched on. She didn't know how long they kissed in the kitchen, with the scent of freshly brewed coffee swirling around them and early morning light casting them in a sparkling beam. All that existed was Case's lips sucking tenderly on hers, his silky tongue stroking and swirling with hers, his spicy and yet sweet taste, and his hand still clutching the back of her thigh.

When she broke the kiss, she was more than dizzy, she was quivering. She didn't want him to feel that, though. Didn't want him to know that kissing him affected her so. Kissing him shouldn't do that. He was a demon. She was part vampire. They were born enemies. As faction leaders, they were further enemies. And the demon got on her damned nerves.

Apparently, in more than one way.

Case's right hand stroked her back. "I know kissing can't be harmful, but the way you're shivering, I'm tempted to ask if you are okay."

"F-fine."

"The shivering is good then?"

She didn't answer.

His other hand glided from her thigh to her jean-clad butt. "Are you sore?"

"No. I have an ass of steel."

His hand clenched her cheek. "That's good to hear."

She shifted back, but his hands wouldn't allow her to put distance between them. "Case, let go. I'm not a possession you can handle past your allotted time."

He released her, and she returned to the counter, set cups, the full coffee pot, a sugar bowl, a saucer of cream, and spoons onto a platinum tray.

The stool scraped over the tile once more. "Why is it that every time I see you, you look paler and paler?"

"Oh, I don't know, perhaps because I'm half-vampire."

"I know a vampire's pallor. This is different. You weren't this pale when we first met."

Tray in hand, she faced him. "Why does it matter?"

"I don't know if it does or not, but if it does, I will find out."

"Good luck with that." She wouldn't let him find out about her issue with feeding.

In the parlor, Aster was telling Thatch about flowers, and he was listening intently, as if flowers and their meanings and magickal properties fascinated him.

Paisley paused in the hallway.

"What about violets?" he asked Aster.

She gave him one of her charming fairy smiles. "A sign of innocence."

Thatch's gaze followed the flowing locks of her

hair. "That's fitting."

Aster cleared her throat. "And is it fitting for you?"

"I don't know if anyone would ever call a demon innocent, but I do my best."

Aster peered at her lap. "Violets also symbolize everlasting love and have been gifted as a declaration to always be true. Medicinally, they are used for breathing problems. Although they are small and delicate, they are quite powerful."

Case whispered in Paisley's ear, "Why are you spying on them?"

"Shh."

"And asters?" Thatch asked.

"Asters have always been thought of as an enchanting flower."

"She is pretty enchanting," Case murmured. "I think Thatch would agree."

"They are a talisman of love and a symbol of patience," Aster said.

"Hm." The sound from Case made Paisley's eyelids fall to slits.

"Their leaves have been burned as an incense to keep serpents away."

Case chuckled under his breath. "I don't think burning aster leaves will keep Thatch's serpent away from her."

Paisley surged forward into the parlor, breaking the moment between fairy and demon. She set the tray on the glass coffee table. "Help yourselves."

Aster spooned in sugar and poured so much cream into her coffee that it was more cream than coffee. Thatch added a small stream of cream, turning the coffee to a dark caramel. Case stirred in two spoonfuls of sugar and enough cream into his cup for a perfectly balanced coffee. His choice of coffee was interesting for a demon.

"What's so amusing about my cup of coffee?" Case asked.

"Nothing." She picked up a cup, poured coffee into it.

"Do you believe the stereotype that demons can only drink black coffee?"

"Well, I've never seen one take their coffee with cream and sugar."

"Let me tell you something, if you had it"—he pointed a finger at Thatch—"this one would take a mountain of whipped cream atop his coffee."

"Hey," Thatch said. "She's not talking about *my* coffee, she's talking about yours."

"And how do you take your coffee?" Case asked her.

She sprinkled in two spoons of sugar and then added cream, watching as the color lightened to a medium caramel. Then she held her cup out beside his. They were identical.

Case's lips quirked at the corners. "So, we're coffee mates?"

She glared. "We're not any kind of mates."

His smirk only grew.

Her eyes widened. The bastard. They may have had sex, but they were *not* mates. Mates were after one thing and one thing only—breeding.

"Paisley is going to come with us to search the grounds," he said, startling her.

"Then I'm coming, too," Aster said.

"Absolutely not," Paisley said.

At the same time, Case said, "Like hell."

Aster set her cup on the table with a clank of porcelain against glass. "I may be small, but I am capable. I'm her lady-in-waiting. Before you, it was my job to stand beside her and protect her. Where she goes, I go."

"I will keep her safe," Thatch offered.

Case breathed out in a huff. "Fine. I guess we're a search party."

After their coffee, the four of them trekked into the woods, searching from the farthest border of the property and making their way around to the back of her house. Paisley and Case led the way. Several feet behind them, Thatch was pointing out herbs and flowers and asking Aster about each one. Their conversation was impossibly cute. Paisley couldn't help but smile.

"Should I be asking you about the local flora?" Case asked.

She shot him a glare. "No."

"Fauna?"

She rolled her eyes.

"Then what would you like to talk about?"

"I would like to talk about nothing. We're not on a stroll. We're searching for a possible dead body, a fairy, one of my own. I'm not in a chit-chat kind of mood." She glanced behind them. "Besides, I have a feeling he's asking her about herbs and flowers to distract her from why we're out here. He gets that, despite her words, she's delicate. And for that, I'm grateful. He's kind and, as you said, very wise."

"And very taken with her."

"I don't want to discuss the two of them screwing."

"It wouldn't be that way with Thatch. He doesn't screw around. He's the gentlest, warmest, tenderest demon you'll ever meet."

Sounded like the perfect match for Aster.

"He would treat her right."

"Stop," Paisley hissed. "I still don't want to discuss or think about them screwing."

They continued on in silence, with Thatch and Aster carrying on a cute conversation about the benefits of rosemary and lavender. The woods were quiet enough that Paisley's ears caught the whistle of a tiny piece of metal zipping through the air.

"Get down!" She dropped to her knees.

The metal whizzed above her head.

An explosion of tree bark shards sprayed her.

Case's arms came around her. His chest pressed to her back. Another whistling sound, and Case jolted against her. "Damn it."

A third whistle.

Case's hold tightened.

A fourth.

A fifth.

Aster screamed, drowning out the sounds of the woods. Paisley couldn't hear if more bullets were headed their way. All that existed were Aster's terrified cries. And then something else met her eardrums. Something closer. A growl started up in Case's throat that grew louder and longer. All the while, Aster was screaming.

Case's growl became a roar that morphed into a yell. Suddenly, he shot into the air and took Paisley with him. She gripped his arms. The force of the wind from how fast he flew and how strong his wings beat the air kept her flat against him. Before she knew it, he was landing on the lawn in front of his mansion. He didn't release her right away but turned with his arms still firmly locked around her as Thatch landed with Aster cradled in his arms.

Thatch set Aster on her feet, and Paisley shook in Case's arms until he let her go. She rushed to Aster. Tears like liquid opal streamed down Aster's cheeks.

"Are you okay?" Paisley demanded.

Thatch held Aster's shoulders as she sobbed. Her voice was tiny when she said, "It's not me." And her gaze lifted to over Paisley's head.

Paisley rotated. "Case?"

His wings were still out. "The two of you are going to stay here." He nodded to Thatch. "Let's go."

When he advanced, Paisley flattened a hand to his abdomen to halt him. "You're not going back without me."

His fingers circled around her forearms. "You're not going near those woods."

"And neither are you."

His fingers flexed briefly as his eyes flared. "Someone shot me eight times in the back to try to get you."

She blinked. "What?"

He inclined his head. "This is fucking personal now." With that, his wings beat the air, and he launched toward the clouds.

The displacement of air from the impact of his wings had her stumbling backward. A second blast of wind struck her back, and she tripped forward on her feet. She rotated to see Thatch flying after his boss—the two of them forces to be reckoned with.

A sniffle had Paisley's gaze lowering to Aster. She grasped Aster's hand. "Let's get you inside." Giving Aster a supportive arm, she ushered her best friend toward the door. She opened it. On the other side, the young demon with long horns stood there, patiently waiting.

"I'm sure you remember me," Paisley said.

"I do."

"We're here because—"

"Case said you're welcome, no explanation needed. Whatever you want or need is yours." He nodded at Aster. "And your lady's."

Paisley's head went back. "Oh." She glanced around. "Where can we wait for their return?"

The young demon showed them into a lush parlor with velvet settees and high-backed chairs. Aster sank onto a settee, looking so fragile that Paisley's heart broke. She sat beside her and embraced her best friend.

Aster buried her face in Paisley's shoulder and sobbed.

"It's okay, it's okay."

"If Case hadn't been there, you'd be dead."

"Ssh." Paisley held her until Aster hiccuped and shifted back to swipe the tears from her cheeks.

"He saved your life, Paisley. I watched him get shot eight times." She sniffed. "I'm never going to

forget that."
     And neither would Paisley.

10

A Damn Feast

Case

*B*rimming with rage, Case flew over Paisley's entire property with Thatch, hunting for any glimpse of who might've tried to kill her and shot eight bullets into his body trying to do so. Eight bullets that were still embedded in his back. They couldn't find a damn thing, though, which only added to his anger. He touched down on his front lawn.

Thatch joined him a second later. "Now what do we do?"

"I'm still thinking that through." He led the way into his mansion.

Paisley and Aster were seated side by side on a velvet settee in the parlor. When he and Thatch entered, Aster sighed. "They're okay."

Paisley popped to her feet. "You son of a bitch!" She forced Case around and yanked his shirt up his back.

"If you want me to strip, darlin', all you have to do is ask."

"Shut up, take your shirt off, and sit down." She faced Thatch. "Can you get me forceps or tweezers, a bowl, a towel, and something to sterilize everything with?"

"On it." Thatch hurried away.

Case shifted to Aster, who was watching them with the biggest, prettiest eyes and hugging herself. The poor thing looked as though she still needed comforting. He wondered whose comforting she needed if Paisley hadn't been able to calm her. Perhaps the gentlest, warmest, tenderest demon was required. Unfortunately, he'd left the room, so that left Case.

"Cutie pie, you don't need to look so worried. I'm perfectly alright. Bullets have little effect on me."

"Still. It was scary…seeing my friend get shot."

Case knelt in front of her and tilted his head. "You consider me a friend?"

"Why not?"

He smiled. Never would he have thought a fairy calling him a friend would mean so much, but it did. "I appreciate that. I am honored to call you a friend, and I *am* okay."

She nodded. "Well, friend, you may want to talk to Paisley."

Paisley was no longer in the room.

"She's mad," Aster whispered.

"Of course she is."

Sighing, he hunted Paisley down in the foyer where she was examining a painting on the wall. He stepped up behind her. "That's the artist's portrayal of Heaven and Hell. The painting is called 'Balance.'"

"Who is the artist?"

"I am."

She rotated around. "You painted this?"

"I did."

"It's stunning."

"Thank you."

"You're a great artist, and a decent protector, but a complete idiot."

"Excuse me?"

"You took eight bullets for me."

"Yes, to protect you, which makes me more than a decent protector."

"Case, someone tried to kill me *while* I was with you. I don't think your presence bothers my would-be assassin very much. Whoever it is, they don't give a damn if you're around or not."

"They *will* care. And let's not ignore the fact that they weren't successful."

"Because I heard the first bullet coming."

He ground his teeth. "And then I covered you."

"I didn't ask you to be my shield."

"My body can handle it. Yours can't." He studied her. "Aster said you're mad. Are you mad because I took bullets for you? Or are you mad that you were concerned for my wellbeing when you found out that I

132

took bullets for you? Or both?"

"I'm mad because you took bullets for me and then left."

"I'm still sensing concern."

"Your senses are off."

"Are they?"

"Yes."

Thatch entered the foyer then with everything Paisley had asked for, as well as a stool. "Come on," she spat. "I'm going to remove the bullets."

While Paisley doused the forceps with whiskey, Case removed his shirt, crumpled it into a ball, and tossed it into a corner. Then he lowered onto the stool.

Paisley stepped behind him and touched his back. "Eight fucking bullets. If you weren't already injured, I'd hurt you myself."

"You can hurt me later, baby. In my bedroom. With a whip, chains, riding crop. Whatever you'd like. I'm game."

"Is sex all you think about?"

He reached back to slide a hand up the side of her thigh. "When it comes to you? Yes."

Without a word of warning, she drenched his back with whiskey.

He seethed.

"Oh, I'm sorry, did I hurt you?"

Smirking, he said, "Give me whatever you've got."

She poked the forceps into a hole to fish out a bullet.

He clamped his hands around his knees when she slipped the forceps deeper. "Darlin', are you trying to dig out a bullet or my spleen?"

"It's deep. Don't move."

"I'm not moving," he ground out between clenched teeth.

The forceps widened in his flesh, and he screwed his eyelids shut.

"I got it." She pulled the tool back out, slower than when it entered his body. When the forceps exited his back, he exhaled.

"Is it iron?" Aster asked.

"Only one way to find out."

Case rotated on the stool to see Paisley holding the crumpled bullet between her thumb and forefinger. After a moment, a gentle hissing sound met his ears. It grew louder. Smoke seeped out from between her fingers and the bullet as the metal burned her. He snatched the bullet away and tossed it into the bowl with a clank. Then he grabbed her hand. Burns marred the pads of her fingers.

"These bullets would've been deadly to you. Even one."

"Any bullet in the right place would've killed me." She extracted her hand from his.

"But an iron bullet buried in your gut?"

She licked the burns on her fingertips, healing them, and nodded. "Yes, the iron would've eaten away at whatever organs it was close to. Slowly, but surely. Whether that or blood loss would've killed me first is a toss-up."

"So, are you going to thank me yet for saving your life?"

She glared. "Turn around. There's seven more."

A jab of forceps. A burning, searing of his flesh.

Then the relief of the instrument withdrawing the bullet buried in his muscle. Finally, a *tink* when the bullet hit the bowl.

"Thank you." It was a whisper in his ear, but it made him smile.

The other six bullets came next.

Paisley set the bloody forceps on the bowl containing the eight shriveled bullets. "Aster, do you have enough fairy dust with you to heal him?"

"Yes."

Paisley stepped aside, but not before Case noticed her hands trembling. He stayed put, considered those tremors, while Aster opened the pouch tied at her waist and dipped her fingers inside it. One at a time, she sprinkled fairy dust onto the bullet holes riddling his back.

As soon as the final wound sealed, he stood, held Aster's delicate hand, lifted it to his lips, and kissed it. "Thank you, cutie pie."

At the side table, Paisley finished wiping the blood off her hands and dropped the soiled towel beside the dish. "Well, you're good now." She wasn't looking, couldn't see what he intended to do. "I have to go to the faye faction, so it's time that Aster and I—"

He spun her around, picked her up, and locked her legs around his waist.

"What are you doing?!"

"I still need nursing. From you." He carried her off.

"Put me down!"

"What? You think they don't know we fuck? Trust me, they know."

"Well, they certainly do now, you idiot!"

He took the stairs two at a time. "I saw your hands shaking."

"I've never had to dig bullets out of someone."

"And here I thought it was because you were developing a soft spot for me." He climbed the stairs three at a time. In seconds, he made it to the top and strode toward his bedroom at the end of the hallway.

She leaned back in his arms to meet his eye. "We need to talk about what happened today."

"We did. Someone tried to shoot you. I stopped them."

"What did you see when you went back?"

"Nothing. Based on the bullets' trajectories, the shooter was high up. There were no bent or broken trees from a giant, which means the culprit had wings." Stepping into his bedroom, he kicked the door closed. "We didn't see anyone fleeing in any direction."

He unwound her legs from his hips.

"Well, that's all important to know, but that's not all that we need to talk about."

He opened her jeans.

"What else do we need to discuss?"

He whisked her pants off her legs.

"You and Thatch leaving me behind."

Her underwear followed suit.

"I'm not weak."

Salivating, he inhaled her scent.

"I'm not a damsel in distress."

His fingers caressed her wet folds. "No, you're not."

Her hands caught his shoulders. "Case, you can't distract me from this."

He penetrated her with a finger, and her eyes literally rolled back.

"Oh, I think I can."

"You're such a jerk."

He chuckled.

"There is no logical reason why your finger can feel so good."

He withdrew his finger and swirled it, slick with her juices, over her clit.

She grabbed his horns and forced his head back. "After we come, we're talking."

"After we come," he agreed and picked her up again so that when he lowered onto the edge of his bed and laid down on the black duvet, she was sitting astride him. "I want you to ride me."

"Is this you living up to your threat to make me do whatever you say?"

"No. When that time comes, you'll know it. Without a shadow of a doubt. This is a request. After I took bullets for you, this is the least you could do for me."

"Is that so?"

"Paisley—" He hauled her up, rubbing her sex against his abdomen.

She gasped.

"I'll beg. Do you want me to beg?" He forced her hips down and then back up. "Please honor my cock with this glorious cunt." And again. "Please slip my cock head over her beautiful, wet lips." And again. "Please take my cock inside her hot cavern." And again. "Please fuck me." And again. "Fuck me senseless." And again.

Love Fey

"Okay, okay, stop." Panting, she gripped his shoulders. "That wasn't so much begging as it was manipulation, which worked." She shifted back. Her hands shook slightly as she opened his pants. His cock broke free. "You have such a beautiful penis," she said. "It's almost not fair for you to *have* such a beautiful penis."

"Why not?"

"Because you're a demon."

"And demons can't have beautiful penises?"

"They shouldn't." The tip of her finger followed a dark gray vein. "Not a single one of you should have a penis this beautiful, this lovely, this tempting."

"So now my penis is lovely?"

She licked the pink head. "Extremely." She swirled her tongue around the wide tip. "And then there's the sinful fact that you can have two extremely beautiful, lovely, tempting penises." Her gaze met his. "Give me two."

That was all she needed to say for his cock to become two.

The corner of Paisley's lips quirked. Then she bent forward. Her hair slipped off her shoulders, brushed the sides of his hips, and curtained his lap while she took his top penis into her mouth a few inches. He'd wanted her pussy, but damn, her hot mouth was just as good. She reared back, bringing his head out of her lips with a pop. When she filled her mouth with his second penis, he moaned. Back and forth, she accepted one into her mouth, and then other.

When she squeezed his balls, a blinding flash of pleasure coaxed a demonic roar from the depths of his

138

core and forced his eyes to roll back. She didn't cease the erotic torment but pushed her lips down on him farther. Her tongue dragged up the underside of his cock.

Pop.

Switch.

Deep.

Lick.

On and on she went.

"Pais—" Twin beads of cum seeped from the slits in his cock heads.

Her lips formed around each, one at a time, sucking the cum down like custard. When she withdrew, a line of saliva mixed with semen connected her mouth with his bottom cock. Meeting his eye, she swiped it away with her thumb and licked her lips. As he watched her swallow, more cum leaked forth.

Still maintaining eye contact, she guided each of his penises over her cunt, gliding his heads through her sweet, dripping labia so that the cum slithering out of him swirled into her creamy fluids. His eyes were closed while he reveled in the slippery feel of his cocks kissing her pussy's divine lips. He wasn't aware she was sinking onto his bottom penis until the head nudged inside her. His eyelids flipped open. She was staring, watching him as she sank lower. He groaned, and he didn't stop groaning until she was fully seated on him.

Her hips rolled.

Yes, finally, yes. Fuck me. Ride me.

The tempo of her hips started slow and then picked up pace. The smacking sound of his cock plowing into her wet pussy heightened his desire. He wanted her to lose control. To unleash herself. To let her pleasure take over. Ride him like a bucking bull she had to stay on top of. Ride him like a wild stallion not meant to be tamed. Ride him like a feral beast during mating season.

Except, her movements slowed to nothing. She lowered on top of him, with their pelvises meshed together and his top penis trapped beneath her. When she rocked her hips, her clit rubbed against his penis, eliciting a moan from her. At the same time, her mons pubis made contact with the base of his cock, causing him to groan. Her hands gripped his shoulders, and she used him to drive herself up and down. The motion was slow, so terribly slow. Not what he'd imagined, but Diablo, it felt stunning. The blasts of warm breath against his neck, and the soft moans told him that she agreed.

"Diablo," he ground out. "You like it. You like the feel of my cock inside you."

"Case." She didn't lift up to look him in the eye. She didn't stop using his shoulders as an anchor to grind herself up and down against him. "Shut up. You want me to ride you, so I'm going to do that my way. Understood?"

"Yes, my queen."

She alternated between using his shoulders to drag herself and bowling her hips. Whichever one she chose, she still did it slowly. "Vibrate."

His penises vibrated at her command.

Immediately, she sucked in a breath. Even with the vibrations tickling her vaginal walls and stimulating her clitoris, she didn't increase her tempo, but she did deepen her movements, applying more pressure. "Goddess." It was a whisper, a gasp, a word of praise, a word of surrender. Gradually, she did pick up speed. Now pulling with his shoulders or rolling her body at random, overcome with the pleasure, unsure of which one awarded her with the most sensation, swapping between them when one became too much.

Gripping her hips while she did what she pleased was all he could do.

When she pumped against him, he thanked Diablo silently and thrust in time with her. Her nails dug deeper into his shoulders, telling him she was close. Their bodies banged wetly.

"Case—" That was the only word of warning he got, and what a word of warning.

Hearing his name when she couldn't take anymore and was at the precipice of her pleasure was more than he could ever ask for.

She dropped onto him. Her fingers tightened. A cry burst from her, followed by two more. Hearing that sent his semen erupting out of the penis buried inside her. The more cum that burst free, the more his body shook in ecstasy. When the streams of his seed surged into her, she, too, shook and cried out.

Once spent, he lay beneath Paisley, utterly delighted.

On top of him, Paisley became lax. "I'd move, but I don't want to just yet."

"You're perfectly fine where you are."

"You really do become a little puppy dog after sex."

"There's nothing little about me."

She laughed. "No, you're right about that."

Minutes later, Paisley didn't say anything else. Or move.

"Pais?" He rubbed her bare legs. "Are you sleeping?"

"Hm. Yeah, sorry."

"Don't be sorry. I've never fucked someone to sleep before. At least not that quickly."

A moment of silence lapsed, and then she said, "By the way, I didn't forget about what we were talking about before. You're good, but you're not that good."

He chuckled. "What do you want to say to me?"

She pushed onto her elbows. "What you did today…leaving me behind…that's not going to happen again. Whatever has to do with threats against me, I want a part in it."

Well, he'd see about that.

She grasped one of his horns and jerked his head. "Are you listening to me?"

"Yes, I am, and let me just say…I like it when you pull on my horns."

She quickly released his horn, making him laugh.

"Case, I mean it."

"And I meant it when I vowed to protect you. Protecting you may involve leaving you behind. You're going to have to deal with that."

She glared.

"Are you going to go all sexy, vampire-eyed on me?"

"No." She untangled herself from him, and her brows furrowed. "I thought…didn't you come?"

"I sure did."

"Then why isn't there cum all over us?"

"Because I can redirect my seed to one of my cocks. Like the one that had been inside you."

"Handy."

"You could say that." He studied her, wondering if it was time to admit the truth. No better time than now. "Pais, I have to tell you something."

"What?"

"I'm a sex demon."

She stilled. "What?"

"You asked me what kind of demon I am. I'm a sex demon."

Her face hardened. "You son of a bitch." She climbed off the bed and yanked on her underwear. "You've been manipulating me into having sex with you, haven't you?"

He sat on the edge of the bed, stunned by her outburst.

"You've been tricking me." She yanked on her pants. "Using your powers on me to get laid." She rounded on him. "Haven't you?!"

He didn't have a chance to answer.

"You are never coming near me again. If you do, I will kill you." She ran to the bedroom door, but he wasn't going to let her leave believing that about him.

He sprang off the bed. In two strides, he caught her as she threw open the door. Seething, he spun her around. Her eyes were burgundy, but he didn't care. "You don't get to toss that kind of accusation at me and not give me a chance to rebuke it."

She hissed.

"Hiss at me all you want, but you will listen to me."

"I don't have to listen to another word you say."

He yanked her onto tiptoe. "I have never tricked anyone into having sex with me. I prefer them to want me naturally, as you did. You wanted me, Paisley. I didn't trick you into that. I didn't have to do a damn thing. Yesterday, all I had to do was sit in a throne and you wanted me."

"And you're telling me that's not a part of your powers?"

"My powers aren't for me, but for the person I'm having sex with. Why do you think I can I have one or two penises? Why they and my tongue can vibrate? That's not for my pleasure but for yours. I'm good at giving pleasure and orgasms *because* I'm a sex demon, but I didn't ask to be. Like you didn't ask to be a hybrid."

She stopped struggling.

"I'm not an incubus. I don't feed off sexual energy. I don't drain someone's lifeforce. I'm a sex demon who can only give pleasure. That's why I've been sought out so much, based on my reputation, by all sorts of creatures. I don't send anything out on purpose. I don't seek anyone out. I don't manipulate. I don't trick."

As he spoke, her eyes returned to normal, degree by degree.

"Does that mean you believe me?"

"Yeah. When you said you didn't ask to be a sex demon. I get that. Unless that was said to be manipulative."

He clenched his jaw. "It wasn't."

"Then I believe you."

"Do you think you're drawn to me because I'm a sex demon?"

"I…" She shifted away. "I don't know. I'm drawn to you for some reason."

"Maybe you're drawn to me…for me. Like how I'm seemingly drawn to you for you." He examined her face, pale despite the orgasm and the anger that had faded only a second ago. "I know you have to go to the faye faction to deal with the murdered fairy, but have dinner with me afterward."

"What? Why?"

"You'll be safe here, and we have some things to discuss. Let me feed you. Fairies, I know, are vegetarian. Vampires, though, eat meat. The rarer the better. What do you eat?"

"I eat meat on occasion, but I'm vegetarian right now."

He nodded. "I'll have a vegetarian dinner prepared. Will you be here?"

She sighed. "I'll be here."

Paisley arrived in a red, sequined spaghetti strap dress with a plunging neckline and two slits in the skirt that revealed her long, pale legs.

Case titled his head. "You look like a feast in that dress, Paisley."

"When you invited me for dinner, I didn't think I'd be on the menu."

"You're always on the menu." He held out his hand. "Come in." She laid her hand in his, and he tucked it in the crook of his arm to lead her to the dining room.

"You're looking like a feast, yourself, in that gothic suit."

He wore all black. The jacket had leather lapels and leather bands around his forearms studded with silver spikes. The vest was also leather, accented with more silver. A thin black belt looped around his hips. "I noticed how much you liked me in all black at the Enchanted Hierarchy Council Meeting, and I don't have to smell the air to know this suit has aroused you."

She made a small noise. "Yes, the suits do it, but the main ingredient is you."

He inhaled. Not to get a whiff of her arousal but to try to contain his own. He led her into the dining room where a small table was set up in the vast space, where a normally larger table sat. Twin white taper candles flickered golden light over the white tablecloth. Crystal goblets of white wine sparkled. Bone china and sterling silver adorned each place setting. He pulled out a chair, and Paisley lowered onto it. The red, sequined columns of her dress parted for her legs. He clenched his jaw.

A damn feast.

Clearing his throat, he moved to the other side of the table and sat.

She was gazing at him from across the table. The candlelight made her eyes glitter. "The cherry on top was how you were sitting in your throne."

"How was I sitting?"

"Like how you're sitting now."

He peered down at himself. His arms were on the armrests, and his legs were spread. When he looked back up, she was nibbling on her bottom lip. "If you continue to do that, we won't get to dinner."

"Then don't sit so sexy."

He tilted his head to the side, considering. "I don't think that's possible." This was how he sat.

"Then dinner may need to be postponed."

They needed a distraction, because the whole point of this dinner was to get food in her, make sure she ate, and hopefully she wouldn't be so damn pale.

"What happened at the faye faction? Do you know whose wings those are?"

She sighed, nodded. "We did a head count…made it seem like it was for a census. We did one for the vampyre faction, too, so no one would be suspicious. And we found her. Mid-thirties, lived alone, single, introverted, a real sweetheart. She wouldn't have hurt a fly."

"Would any fairy hurt a fly?"

Her smile was fleeting. "I knew her in school. Aside from Aster, she was the only one who never made fun of me. She was always too busy reading to be a bully. Shy and quiet. Now, she's dead, because of me."

"No, not because of you. Cowards killed her."

"*Because* of me, Case."

His jaw clenched. "I'll make them pay for it."

"She was a fairy, not a demon."

"You think that fucking matters? She was innocent."

"How about you hold them down for me, while I

kill them?"

He grinned. "I'd be happy to assist." His gaze lowered to the place setting, and he spotted the silverware. His fucking staff had set *silver* on the table. For the vampire queen.

"I will *kill* my staff," he muttered.

Every single one of them.

"What are you talking about?"

"The silver." He rose, gathered the silverware at his place, and reached across the table.

She held up a hand. "Oh, no, it's okay. No need to kill your staff over the cutlery. Silver doesn't bother me. I can touch it, wear it, eat with it, *but* ingesting it would cause damage."

He lowered back down. "So unlike iron, where touching it can harm you?"

"Small quantities don't impact me much, but the more there is, yeah, iron will hurt me."

"What about the sun? You're beautifully pale, but I've seen you in the sun."

She smiled. "No deadly allergy to the sun here. I just don't prefer it much."

"What about blood?"

"What about it?"

"Being half vampire, do you get the thirst for blood?"

"I do."

"How does your fairy-half feel about that?"

"I don't have a split personality, Case. It doesn't work like that. I have the traits of two different beings, but one mind."

"You get the thirst for blood, then. Do you give

over to that thirst? Do you feed?"

Her eyelids fell to slits.

Ah, so he was getting somewhere.

"I feed when I need to."

"Do you?"

"Yes."

If he pushed, he'd get the truth out of her. "When was the last time you fed?"

"When I needed to."

"When was that exactly?"

She let out an aggravated huff. "Why are you asking?"

"Because you look as though you don't have much blood in you."

"Well, being half-vampire, that makes sense, doesn't it?"

He shook his head. "No, because vampires feed on blood multiple times a day, and you can't tell me when you last had blood."

"Can't and *won't* are two different things. You don't need to know *anything* about me, Case."

"I don't?"

"No. I'm a being you find repulsive. Remember?"

"The package isn't revolting."

Paisley snorted. "You're essentially telling a woman she looks good on the outside but everything she has on the inside, everything that *makes* her, is revolting. Smooth, real smooth."

He met her eye. "Let's not sit here and pretend you hadn't called me disgusting."

"I said that *fairies* think demons are disgusting. I didn't say that I do. After all, I'm a vampire. Some would say vampires are demons. You, though, called me revolting, and I'm not going to forget that, which reminds me." She rose. "Why did I agree to have dinner with you? Sex is one thing. Dinner is another. I'm leaving."

Case caught her arm. "Sit."

"I don't do what you say."

"My staff is making you dinner. The least you could do is eat it."

"I don't care."

He stood, towering over her.

"Your height doesn't intimidate me."

Anger surged. "You should show a little more gratitude to someone who wants to give you a nice dinner."

Paisley scoffed. The gothic, glittery queen literally scoffed at him. "Please. You want to fuck me. This dinner is just a ruse to stick your cock in me again."

"I invited you to dinner because this morning, you looked peckish. Now, you're paler, and the sparkles in your eyes have all but faded. What's going on?"

She backed away. "Don't pretend like you care."

"I care."

"The hell you do." Despite her fiery attitude, her face had gone too pale. "All you care about is getting laid, and that's not happening. You can throw all the fancy dinners and candlelight at me that you want, but I'm not opening my legs for you again."

Sneering, he advanced. "That sounds like a challenge."

"It's not." She retreated. "Just because you're good at sex, Mr. Sex Demon, doesn't mean you win. You think I'm a joke."

The anger suddenly morphed into rage. "I *don't* think you're a joke."

"Yes, you do. I'm a combination of your biggest enemy and...what was it? The 'fruitiest' creature in our hierarchy?" She glanced around as if she had no idea where she was. "Why did I come here?"

"I wager it was because you're curious about me, too."

She snorted and rolled her eyes. "Don't flatter yourself. I'm leaving." When she spun around, her entire body swayed. She righted herself and settled a hand to her head.

He was behind her instantly, supporting her with an arm around her waist. "What the hell was that?" he demanded.

"Nothing. I'm fine."

"Fine, my ass. Sit down. Eat something."

She fought against his hold, but it was weak. "Let go."

"I let you go, and you're going to crumple. How can I fight with my favorite hybrid if she falls unconscious at my feet?"

"Know many hybrids?"

"One."

"Then I can't be your favorite if I'm the only one, and I'm certainly not your favorite anything."

He brushed his mouth over the shell of her ear. "You're my favorite pussy."

She was leaning against him now, but not out of passion.

"Paisley?"

She fell limp.

Cursing, he lifted her into his arms. Her head fell back and lolled from side to side. "Damn it." He carried her to his chair. She draped over his lap as if she didn't have a bone in her body. "How the hell do you wake an unconscious vampire-fairy?"

He didn't know what would jar a fairy awake, but he knew what would get a vampire kicking. With the sharp point of his fang, he pierced the pad of his thumb. A bubble of blood formed. He slipped his thumb between her lips and past her teeth. "Don't bite it off," he whispered while wiping the blood onto her hot, sleek tongue. He kept the pad of his thumb to her tongue, letting his blood seep from the puncture and slide over her taste buds.

"Come on, Pais, you're not nearly as much fun unconscious."

She didn't stir.

"I like you better when you're giving me grief, so wake up and spit some of that hotheaded vitriol at me."

A soft groan left her, and her throat worked as she swallowed. Her entire body flinched at the hit of his blood in her system.

"That's it," he muttered. "Wake up, my little vexation."

Her hands closed around his. He didn't like how cold her fingers felt. When she'd touched him before, she hadn't had the frigid touch of a vampire, but the warmth of something strange and wonderful. That warmth needed to come back.

The pressure of her teeth against the cut was gentle, but he could feel his blood streaming along the pad of his thumb. He studied her, getting oddly turned on as her teeth coaxed his blood free and her lips sucked on his thumb.

She moaned.

Her eyelashes fluttered.

She shifted in his arms.

Then her eyelids flipped open, and she yanked his thumb from her mouth, disappointing him more than he could say, and struggled to a sitting position.

"What are you doing?" she demanded.

"Waking your ass up. You're welcome."

"Let go."

"No." He picked her up and resettled her on his lap so she straddled him.

"What are you doing?" She was so weak that her head fell forward onto his shoulder.

"That was a thimble's worth of blood. You need more." He caught her chin with his fingers and guided her head so that her nose brushed the side of his neck. "Drink."

"What? No!" She shoved against his chest, but he held her still.

"Don't ask me why, but I want you to feed on me."

"I don't—"

"Pais, what's going on with you? You need to feed, so do it."

"Because, you infuriating asshole! You hit the nail on the head. Is that what you want to hear? That you're right? I *do* have a problem with feeding. There, I said it. Congratulations. Now, let me go."

He grasped the sides of her head. "Look at me." She was still pale as fuck, but her glare was spitting

153

daggers. "Don't you dare congratulate me for something that made you pass out, unless it was caused by an orgasm I gave you. Otherwise, I don't want to hear it. I didn't want to be right about this. I was curious. That's it. But right now, you're as limp as spaghetti in my arms, and I don't fucking like it. I'd rather have you bucking wild or attempting to scratch my eyes out. Maybe both at the same time, but you can barely sit up. You need blood. So you have a moral quandary with feeding. I get it. That's why I asked in the first place. Knowing that you do have a problem with feeding, I can help you out with that. Use me as your personal tap."

She blinked. "You don't know what you're asking."

"I'm not an idiot. You need blood, but you don't want to get it from innocent people, critters, or even blood banks that need it more, am I right?"

She nodded.

"Wouldn't drinking from one source every time you need it make the act easier?"

Her gaze shifted from his as she considered his words. "I suppose."

"And wouldn't feeding off me, a demon you despise but have amazing sex with, make the act easier?"

She peered back. "I guess so."

"Then let's test it out."

"I've never fed on a demon before."

"If my blood makes you spew vomit afterward, I give you free reign to tell me how revolting *I am*, and you can rub it in all you want."

"But what if…"

He cocked his head to the side. "'What if' what?"

"What if I like your blood?"

"That'd be a good thing."

"What if I crave it?"

"Then you can come to me whenever you need blood."

"That's a lot to ask of you."

"Not if I'm the one offering." With that, he tugged the tie from his neck, dropped it to the floor, and unbuttoned his collar. "Drink up, darlin'."

She breathed hard and fast.

"You want to. I can tell. What's holding you back? When was the last time you sank your teeth into someone?"

She swallowed. "Years. I've been using blood bags."

"Would it help if I sank my teeth into you first?"

She laughed. "Maybe." Her hands slipped up to his neck, making his breath catch. "Are you sure?"

"This is becoming like delayed sexual gratification, Pais. I've been waiting for you to feed on me for a good five minutes now. Yes, I'm fucking sure."

"It'll hurt."

"Pain is one of my kinks."

"Okay." She brought her face to his neck. The tip of her nose slid over his artery. The soft skin of her lips brushed him. For a moment, she did nothing but that, and he realized—

"Are you nuzzling me?"

"I'm preparing myself." Her lips grazed his skin. Her breath warmed him. "I told you, I haven't done this

155

in a long time. Give me a minute."

"I'll give you all of them."

Her hand slid around to the other side of his neck. She inched back and laid the fingers of her right hand in place of where her lips had rested. Her thumb stroked his artery now, up and down, as if testing herself and readying his body for the invasion. His heart raced. Beneath her thumb, his pulse throbbed. Diablo, he desired those sexy sharp fangs of hers to pierce him, for her plump, soft lips to suckle his neck. He was close to begging when her fangs scraped over his skin. The feel of her fangs was like a game of foreplay.

Her mouth opened. The points of her fangs touched his skin. He inhaled and held his body stiff in anticipation. Then her fangs sank into him, puncturing his artery, and he moaned. A flash of pain, of wonderful pleasure. She eased back, slipped her fangs free of his flesh, and he moaned again from another flash of erotic pain. Her lips formed around the puncture holes, and she suckled.

"Oh, damn. Paisley." He clutched her hips, digging his fingers into her flesh. "Diablo, that feels good."

Pleasure radiated from the holes in his neck, down his spine to his abdomen. Blood rushed to his cock even as Paisley drew blood from his artery. His shaft filled with the glorious surge. Filled until his penis became engorged—as hard as stone, threatening to tear the threads of his expensive duds—and pressed roughly to Paisley's underside. He attempted to shift, to allow his cock a little wiggle room, but that wiggle only sent a flare of painful pleasure zipping from the head of his penis to his balls. "Fuck."

Paisley shifted back on his lap, allowing his cock space to stand, but his pants still kept him restrained. If he expanded anymore, grew another centimeter, his pants would surely give to the pressure. Desperate, he reached between them. His fingers shook as he undid his belt and yanked down his zipper, damn near breaking it. He sighed as his penis sprang free.

She didn't stop drinking. Her tongue lavished, drawing out blood from the punctures. She sucked, swallowed, sucked some more. A tiny hum left her. It was the sound of someone tasting something that they enjoyed and wanted more of.

"You like it. You like feeding on me."

She sighed.

"I like it, too."

Her hips rocked forward, right into his unsheathed cock.

He grunted.

She rolled her body into him again.

He grasped her waist, unsure if he wanted to still her or drag her closer. The latter temptation won out, and he tugged her up his lap so her pubic bone was flush against him. She gasped against his neck but didn't cease lapping up his blood. Her fingers wrapped around him and gave a squeeze that made him groan until she finally released him.

While she fed on him, she caused him the sweetest agony with her palpating hand. She glided her hand down the length of him. When her hand tightened around his balls, he choked on a grunt. Her other hand left his neck and formed around his shaft. His eyes rolled back as she dragged her nails up his cock, a few of them following pulsating veins. Pleasure momentarily blinded him. He blinked against the candlelight, seeing splotches.

Her thumb and forefinger lightly pinched below the head, and he saw double. He seethed as her fingers rubbed his head, as if rolling something precious, like a jewel or a bead. His eyelids descended the instant the tip of her finger laid over his slit. She followed the line back and forth. In one direction, he had the softness of the pad of her finger. In the other, the scratch of her nail. Comfort and then pain. Soothing and then harsh. His dick vibrated on its own accord.

Her lips left his neck, causing him to groan in disappointment, for her suckling on him had increased his pleasure to a place he never thought it could go. Who would've thought a vampire feeding on him could cause him so much pleasure? Stiffening his cock to excruciating arousal, making him delirious for release?

She slicked her warm tongue over his throat, and the slight throbbing pain in his neck disappeared—healed.

"Did you get your fill?" he asked, panting.

"Yes, but I still want to be filled." She stood, swept the column of her dress away so that he caught sight of her cunt before she straddled him again, placing her knees on either side of his hips and hooking her feet around his legs. When she raised herself up, a hand around his dick, his lust-soaked brain momentarily cleared.

"Pais, I'm too large for you, let me—"

She sank onto the head of his penis, silencing him. Slowly, she lowered herself. Her breath caught, she stilled, sucked in a breath, and then sank even lower, only for her breath to catch once more. She repeated the process until she was seated on him, with his balls snug against her pretty cunt. Her pussy was tight around him. So tight that if they moved, he could slip his seed prematurely. He held her hips as she panted.

"If it's too much—"

She stole the words from him by stamping her mouth to his. Her lips tasted of metal from his own blood, but he didn't care. The pliancy of her lips, the stroke of her tongue was all that mattered. Until she rose on her knees and ground against him, taking him yet deeper. Then all that mattered was the way her cunt tightened around his cock, but he wasn't so caught up in himself that he couldn't make out the knot between her brows from the frown she wore. Or the way her teeth bit into her bottom lip. Not out of pleasure but because of pain.

"No," he ground out. "I want you to feel pleasure, too. That's the whole point, Pais." He made his cock vibrate, like flipping on a switch, and she gasped. She leaned against him as she enjoyed the feel of his shaft vibrating against her tensed vaginal muscles. Gradually, he felt them give, loosen, relax. A creamy heat swirled around him as arousal overcame her, turning her vagina into a hot pool of passion.

He dipped his hand beneath the bodice of her dress and scooped out her right breast. In the candlelight, her areola was the palest, lushest pink. He'd never seen an areola so light before, not on any creature or human. In the center of the blush-pink circle, her nipple was the color of rouge. Such a fascinating contrast.

Innocence—her sweet areola—coupled with carnality—her sinful nipple. When he'd lavished her breasts before, in the darkness of her bedroom, he'd been right in thinking that they were lovely, and they were. He drew out her other breast to admire the pair. So fucking lovely. Two succulent peaks pointing in opposite directions at the tip of her wide-set breasts. The sight of them summoned a growl of hunger.

Bending his neck, he swirled his tongue around one areola and then the other. Then his lips formed around her right nipple, and he supped on it. Each tug of her nipple into his mouth had Paisley gasping. He released her nipple with a pop before taking the other into his mouth and sucking on it hard. Her hands gripped his shoulders, and she resumed the movements of her hips. A tiny mewling sound he wasn't accustomed to hearing from her curled up from her vocal cords.

"There you go," he cooed. "Do you like this? What I'm doing to your nipples?"

She nodded.

"I like it, too. You have the sweetest nipples. My mouth waters from looking at them." He stared. "I need them, Paisley. If I could get them to milk for me, I'd never stop sucking on them. As it is, they can't give me anything but their texture, and that's enough." He groaned. "That's bloody enough." And he drew her nipple into his mouth again.

Paisley's mewling became cries that wrenched out of her.

"Just like that. Cry out for me just like that."

Gradually her pace increased, and the sounds coming from her became louder, more frequent. He let go of her nipple and used his hands on her hips to help lift her before dropping her back down. Up high so that her pussy released most of his shaft, slick with her. Slowly, slowly. Nearly to the tip. Then back down, fast, striking her cunt with his balls and her cervix with his head. She assisted him, lifting onto her knees and sitting back down.

Thump, thump, thump.

Her knees and thighs clenched him. Her feet slid off his legs as they flexed. She was racing toward climax, body quivering. Suddenly, she stilled. He didn't stop, though, and hefted her up and down to push her over the brink. Her perky breasts bounced. The sight of them increased his hunger. He'd take them into his mouth again, because he didn't dare stop, wouldn't take his hands off her hips, so he tore his gaze from her pretty, bouncing breasts to see her looking down at him. The sparkles in her irises glinted brighter than ever, like sun on broken pieces of black mirror. He stared into them, overtaken by their beauty.

She rammed into him as her body shuddered. The contraction of her muscles made his cock rear like a beast inside her. He lifted his hips off the chair. A strangled roar ripped from his throat as his cock pulsed and purged a surge of semen into her.

Eventually, he lowered his hips.

Her forehead was back on his shoulder as she panted.

"Have you had your fill now, darlin'?"

She gave a small laugh. "Yes."

Cradling the back of her head, he eased her back to get a good look at her. "Your eyes are sparkling again, and your skin has a peach undertone. It appears my blood did the trick. Did you like feeding on me as much as I liked you feeding on me?"

"It's not supposed to be enjoyable for the prey."

He smirked. "Well, being your prey is quite enjoyable for me, or was that not made clear by my monstrous erection?"

"No, that was made quite clear." She lifted off him. As his limp cock slipped out of her, she winced.

His hands hugged her hips. "Are you okay?" His penis lay heavy and depleted against his thigh. "You didn't have to take all of me before you were ready."

"But I *was* ready." She laid a fingertip to the side of his neck, where she'd bitten him. "Thank you for that."

"You're welcome, and what I said before, I stand by it. You can use me as your personal tap whenever you need blood. Don't let your hunger get so bad to where you faint in the middle of a row with me."

Her brows furrowed.

"What is it?"

"I don't want to rely on you for blood. You're a demon."

He rolled his eyes. "We've established that. Several times. I'm a demon. You're a hybrid. We're natural born enemies. Yada, yada, yada. We've also established that we have a craving for each other's bodies. You have an extra craving. Fine. Enemies with benefits can include feedings. I'm fine with that. You can be fine with it, too."

"I have a complicated relationship with feeding."

"Well, you have a complicated relationship with

162

me, too, but that hasn't stopped you from getting off on me."

With that, she climbed off his lap and righted her dress, covering her pretty breasts. "Is there a bathroom that I may use?"

"Of course. Down the hall. Third door to the right. I'll check on the food."

She opened her mouth, but he cut her off.

"You might've had blood, but you still need to eat actual food. Don't run off. I expect to see you at this table when I return."

And if she wasn't there, he'd hunt her down and drag her back. Or at the very least, wrap up the plate, deliver it to her, and watch her eat every bite. Despite popular opinion, even demons could be gentle and nurturing.

11

The Arrangement

Paisley

aisley cleaned herself up and rinsed out her mouth. The water was tainted pink from the remnants of Case's blood clinging to her teeth and gums. She held onto the porcelain bowl and stared at her reflection in the antique, black lacquered mirror. No shame, no guilt, no revulsion at what she'd done twisted her insides. Not like there usually was, even if she resorted to a bag of blood for her feeding. She didn't understand why Case would do this, offer his blood whenever she needed it. He claimed to know what he was doing, but she wondered if he truly did. While she didn't need blood as much or as often as a full vampire, she still required a dose of blood to keep her strong and healthy. Blood to a vampire was personal, a matter of survival.

Case's blood had tasted good, as she feared it would. No one's blood had ever stirred her taste buds before. No one's blood had ever caused any sort of craving in her, but Case's did. Now, she would need him for more than sex. She didn't want to need him. Not him. Not anyone. Damn him for making her dependent on him for sex *and* blood.

She left the bathroom. In the dining room, Case was seated at the table. He started to rise as she entered, but she held up a hand to stop him. "It's okay. I can seat myself." She resumed her place across from him. "This is a rather intimate set-up."

He smiled. "So maybe I was trying to seduce you."

"You seduce me just by being, Case."

His chest rose. "You do the same to me." He leaned forward. "I'm going to want you more and more, Pais. Show me you understand."

She nodded.

"Do you think you're going to want me again?"

She swallowed, nodded once more.

"Then I think we need to establish some ground rules."

Her eyelids fell to slits. "What kind of rules?"

"One, whenever we want each other, we can come to each other. Day or night."

"Okay."

"Two, if I come to you for sex, and you're willing, I take the reins. But you can always tell me if you don't want to do something. Understand?"

"Yes."

"Three, if you come to me, I'm all yours. Do with me what you will. Ask me to do whatever you want."

She crossed her legs, clenched her thighs, liking that idea very much.

"Four, we're monogamous."

His words took her aback. "So, you're not going to want a threesome?"

"Hell no. I don't want anyone else touching you. And if I find out someone else does touch you, I'll kill them."

She snorted. "Be serious."

A growl of dominance. "What about me makes you think I'm not being serious?"

Silence. She had nothing to say to that.

"Five, no matter how pissed off we may become with one another, this arrangement can't be broken off with a fight."

"Considering that fighting makes us horny, I'm sure that won't be a problem."

He smirked.

"Is that all of your rules?"

"That's all. Do you have any you want to add?"

"One thing to include with rule number four." She slipped around the table and stood behind his chair. Bending forward, she let her breasts brush his shoulder as she whispered in his ear, "If someone else touches *you*, I'll kill them. And if you touch someone else…" She stroked a hand down his chest to his crotch, grasped his dick in a death grip. "I'll castrate you. Do *you* understand *me*?"

He laid a hand over hers, forcing her fingers to tighten. "Loud and clear, my queen, and let's add your threats to the list of things that make me horny for you."

She pried her hand out from under his and returned to her chair.

His gaze was hot on her when he said, "I'm never going to want anyone else but you, Paisley."

"You don't know that."

"Except, I do know that. I've never felt this intense desire for anyone else before. I've never even had sex with the same person twice."

"Really?" But he was a sex demon. How did that make sense?

"Really. You're something special, Paisley."

She couldn't look away from him now.

"You're in my body, my blood, my thoughts. I don't care if we're supposed to be enemies. I don't care if we have rival factions. I don't care if we get on each other's nerves. All of that can be true at once." He was breathing hard now. "Do you accept my terms, this arrangement?"

She opened her mouth.

"Before you answer, remember, this arrangement can't be broken with a fight."

"What could break it off?"

"Betrayal. Mutual agreement."

She nodded slowly. "I accept."

His hands gripped the armrests of his chair. She sensed he wanted to do something right then to seal the deal, but his staff stepped into the dining room with two trays of food, preventing him from doing whatever he had in mind.

They ate salad that would make fairies swoon, a pasta with the tastiest sauce she'd ever had, and the richest Devil's food cake that made her moan with pleasure. While they ate each course, they chatted, asked casual questions, and shared laughter. During the cheese and wine course, Paisley thought of something crucial.

"We haven't been very smart."

Case's brow raised. "How so?"

"Well, paranormal creatures can't contract sexually transmitted diseases, but they can get pregnant."

He stilled at her words.

"You've come inside me three times now, and you never asked if I could be ovulating."

Now he was the one looking rather pale.

"I'm not ovulating, rest assured, but since we intend to continue this, we need to discuss this."

"It appears we do. I apologize for not realizing it sooner and for being irresponsible."

"Apology accepted."

"So...this means, you do ovulate."

She smirked. "Yes, I do. Vampire womb holders do not, as you well know. They don't have menstrual cycles at all, but fairies do."

"And you're part fairy." He closed his eyes. "And I'm an idiot."

"A horny idiot."

He snorted out a laugh.

"Fairies have different cycles than humans. Fairies are fertile during the spring and summer."

His eyelids popped open wide. "It's spring."

"It is. We ovulate during every full moon in the

spring and summer."

"What's the moon phase right now?"

Her smirk grew. "Waning. We're heading toward the new moon when I'll be menstruating. I'm past ovulation this month. We're safe." She studied the relief on his face. "You've never had to deal with this before with anyone else?"

"Usually, I'm in my right mind enough to alter my semen before it dispenses."

"You can alter your semen?"

"I can."

"You mean…you can make your semen infertile?"

"I can," he repeated. "But with you, I'm never in my right mind to make that adjustment. With you, I want to come. Inside you. Come and never stop."

She clenched her thighs from the mention of him coming inside her. "By your reaction, I assume you never want to have kids."

He picked up his wine glass. "I wouldn't want to have a kid that's unwanted."

"If it's yours, why would it be unwanted?"

He sipped wine, set down his glass. "My mother was a succubus. It's not possible for them to get pregnant by their prey. Rumor is that my father is Diablo himself and that's how she got knocked up. She was pissed. She couldn't fuck with a baby bump. Why she didn't abort me, I don't know, but she carried me to term and then tossed me as soon as the cord was cut. I grew up unwanted. I know what it's like."

"I'm so sorry, Case." Hearing the sorrow in his voice clenched her heart. He was so large, so strong, so virile that the heartbreak was out of place.

He slid his wine glass away with his fingers. "What about you? Do you want kids?"

She shook her head. "If I had a child with anyone who wasn't a fairy, that child would be a tribrid. Our world had no idea what to do with me. Could you imagine how they'd react if I had a tribrid? The Enchanted Hierarchy would implode."

"Speaking of, how did your mother become pregnant by a vampire?"

A chuckle escaped her. "Being a fairy, my mother's womb was magickal. It zapped my father's sperm to life, and *voilà*." She lifted her hands to indicate herself.

"Then a vampire *could* potentially impregnant you?"

"I doubt it. I'm only half-fairy. I don't think my womb would be strong enough to pull that kind of magick trick. Plus, I think love had something to do with it. The great force of love. That kind of thing."

"So, you don't want kids, either?"

"I wouldn't want to put an innocent child through the kind of crap I experienced, which for any child of mine would be three times as worse."

"They're all fucking idiots."

"*You* made fun of me for being a hybrid."

"I'm a fucking idiot."

She tossed her head back in laughter, not expecting him to say that.

"Are you ever going to let me forget what I said when we first met?"

"Eventually."

"I can prove that I don't think any part of you, inside or out, is revolting."

"You think you can?"

Case rose to his feet, stalked around the table. When he bent over her, bracing one hand on the table and the other on the back of the chair, she quivered with longing. His eyes stared into hers. "I know I can." Then he lifted her out of the chair. He didn't say anything else but carried her up the stairs to his room and laid her on the bed. Stretched out on top of her, he cradled her head in his hands and kissed her in a way that made her lightheaded.

"You're so good at that."

He planted kisses over her face.

"I know what kind of demon you are, but the fact that you didn't used to kiss until now makes me want to call BS. There's no way."

"I wouldn't lie about that." He slicked his tongue into her mouth and then laid a curled finger under her chin. "Keep your eyes open." His hand on her knee made her lips part. "No matter what I do."

His promise came to mind. *One day, whether it's in your bed or mine, you will do everything that I ask you to do.*

His palm glided up her thigh. "Keep your eyes on mine." His fingers spread her labia. "On mine." He massaged her pussy, and it was all she could do to keep her eyes open.

Goddess, his fingers were exquisite.

Gazes locked, he slipped a finger inside her.

She exhaled.

He curled his finger, stroking her inner flesh. At

the same time, the thumb of his other hand made lazy circles over her clitoris.

A tiny moan fluttered up her throat. She kept her eyes open, even when he eased a second finger into her, stretching her.

With two fingers now, he massaged her g-zone.

Unable to resist, she drove her hips up, taking his fingers deeper, encouraging his thumb to press firmer. His thumb answered. His fingers accepted. She wasn't aware that her eyelids had drifted shut until Case said, "Open your eyes, Paisley."

She blinked her eyelids open.

He changed the direction of his thumb from circular motions to up and down.

Her hips elevated off the bed. "I'm going to squirt."

"Then squirt."

Her back arched, and she sucked in a breath.

But she didn't expel it.

"Breathe, Pais, breathe."

She forced herself to draw in oxygen and let it out.

"Good. That's good."

When she squirted, it was a lovely release. She lowered her hips and accidentally closed her eyes.

"Eyes open."

She did.

"Don't shut them again or I'll stop."

"Damn it, Case."

His fingers and thumb were relentless, and she hoped she'd orgasm quickly, because she wasn't sure how much longer she could keep her eyes on him. She fisted her hands into the black comforter beneath her.

Her back arched. Her eyelids fell to slits, but she continued to watch him.

"Paisley—"

"I see you. I see you." She touched his face to prove it. Then she dropped her hand to the mattress, punching it as the sensation heightened. She twisted her body, seeking an escape even as she silently pleaded for orgasm. When it came nearer, she elevated her hips toward the ceiling and panted, reminding herself to breathe. Keep breathing.

Warmth spiraled in her core, exploding outward. A cry broke from her that echoed in the room. Somehow, she managed to keep her eyes open, and she watched Case bend down, a second before his lips touched her cunt. He kissed her clit and then he eased his fingers out of her and placed a kiss to the very center where she throbbed.

"Case."

"What I said earlier…I haven't proven anything, yet, but I will." He kissed his way down

her thigh to her knee.

Several seconds later, she realized what he meant. Earlier, he'd said he'd prove that he didn't think any part of her—inside or out—was revolting. What in the world did he have in mind if he thought he hadn't proven anything yet. Hadn't he?

She thought about it.

Well, maybe not yet. So far, all he'd proven, which he'd demonstrated plenty of times before, was that he loved every centimeter of her pussy. That was no secret. He'd claimed that before he'd even laid eyes on it, when all he'd done was suck it through the cotton of her underwear. Perhaps, that night, at the tiny dining room table, he'd shown her how much he adored her breasts. He'd done it extremely well. With words. With mouth. With tongue. But she was more than her tits and cunt.

Case kissed his way all the way to her ankles. His fingers picked at the thin straps, and he removed the red, glittery heels from her feet. He shifted his hands to her other foot, and he slipped off that shoe, too. A smile touched his lips.

"Even your toes are fucking adorable. It's not fair." He bent his neck, kissed each one. The pad of her pinky toe he scraped with his teeth, giving her chills. He worked his way back up her legs. At her hips, his hands cupped her curves beneath her dress. "Sit up for me."

She did as he asked.

His hands trailed up her body, lifting her dress over her head. Once he deposited her dress to the side, he said, "Back down."

She lay flat on the soft comforter.

Case hovered over her. "You should be naked more often."

"I'll keep that in mind."

He pinched her chin. "With me." His hands followed the lines of her body. "Diablo, you're stunning. I've seen countless bodies before, but only yours has ever captivated me. I…" He bent over her and planted kisses along her collarbone.

"Can I close my eyes now?"

A chuckle escaped him. It vibrated against her chest. "Yes, you can close your eyes."

With her eyelids shut, she sank into the sensations

he gave her. Never would she think a demon could lavish her like this, make her skin tingle with his kisses and the touch of his fingers, but Case was managing like no other. She hummed beneath him. Soon, he had her more than humming. She was purring. Then she was mewling for more. Whatever he could give her.

How could a demon do what he was doing? Even given his specialty, she didn't understand how he could treat her with this much intimacy. She'd never experienced it with any other creature. Not even once. Before Case, the creatures she'd had sex with it, it had just been that...sex. Nothing more. Nothing less. Nothing special. Nothing in the least bit intimate. After all, how could there be intimacy without feelings, without something more than sheer lust and the need to feel pleasure, the need to orgasm quickly.

Case exhibited a level of intimacy that made her dizzy. He kissed every inch of her body, touched every bit, murmured praises against her skin. Everything he did dripped with affection. She writhed. His attention was too much. Far too much.

"Have I proven it?" he asked. His lips brushed the shell of her ear.

Proven that he did not think a single part of her was revolting?

"Yes, yes, you have."

No way would he have managed to do what he'd done if he believed otherwise.

"I'm still not done."

Her eyelids drifted open. "You're not?"

"No."

He climbed off the bed and unbutton his jacket. On

her elbows, she watched him strip. With each item he discarded, her anticipation expanded. Once he was naked, he sat cross-legged on the bed. Then he held out his hand. "Come here."

Trembling, she held his hand and straddled him.

"I'll split my cock in two, but use the top one."

"No, I want one."

He trailed a finger along her jaw. "Are you sure? After you took all of me an hour ago, it could be too much too soon."

"I'm sure. I want all of you."

He inhaled. "You've got all of me, Paisley."

She gaped. "Case—"

"Rule Number Three, I'm all yours."

Right, of course. Rule Number Three.

"And I hope you can agree that you're all mine."

"After what you just did…yeah, I'm all yours." With that, she wrapped her hand around his penis and guided the wide head to her sex. While she scooted closer, he pulled her to him. His cock sank into her gradually. The deeper his shaft penetrated her, the more her mouth parted.

"Paisley, if—"

She laid a finger over his lips. His concern over her comfort touched her, but she wasn't in an ounce of pain. "This is pleasure, Case. Not pain." And she rocked her hips to take him in as far as he could fit. A gasp fluttered from her lips, and she wound her arms around his neck.

He wrapped his arms about her waist. "I want you to keep your eyes open again and on mine the entire time."

"Okay." At this point, she'd do whatever he wanted. Without question. Without hesitation. But with plenty of curiosity and enthusiasm.

Chest to chest, eye to eye, they engaged in tantric sex, another first for Paisley. Being that close to Case, with him inside her, stole her breath. Part of her thought this wasn't right, but she was tired of reminding herself of how different they were as creatures or that they've been on opposite sides of battles for centuries. None of that mattered while their bodies were melded together in such a way. None of that mattered while she felt such incredible things from their bodies *being* melded together in such a way.

Small noises left her.

Case touched his forehead to hers. His golden eyes glowed.

Their movements deepened, and their breaths intertwined.

The head of his penis massaged her cervix with soft taps, and with each grinding motion forward, her clitoris rubbed against the top of his shaft. Sparkling warmth bubbled in her womb. Gazing into his eyes, she nodded, telling him she was on the edge of the cliff, ready to bask in the glow of orgasm. He cupped her ass and towed her up his lap. His penis glided in and out.

The sparkling became a sensual simmer. The warmth became a sexy sear. She came with a surge of simmering, searing fireworks throughout her body.

Case pumped his hips while heaving her along his length. When he came with a grunt, a burst of his seed pummeled into her cervix. Her toes curled, and she wailed. A second spurt had her calling out her pleasure with him. Each time more of his cum shot out of his penis, they moaned together. Finally, he relaxed, and her tensed body slackened.

Case swooped her around so that they lay on their sides. "Three orgasms in one day."

"Technically, I had four."

His hand stroked up and down her sweat-misted back. "I wonder how many we could accomplish in a full twenty-four hours." Her left leg was hooked over him, and he ran his hand along her thigh now. "Stay with me tomorrow, and we could find out."

"We'd have to sleep."

"We could sleep."

"And eat."

"I wouldn't let you starve."

She smiled. "Case, we probably shouldn't push this."

"Push what?"

"Our arrangement. We agreed to it a couple of hours ago. We shouldn't rush into a marathon sex day so soon."

Groaning, he sniffed the side of her neck. "Or it's precisely how we should kick off our arrangement."

She propped herself up on an elbow. "Once a sex demon, always a sex demon?"

"I couldn't be anything else."

"I don't think I'd want you to be anything else."

"I don't want you to be anything else, either, Pais. Hybrid. Queen. Pain in my ass. Be it all…and spend the entire day with me tomorrow."

"Is that your answer to protecting me? Lock me up inside and have your way with me?"

"If it works, it works."

"You really think I'll be safe here? Four vampires broke in, with you inside, and you had no clue. If my people can do that, then someone who wants to kill me could figure it out."

"I'd like to see them try. I have a demon posted every twenty feet around my property and at every entrance. No one is getting in."

"If someone is desperate enough, that won't stop them."

"Then *I* will stop them. Do you really think someone could hurt you while you're lying beside me? While my cock is inside you?"

"I'd rather not find out."

"You'll be safer here than at home. I can promise you that." He kissed her bare shoulder. "Stay with me. Please. I'll make it worth your time. A different orgasm or sex position or both each time."

Well…how could she resist an invitation like that?

So, they spent the next day from sun up to sunset together. Five hours of sleep total. Three meals and plenty of snacks for sustenance between orgasms. Sex all over the mansion. On every surface imaginable. Every position thinkable. And every orgasm possible. It was quite the twenty-four hours.

12

The Midnight Lair

Case

They saw each other every day after that. When Case wasn't with Paisley, she was with her vampire and fairy councils getting updates on the investigation into her parents' murders, discussing the threats to her life, and making sure that her factions were safe from potential attacks. Right now, though, she was asleep beside him, right where Case liked having her.

He picked up a lock of her hair and swirled the tip of it over her chest. A small humming sound left her, and her eyelids cracked open.

"Good morning, beautiful."

"Morning."

He drew a swirl on her shoulder. "It's been two weeks, Pais."

"You're keeping track?"

"I am. For two reasons. One, our arrangement has been going strong for that long. And two, no other assassination attempts have occurred."

She shook her head. "If you think they've forgotten, they haven't. This is what they do. They wait. They let you think they've moved on so you'll let your guard down. But believe me when I say, they're planning their next attempt and waiting for the opportune moment."

"Or they're proving you wrong and they can't get to you while you're with me."

"Yeah, well, you're not going to be with me today."

Right, because today would be their first day apart. Paisley felt bad for spending more time with Case than with her best friend and wanted to make it up to Aster. Girls' day meant he couldn't be anywhere near Paisley, which meant her assassins could have an opening.

"That's precisely why Thatch will be there," he said.

She sat up. "They're going to come for me sooner or later. You know that, Case. And it won't matter who is with me or where I am. If you're right, then I need to be away from you to draw them out. Not just today, but more often."

"Fuck that."

"Case—"

181

He lay her flat against the mattress and stretched out on top of her. "I'm not giving them opportunities to try to kill you, Paisley."

"You're just delaying the inevitable, and it's pointless."

"Do you mean another attempt or your death?"

She elbowed him off her and slipped out of his reach. "Both."

He stood. "And again, I say, fuck that."

A sigh left her as she slipped on her dress. "Case, we'll never find out who they are if they don't have a chance."

Jaw clenched, he tugged on a pair of sweatpants. "We'll discuss this later. You have a fun day with Aster, but I swear, if something happens, you better call me."

She didn't say she would. Instead, she said, "I'll see you tomorrow." And walked out.

It took everything in him not to follow her, to make sure she was safe.

The day was long. He kept looking at his phone, expecting a call. If Paisley was right, whoever wanted her dead could take her out while she was off having fun with her bestie. But a call never came. After a council meeting, Case strode into the parlor for a drink.

Thatch followed him. "No plans with Paisley tonight?"

"Nope. Paisley and Aster have decided to extend it to a girls' night, which you should know as Aster's bodyguard."

"I do know that. You didn't ask Paisley what their plans were?"

Case poured a finger of whiskey into a highball glass. "It's none of my business what they do during girls' time."

"So, you don't know what they did today?"

"I do not."

"They spent the day at The Faye Time Spa. A sauna and full-body massages were on the agenda."

Case would not take the bait about the massages. "Relaxing."

"Followed by facials and getting their nails, hair, and makeup done."

"Sounds like a complete spa day."

"Indeed, and tonight they're planning to dance and have drinks."

Case's gaze flicked up from his glass to the wall. "Girls' night wouldn't be girls' night without dancing and a couple of drinks."

"At the club that opened recently…The Midnight Lair."

His fingers tightened around the glass. The Midnight Lair was run by demons and frequented by demons looking for one-night stands. All manner of creatures frequented that bar for a good time. After all, it was the newest, hottest nightspot, but none of them knew that by going there they were putting themselves on the menu for horny demons.

"I told Aster I will go to the club with them, to protect her, even during girls' night."

"As I would expect you to."

"Well—" Thatch stood. "They plan to get to the club by ten."

A quick look at the time showed Thatch had ten

minutes to get there. "You better hurry."

"My priority is Aster, but I'll keep an eye on Paisley, too. It shouldn't be too hard if they stick together."

Case knocked back the whiskey in his glass. "You're going to a club, Thatch. Have a little fun and dance with the cute fairy."

Thatch flinched. "I couldn't do that."

"Yes, you could. Have a little liquid courage and dance with Aster. Consider that an order. Now go. Get there before they do."

Thatch nodded. "I'll contact you if anything happens."

"Appreciate it."

Thatch left, and Case eyed the bottle of whiskey. He flipped his glass upside down on the tabletop. Ten o'clock came, and he wondered what Paisley was wearing. At ten-fifteen he was sure they'd had their first drinks. What kind of drinker was Paisley? Did she go for a shot, a pint, a martini, or a glass of wine? He could picture her enjoying all types of alcohol suited to the appropriate occasion. Nothing too lowbrow or sophisticated for her. He bet she could throw back shots and chug beer as well as she could sip expensive champagne.

By ten-thirty, he imagined her dancing and wondered what songs were playing. Ten-fifty, he was positive every male demon in that club was trying to get into her pants. Come ten-fifty-five, he was flying toward The Midnight Lair.

The club was packed with demons of every make, and several other creatures thrown into the mix. He spotted Paisley and Aster easily. Aster was the only fairy in the joint, and Paisley wasn't hard to miss. Not in the leather strapless corset that zipped up the front or the black wrap skirt with a sexy, upside-down vee in the center. His fingers itched to pull that zipper down, to unwrap that skirt from her hips. If he had those urges, then countless other demons did, too.

Case joined Thatch at the bar.

Thatch didn't take his eyes off Paisley and Aster, but he laughed out loud. "I had a feeling you'd come."

"I thought it would be nice to have a drink out. That's all."

"Sure."

Paisley and Aster danced together, not paying a lick of attention to anyone else on that dance floor. A song he'd never heard before pumped through the speakers with an interesting trumpet tune and finger snaps. The female singer rapped about being the devil and painting the town red. Paisley and Aster laughed together while singing. The lyrics were rather naughty to be coming out of sweet, little Aster's mouth.

Case glanced at Thatch. The demon was transfixed by the fairy singing some rather dirty lyrics.

When Case looked back, he saw a demon laying a hand on Aster's shoulder. He made a move, but Thatch halted him with an arm to block his path.

On the dance floor, Paisley grabbed the demon's wrist, wrenched it off Aster's shoulder, and opened her mouth in a threatening hiss that revealed the points of her fangs.

The demon retreated.

"They've been scaring demons off each other since

they got here," Thatch explained. "You should've seen the wing slap Aster gave an incubus when he moved in on Paisley. It knocked him on his ass, and then Aster stomped her dainty foot right on his crotch. She apologized innocently while the demon slunk off holding his junk."

"I wish I'd seen that."

"Yeah, turns out I'm not really needed."

Back on the dance floor, Paisley sang about being a demon, and the grin that split Case's face was lightning fast. "I'm going to let Paisley know I'm here. I'm not going to hide it, but I'll be back. Girls' night is still in full swing." He wound his way through the dancing bodies.

A few feet behind Paisley, Aster noticed him. She smiled. "Don't hurt this demon."

Paisley's dancing slowed. "What?"

Case slipped his arms around her, hauled her to his chest, and said into her ear, "So you want to be a demon, huh?"

She rotated. Her eyelids fell to slits. "Are you checking up on me?"

"No, I'm checking up on everyone else here. I hear the two of you have been taking no prisoners. There's an incubus somewhere with a dislocated shoulder and crushed balls."

"I did *not* dislocate his shoulder," Aster protested.

"You don't disagree about crushing his balls, though?"

"Oh, no, I did that."

Case laughed.

Thatch joined them. "Can we get you ladies something to drink?"

"Long Island Iced Tea," Paisley said.

Aster beamed up at Thatch. "Water for me."

"She's a lightweight," Paisley said.

Case jabbed a thumb in Thatch's direction. "So is he."

"I'm not a lightweight," Thatch objected. "I don't drink. There's a difference."

"Come on, Thatch." Aster slipped her petite hand into his large one. "We can be lightweights together." She led Thatch to the bar. "We'll get the drinks."

When they left, Paisley looped her arms around Case's neck. "Do you dance?"

"No, but you can use me as a stripper pole anytime you like."

He didn't think she'd take him up on his offer when she suddenly hooked his hip with her leg and moved her body in a wave against him. One hand on her waist, the other on her thigh, he let out a half growl, half groan. "I swear I didn't come here to ruin girls' night."

"No one said that once girls' night ended and Aster went to bed that *my* night needed to end."

He slid his hand up the back of her thigh. "Come see me when you're ready."

"Do you still think you'll be awake?"

His hand continued to glide beneath the tight, tiny strip of fabric that was her skirt. "I'll be awake and waiting." He felt the curve of her ass and a searing sensation in his eyes with the flash of anger that came over him. "Are you not wearing underwear, Paisley?"

"Nope."

He forced himself to breathe. "The next time you're around other demons, you better be wearing underwear."

"Or what?"

"Or I'll lock you up in my dungeon."

"You wouldn't."

"Wanna bet?"

A throat cleared before either of them could say more.

Thatch and Aster stood behind Paisley, drinks in hand.

"Hand off my ass," Paisley hissed.

He extracted his hand out from under her skirt.

Paisley accepted her Long Island Iced Tea from Thatch. "Thank you."

Aster handed Case a glass of whiskey.

"Thanks, cutie pie."

"Thatch ordered it for you," she said.

Case smirked at Thatch. "Thanks, cutie pie."

Aster giggled the sweetest laugh, and Thatch grumbled.

Paisley observed everything while taking a long sip of her drink through a skinny black straw. "Alright," she said and handed Case her glass. "Girls' night commences. Men to the bar, ladies to the dance floor. No more interruptions."

"Yes, ma'am." Case led the way back to the bar.

Paisley danced to a song that was startlingly accurate. The singer sang about being Aphrodite, and Paisley *was* his Aphrodite. They were teetering back and forth between enemies and something undefinable, and, yeah, as far as he was concerned, there was no turning back. Then the damn rap portion of the song came on. He was convinced the songwriters had him— and other foolish, sprung demons—in mind when they'd written it. No other explanation made sense but enchantment; she captivated him.

He glanced over at Thatch when the chorus returned and threw his head back in laughter at the sight of his best friend staring so intently at Aster.

"What?" Thatch asked, finally tearing his gaze away.

"We're both so fucking gone that it's not even funny."

"And yet you're laughing."

Case nodded once. "And yet I'm laughing."

"What do we do about it?"

"You? You go tell Aster that she's the most adorable creature you've ever seen and are utterly fond of her. And then you enjoy whatever happens next. Me?" Case cocked his head toward Paisley. "I hang on for the ride and hope I don't lose everything."

A pair of demons blocked their view of Paisley and Aster. The demon directly in front of Case nudged his buddy. "Diablo, I'd give anything to rail her against one of those speakers. I don't care if she is a hybrid. She looks like she could take a good fucking and dish one out."

Rage roared through Case's veins. The desire to snap the demon's neck was fierce. Case shoved to his feet, envisioning killing the demon, but Thatch restrained him.

"Haven't you heard the rumor that she's been seen

with Lord Case? A lot?" the demon's friend said. "Apparently, she's taking a good fucking from him."

The demon snorted. "She hasn't been fucked by a true incubus. Once she is, she'll ditch Case and come crawling to me, leaving a trail of cum behind her."

Red. Case saw red.

"Well, you can have the queen all you want. I'll take the little fairy."

Thatch whipped toward the other demon.

Now Case thrust an arm out to halt him. Two demons holding each other back.

"She's so damn small. I could pick her up, fuck her like a rag doll, and come inside her until my seed spills out of her and gushes down her legs."

Case couldn't even see anymore he was so blinded by rage. He released Thatch. Let Thatch snap the demon's neck if he wanted.

"Go for it," the incubus said. "While you do that, I'm going to get the queen to bend the knee for me and worship my cock with her mouth."

Thatch released Case. The action spoke volumes; the wise council was relenting, letting Case do something drastic, final.

Case stepped up behind the incubus. "That's *my* queen you're talking about."

"And that's *my* fairy." Thatch towered over the other demon.

The demons faced them, and the incubus in front of Case sneered. "Afraid she'll like my cock more, *Lord* Case?"

"No, but you should be afraid of losing yours."

"You both should," Thatch added.

The demon in front of Thatch retreated. His friend wasn't backing down, though. "Let's fight for her," the incubus said. "The winner gets the royal cunt."

"You don't want to fight me. There's a reason why I'm the demon lord. I've won every fight to the death I've been in, and that was when I didn't have anything to fight for but my own life."

The incubus angled his head to the side. "My, she must have an amazing pussy to give Lord Case something to fight for. You make a good salesman. I want her even more."

Growling, Case surged forward, but Thatch held him back to edge forward instead. "Talking to your lord in that way is a death sentence. If you want to keep your life, you should walk away now."

The incubus's friend tugged him back. "Let's go. It's not worth it."

The incubus eyed Case up and down. "Enjoy her while you have her."

When they backed off, Thatch pushed Case's glass into his hand. "Drink."

Case swallowed it down and eyed the glass Thatch held. "Are you sure you don't want something stronger than sparkling water?"

"I'm sure."

On the dance floor, Paisley and Aster were dancing, unaware of the disgusting, degrading things two demons had said about them. Seeing innocent Aster in a flowing, pink dress that swished as she danced and recalling the demon's graphic detail of what he wanted to do made Case's blood boil even more.

"You should've ripped out that demon's spine."

"I was tempted."

His blood was rapidly becoming lava in his veins. Spying on a demon closing in on Paisley and Aster only made him burn with rage even hotter. "I'm going to make it perfectly clear to every demon in the faction that Paisley and dear, sweet Aster are off limits."

That demon groped Paisley's ass.

Case was storming toward them even as Paisley twisted the demon's arm. Words exchanged between them, but the demon wasn't getting the hint. He was trying to dance with her, despite her refusal. While shoving him back with one hand, Paisley also kept an arm in front of Aster, preventing her best friend from getting into the mix.

Paisley's voice carried over the music. "I said no."

The demon stole Paisley's hips and yanked her toward him.

"Hey," Aster shouted. "Let her go!"

As Case came up behind the demon, Thatch reached Aster. He stuck a supportive arm in front of her to keep her from advancing, and she clung to him.

The demon, though, was oblivious to what was going on around him.

Case clamped a hand onto the demon's shoulder and jerked him around. Glaring into the demon's eyes, he let his full rage simmer through, turning his eyes to a searing gold. Baring his teeth, he said, "Mine."

The demon surrendered immediately.

"Seriously?" Paisley said. "You did not just say 'mine.'"

Case faced her, still seething with rage. He'd scared off multiple demons who didn't want to take no for an answer and she had the nerve to be pissed off over how he did it?

"I did. I thought we established that already. Rule Number Three." Before he knew what he was doing, he was branding an arm around her and yanking her to him, so that they were chest to chest. "And I'll say it again." He slipped a hand between her legs and vised a hand around her pussy. With his lips to the shell of her ear, he growled so that his voice rumbled with every ounce of anger he had in him, "Mine."

Her grip on his arms tightened. Beneath his palm, her loins pulsed with desire. He leaned back to leer. "And you like that. You like hearing me say that you're mine." He lifted his hand from between her legs to trail a finger down her cheek. "You like *being* mine."

She slapped his hand away. The look she gave him burned him. "Go to Hell." And she shouldered past him.

Immediately, he regretted what he'd done. He'd meant to protect her from the unwanted advances and molestation of lustful demons, and then he'd done exactly as they had wanted. The unfortunate truth was that Paisley made it hard to think rationally. He never would've grabbed her like that. Maybe he would've said the same things, but he would've shown some damn restraint in public.

"Pais—"

She was shouldering her way out of the bar.

A small hand whacked him in the arm. He peered down at Aster. Though her hand was dainty, it was no less tough.

"You idiot."

He winced. "I know. I—"

"You can't let her fly home alone. Someone with wings tried to shoot her. If they're following her, they'll get their chance."

"She's right," Thatch said. "You need to go after her."

Case nodded. "Stay with Aster."

"She won't be without me."

Case's lips quirked up at the corners, and Thatch glared.

Aster's tiny hand smacked him again. "Go!"

"See you two later." He spun on his heel and parted the crowd as he left.

Outside, he scanned the night sky. Wings slapping against air drew his gaze above the club. A shadow flew toward the night sky.

His wings erupted from his back, and he shot straight up. A few strokes of his wings and he was directly below Paisley. Against the darkness, he couldn't see her wings. They were black, like his, and blended with the night. The desire to see them welled inside him. He caught Paisley's ankle and tugged her down. The yank would've only halted her mid-air. Instead, she fell straight down. He caught her with his hands at her waist to see that she'd tucked her wings out of sight the instant he'd touched her. Fresh anger rushed through his veins.

"Why won't you let me see your wings?"

"Only a privileged few have seen them."

"So, I'm not privileged?"

She peered into his eyes, but didn't answer, which was an answer in of itself.

"I'm good enough to fuck but not to see your wings? The biggest part of you? The thing that makes it so you can fly?"

"This isn't about you, Case. I don't show my wings to anyone."

"What in the world do they look like for you to keep them hidden? Are they skeletal?"

"No."

"You've seen my wings, and I've seen all manner of demon wings. Some are downright hideous. I know what vampire wings look like, and no two fairy wings are alike, so what's so secretive about yours?"

"My wings aren't like any vampire's or fairy's. I stopped showing them when I was a kid, when I was laughed at by other kids and called an abomination by their parents."

"They were wrong."

"I'm not showing you my wings, Case."

"If I were to drop you?"

"I'd fall."

"You'd risk death, or at the very least broken legs, to keep your wings hidden from me?"

"Yes."

"Paisley, that's—"

"It's an insecurity, Case. Drop it."

He bit his tongue. For now. "I can't let you fly home alone. There's a threat out there, but Aster is a bigger threat at the moment. She'll skin me alive if I let you go."

Paisley's lips twitched. "Aster is a threat unlike any other."

"I'm beginning to see that."

She sighed. "If you insist on bringing me home, land so we can walk."

He shook his head gently. "I'll fly you home. It's faster." He slipped his arms securely across her back. "Wrap your legs around me."

When she did—tying her arms about his neck to boot—he closed his eyes a moment to relish in the feel of her limbs knotted around him. He meant to fly slowly, but it didn't take long to reach her house. At her front door, he continued to hold her, only now his hands clasped the backs of her thighs.

"Do you have keys somewhere on your person?" If she did, he wanted to get them.

"No, it's unlocked."

He dropped her to her feet. With a hand on her shoulder, he backed her up against the door. Anger was swift, so he stared at their feet while taking a few careful breaths. "Someone has actively tried to assassinate you, and you didn't lock your fucking door?"

"I never do."

He exhaled through his nose. "You stubborn, reckless little hybrid." Taking her hand, he opened the door. On the other side, he glared. "Do not move."

Briming with rage, he searched her home. Every room. Every closet. Every corner. Every potential hiding place.

Surprisingly, Paisley still waited at the front door when he finished. She leaned against it with her arms and legs crossed. That pose did two things—infuriated him because it was cocky and turned him on because it was sexy.

"It's clear," he said.

"Good." She stepped away from the door. "Now you can leave."

"Can we talk first?"

She edged past him. "Fine."

He followed her into the kitchen. She lugged a pitcher of water from the fridge and poured each of them a glass. "Thank you," he said.

They sat at opposite sides of the small table.

"What'd you want to talk about?"

No point in delaying or cushioning his pride. "I need to apologize. It's no secret that I'm in love with your pussy."

She tilted her head. "You're in *love*—"

"I want to touch her, kiss her, lick her, fill her every moment of every day, but I shouldn't have grabbed her like that in public. I'm sorry."

She squirmed in her chair but didn't say anything.

"Pais, I won't ever do that again. I promise. I'm not trying to keep us a secret. That's not what this is, but what we do together…that is private. It's for us, between us. You and me. I won't cross that line again."

She nodded. "Apology accepted, but did you really have to get that detailed about it? Touch her, kiss her, lick her, fill her?"

The corner of his mouth lifted. "I did. What did my words do to her?"

"She's throbbing like a second heart." Paisley squirmed again. "Remember when you said I wouldn't have to do much?"

He inclined his head.

She rotated on the stool and opened her legs.

He sprang to his feet before a single thought could form in his head, and he was on his knees in front of her before he could even blink. "What does she want?"

"She hasn't decided yet."

Hands on her hips, he turned her ninety-degrees so her back was to the table. Then he unraveled her skirt. The fabric draped over the sides of the stool. Now, with his hands molded around her knees, he pushed her thighs apart. "I can give her a sample of each until she decides."

She settled her hands on his. "Not necessary. She wants you to kiss her, lick her…"

He tugged her forward, suddenly famished.

"…drink her, eat her."

He closed his eyes as they rolled back from the sheer pleasure her words had conjured. "It seems I forgot two verbs."

Drink her pussy's goodness.

Eat her pussy out while she screamed.

"The tastiest verbs." He gazed at her pretty cunt. "Is she ready?"

"She's just waiting for you."

With that, he ducked his head between her thighs. He kissed the sweet bundle of her clitoris gland, and she sighed. Forming his lips around it, he sucked on her clit, enticing it to swell into an aroused bump. A tiny moan fluttered from her mouth. He didn't want to give her a release so quickly, though. After all, he had a lot more kissing, licking, drinking, and eating to do, so his lips suctioned around her urethra. A soft kiss. A gentle suck. A little lick.

Lower down, he laid his lips against her vaginal

opening. Her sigh was longer. She was still sighing when he dipped his tongue inside her, causing that exhale of breath to halt and reverse in a gasp. He treated her vaginal opening like her mouth, and her pussy's lips like her face's lips. With his head angled, he made out with her cunt, massaging her labia with his mouth, slipping his tongue into her to draw out her unique, sweet and salty flavors.

Kiss—check.

Drink—check.

Eat—check.

He frenched her pussy for an unknowable amount of time. The only thing that broke his concentration was when he realized she was rolling her hips to pull his tongue deeper, and his nose was rubbing against her clit.

He shifted back to admire her cunt. "Everything about her is so fucking lovely."

"It seems…that you are…having an affair…with my pussy."

He peered up. "I most definitely am."

Now it was time to lick her cunt. Every centimeter of it. With the tip of his tongue, he traced her outer labia.

She moaned. The sound was soft, but it was enough.

He drew her lovely shape, following the inner contours, circling her vaginal opening, teasing her urethra, and finally, swirling over her clitoris. A single thought was all it required to activate his tongue, to turn it into a sex toy, to make it vibrate. Instantly, her hips drove up, and she cried out. He slipped two fingers into her wet opening. Using the tips of his fingers, he played with her g-zone, and her hips lifted higher.

Panting sounds met his ears. He continued the relentless attack on her g-zone with his fingers and on her clit with his vibrating tongue. Knowing exactly how she liked it, he applied pressure and worked the tip of his tongue up and down. She came fast, and her cries echoed throughout the kitchen.

Case looked up to see her bent backward over the table. He stood and planted kisses up her center to the tip of her chin. Arms supporting her upper back, he lifted her into an upright position. "Was that good for her?"

Paisley nodded. "It was perfect."

"Good. I'm glad I could satisfy her."

"You're very good at that."

"Happy to be of service."

"Do *you* need to be serviced?"

The sound of the front door opening had him straightening.

"That's probably Aster." Paisley knotted the skirt around her hips and climbed off the stool.

"Let's see if she persuaded Thatch to dance with her," he said.

At the entrance to the kitchen, Paisley pulled up short.

Over her head, Case saw Thatch and Aster in the doorway. Thatch looped his arms around Aster and lifted her off her feet. As he did so, her body slid against Thatch's until they were eye to eye. Case had to admire that. "Clever move."

One arm braced beneath Aster's shapely behind,

Thatch slipped his fingers into her hair with his other hand. He said something that Case couldn't make out but that made Aster's wings flutter rapidly. Her violet hair streamed over Thatch's fingers, and Aster laid a hand against his cheek. Whatever she said in that moment had Thatch exhaling, his jaw clenching, and his head nodding. Then Aster leaned in and kissed him.

Case wasn't sure who was the most surprised — him, Thatch, or Paisley.

Thatch lifted his hand to the back of her head, cupping her skull with the width of his palm. They shared a delicate meeting of lips that spoke volumes. Thatch kissed Aster with tender care, and Aster kissed Thatch with sweet curiosity. When their lips parted, Thatch's stare was one of absolute worship. Gazes locked, Thatch let Aster slide down his body to her dainty feet.

"Have a good night, Aster."

"You, too, Thatch." She stepped back, and Thatch shut the door.

Aster's wings twittered as she headed toward the staircase.

"Who would've thought that a sex demon could make such a good matchmaker?" Case whispered.

Paisley jabbed an elbow into Case's stomach.

Breath whooshed out of his lungs.

Aster froze. When she peered at them in the kitchen entryway, her adorable cheeks changed from a happy flush to an embarrassed pink. "Hi," she squeaked.

Case grinned. "Hi there, cutie pie."

"Did the two of you see—" She gestured toward

the door.

"Oh, yeah."

Her face burned red from the tip of her chin to her hairline. "It was...we were...I...goodnight." She rushed off, wings stiff on her back.

Paisley let out a small chuckle. "They do make an insanely cute couple."

"And imagine...they'd make the first demon-fairy in existence."

"Don't joke about that."

"I'm not joking. A demon-fairy would be adorable as hell."

"You're the only one who would think that."

"I'm sure they'd think that, being the parents and all. Wouldn't you think so?"

"I'm not discussing hybrid babies with you. You can see yourself out now, Case."

Touchy subject. Hell, babies in general were a touchy subject for him, given his own history, so he knew better than to push. "When I leave—"

She met his eye.

"Lock the fucking door."

13

Paisley

A week passed and still nothing happened. No more assassination attempts. No death threats. Nothing. Despite what she said to Case, she didn't believe that her would-be assassins were stupid enough to think she'd forget about them. Because no matter how much sex she was having, she'd always remember that someone had murdered her parents and wanted her dead. The problem was, they still had no leads, even with Jude, Lena, and Phoenix using members of their own councils to investigate within their factions. All she had left was playing into their hand and pretending to have forgotten, because she fully believed the other thing she had told Case. That they'd come eventually, at the moment they thought her guard was down. And she may be able to draw out someone at the Enchanted Hierarchy Council Meeting with her act.

So, she chose a burgundy and black corset dress with a slit through layers of tulle that made her feel every bit like the vampire queen she was. When she entered the hall, she saw she wasn't the last to arrive. Case was already there, though. He was talking to Jude but suddenly jerked around when she stepped across the threshold, as if he could sense her presence.

Jude bowed in her direction.

She honored him in return with a nod.

Case, though, came right toward her. He wore all black again and looked sinisterly good.

He cut her off on the way to her throne. "Did you dress like a vampire to make a point?"

She squinted her eyelids. "And what point would that be?"

"The last time we were here, you were hellbent on making sure everyone knew you didn't want anything to do with me...the demon lord, your enemy."

"And in your mind, I wore this dress why?"

"So everyone would see that we're on opposite sides. That we have nothing to do with each other."

"Case...everyone knows about us. Everyone. We haven't been subtle. We've been having sex every opportunity we could get since the last time we were here. Your faction has seen me. Word spread from one demonic mouth to the next until it seeped across factions. I heard the whispers at the club. Whispers about us...about me."

His jaw clenched. "I didn't think you were aware of what they were saying."

"I was, but I chose to ignore it so I could have a good time with my best friend. And if I was worried about others seeing us together, do you think I would've danced up against you?" She shook her head. "I've always been a topic of discussion, of ridicule, of debate, but I no longer care if anyone talks about me or what I am or who I choose to be with, so, no, I did not put this dress on to make a point. Not about you anyway. About me. I *am* the vampire queen."

A thought struck her right then. Of course. She *was* the vampire queen. So far, vampires were at the heart of everything that had happened, so that could mean one thing...

She stepped closer to Case. "I think I figured something out."

"What?"

Zara entered then. "Everyone, please take your seats."

Paisley stared at Case, wishing they had a few more minutes.

"Pais."

"After," she whispered and continued to her throne.

When she sat, Case lowered onto his throne across from her. The meeting started with various topics, but she couldn't pay attention to a word that was discussed, because she was too busy ogling Case, who, unlike her, was listening intently. Her gaze followed the seams of his pants and the fabric that stretched over his thighs.

Goddess, his thighs were so thick. She imagined biting them as a part of foreplay, and then dry humping one of his thighs until she came. His thighs were super grindable. She'd never seen a pair like them before. Why hadn't she done that yet? Maybe she would after the meeting ended. She couldn't think of anything better to do on a throne than worship the sexy demon lounging on it.

Case's hand settled on his thigh. His hand rotated, palm up, and formed into a loose fist with his index finger out. She followed it as he lifted his hand to point at his face. When she focused, he was staring right at her. "Stop," he mouthed.

The whole time he'd been aware of her eyeing him like a piece of meat, and that made her feel awful. "Sorry," she mouthed back.

But could he blame her?

"On to the next topic," Zara announced. "Does anyone here have anything they'd like to add to today's agenda?"

"I do," Alaric said. "We need to discuss two faction leaders fucking each other."

Paisley didn't look away from Case, even when he directed his glare to Alaric.

"That language is unnecessary," Zara said. "Whom are you talking about?"

"I'm talking about the lord of demons railing the vampire and fairy queen."

Case's eyes flared gold.

Paisley angled her head to meet the stare of the werewolf shifter sitting beside her. "I don't see how that's anyone's business but ours."

"It's our business because you're a part of this council," Alaric spat.

"I still don't see why the council needs to know what goes on in my bedroom."

Or outside her bedroom, as it were.

"Two faction leaders fucking each other throws everything out of balance, like how your parents threw the hierarchy out of balance."

The mention of her parents sent her blood boiling with rage. She rose to her feet and stalked toward the shifter king. "You want to know what really threw things out of balance? Someone killing them!"

"Exactly, you being here ruins the balance. If they'd never had you, if you didn't exist, there would be two thrones, two leaders. There would be a full-bloodied vampire and full-bloodied fairy here, not you."

She sneered. "Right, but I do exist, and I do claim two thrones, whether you or anyone else on this council likes it or not."

Alaric shoved his feet to glare into her eyes. "You're a bigger threat to this council than your parents ever were. You're a mutt, you claim two thrones, and you're fucking the demon lord. No wonder why someone tried to assassinate you."

A gray hand lashed out past Paisley's shoulder and clamped around Alaric's neck. "I should snap your neck for that."

"Enough!" the enchantress yelled.

Paisley grabbed Case's arm. "Don't."

Case released Alaric's neck but stayed rooted in place while Alaric coughed through his damaged trachea. "The threats toward Paisley have been a concern," Case said, "and you're looking fucking suspicious right now, Shifter King."

"I would have to agree," Zara said. "This outburst doesn't help you any."

"I didn't have anything to do with the assassination attempt," Alaric rasped. "I have a problem with Paisley, but not one big enough to kill her over it." He sneered at Paisley now. "To get you kicked off the Enchanted Hierarchy Council? Now that I don't have a problem with."

Paisley glared. "I didn't ask for this. I didn't want to be queen of *anything*. A killer did that when they murdered my parents. So, if you have a problem with me being on the council, take it up with their murderer. And if you have a problem with me and Case—"

"Then you can take it up with me," Case growled.

Alaric laughed. "Is her cunt already making decisions for you?"

"Excuse me?" Paisley said.

"That's what happens when a man, demon or otherwise, gets too much pussy."

Zara's voice boomed. "I said, that's enough!"

A flash of yellow light blinded Paisley. She shielded her eyes. But even beneath her hands and eyelids, the glare burned her retinas.

A second. That was how long the light lasted, which was all it took to silence the fighting and have them all yelling in pain. When Paisley opened her eyes, and her vision cleared, she found Case's chest in front of her. His hand was at the back of her head.

"Are you okay?" Case's voice was a whisper in her ear.

She nodded. "Yeah. You?" He had grabbed her to block her from the brunt of the flare, with no consideration to himself.

"I'll be better once we're out of here."

The enchantress still glowed, radiating power and anger. "That sort of vile language is forbidden in this space. There will be no more talk about who anyone on this council is sleeping with. Even if it is each other. Nor will there be any more talk about kicking Paisley off this council. She is one of us. She belongs. The assassination attempt on her is a serious matter. One that will have dire consequences, and we will not stop investigating until we do find the culprits. Now, this council meeting is adjourned."

Everyone started to leave.

Everyone except for Paisley, Case, and Alaric.

Jude stomped over with his arms crossed over his chest. He towered over Alaric. "The next time I hear you talk about my goddaughter like that, I will trample you until every bone in your body is broken and you're a pulverized mess beneath my hooves. Got it?"

Alaric eyed him, and then Case, and then Paisley. "I'm not the one you need to worry about." Sneering, he left the three of them standing there.

Jude peered between her and Case. "You apparently took my suggestion from the last meeting, and you're still apparently taking my suggestion." Now he spoke directly to Case. "You and I are friends and allies, but if you do anything to hurt Paisley or her factions, *I* will hurt you. That's not a promise. That's a vow."

"If I hurt Paisley or her factions, I will *let you* trample my body to a pulverized mess."

Jude nodded. "Good answer. Now, the two of you should get out of here. After what went down, I wouldn't trust any of these other faction leaders."

Case nodded. "At the end of every meeting, you say the smartest damn thing." His hand settled on her lower back. "Let's go."

She let him guide her down the hall and outside.

A few faction leaders were there.

"You don't fly around anyone, so—" He swept her into his arms and flew off. At her doorstep, he set her on her feet and tried the doorhandle. "It's locked."

"Well, you told me to lock it."

"You mean to tell me that you actually did something I asked?"

"It appears so."

His gaze scanned her dress. "Where's the key?"

"Where do you think it is?"

He studied her bodice.

"Mm-hm. Why don't you get it?"

Holding eye contact, he molded one hand to the side of her bodice, under her arm, and dipped the fingers of his other hand between the crevice of her breasts. She held still. The feel of his fingers rubbing against the sensitive skin of her breasts gave her a chill before she could stop it. He removed the skeleton key, warmed by the heat of her skin.

"My new favorite hiding place," he murmured.

Hand on her hip, he shifted her to the side and unlocked the door himself.

A note on a side table caught her attention as she stepped over the threshold. The script flowed in Aster's fancy handwriting. She plucked it up and read the message. "Thatch and Aster went out for a picnic."

"Is that so? The two of them are so cute, it's sickening."

"That's what the note says. They packed a lunch and went for a picnic. She's going to show him—" Paisley grinned.

Case arched a brow. "She's going to show him what?"

"A thatch of asters." Her grin softened. "I've seen it. It's covering a little cabin made of bamboo. I used to go there as a girl. It's actually where I met Aster." She laid down the note and directed her smile to Case. "She was making it. She was making the aster grow throughout the thatch. Ever since, that aster thatch has thrived. I'd forgotten all about it until now."

"What are the odds that an aster thatch exists because of our sweet little Aster?"

"I'd say fate is a tricky little pixie."

Case tilted his head. "Can I ask you a question?"

She wasn't sure if she liked his questions, but she nodded anyway.

"Thatch and Aster…what do you think about them being together?"

"What do you mean?"

"Would you object to them being a couple?"

"It's not up to me to object or grant approval."

"But would you be happy for them?"

"Of course. I *am* happy for them. I wouldn't get in their way if it's what they want. It'd be damn hypocritical of me if I did. Given my origins, how could I stop two different creatures from having the love that my parents had?" Now she studied him. "Why do you ask?"

"Because you had a problem with me being a demon."

She frowned. "That's not the same. Aster isn't a queen facing death threats that initially looked like they were coming from the daemon faction, and Thatch isn't the demon lord. They're not us."

"No, they're not." He paused. "Speaking of your parents…how are you after the meeting and everything that was said?"

"Fine. How are you?"

"Fine."

"Right. A werewolf shifter claimed you're pussy-whipped, and you're okay with that?"

"Yes, I am." He stepped closer. "You can control me all you want. I will gladly be your submissive. Want me to wear a dog collar? Because I will."

The visual of a leather collar around Case's neck, attached to a leash, made her smile. "You really are kinky."

"You have no idea."

"As much as I'm sure discussing your kinky ways would be entertaining, there's actually something else we need to discuss. Remember when I said I figured something out? Before the meeting got underway?"

"I do. What did you figure out?"

"Vampires. Something is telling me that vampires are a part of this, more than we know. I'm the vampire queen now. Vampires were sent after you, and no one knows by whom. My uncle has been interrogating vampires, and he hasn't found anyone who harbors any sort of ill contempt toward me. Then there's the first threat, right after I took the throne…bats."

"But a fairy was killed."

"Maybe killed as a diversion. Let's face it, fairies are no threat. Fairies are neutral in conflict. They're pacifists. They're no one's enemy, but vampires? Vampires are everyone's enemy. They like conflict and drama. They like blood. To feed on it, and to take it. Vampires are greedy. They don't have allies."

"I've never known a good vampire," Case said. "Well, before you."

"Then you must not have known my dad well. He was good. How else do you think a fairy could fall in love with him? But he was the exception. He was different. The rest of my vampire family…" She shook her head. "Well, they're not a picnic. Except for my uncle and one cousin of mine. Cinda."

"So…you figured out that vampires are what exactly?"

"The reason behind the threats. Someone could want me dead to take the throne."

"I thought you said your uncle was helping you to interrogate vampires."

"He might not be looking at the right people. He's questioning heads of powerful vampire families. The culprits could be someone we'd never look at. Someone who has made a point out of being inconspicuous. Or…"

"Or what?"

"Or whoever wants me dead wants to defeat the

vamprye faction in its entirety."

"Neither will happen if I have anything to say about it."

His intensity over wanting to protect her would never cease to shock her. She didn't know what to say to that or how to react, so she chose to deflect. "We're not going to figure it out right now, so I'm going to change into something more comfortable. Stay here." When his gaze trailed down her dress, she added, "I mean it, Case."

He held up his hands. "I'll stay."

While heading for the stairs, she gathered her hair into her hands and pulled it over her shoulder. She couldn't wait to get out of the dress. Corsets were aesthetically amazing, but they were hell on the body and severely uncomfortable. Beauty was indeed pain. For women, at least.

"Show me your wings, Paisley."

Case's words halted her. "What?"

"You moved your hair from your back. I can see your sexy shoulder blades, and I can't stop myself from wondering what your wings look like. Show me."

She rounded on him.

He hadn't moved from the side table by the door.

"No."

"Please." He begged so gently, so sweetly, so softly.

"W-why do you want to see them so badly?"

"I don't know, but I do. It's a clawing need inside me. I am dying to see them."

"You don't look like you're dying."

"Pais, let me see all of you. Just once."

"If I show you once, you'll drop it? You won't ask to see them again?"

"You have my word."

"Fine," she said again, only this time, she bit the word out. "Once and only once."

Eyes closed, she prepared for what she was about to do. The last time she'd shown anyone her wings, it had been ten years ago, when she was eighteen, dating a vampire who she thought liked her for her, not because she was a princess.

One night, he'd convinced her to reveal her wings, right after taking her virginity. She believed him when he said he had feelings for her, believed him when he said he thought she was beautiful. As soon as she had showed him her wings, though, he'd laughed his ass off, and all of his buddies jumped out of hiding places to make fun of her. They'd been there, watching them have sex. Paisley had never felt more defiled in her life.

Since then, she'd kept her wings tucked into her body, but here she was, about to show the demon who she'd been having sex with for the past month. Case did know every inch of her body, but that didn't make this any easier.

"Paisley."

She held up a hand. Taking a deep breath, she summoned her wings. They sprang out of her back and stretched out on either side of her. Keeping her eyelids sealed, she braced. Silence resumed while Case took in the sight of her wings, but when he let out a laugh, she had every right to brace, every right to not want him to see her wings, her biggest insecurity.

Humiliated and full of hatred, she glared. "Screw

215

you, Case. This is exactly why I didn't want to show you my wings. Get the hell out of my house."

"Paisley—"

"No! I told you I didn't like anyone to see my wings, but you pushed and pushed. Now, go and don't ever come back."

"Paisley. Look. Down."

"Look down at what?!"

At his erection.

She gawked in bewilderment. "Seriously?"

"*This* is why I was laughing." He waved a hand over his erection. "I wasn't laughing at your wings, Paisley, but at myself. The second you let your wings out, they turned me on."

She shook her head. "There's no way."

"Can you refute this?" He indicated at his crotch.

"You're a sex demon. That could happen at the drop of a dime."

"No, Paisley. It's your wings. They're…"

"They're what? I've heard them described as laughable, disgraceful, ridiculous, wrong, silly, dumb. Goddess, I should've kept a list. So, what would you like to add? What are they? Hmm?"

"Stunning."

"Don't mock me."

"I would never." Suddenly, his body jerked, and he rolled his shoulders back.

She blinked. "What was that?"

Clearing his throat, he rotated his neck in a circle, cracking bone. "Your wings are calling to mine."

"What do you mean?"

"My wings want to come out."

"Your wings want to come out because my wings are out?"

"I guess you could say your wings are making my wings hard." He sucked in a deep breath. "You can't tell me that no one has ever called your wings beautiful."

"My parents. And Aster."

"And now me." His shoulders rotated. "Fuck." He spun toward the small table and gripped the sides of it. From where she stood, she could hear him seething. His upper half jerked back, and he lunged forward. A growl grew, louder and louder, as if he fought to control his wings. "I can't keep them in. I have to let them out." His wings erupted from his back and slapped the air. The moment they burst free, he let out a roar that sounded identical to the noise he made while coming. "Diablo, that felt good." He held onto the table, panting, while his wings shivered.

"Are...are you okay?"

"Yeah."

"Did you...orgasm?"

"Wingasm. I never knew it was possible." He angled his head toward her and chuckled. "I have you to thank for that."

"So, I gave a sex demon a never-before-had orgasm?"

"Yes, you did." He straightened off the side table. "You're something else."

She swallowed. "Why are you so different?"

He stepped toward her.

She had the urge to retreat but held still. "Why do you like my wings?"

He shrugged a shoulder as he advanced. "Your wings *are* beautiful, Paisley. They have the framework of a vampire's wings, but they're purple instead of black, and the rest is like…lace…the sexiest black lace." He tilted his head. "Are those roses?"

"Y-yes." She held perfectly still as he came nearer.

"Roses outlined in glittering purple. That's very you." He shifted behind her. "Can I touch them?"

Startled, she stared over her shoulder. "What?"

"I won't ask again, but I've touched you everywhere. Except your wings. May I?"

She nodded.

His hand stroked the top of her right wing, following the radius. She sucked in a breath and closed her eyes. A full-bodied shiver stole her. He did the same to her left wing, coaxing out another shiver.

"Does that feel good?"

"Yes." She was breathless.

"Have your wings ever been touched before?"

"Never."

"You've been depriving them, then. That ends now." He held her hand and coaxed her around.

"What are you doing?"

He started up the stairs. "Your wings need attention, Pais, and I'm going to give it to them. I'm going to massage your wings from tip to tip."

In her room, he pointed at her bed. "Lay down on your stomach."

Jittering with a mixture of nerves and excitement, she bunched up the skirt of her dress, crawled onto the bed, and hugged a pillow to her head.

The bed beneath her shifted.

Then Case was straddling her. The tip of his finger followed the lines of a rose. "They look delicate."

"They can withstand more than you know."

"Like you." He caressed her wings. First the purple edge that resembled smooth leather as he stroked their lines with his hands. Then he worked his fingers on them, kneading gently from where her wings sprouted out of her shoulder blades to their points.

Her eyelids descended. Satisfied moans came from her.

"That's right," Case said. "Let them feel what they've been missing."

When he finished massaging the outer skeletal, he transitioned to the lacey mainsail portion of her wings. His touch was more than careful, more than soft. It was tender. Damn near affectionate. He used his fingertips, following the patterns.

She tried to decipher the touch. Was it curiosity? Awe? Both? "H-how you touch me…is that a sex demon thing?"

"How am I touching you?"

"You *know* how you're touching me."

"Describe it."

Hands in fists in her purple comforter, she said, "Intimate. It's intimate. How can you touch me with so much intimacy? It has to be a sex demon thing, right?"

"I can touch you this way because this is how you deserve to be touched."

The feel of his lips on the lacey part of her right wing had her eyelids flipping open. "Case, what are—"

"Let me live up to my promise."

She had no clue what he meant. "What promise?"

219

"To kiss every inch of your body."

"That wasn't a promise you made me."

"I made it silently, but I'm sure I made my intentions loud and clear. I haven't kissed your wings yet. I need to."

"You *need* to?"

"Yes." And so he did. He kissed each rose, the center of every swirl, and down the length of their radius bones. By the time he finished, her wings were quivering, and no matter how hard she tried to settle them, they wouldn't calm. They matched what she felt on the inside, how her heart raced. He swung his leg off her. "Come here, Pais."

She turned over. As she did so, she tucked her wings back into her body.

"No." He snatched her up and hitched her onto his hips, making her gasp. "If this is the one and only time I get to see your gorgeous wings, I want to have sex with our wings out." He carried her off the bed, opened her balcony doors, and stepped outside. The sun was setting, sending the sky into a riot of oranges and pinks. He set her on the railing. "Bring them back out, Pais." His hand stroked up the middle of her back. "I'll coax them out of you. You know I can." The palms of his hands made circles over her shoulder blades.

"Case, you're not playing fair."

"It wasn't fair of you to hide them away for good before I was finished."

The pressure of his palms increased, and the circular motion continued.

"I want to come while looking at them."

She arched her back. A tingle formed beneath her skin. Although her wings weren't visible, they were real, and they were beating inside her body, begging to be released. Was this what it had felt like for Case? Keeping them restrained when they so badly wanted to come out, to expand, to beat? She didn't know how Case had held out as long as he had. Her wings unfurled with a slap. With them, a sigh left her lips.

"Thank you," he said.

They fought with the tulle of her skirt to uncover her legs and to give him access. The tulle spilled around them and bunched as they tackled the belt and zipper of his pants next. Once he was freed, both of their hands sought his cock, wrapped around his hard, hot shaft, and directed him to her opening. Case thrust inside her with one smooth movement, filling her. Her breath fled from her lungs, and she locked her arms around his neck, clutching him.

"Thank you," he repeated in her ear, even while pumping into her. His wings were lifted high and spanned the entire length of the balcony.

She pulled him in deeper, wrapped her legs around him tighter. As she did so, her wings came around him so that she held onto him with all of herself.

Case shivered from the contact. The fact that her wings could elicit such a reaction from him didn't make sense. *Why was he* so different from everyone else? *Why was he* so enamored with her wings? Her wings that had made her an outcast. Her wings that had caused her countless tears. Her wings that had been her bane. Her wings that she had tried to cut off when she was thirteen. Tears came to her eyes, and she buried her face in his collar.

His wings surrounded her, too, cocooning them.

He stroked inside her, inching her toward climax.

Still, her tears fell.

Her insides warmed. Her growing orgasm bloomed.

Still, her tears fell.

She came with a moan. And a sob.

Awash in the afterglow of her climax, still, her tears fell.

She sniffed, and Case jerked back. He stiffened as still more tears fell.

"The hell?" He cupped her face with his hands. "What's wrong?"

She swiped her hands over her cheeks. "Nothing."

"Those aren't tears from a happy orgasm. Those are tears from a broken heart."

"No, they're not."

"Paisley."

"They're not." She pushed him back and slipped off the rail. While she righted her dress, he fixed his pants.

"Then what are they from?"

He apparently wouldn't let it go unless she told him.

"My wings, Case. My wings." They were still out, although she badly wanted to hide them again. "My relationship with them is nothing like your relationship with my wings, which is where my tears came from. When I was thirteen, I got so fed up with the bullies that I...I tried to cut my wings off."

His face slackened. "No, you didn't."

She turned. "Left wing. By my shoulder."

His finger touched the scar where she'd worked a saw against her own flesh.

She inhaled sharply.

"Pais—" His voice gave out on a whisper of breath. "How did I never notice…?"

"My father caught me, stopped me. I doubt I would've been able to finish it. I certainly wouldn't have been able to cut them both off, but the intent was there."

"I'm glad you didn't."

Facing Case, she tucked her wings back into her body. "Why are you so different?"

His brows furrowed over his golden eyes. "What do you mean?"

"Why do you like them?"

"Paisley, there's absolutely nothing wrong with your wings. I suspect people called them hideous and whatever bullshit thing they ever said because they didn't want to admit how stunning your wings are. They are jealous, close-minded sheep who deserve to have *their* wings sawed off *their* backs." He stilled. "Wait. You tried to saw your wings off?"

She nodded.

"Wings were sawed off a fairy and left here for you to find. Who knows about what you tried to do when you were a child?"

"Just my parents. And Aster. I don't think my father told anyone. Not even Jude."

"They could've told someone that you're not aware of. Your uncle was your father's longest friend and his

223

right hand. He could've been told in confidence."

"My uncle wouldn't have broken that confidence."

"Is there someone your mother would've told? If she needed advice?"

"Lena, possibly, but I'm not going to ask her if my mother shared a secret that I don't want people to know." A secret she'd just revealed to Case. That meant something that she didn't want to evaluate right now. She cleared her throat and slipped past him into her room. "I'm going to change into something more comfortable."

"Do I need to leave for that?"

She paused in front of her dresser. "I suppose not. You've seen my body in every lighting, every pose imaginable."

His gaze trailed over her. "Yes, I have, and I won't tire of it."

She opened the top dresser drawer. "You will eventually."

Case's hand came out and shoved the drawer closed. He stood beside her, making her feel small in such close proximity. "Don't you remember what I said?" he asked. "I've never had sex with someone twice. Not even a second time an hour later. Now you..." He skimmed a finger down her arm. "...I've had in every way, countless times, and I still want you. If I haven't tired of you or your body yet, I don't think I ever will." He leaned in and spoke into her ear. "You've tamed a sex demon, Paisley."

Instant arousal, even moments after reaching climax.

Case inhaled slow and deep, and she knew he was drawing in not only the smell of their cum still on her body, but her fresh arousal and pheromones.

"I don't think I've tamed you, Case. If I did, you wouldn't need or want to have sex every day, certainly not multiple times in one day."

He chuckled. "True enough. Perhaps I should say that you *hooked* a sex demon. I'm hooked, Paisley." He licked the shell of her ear. "And I like it."

She swallowed. "I need to change."

"Alright." He removed his hand. "What do you have in mind? What's in here?"

"See for yourself." She stepped back to give him access to the drawer.

Standing in front of it, he slid the drawer open and scanned the contents—stacks of silk and satin and lace. From the top of one pile, he curled his fingers through thin loops and lifted out a black floor-length nightgown. The satin flowed like water as he lowered it back into the drawer. "May I choose?"

"Sure."

She sat on the edge of the bed while he examined each nightgown. Not a single nightgown escaped his scrutiny before he made his decision.

"This one." He held up a tiny, satin purple nightgown with a sheer lace bodice.

"It's see-through." Not what she had in mind when she intended to go downstairs and get some food. The last thing she wanted was to run into Thatch and Aster with her nipples visible. This sort of nightgown was one she wore only to bed.

"Yes, it is. I like to see your nipples."

Said nipples puckered as if he could see them.

"Since you're so convincing…" She stood. "Help me with the corset."

He worked on the ties, loosening them as he went down. The corset gave. He removed her dress while his gaze appraised her. "I'll say it…" He peered into her eyes. "One day, I hope you'll bless me with being able to see your wings while you're stark naked." His gaze shifted to above her shoulders, as if they were out. "That'd be a sight worth seeing."

"Maybe…one day…" But first, she had a lot of healing to do where her wings were concerned.

"One day would be good," he said and lifted the nightgown.

She raised her arms, and the satin shimmied down her curves.

"Delectable." His thumb glided over her left nipple through the sheer lace. "If I had it my way, I'd see these beauties all day long, whenever I wanted to."

She brushed his hand away. "That's enough of that. Are you hungry for food?"

"Starved." Taking her hand in his, he led her out of the room and down the hall. In the kitchen they found a wicker picnic basket sitting on the counter. "Our lovebirds are back."

"I wonder if they left us anything. We could have a secondhand picnic." She opened one of the flaps and peeked inside. "Look at that." Smiling, she extracted the leftovers. "Cheese, cold chicken, olives, strawberries, cherries, figs, chocolate…holy crap, this was a romantic picnic. Could you get us plates?" She pointed at a cabinet behind him.

"Sure."

As Case fetched plates, the window beside her shattered. She saw a flaming bottle seconds before it smashed into the tile at her feet.

14

Whiskey, Wrestling, & Wanking

Case

*I*t all happened as if in slow motion. The bottle exploded on the tile, spraying liquor and fire at Paisley. Flames latched onto her legs and feet. In the blink of an eye, she was ignited from the waist down. She looked at him, and in that split second, he saw fear and acceptance in her eyes; she thought this was it—her death.

He snatched her up as his wings burst free. They wrapped around her like a fire blanket. He held on for several seconds while the flames suffocated. Then he pulled back and peered at her legs. From the tips of her toes to mid-thigh, her skin was raw, blistered, bleeding, and weeping. The bottom of her nightgown was singed.

He picked her up and set her on the counter. "Aster!" His hands framed Paisley's face. "Paisley, baby, look at me."

She wasn't looking at him, though; she was staring at her legs with wide eyes. "Oh Goddess," she whispered. "Oh Goddess." Her body trembled.

He stripped out of his jacket and draped it over her shoulders. "Aster!"

Paisley finally met his eye. Tears filled hers. "It hurts."

"I know, baby. I know." He eyed the kitchen entrance. "Aster!"

Aster and Thatch rushed into the kitchen.

"Oh my—!" Aster slapped a hand to her mouth.

Case shot an order at Thatch. "Stay with them." Then he dove through the shattered window. The second he was through, his wings slapped the air, and he shot straight up above the property to survey the land and the skies. Nothing. Not a flash of color. Not a whoosh of wings. Not a clue as to who tried to kill Paisley right before his eyes.

He touched back down and climbed through the window to see Thatch's hand supporting Paisley's back, sparkling fairy dust falling from Aster's fingers, and the last of the burns fading away. Tears still filled Paisley's eyes, though, and he hated it.

"Anything?" Thatch asked.

He shook his head.

229

Thatch and Aster exchanged looks. "Why don't the two of you go into the parlor so we can clean this up and patch up the window?" Thatch said to her.

"Okay, yeah." Aster held out a hand to Paisley.

She didn't say anything but slid off the counter, clasped Aster's hand, and let her best friend take her away.

Case and Thatch didn't say a word, either, as they swept up broken glass, mopped up liquor, and boarded the window with a sheet of plywood they discovered in the gardening shed. Then they found Paisley and Aster in the parlor, sitting next to each other on the love seat. Thatch sat in a high-backed chair across from Aster, and Case claimed the one across from Paisley. She'd buttoned his jacket. It covered her to mid-thigh and dwarfed her, making her look fragile.

He clasped his hands in front of him and bent his neck. None of them spoke. What had happened, what they had witnessed, what Paisley had felt was too much for any of them to process. Gaze downcast, he finally said, "It's not safe for you to stay here. For either of you."

"This was my parents' home. I grew up here. I'm not leaving."

"Until the threat is gone."

"*This* threat."

He lifted his gaze.

"There's always going to be a threat, Case. My parents...they tried to hide it, but they received death threats all the time. They also received threats aimed at me. More than what they got for themselves. I never let that stop me from living, and I'm not going to let that stop me now."

Case angled his head toward Thatch, who lifted a shoulder in a shrug. He could practically hear Thatch's thought, *It's her choice.*

"It was dragon's breath," he said, his stare pinned to Thatch.

Thatch stiffened.

"What?" Paisley's voice was small.

"It was dragon's breath. Not even a Molotov cocktail could be as powerful as that was. I felt it against my wings. It was dragon's breath."

Aster laid a hand on Paisley's. "Tell him."

He looked from one to the other. "Tell me what?"

Paisley sighed. "Witnesses said my father caught fire so quickly that it had to be dragon's breath, but they couldn't find any proof. He was a torch...and no one could do anything."

"We have to tell Zara. And Jude. They need to know."

"Neither of them have phones. I'll have to write to them."

"I can get a demon I trust to deliver the messages, if you trust me with that."

She nodded.

None of them spoke while she wrote the letters. When she finished, Case texted Wren, who arrived shortly after. Case gave him the sealed envelopes. "Get these to Zara and Jude right away, and be careful."

"Yes, sire."

Wren left, and they lapsed into silence again.

Case didn't want Paisley staying in this house tonight. Or ever again. But he wouldn't be able to convince her to leave. Her mind was set. "If you're going to stay here, I'm going to station members of my faction around the property day and night. No one— absolutely *no one*—will get past them to harm you again. I promise you that."

Paisley shifted to Aster, who nodded.

"Okay," Paisley relented.

That was something.

"And I'm staying here tonight," he added.

"I guess we're going to have a slumber party then." Paisley got up. "I'm going to shower. Night, everyone."

She left quietly.

"I've never seen her like this," Aster said. "She's more than shaken. She's...withdrawn." Thatch sat beside Aster and slung an arm around her shoulders. Aster gave him a small smile and leaned into him, but her gaze returned to Case. "She...she was with him when it happened."

"What are you talking about?"

"The night her parents were killed, they were visiting their factions. Her mother went to the faye faction, and Paisley joined her father at the vampyre faction. She was inside, but she heard the screams, and she came out to see her father burn. She doesn't talk about it. All she's ever said to me was that the fire was blinding and so big that she couldn't believe her father was in the center of it."

The sound of a shower upstairs met his ears.

They sat in silence while the water ran through the house's pipes.

When the shower switched off, Case stood. "I'll check on her."

In her room, Paisley sat on the edge of her bed in an ankle-length silk nightgown. His jacket was folded neatly in her arms, and she hugged it to her chest. The fragility that came off her clenched an invisible hand around his throat. He lowered onto his knees before her.

"Here." She held out his jacket.

He set it aside. "When that bottle broke, and you looked at me, that look on your face...I never want to see it again."

"I couldn't feel anything," she whispered, with her gaze lowered. "I couldn't feel the flames eating away at my skin. Seeing them was so strange. And for a split second, I wondered if my father had felt any pain. The screams weren't his but the vampires who saw him go up in flames. When the flames died, nothing remained of him but ash." She met his eye now. "Enya was questioned by Zara's people, and the entire fier faction investigated, but no one could find proof that actual dragon's breath had been used."

"I know what I saw, what I felt. There's no other explanation." And he would find the proof if it killed him.

"What you felt..." She grabbed his shoulders. "Oh my Goddess! Did you get burned? Your wings. Are your wings okay?"

He caught her, stilling her. "They're fine. I'm fine. Dragon's breath can't hurt me."

"It can't?"

"No, it can't."

She checked him over. "Bullets do little damage. Dragon's breath does no damage. *Can* something hurt you? Do you have a weakness? What would I have to protect you from? Anything?"

He rubbed her arms. "Relax, Paisley."

"I can't relax, Case. Someone just tried to kill me in front of you. Again. Could someone kill you in front of me? What would they have to do?"

"They'd have to cut my head off."

She blinked. "Really? That...that's it? I don't mean for it to sound like how that came out, but really? Decapitation is what it'd take? You're that indestructible?"

"I'm not indestructible. Bullets can penetrate, and so can blades, but they don't pose a serious threat."

"Then I just have to make sure no one comes near you with a sharp axe?"

"That or a sword."

"Alright. Easy enough, I guess." Her body slackened. "I'm tired. I'm *really* tired."

"Of course you are." At the head of the bed, he drew back the comforter. "Come on. I'll tuck you in."

She slipped beneath the covers and held the pillow to her head.

He slid in behind her and took her in his arms so that her body curved into his.

"Case, what are you doing?"

"I'm staying with you so that you can sleep safely, but if you don't want me here, I'll go downstairs. Tell me what you want."

She sighed and cuddled back against him even more snuggly. "Stay."

He stayed.

In the middle of the night, he ventured to the kitchen for a glass of water and peeked into the parlor.

Aster was curled up on the love seat beneath a quilt, and Thatch was stretched out on the floor beside it. The two had become inseparable, and it conjured a smile to Case's face. He didn't know anyone more worthy of finding the love he deserved than Thatch.

After getting a drink, he returned to Paisley's room. She had turned onto her other side, facing where Case had been sleeping, and one of her legs had slipped out from beneath the comforter. The sight of her pale, smooth skin knotted his stomach. No burns. No scars. He trailed a finger up her shin. A small sound left her lips.

He crawled back into place. Paisley's face was serene and the most beautiful thing he'd ever seen. Her arched eyebrows, her purple-tinted eyelids, her sweeping lashes, her sharp cheekbones, her slim nose with a single freckle in the place of where a nose ring would be, and her full lips slightly parted. Diablo, she was gorgeous. And she'd almost been nothing but ash.

His hand curled over her cheek.

Her lashes fluttered as her eyelids peeled apart.

"Sorry," he whispered. "I didn't mean to wake you. I couldn't help myself."

She stared at him in the darkness. "Could you not help yourself even more?"

His brows lowered. "What do you mean?"

"Kiss me."

He didn't need to be asked twice. Thumb stroking her cheek, he brought his lips to hers.

They kissed leisurely. Emotions were behind the kiss. There was relief. He knew that one. Relief that she was okay. There was fear. Sure, that one was easy to identify, too. Fear because she'd almost died, and still could. And, okay, there was happiness. Happiness that she was in his arms right then. Not hurt. And asking him to kiss her. She'd never done that. All the weeks they'd been seeing each other, she came to him when she was horny, but she never came to him for tenderness, for kisses, for caresses. That was him. He sought her out whenever he wanted to sink into a kiss with her, lavish her, fondle her.

Their kiss spiraled out. Lips sucking. Tongues nuzzling. Moans growing.

She hitched up the skirt of her nightgown and hooked her leg over his.

He hauled her closer.

"Case, I want you inside me."

He wanted that, too.

His fingers worked open his belt and zipper. He entered her slowly. "Diablo, you feel good."

"I'm sure every woman feels—"

He covered her mouth with his hand. "Don't you dare say that to me right now. I don't even remember what anyone else felt like. There's just you now. Engraved in my mind. Branded on my body." He pumped his hips. "Just you."

"I like that."

"I like that, too."

She scooted even closer, laid her head in the crook of his neck. "You feel good, too."

Lying on their sides, embracing each other, they made slow, sweet love. Yes, *love*. No other word fit for what they were sharing in that moment, hours after she could've died.

Case accepted that, and he liked it, too.

In the morning, he kissed her shoulder until she hummed and opened her eyelids. "I'm heading to my faction. I'll be sending demons I personally vetted to stand guard on your property. There will be demons here around the clock. To top it off, Thatch will likely stay inside, as close to Aster as he can get. And I don't mean sexually, but if it gets the job done..."

She whacked him in the arm, and he chuckled.

"Go back to sleep."

"Yes, sir."

"Sir...that's close to sire." Another kiss to her shoulder, and then he got up. "I'll see you later."

He purposefully didn't tell her he'd see her that night, because he wasn't going to be there. Not in Paisley's home. Not in his home. Not at the daemon faction. No, he intended to go to the fier faction, up in the mountains, to question the queen face to face and visit every single dragon clan. He wouldn't rest until he found the bastard who tried to kill Paisley.

After stopping at his faction and deploying demons to stand guard around Paisley's property, with an additional set on standby for the next shift, he returned home to pack. Thatch was there for a quick visit, too, getting reports from their council.

Case wasn't home for more than thirty minutes before someone pounded on his front door. Curious as to who it could be, and furious that they had the balls to hit his door as if they wanted to break it down, he opened it and found Jude.

"I received correspondence from Paisley. She said someone tried to kill her using dragon's breath."

Case nodded. "It's true."

"She also said you saved her life. Thank you."

Exhaling, he inclined his head.

"I know you. You're not going to let this go. What's your plan?"

"I'm going to the fier faction. Now."

Thatch spoke up from behind Case. "As your right-hand, it's my job to tell you when you're making a big mistake…and you're making a big mistake."

Case faced him.

"Not telling Paisley, going behind her back…not smart."

"I'm doing what I have to do."

Thatch lifted a hand. "Whatever, it's your decision, it's your funeral."

"I'm coming with you," Jude said.

Case turned back.

"She's my goddaughter. I'm not letting her fall to the same fate as my best friend."

"I'm ready to go if you are."

"Race you there."

Grinning, Case picked up a leather backpack from beside the door and peered at Thatch.

"I know Aster is your priority, but can you keep an eye on Paisley for me while I'm gone?"

"If she lets me, I will."

"Thank you." Case slung the pack over his shoulder. "Let's go," he said to Jude, who galloped off. Case launched into the sky. He flew low, keeping pace with Jude.

They traveled for hours past valleys, lakes, streams, and woods to where the fier faction resided, deep in an underground network of caves spanning an entire mountain range. Side by side, they made their way into a cavern where dragon shifters stood guard.

Case approached them. "Tell Queen Enya that the Demon Lord and Centaur King are here to see her."

The guards escorted them deep into the cavern to where Enya lounged on a lava rock throne. Beside her sat her daughter, Phoenix Carnelian. While the queen was in her dragon shifter form with her blood-red scales glinting in the light of torches glowing with dragon's breath, Phoenix was in human form. She had red hair, tan skin, and eyes like emeralds.

"Well, well, well, what can I do for the Demon Lord and Centaur King this fine day?" Queen Enya asked.

"You can cut the holier-than-thou attitude," Case spat. "We're all faction leaders here, and this isn't a conversation where you should be showing an ounce of disrespect."

"You're in my home right now, Lord Case. You need to show *me* some respect."

"You'll get it after you give it."

The queen eyed him.

Beside her, Phoenix rolled her eyes. "Mom, seriously, stop. You know why they're here without them having to say it."

Case lifted a brow.

"Paisley is my friend. If something happened, I want to know."

"Paisley is *not* your friend." The queen wrinkled her nose in disgust. "She's a faction leader, and faction leaders can't be friends." She cast a look at Case.

239

"Unless, of course, you're banging one."

Case's jaw clenched.

"We're friends," Jude cut in, indicating at himself and Case. "And we're not banging each other, no matter how much Case may want this hot horse bod of mine."

Case snorted.

Phoenix held back laughter. "I can see his temptation, King Jude." Grinning, she faced her mom again. "Paisley *is* my friend, Mom, and she will continue to be my friend when *I'm* queen." She nodded. "Has something happened?"

"Something has. Paisley was hit with a Molotov cocktail made of dragon's breath."

Phoenix gasped. Her eyes widened. "Is she…is she okay? She's not—"

"She's alive."

Phoenix sighed but quickly straightened. "Dragon's breath?"

"That's right. I felt it. There's no mistaking it."

Her face paled.

Queen Enya spoke up then. "Are you claiming that we had something to do with it?"

"Don't answer that, Lord Case. It's not necessary." Phoenix sent a glare toward her mom that clearly told the queen to zip it. "This morning, we found a dragon shifter outside. He was dead. Whoever killed him did it to steal his dragon's breath, and now I know why…they wanted to kill Paisley with it and frame us, but I promise you that, despite my mother's disdain, I won't allow this faction to hurt Paisley."

Case nodded, believing her, but that didn't mean

someone wasn't doing anything behind her back. "Can we be given access to the dragon clans to talk to each leader?"

Phoenix eyed her mother. "Mom…"

Queen Enya seethed quietly. "Fine, but I can't guarantee that you'll get a friendly reception."

"That's fine with me, because I don't feel like being all that friendly." Case spun on his heel. "I need some fresh air." Vibrating with anger, he marched topside and sucked in air that didn't smell like a musky cave.

Jude followed him up and watched him pace in the grass.

His cell phone's ringtone cut through the sound of his seething. Thatch's name on the screen halted his feet. He answered the call. "Hey, is everything okay?"

"I'm not sure if I would describe this as okay."

"What do you mean?"

Jude came up beside him. "Was there another attempt?"

Case lifted a hand. "Did something happen?"

Thatch let out a breath. "You could say that. Paisley asked me where you were, so I told her the truth. I wasn't going to lie. She's pissed, Case, as I knew she would be. She told me that the next time I talk to you to say these words exactly, 'The arrangement is over.'"

Case closed his eyes. The sun was sweltering, but cold panic washed over him. "Are you

there now?"

"I am."

"Give her your phone. I'll talk to her."

241

"Alright."

He waited.

"Who is it?" Paisley asked.

A shuffling sound, and then, "You've got to be kidding me."

The line disconnected.

He called Thatch back.

"I knew that'd go that way," Thatch said.

"Find her and put me on speaker."

"I told you this would be your funeral. Don't make it mine, too."

In the background, Aster's soft voice said, "Give it to me." A moment later, she said into Case's ear, "What do you need me to do?"

"Put me on speaker wherever she is."

"Okay."

He listened as Aster headed to wherever Paisley had retreated to.

"Go," she said.

"Paisley —"

"Oh my Goddess. You and Thatch need to stop. I don't want to talk to him. He made his choice. He left."

"I didn't leave *you*," he said, hoping she'd hear him out. "I left, yes, but I left to find out where the dragon's breath came from."

"You did it behind my back, Case. My parents kept me in the dark, too, because they thought it was for my own good. And, in the end, that's what got them killed. I already asked you not to leave me out of anything that has to do with threats against me. I *asked* you. Going behind my back, like you did, is something I will never tolerate. In case Thatch didn't already tell you, I'll say it now, and it's the last thing I'm going to say to you…our arrangement is over."

The call ended.

"Damn it!" With his hand wrapped around his phone, he rammed his fist into the cave. A chunk of rock broke off.

"She'll get over it eventually."

"Have you known your goddaughter to get over anything eventually…or ever?"

"Now that you mention it…"

"Let's talk to these damn clan leaders. The faster we get answers, the faster we can get back." And he could try to find some way to mend things with Paisley.

Except, it took two days.

Two days to question twenty clan leaders.

Two days of issuing blatant threats.

Two days of dealing with cocky dragon shifters.

Two days, and they weren't any closer to knowing who tried to kill Paisley.

Case returned the morning of the third day and went straight to her. She opened the door and promptly slammed it in his face. He braced his hands on the doorframe. "Paisley, come on. We need to talk."

"Go to hell." Her voice was distant. she was leaving him there on the doorstep, not intending to open the door again no matter how much he knocked or pleaded.

But she had to hear him out. If she did, she'd see. She'd understand.

He flew to her balcony. The fact he found the door unsecured relieved him while also angering him. He let himself in, journeyed through her bedroom, and out into the hall. She was at the other end of that hall, heading toward him. When she saw him, she jolted to a stop. Then her eyes flared burgundy, and she rushed at him so fast that she was a blur of black and purple. She plowed into him.

His body collided into the wall, and plaster caved in around him.

"Breaking into my house is a death sentence," she growled.

"Hear me out and then you can kill me if you still want to."

"I don't want to hear a thing you have to say, Case." She shoved him before taking a step back. "Get out of my house."

"Pais, please."

"No! I don't want to hear it. What you did was betrayal. You violated my trust in you. How can I trust you not to do anything else behind my back because you're 'looking out for me'?" She made air quotes for emphasis.

"Because I won't ever do it again."

"You shouldn't have done it this time. You already knew that I didn't like being left behind when you and Thatch returned to my land after you were shot. Before that, you knew I wanted to search the area with the two of you. Before that, you were aware that I wanted to take care of the fairy wings because they were on my property. This is a pattern, Case. A pattern of me wanting to be included, and a pattern of you deciding *for me* what would be best. We could've sat, you and I, or even the four of us, and come to a compromise, but you took it upon yourself. So, I'm taking it upon myself to squash us for good. Our arrangement is over. Now, go."

He stood there, staring, unable to form a response.

"Get out of my house!"

Feeling as dead as their arrangement, he passed through her bedroom and onto her balcony, where he launched into the air and flew home.

Case sat on a couch with a glass of whiskey. His third one for the evening. Around the glass, his knuckles were bruised from a match against another demon. Nothing felt better than beating up demons in a ring to get out pent-up aggression. He'd been doing it for the past three weeks.

Thatch stepped into the parlor with his arms crossed and a disapproving look on his face. "What the hell are you doing?"

"Isn't it obvious?" Case lifted his glass.

"Oh, no, it's pretty obvious to me that you're being a coward, but I'm wondering if *you're* aware that you're being a coward. All you seem to care about these days are the three W's. Whiskey, wrestling, and wanking."

"It's all I feel like doing."

"You've even stopped attending our council meetings about the threats to Paisley."

"Are we any closer to knowing who tried to kill her?"

"No."

"Then you don't need me there."

"Look…" Thatch came closer. "I don't pretend to understand your relationship. Or whatever arrangement the two of you had. I do know that the two of you were having sex and were seeing each other daily up until you left. I tried to warn you that there'd be consequences for not talking to Paisley about it first. Now you're facing them. Paisley dumped you."

"Dumped me?"

"She kicked your ass to the curb. Do you like that phrasing better?"

"I guess, but I'm surprised that you said 'ass.'"

Thatch stared up at the ceiling a moment before meeting Case's eye. "You're miserable, and Aster says Paisley isn't the same, either. Again, I don't know what the two of you had going on, but it's obvious to me that whatever it was…you've fucked each other up."

Case raised a brow.

"Yeah, I said it. You've fucked each other up. The two of you are headstrong and are ready to throw away whatever you had because one of you is an idiot and the other feels betrayed, but you both clearly miss each other. For whatever reason. You may not even understand why, and you don't have to. Why will come later. The two of you were happy together. If 'together' is even the right word. You decide. But you won't get that back, you won't get *her* back, unless you fix it."

"I. Don't. Know. How."

"I think you do, but I'll say it again, you're being a coward. Suck it up and do what you have to do because the three W's aren't working for you. But one thing had worked for you. One thing had changed you. And that was a certain beautiful hybrid."

Thatch left, and Case drained the rest of his whiskey in one swallow.

He did miss Paisley.

He missed the smell of her skin.

The smell of her hair.

The smell of her on his bedsheets.

He missed the sound of her laughter.

The sound of her voice.

The way she said his name right before she came.

He missed the feel of her in his arms.

The feel of her on top of him.

And, yeah, his cock missed the feel of her cunt.

He missed seeing her gorgeous face.

Her pale skin.

Her sweet breasts.

He missed talking to her, being around her, knowing that if he wanted her or needed her at any time, he could go to her.

Damn it, he fucking missed her, and that was a foreign concept. Thatch was right; Paisley had changed him. Somehow, she'd changed a sex demon's habits. Sex demons didn't develop attachments to one being. Sex demons didn't rely on one being for pleasure. Sex demons didn't want anything other than sex. But here Case was, a sex demon *and* the demon lord, and he had developed an attachment that requested more than sex.

What did he want with Paisley? An actual relationship? To be her boyfriend?

Diablo.

He cringed at the word *boyfriend*. Nothing sounded sillier or more childish than thinking of himself as someone's boyfriend.

Did he want to be her lover? Lover wasn't as ridiculous sounding as boyfriend, but sex demons didn't fall in love. Lovers had deep feelings for each other, and while he considered the last time they'd been together an act of "making love," because of the very nature of the moment, he wouldn't say that their arrangement had anything to do with love. It had to do with desire. Temptation. Lust. Carnal passion.

Are sexers a thing? He cracked a smile. *Better yet, lusters.*

Still, he couldn't deny that there wasn't something more, but he didn't know how to define it. Thatch said he didn't need to define it now. What he needed to do was get it back, then the definition—the why—would come later, but he could be a coward for the rest of the night, at least. Until the Enchanted Hierarchy Council Meeting tomorrow when he'd have to face Paisley.

When he arrived at the meeting, she was already there, sitting in her throne, looking regal in a black dress with a piece of metal armor that covered her chest. That armor was a clear statement of the assassination attempts and the fact that she'd survived them. More metal looped up her bare arms from wrists to shoulders. Her hair was up, showing off her lovely neck, and her lips were painted an intriguing metallic silver to match her armor.

Lena stood in front of her, and the two of them

were carrying on a conversation. He had no choice but to sit down. When Lena left to go to her seat, his view of Paisley was unobscured. He expected to meet Paisley's eye, but she diverted her gaze away. That rejection had him curling his hands around the edges of the armrests.

Look at me, baby. Come on.

She wouldn't look at him.

During the entire hour they were there, discussing one thing after the other, she didn't glance his way once.

"I purposefully left this for last, because it's the most important topic," Zara said. "The attempt on Paisley's life using dragon's breath."

Paisley stiffened in her throne.

Queen Enya huffed. "I will tell everyone exactly what I told Lord Case and King Jude when they marched into my home, questioning me and my faction."

Paisley's head angled toward the queen, but she kept her gaze trained on the floor, as she had during each topic of discussion.

"We did not have anything to do with the attempt on Paisley's life. In fact, one of my own showed up dead, drained of his life-fire. We believe that whoever killed the shifter tried to kill Paisley and frame us. Like someone tried to frame Case. Now, I don't know if I need to have sex with Paisley to get everyone to believe my innocence"—she bent forward to wink at Paisley—"but I will if she will."

"Seriously?" Case snapped.

Enya smirked. "Threesome?"

"You've got to be fucking kidding me," Paisley mumbled.

Zara's voice rose. "I thought I made it clear that talk of hierarchy leaders having sex with each other would not be brought up here again. Let me add that no one will shame another, especially not a woman, for whom they're having sex with."

Enya sat back. That smirk remained on her face, though.

Zara cut in. "The entire Enchanted Hierarchy has been on high alert since the attack and will remain so. Curfews are still active. Make sure your people are following them. Only the werewolf shifters have an exception during the full moon, but they must stay within their faction's bounds." She said that to Alaric, who nodded. "Enya, the clan leaders are still doing nightly head counts?"

"They are. And in the morning. No one will kill another one of us to try to kill *her*."

Case's jaw clenched. That *her* made it sound like Paisley was a bug.

Zara's voice drew his attention when she directed her next question to him. "Case, your demons are still posted around Paisley's property?"

"They are, and they will continue to be until the bastards behind this are found."

Paisley still didn't meet his eye. Not even after that vow.

"And my people will begin a new round of interrogations with truth potions," Zara said. "Last time, we exempted faction leaders from the interrogations, but now each of you should expect to be questioned.

And don't even try to find a way to trick the truth potions. It won't work. That's it for today, but I'll remind each and every one of you to be vigilant."

Case shoved to his feet. If he didn't act fast, Paisley would rush out of there to escape him. In a few strides, he was in front of her. She hadn't even had a chance to shift in her throne. "We need to talk, Pais."

"No, we don't."

"Yes, we do."

She shifted her head away.

"Look at me, Paisley."

She didn't.

He bent forward, planting his hands on the armrests of her throne. "Look at me."

Her eyes flicked to his. "I'm looking at you. Now back up. People are staring."

"I don't care." He shifted closer. "I miss you."

"Then you should've thought of that."

"I did, but I thought about how much I'd miss you if someone were to kill you. I didn't think about how much I'd miss you if you were still alive and avoiding me."

"Your mistake. Your loss." She propelled to her feet.

He straightened, but he didn't back away. They stood so close that they were touching. He curled his hands around her shoulders and caressed her soft skin with his palms. "It *was* my mistake." He slipped his hands to the backs of her shoulders, remembering her wings. "But is it really just *my* loss?"

Her eyelids drifted shut. "Stop touching me."

"I would, but you closed your eyes, which means

you like it." His thumbs stroked over the bones of her shoulders, where her wings would appear if she let them. "You're not feeling any kind of loss? You're not missing me at all? My touch?"

When his hands stroked past her shoulders, down her back, she shivered.

"My presence? Nothing?" He raised his right hand to the back of her neck and angled his head, craving a kiss. Diablo, he hadn't kissed her in nearly a month.

She sucked in a breath. "Don't, Case. Don't."

He held back despite his urges. "Paisley, I went to the fier faction for you, and I was only gone two days."

"It's not the length of time that you were gone. It's the fact that you didn't think I should know. I was the one who got burned, but the way you burned me by leaving me behind without a word, that hurt me even more than the dragon's breath did."

He lifted his other hand to the side of her face. "Can't you understand that after what I had witnessed, I didn't want to risk you and your beautiful life?"

She swallowed and angled her head to avoid his eye, but when she did, she'd pressed her cheek right into his palm. Her eyelids closed again. "You could've done both," she whispered. "You could've kept me in the loop *and* kept me safe. And if I had demanded to go with you— because it *is* my life, and it was my father's life, my mother's life—wouldn't you have stayed by my side to keep me safe?"

"Yes."

"Then you decided on your own to leave me out of it when you still could've accomplished the same with me there." She met his eye now. "I can't trust you. You make decisions without me, and you expect me to abide by them. That's not any kind of relationship.

You started this arrangement. Well, now I'm the one ending it." And she tore out of his hold.

Instantly, his hands felt empty, cold, lifeless.

Jude joined him. "I see she's still giving you the cold shoulder."

"But what a beautiful shoulder it is," he mumbled as she disappeared from sight.

Jude lifted a brow. "Do I need to have a talk with you about my goddaughter?"

Case let out a laugh. "You should've done that before you told us to fuck each other. Better yet, you shouldn't have told us to do that at all."

"Hey, don't blame me. The two of you would've gotten around to it at some point."

True enough.

"What I meant is…you are clearly feeling a certain way about her."

Case arched a brow. "A certain way? Care to tell me what that way is?" Because he didn't fucking know.

"You said it yourself."

Case's brows furrowed now.

"*Care*. You *care* about her. It's not just about sex."

He slipped his hands into his pockets. "Not for me anyway."

"Do you love her?"

His head knocked back as if Jude had clocked him in the jaw. "Love? Now, hold your horses."

Jude crossed his arms and pawed the tile with a hoof. "That's incredibly offensive."

"Shit. Sorry. But you know what I meant."

"I do. I'm busting your balls. You're good." He gave Case a friendly punch to the shoulder. "But *do you* love her?"

"I wouldn't call what I feel love. Hell, I don't even know what love feels like. You know as well as I do that sex demons are incapable of love, but I do enjoy her body. All day, all night, I enjoy her body. I'm addicted to her. I find myself thinking about her body all the time and I want to—"

"Whoa. Okay. I know I told the two of you to fuck each other but saying it and hearing the details are two different things. I knew her as a little girl."

"I was going to say that I want to hold her all the time. Simply hold her."

"And you never wanted to do that with anyone else?"

"Diablo, no. I had never even kissed anyone before her. She's got me fucking addicted. I'm a fiend. Ask Thatch. This past month, I've been a wreck. She's *wrecked* me."

Jude grimaced. "I'm sorry, man, but…"

"But what?"

"But you've wrecked her, too. I've never seen her shrink away from someone confronting her about something. That's not like her. She would've chewed Enya up and spat her out for that."

The memory of Paisley saying she'd chew him up and spit him out, and teasing him with a kiss, blazed to the front of his mind. Diablo, he had wanted to kiss her so badly a moment ago. If she'd allowed him to, he would've gotten her to melt into his arms. With his lips on hers, he would've managed to get her to surrender, to forgive him, and leave with him.

"Did you notice she's paler than usual, too?"

"I did."

About a month had gone by since she'd last fed on him. His blood couldn't sustain her for that long, so what had she been doing all this time? He hoped she wasn't starving herself.

"I know all about her struggles with drinking blood. Her father told me about it. He felt so guilty about it, too, because it was his fault that she needed blood. I noticed, though, that while the two of you were...whatever the two of you were...she looked healthier than ever."

He didn't think Paisley would want Jude to know that she'd been drinking Case's blood, so he didn't say a word.

"The two of you were good for each other, so whatever you have to do to fix it, do it."

Case stared up at the ceiling. "Easier said than done, my friend."

"I know it, which is why I'm going to wish you luck. You'll need it."

Luck was an understatement. He needed the universe on his side.

15

Breakfast of Champions

Paisley

*S*eeing Case had shaken her more than she had thought it would. She'd been doing relatively well up to the point when he came close and she could smell him, feel his body heat. Then he had to go and touch her. Why the hell did he have to do that? It had shattered her resolve. For a moment, she'd forgotten the reason behind her anger, the reason behind her determination to not see him, not need him. For anything. She'd questioned if her anger was worth not being near him, with him. He'd weakened her. That weakness had stayed with her until she made it home. Now, she was pissed all over again.

She headed toward the staircase. Two steps up and dizziness snatched her in a spiraling grasp. She gripped the banister and squeezed her eyelids shut. Willing the dizziness to abate, she focused on her breathing. Nice lungfuls of oxygen. Gradually, the spinning stopped, and she resumed her trek up the stairs. Still, she climbed up carefully, and her hand didn't leave the banister in case she needed support. Tumbling down the stairs and cracking her head open was not her plan for the day.

In her bedroom, she changed into jeans and a dark purple tank top. Both would hide dirt stains from gardening. Her rose bushes needed care, and tending them always helped to calm her. After seeing Case, she was in desperate need of some rose therapy. First, she needed water. She could feel her dizzy spell clinging to the edges of her vision. Water wasn't what her body required, but she hoped she could fool it into thinking water was precisely what she lacked.

She retrieved a glass from a cabinet in the kitchen. While it filled, her gaze trailed over to the window. Thatch had repaired it the day after, but she still stood well out of its way. Even with demons posted around the perimeter of her property, she didn't trust that window. Didn't trust that someone wouldn't send something else flying through it in the hopes of killing her once and for all. So, she sipped water with her back to the counter.

Aster stepped into the kitchen then. In her hand was a blood bag.

Paisley eyed it suspiciously. Not even blood bags helped her anymore. The problem wasn't simply a moral issue of not wanting to drink blood. Nor was it about the unappealing taste. Now, her stomach revolted at a drop of blood that wasn't Case's. This was not ideal. Not in the least. "What's that?"

"I got my hands on a bag of AB Negative, donated by a seventeen-year-old. As far as blood bank blood goes, this is as pure as you can get." Aster held it out. "It could help."

Sighing, Paisley cut into the top with a pair of scissors. "Bottom's up." She tipped the bag upside down and sucked out room temperature blood. As it poured into her mouth, slithered over her tongue, her body clenched. She had a hard time swallowing it down because of what usually happened immediately afterward—stomach cramps, gagging, and then the blood reversing up her esophagus.

The blood coursed smoothly down her throat. She held still, counting to twenty. When nothing happened, she met Aster's eye.

Aster exhaled. "So...how'd it taste?"

"Not bad compared to other sources or other bags."

Still, it wasn't Case's blood. His blood was something special. She'd started to wake up in the night in a cold sweat from craving his blood. I suppose the answer is the rarest blood of all. AB Negative blood from a freaking teenager. She didn't want to think about having to find blood like this for the rest of her life, so instead she raised the bag back to her mouth and sucked out another swallow. It went down easily.

On the third swallow, though, her stomach muscles clenched.

No, no, no.

She spun and bent over the sink. The rarest blood of all choked her as her body expelled it. Tears streamed down her cheeks. Even when the last drop was out of her system, she continued to dry heave. Several minutes passed before her stomach settled. When it did, she slid to the floor, unable to withhold the tears as her frustrations poured out of her.

"I hate this," she sobbed.

Aster rubbed her back. "I thought for sure that'd work."

Paisley swiped the tears from her cheeks. "I don't know what to do."

"Maybe…maybe we have to go younger."

"What do you mean?"

"Well, the purer we go the better your stomach handles the blood, but we haven't tried an infant's blood."

"No, absolutely not. I am not going to feed on babies. I'm not a monster."

"I'm sorry. I didn't mean to suggest…but I don't know what to do. I hate seeing you like this. You're suffering, Paisley. You're going to hate this suggestion, maybe more than infant blood, but I think…" She inhaled deeply. "…you need to consider talking to Case."

"No."

"His blood was the only thing you could tolerate."

"I said, no."

"You're going to die!"

Paisley looked away from Aster, because that truth had crossed her mind. If she couldn't figure out what to do, she would die from starvation and malnutrition. "I don't need Case."

"You do. In more than one way, but you don't want to admit it."

Paisley didn't say anything to that.

"Maybe it's human blood that is bad for your system. We could try to get donors from the factions."

"I don't want the other factions to know."

"What if I asked Thatch—"

"I'm not going to use your boyfriend as my blood source."

Aster's cheeks flamed red. "What about…? What about my blood? Fairy blood might not give you the same reaction. Every part of our being is magical. It could work. And you know I would do anything for you."

She did know that, but she didn't want to use her bestie as her personal blood farm, either. "I'll think about it." Only that reply would get Aster off her back. "I'm going to spend some time with my roses."

"Stay inside the perimeter."

Rolling her eyes, she rose to a shaky stand. "I will."

In the backyard, she opened the door to the gardening shed. A bench contained gloves, seed packets, shearers, and a handheld cultivator. She picked up the gloves and shearers and watched a shadow grow up the back wall of the shed. Fear didn't come with the shadow. Rage did, because she recognized the build.

"Get the hell off my property."

"I can't," Case said. "You need to feed. Feed on me and then I'll go."

She reached for a shovel propped against the wall and gripped it, contemplating bashing his head in. "I don't want your blood."

"You may not want it, but you need it. I know you. I know the signs. You're too pale. You're moving slower. You're shaking."

"I'm shaking out of anger."

"If you want me to leave, feed on me."

She whirled around, breathing ragged. Seeing Case standing there in the doorway summoned a surge of emotions, from rage to lust, but underneath both powerful emotions was another—happiness. Case's presence, no matter how much it inspired her to want to bang him and snap his neck, also evoked happiness in her. She didn't understand it, but she couldn't deny that Case brought her a sense of peace and joy. That realization, in that moment, only tripled her wrath, as well as her hunger.

She leapt onto him.

He caught her, and she sank her fangs into the side of his neck.

A satisfied groan rumbled in his throat and tickled her tongue as she sucked.

He backed her into the wall. His hold on her was fierce. She never could grasp how her feeding on him could cause him so much pleasure, but he got off on it each time, and him being turned on by the act stirred her loins equally. Unable to contain it, she rocked her pelvis into him.

He responded by grinding his erection against her crotch. The friction was exquisite.

"Paisley." His voice was like thunder. "If you don't want this, stop moving your hips."

She hitched herself higher up his body and pistoned her hips faster, clearly telling him she wanted this. She wanted this more than she could voice, more than she understood, more than she dared to consider. All the while, she didn't stop feeding. Both pleasures drove her mad with desire. The second she got her fill, she slicked her tongue over the puncture holes, sealing them instantly.

In his ear she ordered, "Fuck me. Now."

He set her on her feet, yanked off her pants and underwear, whipped her around, and bent her over the bench.

"Two, one inside, vibrate."

He sank one penis into her soaking pussy, while the other lay snug against her vulva and clit. Both vibrated.

She moaned and gripped the sides of the bench.

Case thrust inside her, and she rocked back against him in a frenzied need to come. Her clit sang as a wet heat bloomed inside her.

That heat surged into her womb, swirled, whirled, spiraled, and expanded.

Case's penises were stunning in their skill, their magick.

Suddenly, the heat collected into a ball in her core. Case plunged into her again, and the heat exploded outward, filling her womb, flowing down her legs to her knees. The orgasm was swift. She didn't cry out as she usually did, but rather sighed and fell limp.

"What was that?" Case asked, stilling. "Did you come already?"

"Um…" For the first time since their arrangement, embarrassment washed over her. Every time he'd made her come, it had been glorious and exactly how she'd wanted it. She'd never batted a lash at how they'd fucked each other before or how she'd orgasmed, but now she was mortified. "…yeah."

"You've never orgasmed that quickly or that softly for me before." He withdrew his penis and guided her around. "How long have you been horny for me, love?"

She diverted her gaze. "Since you left."

"Why didn't you come to me sooner?"

She met his eye now. "Because I am tired of wanting you and needing you."

"And how did that work out for you?"

"It didn't. Obviously, and that's the problem."

"What are you talking about?"

"You've called me yours, and I. Am. Yours. You're the only one who knows how to fuck me so good. Every time. You're the only one I want, and that's the problem." She wasn't ready to admit that she could only tolerate his blood. That was more than pleasure. That was actual survival, and telling him that she needed him to stay alive, well, that was a whole other thing.

"You think it's easy for me wanting you all the time? And only you? Because it's not. But I'm not questioning it. I'm fine with wanting you, no matter how bloody inconvenient it is." He stepped closer. The head of his penis dug into her abdomen. He plunged his hands into her hair, curled his fingers around her locks, and pulled slowly so her throat was exposed to him. His teeth scraped along her trachea. Hands around her skull, he lowered her head and settled his mouth next to her ear. "The difference between us is that I like being yours."

"I'm used to being an independent woman. Having to rely on you is difficult for me to reconcile."

"You're still an independent woman, Pais, whether you need my cock or not."

She kept a hand flat to his chest. "You claim to like being mine, but then you do things without me."

"I made a mistake. You may not believe me, but I thought I was doing it out of your best interest. Keeping you safe. I didn't realize I was damaging your trust in me. If I had known you wouldn't have forgiven me, given me a chance to explain myself, I would've chosen differently."

"Would you have?"

"Yes." He toyed with a lock of her hair. "When you broke our arrangement, a part of me broke with it."

She frowned, because that was what had happened to her. "What are we doing to each other, Case?"

"I don't know, but I'm not complaining." He twirled her hair around his finger. "Now, as for our arrangement, do you want to reinstate it? Because if you do…it can't be broken in that way again. Rash. Without giving the other person a chance to explain, to defend themselves."

"What could break the arrangement then?"

Case tugged on her locks. "Nothing, if I have anything to say about it."

"Be reasonable, Case."

"I am, but…if you feel like you need an out…true betrayal. If one of us has sex with another." He clasped her chin gently, but his next words made the touch firm. "Even kisses another. That'll be the end of the arrangement for good. If one of us does something against our factions, that would do it, too."

She nodded. "One more thing. I need you to swear something to me."

"What's that?"

"From now on, we don't do anything without talking to the other first. You won't go off to do your own thing. If it has to do with me, my factions, the threats, you will include me. Hell, if it has to do with you, your safety, and the possibility of you disappearing for days at a time, you will include me in that, too."

He titled his head. "Is that you caring about my wellbeing?"

She clenched her jaw. "Well, you care about mine, don't you? Now swear to me."

"I swear. Will you swear not to end our arrangement rashly again?"

"I swear."

"Good. Now—" He peered down at his penis. "You robbed me of riding you to bliss and hearing you cry out loud and long. I don't like it when someone robs me." He picked her up and set her on the bench. While looking at her pussy, he nudged the head of his penis into her. Then his hands molded around her hips. His fingers dug into her flesh, and he suddenly yanked her onto him so that he impaled her in totality.

She gasped from the fullness.

265

"You're not done until I say you're done."

"Yes, sir."

His grin was quick. He lifted her up, and she locked her legs around him. When he held her against the wall, he stroked inside her, long and deep. "Call me sire."

Biting her bottom lip, she stared into his eyes.

"I want to hear you call me sire." He pumped his hips faster. "Pais…"

She moaned. Hearing him call her "Pais" while his penis caressed her dripping vaginal walls was enough to reignite her arousal.

When his penis vibrated at a speed she'd never felt before, she knocked her head back. "Fuck." She cried out again and again, but the pleasure building inside her was too intense. Too much.

"You're holding yourself back, love. Don't hold back on me."

"I don't know if I can."

"You can."

"I can't, I can't."

"Yes, you can." He pounded into her faster but kept each stroke deep. "You can."

She held onto him for dear life and let his penis push her over the edge. This time when she came, she clutched him, dug her nails into him, and let loose a loud, long moan. The orgasm rippled throughout her body, coaxing another moan from her that stretched on and on. He hadn't finished yet, though, and continued to sink into her. Ten seconds after her orgasm finished, another one startled her and had her crying out again.

With a roar that signified him purging his seed,

Case came, too.

Panting, they held onto each other.

"Yes, sire," she whispered.

Chuckling, he leaned back. She was latched onto him—arms and legs—so he was able to move his hands from her hips to cradle her face. He kissed her so thoroughly that she melted even more around him.

"Case, I need to talk to you about something."

"If you're going to ruin this moment, stop now."

"I might, but not in the way you think."

He peered into her eyes. "What way is that?"

"If you think I'm going to tell you this was a one-time, last-time thing…a mistake…that I'm taking back what I said about reinstating our arrangement…I'm not."

"Good." He slipped out of her. Both hands on her hips, he helped her to a stand when she unraveled her legs from his waist.

She pulled on her underwear and pants.

"What do you want to talk about?"

She picked up her gardening gloves. "Grab those shearers and follow me."

Kneeling in front of one of her beloved rose bushes, she pruned the branches. Case knelt beside her. "So…" She clipped a branch. "Drinking your blood only made it harder on me."

"What do you mean?"

"Over the past month, I tried every source of blood I could think of." She knocked her head to the side to amend that. "Human blood. But nothing worked. Before you showed up, I tried AB Negative blood, donated by a seventeen-year-old. At first, I thought it was working, but then it came back up." She cut away a dead branch. "As it turns out, your blood is the only blood my body can tolerate."

"Whenever you need my blood, Paisley, you've got it."

"It's not that, Case...it's..." She trimmed a branch shorter. "I was slowly starving to death. If your blood is the only blood I can take, if something were to happen to you...if you died...I wouldn't be long behind you."

He didn't say anything.

"Talk about a fun conversation when we're not even in that kind of relationship, huh?"

"What kind of relationship are we in?"

"Not the kind that warrants conversations about what would happen if you were to ever die."

"I disagree."

She snipped a few inches off a branch.

"Our relationship started because of death threats aimed at you. Since that Molotov cocktail nearly took your life, I haven't been able to stop thinking about what would happen if you died." He traced the underside of her jaw with the tip of his finger. "This past month without you, I lost all control."

She tilted her head to him now.

"Thatch said I was only interested in the three W's—wrestling, whiskey, and wanking." He snorted. "That's all I did. Fight, drink, and jerk off while thinking about you. I was a mess, Pais. You asked, 'What are we doing to each other?' And I don't know. Thatch claims we fucked each other up. Jude says we wrecked each other. That was us not being together, so to me, the answer is clear. We can't be apart."

She arched a brow. "That…that sounds serious."

"I am serious."

"Case, that's a lot to throw at me moments after we picked up our arrangement."

"I know it is."

"Since the Molotov cocktail, you've called me baby. And since you came here, you've called me love. Twice. Baby and love are pretty serious terms of endearment."

"And yet they feel natural for me to say. Did you prefer me calling you darlin'?"

"I didn't mind it."

The truth was, she didn't hate hearing him call her baby or love, but it was hard to admit that. To Case it'd be even harder.

"Then, darlin', I'm going to leave you to think about that. I'll see you later."

She watched him leave, all long legs and muscular back. Flattening her hands to the soil around the rose bush, she bent her neck. Sometimes, Case was too passionate, too enormous, too magnetic. And the things he said threw her for a loop. But her attraction to him was undeniable. Her need to be near him, feel him, enjoy him was startling. She'd never needed to be near anyone else, feel anyone else, enjoy anyone else as much as Case.

That night, she woke up, aroused, famished, and wet. Except, when she climbed out of bed to go to the bathroom, she was wet for an entirely different reason than being turned on. Her moon time had come two days earlier than the new moon, and her blood wet the inside of her thighs. She inserted a menstrual cup so she could ritually collect her precious blood and give it back to Mother Earth in thanks and ceremony, as all fairies did in honor of nature.

Feeling a bit faint, she laid back down and fell asleep.

In the morning, she woke to a dinging sound from her cell phone. She hated the thing and never used it. The only reason why it was charged and on was because Aster had begged her to keep it charged and on at all times, especially if Aster left the house with Thatch, leaving Paisley alone. As far as Paisley knew, Aster was the only one with the number. She picked it up from the nightstand. On the screen was a text with two emojis—a tongue and a taco. She didn't recognize the number.

Frowning, she changed into soft black pants and a baggy shirt that slipped off her shoulder, and she carried the phone downstairs to ask Aster if she knew the number. On her way to the kitchen, though, a knock came from the front door.

Case stood on the other side of it.

"What are you doing here so early?" she asked.

"I texted."

She held up her phone and showed him the screen. "You sent this to me?"

"Who else would send that to you?"

A sliver of anger shimmered over his eyes in a quick glimmer of gold.

She didn't understand that reaction. "I don't know. What does it mean?"

The corner of his mouth tilted up. "Really?"

"What?" She shrugged. "I don't speak emoji. I

don't even text. What does it mean?"

He pointed at the screen. "That's a tongue."

"I see that."

"And that's a taco."

"Also obvious. Do you want tacos? Because if you do, I don't have the makings for them. We'll have to go out."

His smirk grew. "That's my mouth."

"Yes, I got that part."

He indicated at the taco again. "And that's your pussy."

"Oh." She studied the text until the meaning crystalized. "Oooooh."

"That's right, darlin', I woke up hungry for her."

Even while her pussy shed menstrual blood, his words made her throb. "Well, um…"

Case stepped over the threshold and shut the door. "What is it?"

She cleared her throat. "Well, it seems the orgasms you gave me yesterday kickstarted my period two days early. I'm bleeding."

"We had sex all throughout your last bleed."

"That's true, but we didn't have oral sex."

"I'm not afraid of your menstrual blood, Paisley. I'm a demon. I rather like blood."

"You want to go down on me while I bleed?"

"I do. What else do you need me to say to make that clear?"

"N-nothing."

"Are you sure? Because I can do more." He picked her up so that her legs were on either side of him. "I can make it quite clear with my actions, but I won't do

271

anything you don't want me to do. Do you want my mouth and tongue on your pretty pussy while she sheds your sweet, matriarchal blood?"

She nodded.

"Then let me worship her and her nectar."

"The first day, my flow is heavy, though."

He carried her to the stairs. "I told you, I'm not afraid of your menstrual blood, Paisley. Knowing that you're bleeding has only made my craving stronger."

"You really are a sex demon."

He threw his head back in laughter. "I really am, and aren't you lucky?"

As he made his way up the stairs, she moved one of his hands from her hip to press his fingers to her sensitive pussy. With a light pressure, she coaxed the pads of his fingers in gentle circles over her clitoris. "Extremely lucky."

In her room, he propped her against a post at her bed's footboard and continued to rove his fingers in a swirling pattern. She leaned her head back. "You asked me if I'd missed you at all. I missed your fingers."

"Mm."

"I missed your hands." The feel of his hand on her hip, claiming that space, felt good. "I missed your lips, your tongue."

"You'll get both soon enough."

"I missed looking into your eyes when they turn golden with pleasure. Hell, even golden with anger is good."

His lips quirked.

"I missed—" She moaned. "I missed your horns."

He chuckled. "I like it when you grip them when I

go down on you, and use them to haul me closer to your pussy."

"I'll do both soon enough," she said, mimicking his words.

"Soon enough is right now." He unwound her legs from his hips and slipped her pants down her legs. On the floor at her feet, he left her pants in a small bundle. He gazed up at her from his kneeling position. His hands were on her hips, beneath her baggy shirt. "Do you have something inside you?"

"A menstrual cup."

"Take it out."

"You can go down on me with a menstrual cup in."

"I want it out."

She tilted her head.

"I want your blood to flow freely while I eat your pretty pussy."

Stunning arousal.

"Okay. I'll be right back." She slipped into the bathroom. With a foot propped up on the ledge of the tub, she extracted the cup. Then she poured her menstrual blood in a bowl that she used to collect her offering and washed the cup with warm water and soap. She placed the cup upside down on a clean paper towel to dry.

On her way back to her room, she could already feel blood trickling out of her. She paused, considered dabbing at herself with toilet paper, but Case's words returned, so she continued on. At the threshold, she pulled up short when she saw Case lying on his back, with his head on her pillows.

"Sleepy?" she asked.

He grinned. "This is how I want to eat you. Me on my back, you straddling my head." He held out a hand. "Come here."

She hesitated a moment. Then she took his hand and climbed onto the bed. Peering down at him, she positioned her knees on either side of his neck.

"Higher. I want your pussy above my face."

Holding onto the headboard, she inched her knees higher.

"That's it. That's the sight I want to see."

A drop of blood landed on his bottom lip. Staring up at her, he licked it away. His eyes flared gold. "That's good." His voice was a growl. "Damn good." He stroked his hands up and down her thighs. "Now sit on my face."

"I'll smother you."

"What a happy way to die."

"Be serious, Case."

"I'm always serious when it comes to oral. No demon has been killed by pussy before, and it's not happening today." He grasped her hips and tugged her down so she sat right on his face.

She grabbed his horns. "Goddess." And she was about to raise herself up, but his hold was too strong. When his mouth molded around her vulva and his tongue plunged into her, she couldn't lift an inch because it felt too damn good. He ate her with purpose. She wasn't sure if that purpose was to consume every last drop of her menstrual blood or if that purpose was to give her an exquisite orgasm. Knowing Case, it was likely both. He ate her with such an intensity that she was paralyzed on top of him, unable to do anything but take it.

Usually, when he went down on her, she rolled her hips, encouraging his tongue deeper, rubbing his nose against her clit, but this time, she couldn't even do that. All she could do was grasp his horns, force herself to breathe, and release moan after moan.

His tongue traced her vulva and tickled her clitoris. Then he sucked at her opening, drawing out her juices and blood. She could feel both leaving her, and the sensation drove her wild. Even while he was relentless, he was gentle, understanding that she was more sensitive during her bleed.

When she came, her orgasm sent a surge of blood forth. Case sucked up what her body gave him and licked her clean. She knew he was done by the gentle kiss he placed on her pussy. Sighing, she eased off him.

His chin and lips were stained red. He grinned. "I've heard humans call eating out a woman first thing in the morning as the breakfast of champions. Now that surely was."

16

Bloody Mary Cocktail

Case

hen Paisley left to reinsert the menstrual cup, Case sat up and swung his legs over the edge of the bed. While his mouth and taste buds had gotten their fill of her, his cock was straining for attention. "Not yet, you little beast," he hissed.

"Little beast?" Paisley stepped out of the bathroom. Her legs were bare. Her shirt slipped off her shoulder to her breast where it clung to her curves. She held a wet hand towel. "Did you call your penis a 'little beast'? Because there's nothing little about it."

He smirked. "My cock is the little beast. I'm the big beast."

Smiling, she wiped the wet towel over his face. "I disagree. Your dick is the big beast. You're the bigger beast."

He chuckled. "You inflate my ego."

"I inflate your cock."

"That you do."

She carried the stained towel into the bathroom, and he got to his feet. When she rejoined him, her hands embraced his waist. "I think it's time that the beast came out to play."

"Not yet, Paisley. You're pale. Your moon time is taking too much of your blood. You need to feed."

Despite his words, she opened his pants, and his cock emerged, ready for whatever she could give it. "I'll feed after," she said.

"No, you need to feed first. I'm not going to have you pass out with my dick in your mouth."

"Case, that won't happen." She sat on the bed, angled him toward her, and closed her hands around his dick.

"Paisley. I'm trying to take care of you."

"Let me take care of you." She swirled her tongue around his cock's head.

Diablo. He wanted her mouth more than he could say. Her mouth, her tongue, her fangs. "Bite it," he ground out.

She jerked back. "What?"

Holding her chin, he said, "I want you to feed on it."

She gaped. "Okay, now you can't be serious."

"I am. My cock is strong, pain is one of my kinks, and I get off whenever you feed on me. And that's my neck. If you want to give me my happy ending, feed on my cock. Take the blood you need, and I can assure you that I'll come."

Burgundy rings formed around her irises. "Alright. Turn to your side."

He shifted.

She held his cock in her hands, opened her mouth wide, and lean forward. The points of her fangs scraped his hot, stretched flesh a second before they plunged into his penis. He sought the bedpost and gripped it. Her fangs slipped out of his flesh, and she closed her lips around the puncture holes. When she sucked, his head wheeled. "Fuck. That's good."

As blood rushed to his penis, she gulped it down. The more she drank, the more blood surged to his erection to replace what she took. His penis throbbed with pleasure.

He shot his other hand to the bedpost and gave it a death grip. His eyelids lowered.

She moaned, and that sound made a bead of cum spurt forth. The fact that she was enjoying feeding on his cock sent a bolt of lust from the base of his spine, through his balls, to the tip of his penis. He stroked a hand over the back of her head, down her hair. "That's it, baby. Take everything my cock can give you. Take it all."

Her hands tightened. Her mouth sucked harder.

He groaned.

Suddenly, she was on her knees in front of him, taking the head of his cock into her mouth. She worked her hands up and down his length while her tongue flicked over his frenulum. It didn't take long for him to come. When he did, she wrapped her lips around the tip and slurped down every drop of cum that he purged.

Once spent, he collapsed onto the bed. "Diablo."

Paisley rose from her knees and settled beside him. "I take it that was good for you."

"Baby, that was phenomenal for me. How was it for you?"

"Demon cock-blood could be a new commodity in the vampyre faction if it becomes known how satisfying it is for both parties. We might've found what could end our centuries-long feud."

Case laughed. "Picturing vampires on their knees, drinking from demon cocks is quite the visual."

She elbowed him. "Not funny."

"A little funny." He stood. "Come on. I need to get some food in you."

"I just fed on you."

"That was like a Bloody Mary Cocktail. You need real food."

She stood. "A Bloody Mary Cocktail? Is that what we're calling me feeding on your cock?"

"We might as well."

She smirked. "Yeah, I suppose that could be our code word for it."

"I'll serve it up whenever, wherever." Hands clasped, he led her out of her room and down the stairs to the kitchen.

Sitting at the table was Thatch and Aster.

"When did you get here?" Thatch asked Case.

"A while ago."

Paisley slipped past Case. "He wanted a taco."

Thatch coughed into his coffee.

Aster patted him on the back. "Are you okay?"

"Fine." His voice was a croak.

Paisley calmly poured two cups of coffee, while Thatch continued to hack.

Case stepped up behind Paisley. He placed his hands on the counter on either side of her hips. "Don't ever talk about tacos like that around Thatch."

"Oh, does he speak emoji?" She turned and held out a cup.

"He does."

"Fortunately, Aster doesn't."

"Oh, damn it." He did not want to think about Thatch eating out Aster. Cup in hand, he faced the pair at the table, sitting side by side. He stilled. Shit, he was thinking about it. "I am going to make you pay for that."

Paisley lifted the cup to her lips, sipped. "You were the one hungry for tacos."

He eyed her.

Shrugging innocently, she sat on a stool across from Aster.

"I made blueberry and cranberry muffins," Aster said.

Sure enough, a plate in the middle of the table contained a pyramid of fluffy muffins. Their fragrance reached Case's nose and made his stomach rumble. "Damn, cutie pie, a demon could get used to this. Right, Thatch?"

Thatch glared.

Paisley elbowed Case again. This time in the ribs.

Grinning, he selected a muffin and set it in front of Paisley before he chose one for himself. She plucked off the soft, sweet tip and plopped it into her mouth. The tiny moan she made clenched his abdomen with a different hunger. Under the table, he shifted his hand to her bare thigh, squeezed.

She slid his muffin closer. "Eat your muffin, Case."

He leaned down so his mouth grazed her ear. "I'd rather eat yours again."

"Oh, so tacos are muffins, too?"

"They are, but there's no muffin emoji."

"Don't forget that Aster made these."

He literally felt the color drain from his face. "Damn it." He growled in her ear with a hint of anger. "I really am going to make you pay for that."

"Eat your muffin, Case."

He stuffed half the muffin into his mouth.

Paisley tore off another lump of pastry. "What do the two of you have planned for today?" she asked Aster and Thatch.

The question summoned a sweet blush on Aster's cheeks. "I plan to force Thatch to watch Pride & Prejudice."

"Ooh. Which one?"

"The one with Keira Knightley and Matthew Macfadyen."

"Good choice. The music makes that movie. I have a feeling you're a demon who can appreciate music," she said to Thatch.

"I am a musical demon."

"He plays the piano," Aster said.

"Ah, so I was right. The piano numbers will

probably make your demonic heart swoon."

Thatch smiled. "I'm looking forward to it."

"What do the two of you have planned?" Aster asked them.

Paisley lifted a shoulder. "We haven't discussed it yet."

What did he want to do with Paisley today? They could take a page out of Aster and Thatch's book and do something romantic. Or at least something borderline romantic. He could handle that, right? A simple stroll. Chilling on the couch while watching a movie. Any movie. It certainly didn't have to be Pride & Prejudice. Not any of the human adaptations or the creature version starring a tall, slender elf and a handsome, brutish orc. Maybe they could have a picnic. He'd never been on one before, and he wouldn't mind trying it for the first time with Paisley.

A crumble of muffin fell from Paisley's fingers, and she suddenly popped to her feet. "Excuse me." She didn't look at any of them when she left.

He glanced after her, curious over her abrupt departure.

Had she been considering what they'd do today? Was she nervous about spending a potentially borderline romantic day together?

He ate two muffins and chatted with Thatch and Aster. Twenty minutes later and Paisley hadn't returned. He grew anxious. What was she up to? He glanced over his shoulder again. Turning back, his gaze lowered to the stool where she'd been sitting. A miniscule puddle of blood sat there. He picked up a paper napkin from the table and swiped it away as discreetly as he could. With the napkin crumpled in his hand, he stood.

"I'm going to check on Paisley."

Still holding the napkin in his fist, he headed up the stairs. He had to restrain himself from running and tipping off Thatch and Aster that something could be wrong. In the doorway of her bedroom, he stilled. She sat on the edge of her bed, with her head bent, and her hands lightly gripping the mattress. "Paisley?"

When she lifted her head to look at him, her lips were pale.

Shocked, he unclenched his hand, and the napkin tumbled from his fingers. He reached her in a few strides and dropped to his knees. "What's going on?"

"I had a period gush." Her chin lifted, indicating behind him. "It was a lot."

He peered back at her bathroom. A white towel—nearly red with blood—lay on the floor. "Has that happened before?"

"No."

Her orgasms yesterday had launched her period ahead of schedule.

"Do you think it happened because of your orgasm this morning?"

"Might've. Orgasms can encourage more uterine lining to come loose."

"So, it is my fault."

"That's not what I meant."

He jumped to his feet. "You lost too much blood and iron. Feeding isn't going to do it. You need a transfusion. And fast." He headed for the door.

"Case." Her voice was so soft that it killed him.

He didn't turn back.

In the kitchen, he spoke to Aster. "Paisley needs a blood transfusion. Now."

Aster jolted. "What?"

"Do you have the equipment?"

"Yes."

"Get it."

She sprang to her feet and hurried out of the kitchen.

Thatch started to rise.

"No." Case held up a hand. "Stay here."

"Case, with all due respect, I looked out for both of them while you were gone, and the month she refused to see you. She's as much my responsibility as Aster is."

"I appreciate that you looked out for her when I couldn't, but I don't think she'd want you there now."

"But she needs a blood transfusion?"

"She does."

"Was she injured?"

"No. It's her moon time, and…"

Thatch nodded. "I want to be close to Aster."

Case returned the nod. "Alright. You can post outside the room."

They climbed the stairs. Thatch positioned his back to the wall and crossed his arms as Case stepped into the room. Aster was there, talking to Paisley, who was shaking her head.

"I'll be fine," Paisley was saying. "I need to rest. I don't need a transfusion."

"The fuck you don't," Case snapped. "You're getting a transfusion."

She swayed when she met his eyes. "Case."

"Goddamn it." He snatched her up. "I caused this."

"Not on purpose."

"That doesn't fucking matter." He laid her out on the bed. "I caused this, so I'm going to help fix it." He faced Aster. "I'm a universal donor, and she can tolerate my blood. Hook me up."

Aster opened her mouth.

"Don't argue with me, cutie pie." He grabbed a chair from the corner of the room, positioned it next to the bed, and sat.

"Case, you don't have to do this," Paisley whispered.

He stole the rubber tubing from Aster and tied it around his own arm. Hard. "I'm doing this." To Aster he said, "Get to it."

She slipped a needle into Paisley's arm that was attached to a thin tube connected to another needle that she expertly slid into Case's vein. "Grip this." She placed a stress ball in his hand, which he strangled. Then she tugged off the tubing cutting off his circulation with a snap.

Blood instantly rushed down the tube and into Paisley's vein. "I'll come back in fifteen minutes.

If you start to get dizzy, call for me."

He lifted his hand. However long it took, it'd take. However much blood Paisley required, he'd give it.

Aster left quietly. Out in the hall, Thatch's and Aster's voices met his ears as they mumbled to each other. Their footsteps sounded when they walked down the hall.

Paisley drifted off to sleep quickly, lured by her

lack of blood.

Guilt ate at him. Like a horny sex demon, he'd taken her that morning because he'd woken up hungry for her, and the fact she was bleeding had only intensified that hunger. But he hadn't considered what that could mean for her...a vampire hybrid who suffered from blood withdrawals and struggled to consume any blood that wasn't his. He was a fucking idiot for not realizing that her moon time could pose a threat and make those withdrawals, the struggle worse. Weakening her with every drop of bled shed. Stealing her vitality. She'd told him that her orgasms yesterday had kick-started her period two full days early, and he hadn't fucking taken a moment to contemplate what an orgasm during her period could do. The fact that they'd had sex during her moon time before and nothing like this had happened had tricked him.

He thought back to that time. She had fed on him a lot more. Sometimes twice a day, and she'd taken to eating steak and spinach salads most nights. She'd been replenishing the blood and iron she'd lost. Had she lost even more from the orgasms he'd given her? Had she hidden it from him? Had Aster given her blood transfusions when he wasn't around?

"Damn it, Paisley."

His blood snaked through the tube.

The fifteen minutes Aster had promised him were gone all too quickly.

"Time's up," Aster said when she entered the room.

"Five more minutes." He'd beg her if he had to.

"It's enough, Case." She jabbed her fingers roughly

286

into his arm and tugged the needle from his vein fast, as if expecting him to restrain her from removing it, and, honestly, he'd considered it. "Hold this." He lifted the tube of leeching blood, so she could open her satchel and sprinkle a bit of fairy dust on his arm.

The pinprick disappeared.

"Hold that up and she'll get the rest of the blood. I'll be back in a moment."

Holding the tube high, he coaxed the rest of his blood through the tube to Paisley's arm.

He wound the tube around his arm as the blood drained. A foot of the tubing remained. He slipped from the chair to kneel on the floor beside her bed. Her color had returned—a sweet peaches and cream shade, and her lips were pink again.

"Pais?"

She didn't stir.

A couple of minutes later, the tube emptied, and Aster returned. He resumed his seat in the chair as she gently removed the needle from Paisley's arm. Even so, Paisley's eyelids opened and a frown formed between her brows. Aster sprinkled fairy dust onto the crease of Paisley's elbow. Before she left, she laid a hand on Case's shoulder, a gesture that was full of affection and assurance.

Paisley turned her head on the pillow. She opened her mouth to speak, but he lifted a finger. He needed to say something first. "I had no idea that your moon time could be potentially dangerous. You didn't tell me, and I never pieced two-and-two together."

She sat up slowly, slinging her legs over the edge of the bed. "Men don't usually want to know about a woman's period."

He frowned. "A man who can't handle discussing his woman's period with her isn't a fucking man and doesn't deserve her or anyone who menstruates."

"I'm your woman?"

She didn't ask that with an arched brow to indicate annoyance at the claim, the possessiveness, the boldness. But still a question lurked behind her words. A question that shouldn't be there.

He stood, hooked her legs with his arm, and lifted her. Sitting on her bed, he placed her on his lap. Still being careful with her, but also wanting to get through to her, he slipped his fingers into her hair and closed his hand into a loose fist. "You're my woman. Try to dispute that."

"I can't. Nor am I looking to dispute it. I just wanted to clarify what you said."

"You're my woman, and I want you to be comfortable talking to me about your period. I want to know when something may affect your health, especially if something I do can impact your health."

"This wasn't your fault, Case."

He wasn't so sure about that. "I'm going to be scared to have sex with you in any way during your moon time now."

She extracted his arms from around her and walked into the bathroom where she picked up the soiled towel and shoved it into a trash pail. "If you can't handle this, then leave."

"What?"

She spun on her feet. "A life-threatening aversion to blood and potentially dangerous moon times. If you can't handle that, then leave. I don't need someone who is going to be scared to have sex with me during my period. I don't need someone who's going to treat me like an invalid while I'm bleeding."

"I'm not treating you like an invalid." He charged forward two big steps before stilling himself. "Someone who will worry about you during your moon time is exactly the kind of person you should be with because it means they fucking care about you!"

They glared at each other. Breathing hard.

A knock made Paisley jump.

Case's glare flicked over to the opened door, to Aster.

"S-sorry, but one of your demons is at the door asking for you. He says it's urgent."

Cursing under his breath, he marched out the room.

Thatch waited in the hallway. "It's Wren."

Wren was one of the demons patrolling Paisley's property.

"Sire." Wren bowed his head. "I need to show you something."

Case glanced over his shoulder at Thatch. "Stay with them."

Thatch nodded once.

Case stepped outside with Wren and tugged the door shut behind him. "What do you need to show me?"

"I found a dead fairy."

Those five words steeled Case's spine.

"I was patrolling when I noticed something glittering beyond Paisley's property line. I looked and found her there." He led Case past the circle of demons, deep into the woods to a fairy's body someone had dumped on a patch of clovers. Her wings lay in a bloody heap several feet from her body. Her satchel of fairy dust lay spilled on the ground. Case didn't recognize her, but she was innocent. And she was dead. Anger swallowed him in one gulp.

A note lay on her chest. He picked it up and unfolded it: *Aster's next. We'll leave her body where her demon boy-toy will find it.*

That anger morphed into rabid rage. He couldn't contain it and knew that when he stepped back into Paisley's house that they could see it in the glow of his eyes and the tension of his muscles. He crooked a finger at Thatch, who hustled over, and passed the note to Thatch, who read the words on the piece of paper and spun toward Aster.

The fear leeching off his best friend was strong enough to slam into Case, and it confirmed something he'd suspected: Thatch was in love with Aster. It wasn't a physical attraction. It wasn't friendship. It was all of that and so much more. Thatch was in love with Aster, and now the people after Paisley were threatening to take Aster's life to get back at him, at Case, at Paisley.

Paisley approached them. "What's going on?" She snatched the note from Thatch and read it. Immediately, her gaze sought Case's.

"Wren found a dead fairy." Case hadn't noticed Aster come close until Thatch attempted to take the note from Paisley, but Aster was faster.

She read the threat, and now she appeared as though she needed a blood transfusion. Her skin became sickly pale. Her wings flattened together, as if

290

she knew that they'd cut the dead fairy's wings from her back. She peered up at Thatch.

Thatch dropped to a knee in front of her and gripped her hands with his. "They're not going to touch you, baby doll. On my life, they won't touch you."

"Get her out of here."

They all faced Paisley.

"She's not safe here, but she'll be safe at your place, right?" she asked Case.

"I will have a fucking ring of demons around my mansion. Day and night. No one will get in to hurt her. No one."

"But I can't leave," Aster protested. "I can't leave you here." She was looking at

Paisley. "I just gave you a blood transfusion, for Goddess's sake."

"I'm fine now, but a fairy was killed and your life is being threatened. You can't stay here." Paisley shoved Thatch's shoulder. "Go."

Thatch swept Aster into his arms.

"No, Thatch, please."

Case opened the front door.

Aster was sobbing now, begging Thatch not to take her away.

Thatch stepped through the doorway, and his wings burst from his back.

"Nononono!"

He launched into the air so fast that the displacement of air had Case staggering backward. Aster's protests vanished. Case stepped outside to make sure they left the perimeter safely, but Thatch was gone.

"You should go, too," Paisley said.

His gaze snapped to her.

"Aster could use you. Help her to understand this is for the best."

"She doesn't need me, Paisley. She needs her best friend. Why don't you come with me? All three of us could help her with the transition."

"I have to deal with the dead fairy and go to the faye faction. I'll have to talk to her family and help prepare her death ceremony. It's crucial for departed fairies to be laid to rest in a specific way. I have work to do."

"When you're done, come to my place. You can check on Aster, and the two of us can continue our conversation, because we will continue that conversation."

"Fine."

One word. "Fine" was better than "no," but not by much.

Still, he carried that one word with him when he left to ensure Aster's safety.

17

Gold Masks

Paisley

*P*aisley showered first. She removed her necklace and placed it in an oyster-shaped dish on her bathroom counter. In the shower, she worked shampoo and conditioner through her hair and lathered her body with rose-scented body wash. With a clean menstrual cup in, she stepped out of her bathroom in a robe and came face to face with three figures. They stood side by side, wearing solid gold masks with almond-shaped eyeholes, but no holes for the mouths. In all black, not a strip of skin showed. Not at their necks or at their wrists.

Dropping into a fighting stance, she hissed. She didn't give them a chance to make the first move and attacked them. Three against one, though; she was outnumbered. When she struck one, the other two were on her, hitting her in return. She tried to keep moving so they wouldn't have a chance to land a blow, but their hands and feet made contact with her ribs, back, and legs. One moment she was fighting, the next she was coming to on cold tile.

Pain radiated at the back of her head. Groaning, she touched her skull, felt a slit in her scalp and the stickiness of blood. Then a crushing weight pinned her down.

Hands grasped her arms.

Shackles clanked around her wrists.

Iron seared her skin.

She cried out.

The hands bruising her arms, yanked her onto her knees.

A piece of paper and a pen landed in front of her.

"Write Case a letter," one of them barked. "Tell him you're leaving and not to come after you."

"No."

The flat side of an iron blade pressed into the back of her hand.

She screamed.

When the iron blade lifted away, a strip of red, raw skin remained.

"Write to him!"

Other hand shaking, she picked up the pen.

"Tell him you're leaving. Tell him not to look for you."

"Make it convincing."

She wrote Case's name at the top of the piece of paper.

"Don't even try to hide a secret message in it."

"No random capitalization. No underlines."

"If you do, we'll burn each of your fingers and make you start over."

Tears blurring her vision, she wrote out a message that she hoped would give Case enough pause so he would question the rest of the note. She needed him to doubt her words. Hell, even if her words enraged him, maybe he would ignore her wish to leave her alone and find out what happened. Because surely the bastards intended to kill her and dump her body where no one would find her or know the truth.

I can't do this anymore. I know we had an agreement. One that I take seriously.

She wrote the rest of the note, hating herself for each sentence. But he would see the truth behind the bullshit. He had to. When she signed her name and dropped the pen, the note was snatched from her. They each read it over, examining it for clues that she tried to slip in under their noses. The note passed their scrutiny. One of them folded the piece of paper and set the note by the door.

Huddled on the floor, she eyed it.

Don't believe a word of it, Case.

Another piece of paper was dropped in front of her.
"Now write to your uncle."
"Tell him you're leaving."
"Make it good."
She scribbled another note while tears leaked down her cheeks. When she finished the hasty letter to her uncle, they stole that one, too. Then a second crack at the back of her head had her collapsing against the tile. Unconscious.

A grimy, dirty floor.
Iron cuffs strangled her wrists.
The cell was a void of darkness.
Head pulsing with pain, Paisley pushed into a sitting position and leaned against the wall. Her head spun. She dusted her fingers off on the robe she still wore and carefully probed the back of her head. The stabbing pain beneath her fingertips made her wince. She needed some of Aster's fairy dust, but she wouldn't be getting it here.

A bang reverberated from somewhere in the darkness. Footsteps approached. She shoved to her knees despite the raging migraine threatening to knock her flat. Even her eyes transforming with burgundy hurt like a bitch.

The three figures appeared on the other side of the iron bars. One of them rammed a key into the lock. A clank echoed. Then they rushed in and plowed into her before she could even move a muscle. They flattened her to the filthy floor.

Gold masks hovered over her. "Renounce your thrones."

"Fuck you."

A blade sliced across her chest.

She yelled.

"Renounce your thrones."

"No."

The blade returned. The tip plunged into her shoulder, and the masked figure dragged it down her arm to her wrist. Her scream bounced off the walls of the cell.

"Renounce your thrones, whore!"

Shaking from pain, as blood leeched from her body, she stared into the eyeholes of the gold mask in front of her. "You'll have to kill me."

"We'll do better than that. We'll slaughter the entire faye faction. Starting with your fairy BFF."

No, no, not Aster. She couldn't let them harm her best friend or her faction for her mistakes. She had to get free and stop them. Somehow.

But they continued to cut every inch of her body while demanding she renounce her thrones. She'd long stopped telling them no. She wasn't going to give up thrones her parents had occupied and lost because murderers had stolen their lives. No doubt those murderers were surrounding her. Torturing her. Why they weren't killing her outright, she didn't know.

Blood was a blanket beneath her.

Unconsciousness crept along the edges of her mind.

"Bring in the blood," one of them said.

A gold mask left.

A moment later, he returned with a plastic tube wrapped around his arm, a funnel, and a bucket with blood streaming down the sides.

Their intentions terrified her. "No. No."

One of them straddled her and pinned her shoulders with his knees. Hands grasped her head, stilling her. Another shoved the end of a tube into her mouth and down her throat. She gagged but couldn't get away. The third poured blood from the bucket into the funnel. It snaked down the tube. Tears leaked from her eyes as she convulsed. She had no choice but to choke on the blood they forced down her throat.

Finally, they yanked the tube out of her mouth and released her. She rolled onto her side and retched. Some of the blood reversed up her esophagus, but the rest stayed down, cramping her stomach.

The three figures left.

The door banged shut behind them.

Lying on the floor, she cried softly. Her tears mixed with the dirt. All the while, the iron shackles around her wrists branded her with burns. Slowly, though, her wounds healed because of the blood they'd force-fed her.

In the darkness, she sought the only comfort she had—her necklace.

Except, her neck was bare. "No. No, no, no!" She searched the ground with her hands, dragging iron chains. From corner to corner, she felt for the gold, diamond-encrusted paisley. "Please. It has to be here." Tears dripped off her face. "Please. Where is it?" She ran her hands over every inch of the ground twice over, but the necklace wasn't there.

Heartbroken and home sick, she curled into a ball on the floor and sobbed.

Her kidnappers returned while her tears were still damp on her cheeks. Again, they demanded she give up her thrones. She refused. Each and every time, she refused. They sliced up her body, poured blood down her throat, waited for her to heal, and repeated the torture on a loop.

18

Underground Tunnel

Case

ase stood outside Paisley's home, knocking on the door and calling her cell phone, which rolled to voicemail. "Paisley?" His hand wrapped around the handle, twisted. When the handle rotated with the motion and the door slid open, anger was swift. "You infuriating little hybrid," he muttered and shoved the door open.

On the other side of the threshold, he shut the door and yelled, "Did I not tell you to lock your fucking door? Will a spanking get that through your head?" He remembered how she'd cried out each time his hand had met with her lovely ass, how she'd come, how she'd been panting afterward, how she'd flirted and teased him. Reliving all of that would be a treat, but this time, he'd do it differently. With her on all fours, he'd sink his penis deep inside her, spank the top of that lovely ass, and stroke his cock in and out before spanking her again. He'd encourage her to squirt and keep on squirting until she came. It'd be kinky and erotic as hell. Turned on, he peered from the parlor to the kitchen to the staircase.

"Pais?" His gaze landed on a piece of paper on the side table. He picked it up.

Paisley's script flowed over the page. It appeared rushed.

Case,

I can't do this anymore. I know we had an agreement. One that I take seriously. We promised not to leave without talking to the other first. Not to end things on a whim. Not unless there was true betrayal or mutual agreement. Or one of us did something against our factions. I received damning evidence that you have been behind the attempts on my life this entire time. I can't ignore that. I can't forgive that. I'm sorry. It's over. I'm leaving. Don't try to find me.

Paisley

Case read the note over again, sure that he hadn't comprehended it right the first time. What the hell was she talking about? What evidence? There was no evidence because he wasn't behind a damn thing. How could she think he was behind everything after all the time they'd spent together? After he'd committed her body to memory with his eyes, hands, lips, and tongue? After he'd gone to the fier faction to find out who'd tried to kill her right in front of him? After he'd told her how wrecked he became when she called off their arrangement the first time?

He'd gotten her back two days ago. One and a half days ago, to be precise, and already he was losing her again? She was ending their arrangement and not letting him defend himself. Again! At least give him a damn chance to prove that he'd never do anything to harm her or her factions. He deserved that much.

He reread the last sentence: *Don't try to find me.*

Brows lowered, he peered toward the staircase. He ventured upstairs to her bedroom. Her bed was perfectly made. He peeked into the bathroom. The tube of matte purple lipstick that never failed to knot his stomach with lust wasn't lying on the counter. Her bottle of rose perfume was missing, too. As well as her toothbrush.

He was backing out of the bathroom when he spotted her paisley necklace resting in the porcelain clam shell dish on the counter. She only removed the necklace to bathe, and then right back on that pretty, kissable neck it went. A gift from her mother that she wore daily, she wouldn't leave it behind. He picked it up and held it in his hand as he stepped into her bedroom.

Half her closet was empty. He slid open each drawer of the dresser to see a sizeable dent gone from her nightgowns, bras, and panties, as if she'd packed up and left, but would she have forgotten her necklace? And if she really meant to stay gone forever, wouldn't she have dug up her prized rose bushes? She'd left without saying a word to her best friend. If Aster knew, she hadn't let on this morning.

According to the note he still held, she'd left because of him.

Because. Of. Him.

His fist closed around the note and necklace, crumpling the paper, embedding the paisley into his palm. Anger simmered beneath the panic. He pulled the front door shut behind himself and flew off. That anger became a rapid boiling rage. His wings beat the air as if he could kick oxygen's ass. Before he knew it, he was home. He threw the door shut with a bang that rattled the windows. The short flight home didn't lessen his fury by so much as a drop.

He stormed into his home and straight to a bottle of whiskey, splashed a couple of fingers into a glass, and knocked it back. Then he chucked the bottle at the wall, followed by the glass. The wrath battering inside him begged to come out, and he wasn't going to deny it.

Shaking, barely able to contain it, he smashed a chair against the tile. He picked up the mahogany leg and whaled it at the rebuilt glass display case holding the liqueur. Once it was shattered and dripping with spirits, he raged around the room, breaking lamps, framed pictures on the walls, and everything else that got in his way. He didn't want to leave a single thing whole in that room. He wanted it all in rubble at his feet, like his relationship with Paisley. In fucking rubble. He intended to go from room to room, demolishing everything.

Thatch's arm locked around his neck to subdue him, but Case broke out of the hold, whirled around, and swung the chair leg into Thatch's head. The wood splintered in his hands and fell apart in several pieces.

"Case!" That shout was the one thing that could stay him.

Seething, he faced Aster. Terror radiated off her, and he hated that he'd done that.

Seeing her standing among glass shards broke what hadn't already shattered in him.

"What's going on?" she asked.

"Paisley left."

"What?"

"She. Fucking. Left." He removed the note from his pocket and held it out.

Glass and bits of wood scattered at her feet when she stepped closer. She took the piece of paper and read it. From the first sentence, she started to shake her head. She didn't stop until she finished reading. "This doesn't make sense. Paisley wouldn't leave without saying anything to me. She wouldn't do that."

"Except she did."

"No. This…this doesn't make sense." She shook

the paper. "Why would she say that she takes your agreement seriously and lay out what the two of you had promised only to go back on that promise? It doesn't make sense. Promises are important to her. Almost sacred. She wouldn't do this."

He pulled the paisley necklace from his pocket. "I found this, too."

Aster touched the chain that dangled from between his fingers, but she didn't take the necklace. And he was glad. If she'd tried, he probably would've growled like a dog protecting its bone from someone who'd dare try to take it away.

"Paisley wouldn't even leave her bedroom without that necklace on. This isn't right. Something's not right, Case."

He inhaled slowly in an attempt to vanquish the anger still whirling inside him and stashed the necklace back in his pocket. "You don't think she could've been so pissed off with me that she'd not realize she hadn't put the necklace back on?"

"Is it possible, even in the slightest chance? I suppose so, especially if she got a call or letter from whoever told her these lies right after showering, but this doesn't feel right to me."

Case met Thatch's eye. "What do you think?"

"Paisley wouldn't have left without telling Aster. I'm confident about that."

"If she had really left, she would've left someone in charge." Case spoke directly to Aster. "I'd think she'd leave you in charge of the faye faction."

Aster lifted a slender shoulder. "Maybe…maybe she left me a note in my bedroom?"

"We'll check."

Aster's eyes widened. "If Paisley is gone…no."

"What is it?"

"The dead fairy. I don't believe she'd leave one of our own in the woods to decompose without a proper burial ceremony. I'm sorry, Case, but I need to check on that first."

"The three of us will. Thatch."

Thatch swept Aster into his arms. "Already got her covered."

Case's lips twitched despite the anger and confusion wrestling for dominance.

They flew to Paisley's. Wren was there, guarding the dead fairy's body. From the dark blue circles around his eyes, it was evident that the demon hadn't slept since he'd found the body; Paisley hadn't come for the fairy as they'd all expected she would.

Aster shook her head. "Paisley wouldn't have left her. She wouldn't have done that."

Case looked to Thatch. "Take Aster to the faye faction." Then to Aster. "Bring Paisley's council here to take care of this fairy. I'll stay here."

Thatch lifted Aster again and took off.

Wren cleared his throat. "Sire, what's going? Why hasn't Paisley come for the fairy herself?"

"She left. Or that's what her note said. Did you see her leave?"

"No, but I don't have a good view of her house from here. You should ask the others."

So Case did. He made his way around the property, questioning his demons. Not a single one of them saw her leave. Not by flying. Not on foot. Not even on freaking unicornback.

By the time he finished, the faye faction had come and gone and taken the fairy with them to begin preparations. Aster would join them later, but for now, she led them into Paisley's house to check her bedroom for a note, but no such note existed. Systematically, they searched the entire house for signs of a struggle but didn't find one. But they did notice that her phone and keys were gone, too. Everything supported what the note said; she'd left.

She'd left *him*, believing a lie rather than everything he'd ever said.

"Where would she go?" Thatch asked.

Aster lifted a hand. "To Jude. Maybe to Phoenix, but considering Queen Enya doesn't like Paisley very much...Jude." She plucked her phone from her bag. "Jude actually does have a cell phone. He just never uses it. He barely keeps it charged. I don't know if he'll answer, but this is faster than a letter." She tapped on the screen and raised the phone to her ear. A moment later, she nodded. "Jude, it's Aster. Is Paisley there? No, Paisley's gone. I mean she left. We don't know where she went. She left a note. It said she was leaving because"—she cast a look at Case—"because she got evidence that Case was behind the attempts on her life. No, Jude, he wouldn't do that. We're...we're at Paisley's. Yes, Case, too. Jude? Hello?" She lowered her phone. "He hung up. I think he's coming. He doesn't sound very happy."

"I imagine not." Case sat on the love seat in the parlor. "When he gets here, point him in my direction." If Jude wanted to trample his ass now, he'd let him.

Ten minutes later, a fist pounded on the front door. Thatch opened it.

Hooves clacked on the tile as Jude made his way into the parlor. When he appeared, he jabbed a finger at Case. "What the hell did you do to my goddaughter, you demonic son-of-a-bitch?"

"Nothing, but if you want to hit me all the same"— Case stood—"I'll give you one good hit."

Aster scrambled between them. "He didn't do anything. It's a lie. It's all lies."

Jude eyed him. "Then why would Paisley believe it?"

Case lifted his hands. "I don't know. I'd think she'd know me a little by now, but she apparently still thinks the worst of me."

"If she's not here, and she's not with me, then where is she?"

"We were hoping you'd know."

"I don't. So, she really left?"

Case handed over the note in way of an answer.

Jude read it over. "What damning evidence is she talking about?"

"There is no evidence. If there is, someone faked it. I swear to you, I swear to Paisley, I swear to Aster, the most innocent person I fucking know, I swear to Diablo himself, that I never did anything to put her in harm's way, and I didn't kill a single fairy. Someone is framing me, just like they did when they burned my brand into Paisley's lawn."

Jude nodded slowly. "Until we find out the truth, let's keep this quiet. We'll wait to see if Paisley comes back. If she doesn't show up for the next meeting, we'll tell the other faction leaders then."

"And until then, what do we do?"

"Hope she comes back."

Case would hope. He'd hope every day, every hour that Paisley would return. "Let's go back to my place. Maybe we can figure out where she went or how to look for her." He took a step, and then a force plowed into him. His back slammed into the wall, cracking plaster, and a hand formed around Case's throat.

"What the fuck did you do?" Silas shouted. "What did you do to Paisley?!"

Case rammed a fist into Silas's solar plexus before cracking his knuckles into Silas's chiseled cheekbone.

Silas dropped to the floor.

"I didn't do a fucking thing," Case roared.

Silas made to get up, but Jude jabbed a hoof onto his chest, holding him down.

"I am sick of everyone thinking I did something to Paisley." Case pointed a finger at Silas. "I didn't do a damn thing but care about her."

Silas laughed. "A sex demon cares about someone?"

Case clenched his jaw. "I will fuck you up and dump your ass outside in the sun to burn to a crisp. Try me."

"Believe Paisley will forgive you for that?"

"Maybe it'll be enough to get her to come back." Case lunged.

Aster blocked him and stuck her hands between them. "Stop, stop, stop! This isn't helping. Paisley wouldn't want us fighting."

"Then maybe she shouldn't have fucking left."

"She left because of you," Silas shouted.

"What the hell do you even know about it? About Paisley and me? Nothing!"

"I know what she wrote me."

Aster stepped closer to Silas. "She gave you a letter?"

"I found it at my door."

"What did it say?"

Silas glared at Jude. "Get your filthy hoof off me."

Jude stepped back.

Silas shoved to his feet and ripped a folded piece of paper from his pocket. "Read it yourself."

Aster unfolded the letter and read it first. Then she handed it to Case.

Uncle Silas,

Something happened. With Case. I have to leave. I can't trust him. I don't know how long

I'll be gone. Maybe forever, so I'm leaving you in charge of the vampyre faction, and Aster will be in charge of the faye faction.

I love you.

Paisley

Case studied the paper. The handwriting belonged to Paisley, and it appeared as rushed as the note she'd left him. Right over the word 'forever' a drop of water had splashed against the paper, distorting the ink. He showed it to Aster. "Does that look like a tear?"

Aster studied it. "It does. If she was upset, there might've been tears."

"And what the fuck did you do to make my niece cry and leave?" Silas demanded.

Aster blocked him when Silas advanced again. "You don't understand. Case didn't do anything."

Case looked to Thatch. "Pick up your beautiful fairy and get her out of the way. I don't want her hurt. If Silas wants to feel more pain, I'll give it to him."

Thatch plucked Aster off her feet and set her on the floor at his side.

Jude stepped into her vacated place when Silas advanced. "Aster's right. Case didn't have anything to do with why Paisley left."

"Her note says he does."

"She was lied to," Aster said.

"By whom?"

"We don't know."

"Convenient. If Paisley says she can't trust Case, then I can't trust him."

"Fine," Case said. "Don't trust me. I don't care what *you* think of me. I care what *she* thinks of me, and I will prove that whatever someone told her is a lie. If you care about your niece, you'll call a truce with me and help."

311

Silas eyed him a moment. "I suppose for my niece I can call a temporary truce, but don't think I'm going to shake your hand."

"Yeah, I'm not fucking touching you unless I'm bruising you." Case peered at Paisley's parlor. The front door was still closed. And, he was right, the sun was still out. "How the hell did you get in here?"

"The underground tunnel."

Case whipped toward Aster. "What fucking underground tunnel?"

Aster grimaced. "Um…the underground tunnel that goes from Paisley's house to the vamprye faction. She…she never told you about it?"

"What do you think?"

The fact Paisley kept that from him, knowing that someone wanted to assassinate her, infuriated him. Anyone could've found out about that tunnel and used it kill her in the middle of the night. He would've come to her house and discovered her in bed, drowning in her blood.

Hands in fists, he said, "Show me."

Aster showed them to the basement and a hidden doorway concealed by a shelf packed with supplies. The shelf swung out to reveal an underground tunnel.

Case's eyes brightened with golden rage. The light illuminated the tight space as he searched the pathway for a sign that someone could've used that tunnel recently. Like Paisley. To escape undetected by his men. The ground wasn't dirt or sand, though. Rather, cobblestone covered the ground, so he couldn't make out any footprints.

Winding along the tunnel, he led the way, with

Aster and Thatch behind him. Silas stomped after them, and Jude followed at the rear. None of them spoke as their footsteps echoed off the walls of the tight enclosure.

The air was dank and musty. The stench of earth and mold clogged his nostrils.

"What was this tunnel used for?" he asked.

"It's an escape route for the royal family," Silas said. "And, in the event of war, the entire vampyre faction could use it to flee an ambush. Like from the daemon faction."

Case whipped around, but Thatch halted him with a hand to his shoulder.

"Don't engage," Thatch said.

Clenching his jaw, Case rotated back. "Who else knows about this?"

"Just Paisley's council."

All potential suspects in his eyes. "I'll want their names."

"Why?"

"Because one of them could've been behind her assassination attempts."

"What does that even matter now? She's gone. Because of you. She believes you're the one behind the attempts on her life."

This time when Case about-faced, Thatch stepped to the side, allowing him the chance to get into Silas's face. "I will find out the truth, and you'll get out of my fucking way so I can. If you interfere in any way, I will break you."

"And start a war with the vampyre faction?"

Not answering, Case continued on.

No, the logic wasn't there, but if she came back, he'd figure something out. He had to believe he could convince her that he wasn't behind anything. Not any threats against her or against her factions.

They reached the end of the tunnel and didn't come across evidence that someone had used it recently. But that didn't mean it hadn't been, because on their way back to Paisley's—minus Silas who left to go home—no proof was left behind that they were retracing their steps.

The four of them stood in Paisley's home a moment, unsure of what to do next. Or even what to say to each other. Case couldn't believe he'd been there a mere twenty-four hours earlier, giving her a blood transfusion and trying to tell her that he cared about her.

Then she left him without giving him a fucking chance.

"I'm leaving," he said.

He didn't go to his punching bag to bruise his hands.

He didn't go to the boxing ring to have it out with other demons.

He didn't go to the bar to drink himself stupid.

He escaped to his house, laid on his bed, and stared up at the ceiling. He couldn't think of doing anything else but lying still. Breathing and staring. Letting depression strangle him.

Nothing else made sense.

Nothing else mattered.

19

Fier Mountain

Paisley

hreats.
Torture.
Blood.
Paisley refusing to give up her thrones.
Threats.
Torture.
Blood.
Paisley refusing to give up her life.
Threats.
Torture.
Blood.

Paisley refusing to give up.
Threats.
Torture.
Blood.
Paisley refusing.
Threats.
Torture.
Blood.

In her cell, concept of day or night didn't exist. Time didn't exist. Paisley didn't know how long she was there. All she knew was the feel of iron searing, iron cutting, the dizziness of hunger, the metallic taste of foreign blood in her mouth, and the gut-clenching pain from that blood filling her stomach.

During the moments they left her alone, she thought about Case.

Please find me. Please find me, Case. Please.
Threats
Tortue.
Blood.

It never stopped.

Paisley couldn't rest. She lay on the floor, huddled in a ball, waiting for the nausea that cramped her stomach to fade. In a ball, she made herself as small as possible, so her kidnappers had less skin to cut, fewer spots they could hit. The repetition and lack of sleep and dizzying hunger and constant pain was enough to fracture her mind. All she was aware of was the footsteps whenever they came because that meant—

Threats.
Torture.
Blood.

She braced for what would come next.

Pain.

Retching.

Pain…pain…pain.

Metal clanked against metal.

The cell door squeaked open.

She peered up at a gold mask.

Gold. The mockery of that didn't escape her. Gold was Case's color. They were framing Case while wearing those ridiculous masks.

The man bent toward her.

A flash of bronze fell toward the ground.

Her gaze followed it to see a bronze key strike the ground two feet from her face.

The man cursed and bent down to retrieve it.

Paisley pounced. Her fingers curled around it first, and she yanked the key and a fistful of dirt and dust away from her kidnapper.

He launched, and she used his momentum against him to send him sailing to the wall behind her. Then she jabbed her fist down, striking the point of the key through the eyehole of the gold mask. Her kidnapper screamed. As he howled, she unlocked her shackles, scrambled to her feet, and ran. She was so weak, though, that she collapsed into the walls and could barely keep herself up.

But she had to get out of there. Tripping on her own feet as if her ankles weren't solid, as if her knees were soft cheese and not bone, wasn't going to stop her. If she couldn't escape now, it'd be all over. For her. For Aster. For the faye faction. Far too much was at stake than her own life. She had to stay alive long enough to make sure the people she cared about would live long past her.

"Stop her!" The shout echoed behind her.

She wound her way this way and that, sensing a hint of breeze ahead that told her a doorway was just ahead.

"Stop her!"

Sunlight streamed into the dingy hall.

"Stop her!"

She turned and found the entry to a cave.

Ten more steps.

Her vampire hearing picked up the sound of two people racing after her.

Five more steps.

"Don't let her get away!"

She dove into the sunlight and rolled onto her back to see who was approaching.

But the pounding footsteps halted.

They didn't want to come out in the open. Vampires? Or did they not have their masks?

She couldn't stay there and ponder that. A look revealed a forest, and through a break in the trees she saw Fier Mountain, where the fier faction resided. *Phoenix*. She shoved to her hands and knees and struggled to her feet. Holding onto trees, she staggered through the forest to the mountain. Sweat slithered down her back and neck. Her heart thudded in her chest. Each step felt like a marathon. She willed herself to keep going; she could collapse once she was safe. And the second she passed into fier faction territory, she dropped.

Dragon Shifters surrounded her.

"Phoenix…Phoenix…Phoenix…" She continued the chant until she passed out.

A hand on her cheek and someone saying her name pried her awake.

"Paisley. Oh my Goddess, what happened?"

"Kidnapped…tortured…"

"Carry her to my chambers. Careful."

Arms lifted her. Then she was laid onto something soft.

"Get her blood now," Phoenix demanded.

"No, no." Paisley maneuvered into a sitting position. "I'm fine. I don't need it."

"Are you serious? You look like you're going to die."

Paisley had never told Phoenix about her blood challenges. "I just need to get home. I need to get back to Case."

"He's probably heading to the Enchanted Hierarchy Council Meeting. My mom already left."

It was the day of the council meeting? They'd had her for a month? Too much time had passed. Anything could've happened. She managed to get to her feet. "I have to go."

"What? No way. You can't go anywhere in the condition you're in. You *look* like you've been kidnapped. If someone sees you like this—"

"I have to get to Case." She made a single step and staggered.

Phoenix caught her. "Okay, but let me help you."

With Phoenix's assistance, she drank, ate, bathed away the sweat and dirt and dried blood, and dressed in a black dress. "Here." Phoenix handed Paisley a pair of elbow-length silk gloves. "To cover the burns on your wrists."

"Thank you." Paisley seethed softly while easing the gloves over her burns. Tears formed before she could stop them.

"You shouldn't go, Paisley. You're in no state to be at that meeting."

"I have to."

"Fine, but we're going to help you get there. You can't fly like this, and you can't walk all that way. Not only would you not make it in time, but you'd pass out after five minutes. We'll escort you."

Paisley nodded. "Okay."

20

Enchanted Hierarchy Council Meeting

Case

month without Paisley felt like six months.

Sitting in his throne in the hall, Case waited for the other leaders to arrive. It was hard to be there again, knowing Paisley wouldn't be coming. No one had heard a word from her. Not Aster. Not Jude. Not Silas. She was gone. As simple and as complicated as that.

Over the past month, Case's life had been put on pause. He wasn't interested in doing anything he normally did. Not even sex. No one interested him. No one aroused him. No one tempted him. Paisley had fucking ruined him. *You're a sex demon, for Diablo's sake! You're not supposed to get hung up on one person!* He'd yelled those words whenever he found himself sitting in silence, thinking about Paisley. *She left. She doesn't fucking want you anymore, so get over her. Get back to your life as Demon Lord and sex fiend. You don't need her.*

Except, he did.

A few days after she'd left, he'd wondered what she was doing about feeding. She'd said his blood was all she could stomach, all that could sustain her. By staying away, was she starving herself? He shouldn't care about that, but he did.

With Aster's help, he filled a cooler of blood bags to leave at Paisley's doorstep. He had no clue if she were home or not, but he knocked anyway before flying off.

A week later, he returned. The cooler still sat there. Squatting down, he opened the lid. The blood bags were there, untouched and spoiled.

At home, he tossed the blood bags in the trash. Then he slammed the cooler into the floor until it caved in on itself and bent out of shape. He didn't bring her any more blood. If she refused it, he couldn't do anything about that. He wasn't going to drain more from his own veins only for it to go unused. Nor was he going to hunt her down to get her to feed, unlike last time. She'd made her choice, and he'd have to stop thinking about her wasting away.

It was impossible not to.

He visited her house one day on a whim, but he didn't go to the door. Instead, he checked on her rose bushes. They were coming to life with vibrant leaves and tightly closed buds encased in green. Weeds sprouted from the rich soil around them. Neglected.

Kneeling in the dirt, he yanked weeds by their roots. "This is the only time I'm doing this," he muttered to the roses. "If your mistress doesn't come back, you're shit outta luck. Maybe Aster will tend to you when she's not too busy with Thatch." He growled at that.

Those two were driving him nuts. They stared moony-eyed at each other all the damn time. They whispered and blushed. Seeing his best friend and right-hand blush was not something Case ever wanted to witness. They were insufferably cute, and it nauseated him. Aster was sweet, though. Once, she had given him a flower she'd picked. He felt like Frankenstein's monster taking it from her, but the last thing he wanted to do was offend her. The flower was, well, cute. Sure, he didn't know what kind it was. It had petals, though. White petals. And a round, yellow middle. Later, when he stared at it in the privacy of his room, it had made him smile. A fleeting occurrence, but Aster's attempt was appreciated.

Beside him, a pile of weeds grew. He ripped out the last weed he could see, gathered them up, and tossed them into the woods. Covered with dirt, he studied the rose bushes. Would Paisley return to see them bloom?

He knew one thing for a fact, *he* wouldn't.

But he needed distractions to keep him from going to her place, from so much as thinking about her. He'd rebuilt the shelves he'd destroyed and restocked the spirits, but he hadn't had a drop. He'd refurbished the furniture, working it all by hand. He'd even bought new art for the walls. Seeing the room finished didn't give him a dose of pride or accomplishment for completing a task. It didn't give him a damn thing. The bottles of whiskey and scotch and vodka were just booze. The neatly carved and varnished and upholstered seats, places for asses to sit. The paintings on the walls, hollow images of life.

To get out of this pit, he dove into his faction leader duties. He held conferences to uncover the bastards who had threatened Paisley's life. She may not want anything to do with him, but he could do that. He could get an answer and end that chapter of his life for good. He went so far as to question each member of Paisley's councils.

When not in meetings or performing interrogations, he visited his faction daily, talked with his people, was invited to many dinners, kindly denied the offer to take many daughters' hands in marriage, and staved off the advances of married men and women, widowers and widows. He wasn't so much as tempted by any of them. Diablo, Paisley really had ruined him.

Sitting in his throne, his annoyance grew as the faction leaders arrived. One of them could've been the one behind the threats. One of them could be framing him. But which one? He eyed each one as they entered.

Lena came first. The beautiful and calm Lena who

had Jude's eye and was friends with Paisley and Paisley's mother before her. He couldn't imagine Lena or the elves doing anything malicious. They were creatures of nature and valued life.

Zeke entered with his hateful glare.

The only factions orcs got along with were the aelf and faye factions, and that was because orcs loved to fuck elves and fairies. It was known far and wide. The size difference got them off. Hey, Case held no judgements. He understood how fun it could be to have sex with a tiny creature, but demons and orcs didn't get along. Orcs didn't like vampires, either. But considering Paisley was half-fairy and the faye queen, he wondered if they thought of her in favorable fuckable terms or unfavorable killable terms. Plus, the king was a hateful son-of-a-bitch. For that reason, he couldn't eliminate them as a possible threat. But they were lower on the list considering they did like fairies.

Next, Langston stomped inside. Giants were gentle beings. He couldn't see them committing harm against any creature.

Atlantica strutted past. And, damn, she could've been on a cat walk. She wore a tiny, shimmering dress that was far too short and showed off her extremely long, pale legs. Before Paisley, Case would've been sprung over that itty-bitty dress and Alantica's endless legs, but the sight of her did nothing to him. Still, he considered her. Queen of Mermaids. She was a darling. No one had any conflicts with her or the oceanus faction. Maybe because they resided in the seas, but they didn't care what happened on land as long as it didn't impact their waters.

Enya had Case glaring. Top of his list. Enough said.

Julius slithered over the tile after Enya. The Basilisk King was a slimy, slithery son-of-a-bitch. Pun fully intended. You couldn't trust a thing Julius said or did. A potential suspect.

Philippa, skai faction queen, came next. Her hooves clicked on the tile. As a Pegasus, Philippa was loyal and kind. She always gave him a friendly nod whenever they were in each other's presence. Like now. And she was an ally to Jude. By hurting his goddaughter in anyway, the skai faction would lose Jude's friendship, protection, and support. He doubted Philippa had a hand—or hoof—in what was going on.

Alaric had Case gripping the armrests of his throne. This fucker was right behind Enya on his list of suspects. He was also on Case's list of assholes he'd like to beat to a pulp. Surprisingly, though, Alaric wasn't in the first-place position. Number one was the piece-of-shit incubus from The Midnight Lair.

Blair shimmered in and out while walking toward her throne. Banshees were as dangerous as they were depressing, but the spiritus faction didn't have any beefs with the daemon, vampyre, or faye factions. That didn't mean that there weren't hidden tensions or resentments that they'd kept under wraps. It was something to investigate further.

Jude followed Blair into the hall. He gave Case a small shake of his head; still no sign or word of Paisley. Jude had requested, as Paisley's godfather, that he be the one to bring up the topic of Paisley as good as forfeiting her thrones. Case didn't doubt that suspicious gazes would look at him, wondering if he'd done something to push Paisley to leave. Maybe he'd been the one behind the threats the whole time and had murdered her. Some would spit those accusations.

Fuck all of them.

Zara finally entered. Perhaps Zara herself wouldn't do anything to harm Paisley, but wizards and enchantresses couldn't be trusted. Not entirely. They always had their own motives. They believed everything they did was for a higher purpose. Could they believe that offing a hybrid, who shouldn't exist, would put balance back into the Enchanted Hierarchy and the universe as a whole? Could they think eliminating Paisley would be an act of good? Case wouldn't take them off the potential suspect list because of that.

Zara took her seat.

Now all the thrones were filled. All but Paisley's.

Zara began the meeting.

Case wasn't listening. He didn't give a damn what they felt was important to bicker over. The matter they needed to discuss Jude would be bringing up at any moment. Case only had to brace for it and the upheaval the news would cause—for the faction leaders and for the entire Enchanted Hierarchy. They'd wanted her gone. Now that she was, they had no idea the damage that would create for them all.

The door opening disrupted the meeting and drew everyone's attentions.

Case's gaze shifted to the entrance. Aside from the faction leaders, the only other people allowed clearance were their right-hands. Except, a faction leader *was* stepping through those doors—Paisley. In a form-fitting, off-the-shoulder, black velvet dress and gloves past her elbows. Her dark purple hair tumbled over bare shoulders.

His chest constricted at the sight of her.

Then in rushed the rage.

What. The. Fuck.

21

All the Beautiful Things

Paisley

*B*eing escorted by Phoenix and her guards to the Enchanted Hierarchy Council Meeting was not something Paisley ever thought would happen, but she was grateful for them when she arrived to the meeting while it was still in session. Her determination to set things straight wavered the second she saw Case. It required every ounce of strength she had left to reach her throne and sit across from him. His wrath pulsed from across the way.

"Sorry, I'm late," she muttered. "Won't happen again."

Zara nodded.

Looking at Case, every part of her being wanted to go to him, throw her arms around him, tell him what'd happened, but she was forced to sit there and endure the daggers of hatred he threw with his eyes. They were searing gold. His hands clenched around the armrests, turning his knuckles white. His chest rose and fell rapidly. He was barely controlling his anger, and she could feel that struggle where she sat.

Case, I'm so sorry. I didn't mean a thing in that note. But the hostility in his eyes told her he may not believe her, even if she was able to voice those words.

On the other end of his silent rage, she struggled to keep her body from swaying with weakness. Beneath the gloves, her burned wrists screamed. She tried not to let her discomfort show on her face or in her eyes. Keeping her eyes from reflecting her pain with burgundy rings was taking all her concentration.

During the meeting, Case's glare didn't shift from her. Not even a fraction.

Whenever she glanced at him, his fury was there to greet her. But the second Zara dismissed them, Case was up and leaving in long strides.

Ignoring her weakness, she shot to her feet and chased after him. Out in the hallway, she caught up to him and grabbed his arm. "Case, please."

He stopped, but he didn't face her.

She slithered around him, still holding his arm for support. "I can explain."

His jaw clenched.

"I swear I can."

Case didn't say a word but yanked his arm free of

her feeble grasp and marched away. The second she didn't have his sturdy body in front of her, she staggered.

A hand steadied her at her back.

She peered up at Jude.

Anger drew his eyebrows down. "Did he hit you?"

"No. He jerked his arm away. That's all."

Jude studied her. "Your note said you left. Where'd you go?"

She cast a glance along the hall to be sure they were alone. "I was forced to make it look like I left of my own free will, but I didn't. I was taken from my home and was held prisoner."

His body shivered, and he struck the ground with a hoof. "What?"

Under her breath, she told him everything.

"You have to tell Case. He needs to know this."

"I want to, but I don't know if he wants to hear a word I have to say."

"You have to make him listen."

"I don't know if I have the strength. I'm so tired, Jude."

"Well, you can't go home. You were already kidnapped there once. We don't need them to snag you again."

"You're right." If they came for her again, they could kill her on the spot.

"I'll bring you to my faction. You can rest, and I'll get a message to Case to meet me there. Then I'll make him listen to you, if I have to kick his ass and pin him to the floor to do it."

She let out a soft chuckle. "No, I can't trick him

like that. I'll…I'll go to him instead and do exactly what you said…make him listen. I could use a ride, though."

"I'd be happy to give you a lift."

Outside, he knelt on one knee, and she sat sidesaddle on his back.

"Hold on."

She secured her arms around his waist, and he took off. In no time they made it to Case's. Unlike last time, she didn't have to use her vampire hypnotism in order to get past the gate or through the doors. The demons on guard let her and Jude in without question.

She slid to the ground. On her feet, she smiled. "I've got it from here. Thank you."

"You're welcome. I'm glad you're back. That you survived." Jude laid a hand on her cheek. "I missed you, and I love you, dear goddaughter."

"I love you, too. Now bend down so I can kiss your cheek."

He chuckled and bent low.

She planted a kiss on his cheek.

He straightened. "I remember when you were a little girl, I'd hold you, and you'd kiss my cheek just like that. Time sure does fly by."

"Maybe one day you'll have a daughter of your own who will kiss your cheek."

"I'm afraid that time has passed."

She tilted her head.

"Don't. I'm not discussing this with you. Besides, I'm happy being a godfather."

"Thank you for that."

He bowed his head. "Good luck getting through to

him."

"I like my odds." And she barged right in just like she did after her coronation. She didn't have much strength, but she was able to slam the door to get Case's attention.

He stepped out of the parlor. The moment he saw her, his body tensed, and his eyes gleamed an outraged gold.

"I know you're pissed," she said. "And you have every right to be."

He exhaled loudly through his nose and stomped toward her.

She backed toward the door before she could stop herself. "I would be as pissed if I were in your shoes, but I didn't leave." Peeling off her gloves, she winced when the fabric scraped against her burns. "I was taken." And she showed him the raw burns on her wrists.

He froze.

Then he dropped to his knees and cradled her hands with his. "I'll kill them all."

His vow didn't shock her. Killing was in his nature. The way he fell to his knees and held her hands while examining her burns, however, did shock the hell out of her.

"I don't know who they were," she said. "They wore solid gold masks. All I know is that there were three of them."

"What did they do?"

"Torture, Case. They tortured me."

His jaw clenched. "How?"

"Cut me with iron and gave me blood to make me

heal so they could do it all again."

Case seethed. "How'd you get free?"

"One came for me, dropped the key to my bonds. I impaled his eye with it and fled."

"That's my feisty hybrid." He stood and lifted her into his arms.

"What are you doing?"

"Taking care of you. Or at least taking you to a fairy who can."

Aster.

"Wait." She curled her fingers in his lapel. "The threat to Aster. It's real. When they took me, they threatened to kill the entire faye faction. Starting with Aster."

"We'll protect the fairies. The first fairy was before I began my watch. The second one happened beyond our protective barrier. We've learned. And no one will be able to get to Aster with Thatch around. I can guarantee you that."

The mention of the second fairy brought the last hours before she was taken rushing back. "Oh my gosh! The fairy that was found...her burial ritual...I need—"

"Aster took care of it. The point is, nothing more will happen to them." He carried her down the hall. "And until this is resolved, you're staying with me. I can't have someone killing the only person I truly enjoy having sex with. No matter how much you annoy and aggravate me." He turned into the library where Aster and Thatch sat side by side on a couch.

"Paisley!" Aster hopped off the couch and rushed over. Her wings fluttered excitedly.

Case set Paisley on her feet.

She opened her arms and accepted her best friend. "I missed you."

"I missed you, too. I was afraid I'd never see you again."

Case stepped forward. "Paisley needs some of your healing magick, cutie pie."

Paisley held out her hands.

Aster gasped. "How'd this happen?"

"Iron restraints."

Aster's face suddenly hardened. "But how?"

"I was kidnapped. That's why I've been gone. I didn't leave. I certainly wouldn't have left and not told you where I was going."

Thatch joined Aster's side. "Who did this?"

"I don't know. They wore gold masks. I think they had wings, though."

"How do you know?"

"It's a hunch, but to bring me where they held me undetected, they likely flew. I was all the way in the mountains, close to Fier Mountain."

"Enya," Case growled.

"I don't think so, though. When I escaped, I stumbled out into the sun, and they didn't follow. They easily could've gotten me back. I couldn't move fast, and two of them could've hunted me down. They either didn't have their masks or...they are vampires."

Case's jaw worked. "If they were vampires, then there's a chance they could've known about the underground tunnel."

Paisley grimaced. She hadn't told Case about that, and her kidnappers using it to get into her house undetected made sense. "Case, I'm sorry I didn't—"

"I get it. You couldn't trust me with the vampyre faction's escape route."

"It's not that, Case. Only a select few knew about it. I didn't consider it because I didn't think it could be used by my enemies. They're not supposed to know about it."

"Well, they found out somehow, which means there is someone you trust who broke that, but it wasn't me, Paisley."

"I know." She laid a hand on his chest. "I know."

He curled his fingers around her arm and examined the burns on her wrist. His gaze shifted to Aster. "Cutie pie, we still need that healing."

"Oh, sorry." Aster untied the pouch of fairy dust from her belt, extracted a pinch, and sprinkled the magickal sparkles over Paisley's wrists.

The burns vanished.

"Thank you, sweetheart." Case guided Paisley around, and he studied her face. "You're still pale. When was the last time you had blood?"

She gazed off to the side to think. "Um…four, five days, maybe, but I couldn't stomach it."

He picked her up again. "I'll show you to your room."

"I can walk," she said as he carried her to the stairs.

"No, you can't. You can barely stand."

She didn't respond.

"You don't even have the energy to argue with me."

True.

"And that pisses me off."

"Sorry."

"Not you. I'm not mad at you. I'm mad at whoever did this *to* you." He opened a door and carried her into a room.

She peered around. "This is *your* room."

"It is." He shut the door. "My room is now yours. Like my body is yours. Like my blood is yours." He stretched out in the middle of the bed so that she was lying on top of him.

Her legs slipped between his. She didn't have the strength to push off him.

"Drink as much as you need."

She nestled her face at his throat. With her hand at the other side of his neck, she nuzzled him. Not having blood for several days, being force-fed unknown blood that she'd vomit up, she became dizzy with hunger and apprehensive with nausea. She laid her head on his shoulder.

"What's wrong?"

"I don't know if I can."

"You can."

"You don't understand. After what they did to me, my progress with feeding has gone five steps in reverse."

"And I'll help you go six steps forward. Here. Close your eyes."

She did as he asked.

"Are they closed?"

"Yes."

His thumb brushed over her lips, leaving behind a warm, wet smear.

"Lick your lips."

She did as he asked again. His blood stained the tip

of her tongue, enough to get the flavor in her mouth.

"Was that okay?"

"Yeah. Yeah, that was fine."

"Are you ready for more?"

"I think so."

"When you fell unconscious during our first dinner, I slipped my thumb in your mouth, and you sucked on it. Do that now."

"Okay."

She touched his hand and guided his thumb to her mouth.

"Take it nice and easy."

She closed her lips around his thumb and pressed her teeth to the callused pad. Blood seeped from the tiny gash he'd pierced into his thumb with his own fang. It dribbled onto her tongue and slithered past her taste buds. She swallowed. His blood went down without any trouble. Her throat didn't constrict. Her gag reflex didn't activate. She drew more of his blood free, swallowed again.

Then she pulled his thumb from her mouth.

"How are you doing?" His other hand stroked her back.

"I'm doing okay. I think...I think I'm ready now." She scooted closer, elevating her face to his neck. Her lips were featherlight against his throat.

It's Case, she reminded herself. *You've sank your fangs into his neck several times. You like it. He likes it. Actually, he downright enjoys it. And his blood tastes good. Tastes amazing. Tastes fucking delicious. It's okay.*

"It's Case," she whispered and pierced him

carefully with her fangs.

His chest lifted her up when he inhaled.

She slipped her fangs free and fixed her mouth against his skin. He let out a sound that was part sigh, part moan. In response, she sighed, too, and melted against him as she suckled. His hands caressed her back, soothing her after her recent trauma. His touch calmed her nerves, and she consumed his blood without a problem. She didn't rush herself, though, and drank slowly. The slower she sipped his blood, the more intimate the moment felt, the more sensual the act became.

When she finished, she licked the wound to heal it and laid her head on his shoulder.

"There you go," he murmured, still rubbing her back. "There you go."

His tenderness filled her with so many unnamed emotions. His tenderness, from the beginning, never failed to stun her, leave her speechless.

She rose up to look at him. Goddess, he was handsome.

Case framed her face with his hands. "Kiss me, Paisley."

She lowered her lips to his. Except, she couldn't lay her lips fully against his and give him the kiss he was yearning. She was so damned confused over what she felt in that moment, what she felt from him, and everything she'd felt while in the hands of her kidnappers.

"Paisley?"

She climbed off him.

"Pais." The bed squeaked.

She held up a hand. "Stay there." She walked to the window and stared at the night sky speckled with stars. The moon was a cute crescent in the shape of a smile. "While I was kidnapped, I kept hoping that you'd become so enraged at me for ghosting you that you would hunt me down to make me pay, but then you'd make *them* pay once you realized the truth."

"I'm sorry. If I had known, I would've done exactly that." The bed squeaked again, and his voice was closer. "I *was* enraged. So much so that it stopped me from going after you because I was waiting for you to come back."

She traced the line of the crescent moon with the tip of her finger. "And what were you planning to do when I returned?"

"Fuck you good to convince you to never leave again."

"Real nice."

"There might've been some spanking involved for good measure."

For some reason, that made her laugh.

"In all seriousness, do you remember how you told Thatch you'd filet him if he hurt or failed to protect Aster?"

"I never forget a threat. Not one I give. Nor one I get."

"Well, you fileted me. Suddenly, all the beautiful things in my life were gone. You stole them from me by leaving. At least that's what I thought when I found that note. That's why I didn't come after you. I was fileted."

His claim staggered her. She faced him. "What are we, Case? Are we still enemies?"

"We'll always be enemies on some level because the daemon and vamprye factions are always going to be enemies no matter we do. So, yeah, we are. But there's a fine line between love and hate, enemies and lovers. We are that line, baby." He inched closer. "We can be so much more than enemies, though."

Her answer was a whisper. "We already are."

His Adam's apple bobbed from a deep swallow. "I have something for you." He stepped around her. When he swept her hair from the back of her neck, she shivered.

Warm metal touched her skin.

She closed her fingers around her necklace as tears formed. "I thought I'd lost this."

"I found it in your bathroom. I kept it...put it in my pocket every day."

She rotated around and kissed him. Beneath her lips, she felt his surprise a second before he caught her hips with his hands. Their kiss was soft but determined. Determined to share, to accept, to forget the hell they'd been through the past month.

Case leaned back. "As much as I want to have a night of reunion sex with you, we need to find out who did this, who took you from me, from all of us. And we can't wait, love. We have to do it tonight."

22

Vampyre Queen

Case

While Thatch contacted Jude and Silas to tell them they needed to get to Case's right now, Case watched Paisley in the privacy of his bedroom. Although there was a bit of coloring to her cheeks now after feeding, she was still pale from everything she'd endured. Even her eyes looked tired. "I know you're exhausted, baby, but we're going to need you to show us where they had you. Do you think you can do that?"

She nodded. "I can do that."

He pressed his lips to her forehead and spoke with his lips touching her skin. "You're so fucking strong, Paisley. So damn strong."

She wrapped her arms around his middle. "I don't feel it."

He moved a hand to the back of her head, tangling his fingers with her hair, and massaged her scalp. "You are. You're stronger than all the demons I know. You're stronger than me, Pais, and that's a fact."

She leaned into him. "Mm. You need to stop massaging my head or I'm going to fall asleep standing up."

He kissed her temple. "I wish you could sleep, but we can't wait."

Sighing, she stepped back. "I know. I'll change. I…I need clothes."

"I'll go to your place and get you pants and T-shirt. Okay?"

She nodded.

"Stay here. Right here. Don't even go downstairs."

"I'll stay right here."

Locking in the memory of her in the black dress, standing before his bed, he opened and then closed the doors to his balcony. Then he flew off to her house. In a moment, he was landing on her bedroom's balcony. He let himself in. Seeing her bedroom empty now was vastly different from when he saw it after her disappearance. Then, everything had mocked him. Now, they reassured him, because she was there to use them. She hadn't actually left anything.

She hadn't left *him*.

He went to her closet and pulled a pair of black pants from a hanger. A long-sleeved black shirt joined the folded pants in his hands. His gaze searched the floor, and he spotted a pair of black ankle boots. Before he left, he stopped in the bathroom and picked up a hair tie from the counter. Considering her hair, he fingered a tiny elastic tie. With a smile, he rolled the tiny elastic onto the tip of his pinky finger.

Then he flew back to his place and stepped through his balcony doors to see her sitting on the edge of his bed, hugging one of his pillows to her chest. The vulnerability of that position tightened his throat. But the level of comfort that exhibited, that she could choose his pillow to embrace when she needed to be soothed, made his heart pound with longing. All he wanted was for her to wrap her arms around him in place of that pillow.

Instead, he held out the clothes and boots.

She took them and stood. Back to him, she said, "Can you get the zipper?"

He didn't say anything as he dragged the zipper down. When it parted, revealing her smooth, pale skin, he bent his neck and pressed a kiss to the scar at her left shoulder blade.

She shimmed out of the dress, slipped on the shirt over a lace bra, and pulled the jeans up her legs. While she laced her boots, Case watched her fingers. Diablo, she had beautiful, long fingers. He truly did adore every part of her body.

"Alright." She rubbed her palms over her thighs. "I'm ready."

"One more thing." He held the hair tie between his

thumb and index finger.

"You thought of everything." She pulled her hair into a pony tail. "I'm ready."

"Not yet." He stepped behind her and took her thick pony tail with his hands.

"What are you doing?"

She started to turn, but he gave a gentle tug on her hair. "Stay still." And he set to work dividing her hair into three sections and twining them together.

"Are you…are you braiding my hair?"

"Mm-hm. You've seen Thatch's braid. All demons are taught how to braid when they're children. We can braid hair and rope."

"Ah. A romantic or deadly skill, depending on the purpose."

"Exactly."

He finished twisting her hair together and secured it with the tiny elastic band he'd slipped onto the tip of his pinky finger. "There." He gave another gentle tug. "Now you're ready."

She pulled her braid over her shoulder and turned. "Wow. A Dutch braid. You're good."

"I'll braid your hair any day, baby." He clasped her hand. "Let's go."

Downstairs, Thatch, Aster, and Wren waited with Jude and Silas.

Silas hurried to Paisley the moment she stepped off the staircase and gathered her close. "Thank God. Thatch said you'd been kidnapped. Do you know who did this to you?"

She shook her head against Silas's shoulder. "No, that's why you're here."

Silas shifted her back and searched her face. "Are you okay?"

She shrugged. "To a degree." Her gaze met Case's. "Better now."

Silas faced Case, too. "Someone kidnapped the vampyre queen. They will pay for this."

Case nodded. "They will pay with their lives."

"Yes, they will."

"Let's go." Thatch turned to Aster. "Baby doll—"

"Don't you dare try to tell me I'm staying here. I'm going with you." Thatch started to shake his head, but Aster grabbed his hand. "She's my family. She's the *only* family I have left. Just as much as Case and Silas want revenge, I do, too. I'm going."

Thatch's jaw flexed.

Case took a step. "Thatch, she's coming, and you'll make sure nothing happens to her."

"That doesn't even need to be said."

Wren stepped forward then. "I'll stay here to make sure the mansion remains secure."

"Thank you, Wren." Case's gaze ran over the others. "Let's go." He followed Paisley past the gate, into a dark patch of woods where the moon's light didn't reach the ground. "Are you sure about flying?"

She nodded. "I trust everyone who is here, and...it's dark. My wings aren't visible against the night sky."

That was true. When she'd left The Midnight Lair, and he'd caught up to her in the air, he hadn't been able to make out a thing about her wings. "Alright, love, bring them out."

"Are you sure you should watch?"

"Bring them out."

"You asked for it." Her wings sprang from her back with a light slap against the air.

Case flinched as lust roared through his veins like a bolt of lightning. He swallowed.

"Diablo, your wings are fucking perfect." She took a small step back, and his gaze leapt to her face. "Don't back away from me, love."

"Keep it together, Case. We have to go. Do you think you can follow me?"

"Follow you? No. I'll be right beside you, every wing stroke of the way." He jerked his chin. "You first."

She leapt into the air, and he launched after her.

He heard the sound of Thatch's and Silas's wings and the beat of hooves pounding against the earth, tipping him off that the others were following. It took them three hours to get to the stretch of woods near Fier Mountain.

Paisley dropped into the woods and Case landed beside her. A moment later, Thatch and Silas touched down as Jude galloped up to them.

Thatch set Aster on her feet.

"It's about a mile from here." She pointed away from Fier Mountain. "We go on foot the rest of the way, so we don't get spotted."

They maintained their formation—Paisley and Case taking the lead, Thatch and Aster, Silas, and then Jude. None of them spoke.

Twenty odd minutes later, they reached the edge of the forest.

Paisley held up a hand to halt their team. From

behind a tree, she pointed at a dark opening in the side of a mountain. "That's the cave," she whispered to Case.

Rage simmered through him. That was where they held her for a month while he'd spiraled out of control. The fuckers would pay for that.

They snuck across the clearing to the cave entrance.

Paisley peeked in, using her vampiric sight to see. She gave Case a nod before stepping inside. With his eyes emitting a soft glow that didn't reach past his own feet, he followed her close behind, prepared to snatch her out of the way if something happened.

They snaked their way through a tunnel.

In the darkness, Paisley's hand touched his.

He inhaled.

Her fingers threaded with his, and he clasped her hand tightly. That contact spoke volumes. At once, it gave him strength because she was reaching for him in that moment, but it also weakened him, because if she weren't feeling unsafe right now, she wouldn't be holding his hand. More than anything, he wanted her to not only feel safe but to *be* safe. And she wasn't safe in this cave. She'd be safe back at his mansion, warm in his bed, sound asleep in his arms.

She halted.

Case bumped into her and wrapped an arm around her waist. "What is it?"

"They're ahead. I can hear them. They're…the fuckers are playing poker."

The others gathered.

"What's the gameplan?" Thatch asked.

"We should round them up," Silas said. "Bring them to your dungeons." He nodded at Case. "I say we torture confessions out of them, find out who put them up to it."

Case liked the idea of torturing them until they begged for mercy and wept their truths.

Jude crossed his arms. "I say we go in, don't even give them a chance, slaughter them, and leave them at the doors to whichever faction they belong to. That'll be a message enough for whoever is in charge not to cross the vampyre queen, or the people who love her, ever again."

Case liked the sound of that, too. Either way, he fully intended to kill them. But what they did wasn't his decision. "What do you think?" He turned to Paisley and froze.

She wasn't beside him anymore.

He whipped around. "Pais?"

The tunnel was empty.

Up ahead, crashing sounds echoed.

"Fuck." He took off, following the noises to a chamber in the cave where Paisley was taking on four masked men by herself. A cheap poker table was flattened to the ground. Cards and poker chips were scattered across the space. She leapt onto one of them, latched her teeth onto his neck, and then ripped out his throat with her fangs. The man crumpled, and she went down with him. Another one of them went to attack her.

Case sprang into action, grasped the bastard's head, and wrenched so hard that his neck didn't just crack. His head rotated completely around.

At the same time, Thatch, Silas, and Jude joined

the fray.

Jude sent one of them flying with a mean kick, and Silas jumped onto the suspect.

Thatch slammed the fourth into a wall when he tried to escape.

Paisley moved in on the fourth suspect before Case could and yelled as she threw a fist. Her knuckles sank into the gold mask, caving it into the man's face.

Behind him, he turned to see Jude crushing a hoof through the third suspects chest.

All four were now dead.

Case went to Paisley. Blood streamed down her chin to her chest, wetting her shirt. He looped one arm around her to support her while she shook and lifted his shirt with his right hand to wipe the blood off her face and neck. "What the hell, Paisley?"

"They tortured me," she panted. "I couldn't let them live."

"Neither could I, but we should've questioned them first."

"I don't think there's any need for that," Thatch said.

They turned to him. He crouched next to one of the dead, holding the gold mask with one hand and parting his lips with his other hand. Fangs. The fucker had fangs.

Aster stood in the entryway. "He was a vampire," she whispered.

Paisley stepped closer as Silas ripped off another mask and Jude flicked the mask of the man whose heart he'd crushed with his hoof. Also vampires.

Case tried to tug off the mask of the man Paisley

had punched, but it was wedged into his face. He peered over his shoulder at Paisley. "Damn, love."

She shrugged.

He pushed to his feet. "Do you recognize them?"

"A little. Low on the chain. Very low."

"Doesn't matter how low they were," Silas said. "They hurt their queen. I will string them up for the entire vampyre faction to see and know we'll do the same to anyone who dares harm their rightful queen."

"No."

They all looked to Paisley.

"I don't want the other factions to know that my own kidnapped me and tried to kill me. No. This is staying between us. We'll burn their bodies, and then we'll move on."

"It's your choice, love, but we don't have fire."

"Yes, we do. We're by Fier Mountain. You and I will go to Phoenix. We'll get dragon's breath. There won't be a trace left of them by the time the fire goes out."

"Then let's get that fire."

The two of them reached Fier Mountain and asked for Phoenix. They told her everything in confidence, and she ordered a dragon shifter she trusted to join them back to the cave, because if she left, her faction would notice.

The others had dragged the dead bodies out into the clearing, and the dragon shifter set them ablaze. While everyone's eyes were on the burning bodies, Paisley lifted off.

Case shot into the air after her and caught up in a few beats of his wings. "Are you trying to sneak off, love?"

She looked over. "No. It's just...I'm not ready for everyone to see my wings. Not even Silas has seen them." She shook her head. "I'm working on it. Plus, I wanted a head start."

"Head start where?"

"To your bed."

23

Holy Feminist Arousal

Paisley

S tepping through the doors of Case's mansion felt like coming home. She never would've expected that, but she never would've expected a lot, like their relationship.

Case picked her up as Thatch and Aster entered behind them. "We're showering together," he told Paisley. "And then I'm going to fuck you to sleep." He cast a glanced toward Thatch. "Feel free to celebrate with Aster in a similar fashion."

Aster's eyes widened.

Paisley smacked Case in the shoulder. "Don't say that to them."

"Baby, they deserve it. Just like we do." He carried her up the stairs.

"Am I ever going to walk these stairs myself?"

"Not when I'm hard."

She laughed. "Which is practically all the time."

He shot her a grin. "Only for you, baby." He brought her into his bathroom, set her on her feet, and stepped behind her.

She shivered when his fingers grazed the back of her neck.

He unhooked her necklace and set it on the counter. "We'll need something to put it in when you bathe here."

"I can bring the porcelain clam dish."

Her statement had him stilling. "You have that at your house."

"Well, I've been here more than there." It was practical.

He nodded slowly. "Whatever you want to bring here, you can. You can have half the closet, and I'll give you a dresser."

Now his statement had *her* stilling. *This is what couples do*, she reminded herself. *They make space for each other. Live together. So, does that mean...are we a couple*? She wasn't ready to ask that yet, so instead she set to work stripping him of his clothes. Standing in front of her, stark naked, he stole her breath. "Goddess."

His cock expanded and lifted under her appraisal. "You don't need to evoke her. You're the only goddess here." And he removed every article of her clothing.

In the shower, they enticed each other with their hands while washing away their sweat and their enemies' blood. Paisley was purring in his embrace as his fingers stroked her pussy.

"You like that, baby?"

She clutched him. "Yes, goddess, yes. Your touch is so good. I've missed your touch."

Groaning, he shut off the shower and hoisted her off her feet with his hands behind her knees. She hooked her legs around his dripping wet waist.

On the edge of his bed, he sat, settling her on his lap. "I want to have you in every way possible," he said, "but right now, I want you like this. With my arms around you." He circled his arms around her waist. "With your arms around me."

She looped her arms around his neck.

"Just like that. Now, rise up and take me inside you."

She lifted onto her knees, scooted closer, and guided him to her. Staring into his eyes, she sank onto him. The deeper he went, the wider her mouth parted as she breathed in and out tiny gasps. Goddess, it felt good to have him inside her again. She'd yearned for this, yearned for *him* for far too long. Except it wasn't just about sex anymore. It was about being close to him again. He was a force in so many ways. A magnet. She couldn't resist him or the things he gave her. She wanted him. She wanted it all.

Case's wide hands cupped her hips. "Am I hurting you?"

"No," she gasped.

"Your eyes are burgundy, love."

"It's not pain."

"Then what is it?"

How to explain to him what she felt? One word came to mind. "Needs."

His jaw clenched as a mask of anger took over his features.

She laid her hand against his jaw. "You can wipe that anger off your face, Case."

"You hate needing me. You've made that clear."

She shook her head. "That was *before* I was held prisoner. Things changed. I needed you every day. And it had nothing to do with blood or sex. I needed *you*."

Case inhaled.

Inside her, she could've sworn his cock had expanded. She squirmed on his lap and sucked in a breath. "Did you get bigger?"

His hands softened. "Did I?"

"You definitely did."

"I'm sorry. I didn't know. I felt…"

She titled her head. "Felt what?"

"I don't know."

She studied him quietly.

He did the same. "Your eyes are still red. I'm bigger than I've ever been inside you. Are you sure you're okay?"

She wrapped her arm around him again. "Positive." And she rocked her hips.

He let out a hiss of pleasure. "Diablo, I missed this." He laid his lips to the side of her neck. "I missed *you*."

Her grip on him tightened.

His own arms responded to that, and he grasped her. "Do you want my cock to vibrate?"

"No." Her voice was a breath in his ear. "I just need you. Nothing extra. Just you."

"You have me."

"Yes, I do."

"And I have you."

"Yes." She hitched herself higher and gyrated her hips faster. "I missed you, too."

That time, she was positive that his cock had grown inside her as he growled with pleasure. Holding onto him, she released a strangled gasp.

"Fuck." He lifted her off his lap. "I'm sorry, baby, I don't know why that keeps happening."

"It's okay."

"No, it's not. I felt it that time. Let me pull out, and I'll divide my cock in two. Give you some relief. That way, if I get bigger while I'm inside you, there's room."

"I'm okay."

He cupped her face with his hands. "I don't want to hurt you, baby."

His words caused a fluttering in the pit of her stomach. She stamped her mouth to his, silencing him with a kiss, knowing damn well that he couldn't resist kissing her. Nor did he resist. As they got lost in the kiss, she seated herself on him again and resumed rocking until she broke off the kiss to moan into his mouth. The sensations of his dick stroking every centimeter of her vaginal muscles washed over her like a wanton tidal wave. Her hips were lightning fast as she rode him.

"Fuck." He grasped her as if to stay afloat in the

wake of her frantic urge to experience all the pleasure his dick could give her. And his dick apparently wanted to give it all.

Suddenly, Case dropped back onto the bed, drawing Paisley down with him. He held her hips captive, preventing her from moving, and lifted his own hips up, plowing into her. The squelching noises of his cock sliding in and out, the wet slaps of their bodies banging into each other, was hot as hell. He thrust faster, pumping in a frenzy.

Paisley clutched him and cried out non-stop. With her face buried in the side of his neck, she squirted. Not once. Not twice. But three times. One right after the other. The dripping wetness didn't slow him. When she squirted for the fourth time, her orgasm popped, and she let out a long wail.

He plunged into her once more. With his hips lifted, he unloaded into her. The moment he emptied, he plopped down, utterly spent, and Paisley draped over him.

Neither of them said a word for several minutes.

"I'm afraid to move," Case muttered.

"Why?"

"Because I think that orgasm shattered me. The only thing keeping me together is you. You're my glue."

"I'm your glue?"

"Mm-hm."

She didn't know want to say to that, so she said, "I'm sorry."

"What are you sorry about?"

"I got you all sorts of wet and your bed is soaked."

"Don't ever apologize for squirting. Female ejaculation is the sexiest thing a woman can do during sex. End of discussion."

"Still. We're going to need to shower again."

"Then we'll shower, and I'll invest in a waterproof blanket that you can go to town on." He risked shattering and rolled over so that Paisley was pinned beneath him, with her legs on either side of his hips and his limp cock still inside her. "I like it when you squirt, Paisley. That was a record for us. Four times. I want to break that record. Five times. Maybe one day we'll make it to ten."

She arched a brow. "Ten times? That's a lot of ejaculating for a woman."

He grinned. "If anyone could do it, you could."

She grinned back. "I could with you."

"Damn straight." He kissed her long and slow. "I'm going to pull out of you now."

She nodded.

Watching her closely, he inched out of her. Once the head of his cock left her body, he kissed her eyelids one at a time. "Your eyes are fucking fascinating. I thought they only became red when you were mad and your vampire side wanted to come out to play."

"Come out to play? You mean come out to kill."

"Mm. You wouldn't kill me."

"I wanted to a couple of times. I tried once." When he delivered a dead vampire to her house, and she attacked him.

"Good thing I'm not easy to kill."

"That's a very good thing."

They showered a second time. Then Case found a

nightgown in his closet that she'd left behind and stripped his bed. She helped him to fit a clean sheet over the mattress. Then she climbed right in without a blanket and hugged one of his pillows to her head.

"Tired, love?"

Her eyelids were closed when she said, "Yeah, I didn't sleep much while…" She didn't say more. Didn't need to.

He climbed onto the bed and held her close. "You can sleep now."

And for the first time since she'd been taken, she *was* able to sleep.

She woke to Case kissing her neck and couldn't help but smile. "Mm. Morning."

"Morning, beautiful." He trailed kisses from her neck and across her collarbones. "I want to stay in this bed with you. All day."

"I want to stay in this bed with you, too, but I can't."

"And why the hell not?"

"Because I want girls' time with Aster. She's missed me, too. And I've missed her."

"Now how can I argue with that? But can we have fun before girls' time kicks off?"

She elevated onto an elbow and gave him a quick peck on the lips. "Abstinence would be good for you."

He knotted his fingers into her hair, keeping her from withdrawing. "Abstinence could kill a sex demon."

She paused. "Really?"

"No, but it'd feel like death."

She studied him and his half-lidded eyes—so damn

sexy. "You'll survive it. Imagine how great it will be when we do have sex. The release."

"When we do have sex, if you've forced me to hold out for long, it won't be a release. It'll be a demolition."

She arched a brow. "You'd demolish me?"

"My orgasm may demolish *me*."

"I'm sure no sex demon has ever been laid to waste by their own orgasm."

"That's actually how most sex demons go."

She stilled. "Okay, seriously?"

"Worried now, are you?" His lips quirked into an infuriatingly cocky smirk.

"Like I said, I think you'll survive." She patted his shoulder.

He didn't release her. "Do you remember the conversation we had before you were taken? About your moon time?"

She thought back to that day and how she'd snapped, accusing him of not being able to handle her issues with blood. "I do."

"We never got to finish that conversation. I'd like to finish it now."

Apprehensive, she nodded. "Okay."

"If you want to have sex while you're bleeding, you should know by now that I'm game, but I need you to be honest with me the entire time. If your flow is heavier than usual, if you feel weak, faint, anything at all, tell me, and I'll transfuse you. Aster showed me how." He ran his hands down her arms. "I don't want what happened last time to happen again."

"Last time, you said that someone who will worry about me is exactly the kind of person I need to be with, and you're right. One hundred percent." She brought her lips to his. They brushed when she said, "And that person is you."

His lips closed around hers. They shared another kiss that was beyond tender; this was one of the ways Case liked to kiss her. She was getting used to receiving that tenderness from him. Truthfully, those kisses were her favorite.

"When you were taken, you were on your period." He studied her face. "They had you for a month. Did you get it again while in that cell?"

"No, not yet. The new moon is in three days, so we'll see, but the body knows. After all the torment it endured, it might not have felt safe to ovulate. I didn't have any of the usual signs, so I may not even get my period."

His jaw ticked.

She smoothed her hands over his tense shoulders. "My cycle will go back to normal when my body feels safe. And I feel safe now."

He kissed her forehead. "When it does, can you share those dates with me? When you ovulate and when your moon time arrives?"

"Of course."

"Good, because I want to start tracking it, too. I want to make sure I'm keeping you safe."

Holy feminist arousal. "That's one of the sexiest things a man could ever say."

His lips quirked up at the corners. "Wanna have sex now?"

Yes, she fucking did, so she leveled on top of him and wrapped her hand around his cock in way of an answer. "We can fuck for half the day, but the other half, I'm spending with Aster. Deal?"

"Deal, baby."

And, goddess, did they fuck. In every way possible.

Satisfied beyond belief, Paisley dressed for the first time since Case had removed her dirty, blood-stained clothes. She peered at him as he zipped a pair of pants. "While I spend time with Aster, to keep you out of trouble, maybe you can have boys' time with Thatch."

He grimaced. "Boys' time?"

"Demons' time?"

"Better."

"What *do* demons do to bond?"

"That question can be answered in multiple ways. There's what I would've done before you, which is very different than what I'd do now. Funny thing is, what Thatch would do now is exactly the same as what he would've done before Aster." He twirled a lock of her hair. "I'm a changed demon."

Could she really have changed so much just because of her?

"And then there's what Thatch *and* I would do."

"Which is?"

He shrugged a shoulder. "Play pool. Box. Fly. What do you think you and Aster will do?"

"I don't know. I'll have to ask her."

They found Thatch and Aster outside, strolling

hand-in-hand on the grass.

"I had to deal with their cuteness all by myself," Case said. "It was torture."

"I would've preferred that torture to literal torture."

Case caught her hand, tugging her to a halt. "I'm sorry. For everything they did to you. I'm so sorry."

"It's not your fault, and they're gone now."

"Thank Diablo *and* your Goddess."

Thatch and Aster turned toward them as they approached.

"Are the two of you finally done?" Thatch asked.

"For the time being," Case said.

"That's surprising."

Aster met Paisley's eye while the two demons teased each other. Then her gaze lowered, and that knowing little smile appeared.

Paisley looked down to see Case was still holding her hand. Or was she still holding his? She didn't look at him when she extracted her hand from his and addressed Thatch. "I'd like to spend some time with my best friend, if you don't mind."

"Of course not." He kissed the back of Aster's hand before releasing it.

"Let's continue the walk," Paisley said. "I haven't been outside much lately."

They ambled ahead.

Aster picked a dandelion from the grass. "I'm so glad you're back, and that you're safe. I missed you so much." Her voice lowered. "Case did, too. I tried to tell him that the letter didn't sound like you and didn't make sense, but he struggled to see past the fact that you said you were leaving."

"We agreed not to do that. Not to jump to conclusions, leave, end things without giving the other a chance to defend themselves. I thought my letter would've provided enough doubt, but my kidnappers made sure I didn't hide any clues in it for him to figure out the truth."

"Did he tell you what it was like for him?"

"No. All I know is the wrath I felt coming from him."

Aster bent her neck, as if she were telling the grass this secret. "When he returned from your place, he wrecked the parlor. Did you notice that everything is different? The chairs, shelves, artwork?"

She hadn't.

"It was in ruins. Thatch had to restrain him or else he might've wrecked the entire mansion."

"He was pissed," Paisley said, understanding that reaction to want to destroy.

"He was heartbroken."

Paisley pulled up short, spun toward Aster, and peered back at Case and Thatch, who trailed behind them, still being their protector selves.

Case and Thatch stopped when they did.

Case's brows lowered.

She quickly shifted forward. "That's not possible," she whispered. "Sex demons can't fall in love. Everyone knows that."

"You don't have to be in love to have a broken heart."

"That's true," she muttered and resumed their stroll.

"Where did that even come from? That sex demons

can't love?"

"I don't know. I assume from the mouths of sex demons."

"That'd make sense, but Case doesn't seem like your normal sex demon, and I'm not saying that because he chose you."

Paisley snorted. "He *chose* me?"

Aster gave her a look. "Hasn't he?"

Paisley couldn't answer that.

"Haven't *you*?"

She stared at her bare feet in the grass.

"You're my best friend. I've known you since we were little sprites. You never kept a lover long. A month, tops. And you never saw them nearly as much."

"I could never trust them," she said, rationalizing over the fact that she used to heave ho her past lovers after four weeks. "And none of them…they didn't…" She wasn't sure what she was trying to say.

None of them impacted her in the same way. They didn't make her feel as if she were a masterpiece the way she was. She'd been a conquest. For each and every one of them. She'd known it, and she used that as a good reason to fuck them and then pitch them to the side. They wanted to tell the tale about railing the hot hybrid, so she gave them a damn good tale to share. When she became queen, she'd expected more and more creatures to line up to seek the hybrid queen's pussy, and she would've shown the ones she picked a good time, but they hadn't even had a chance to form a line. The day of her coronation, she'd met Case, and just like that, her hybrid queen pussy became his.

"None of them were Case," Aster finished. "They

didn't make you feel the way he does."

"So maybe I have chosen him," she hissed. "But if you're trying to get me to say that I'm in love with him, it's not going to happen."

Aster laid a hand on her arm. "I'm sorry. I didn't mean to upset you. I'm curious. We haven't had much of a chance to talk. I want to know what's going on with you. Internally."

"You mean emotionally."

"Well…" Aster shrugged.

"I do feel things for Case. Okay? And I do care about him, but I'm not *in* love with him."

"Okay." Aster cleared her throat. "Um…change of subject…you know the Enchanted Hierarchy Ball?"

Paisley's parents used to go to the ball every year, since it was mandatory for all faction leaders to attend. Her mother would wear the most stunning dresses. "What about it?"

"It's next week."

She'd lost her sense of time in that cave. "Right, it is that time of the year."

"Since Case is required to be there, Thatch is going, and…he asked me to go with him. I said yes." Aster peered at the dandelion she twirled between her fingers. "I think…I think Case would like to go with you."

Paisley glanced back at Case.

He tilted his head.

"I think I'd like to go with him, too."

When she looked back, Aster was smiling at the dandelion.

Paisley didn't know what to say about the fact that

she wanted to go to the ball with Case, so she fell silent. The quiet weighed on her, though. "What do you usually do here?"

"Thatch and I take a lot of walks."

Now Paisley gave Aster a knowing smile.

Aster's cheeks brightened. "What?"

"You know that demon worships the ground you walk on, right? The two of you spend a lot of time together?"

Aster nodded.

"Do you love him?"

Aster tripped on her dainty feet, and Paisley caught her. Eyes wide, Aster shot a quick glance back at Thatch, who jolted to a stop beside Case.

Now both demons were frowning.

From the space between them, Paisley read Thatch's lips: "What the hell?"

At the same time, Case said, "What the fuck?"

Paisley laughed out loud. She slung an arm around Aster's shoulders to turn her around and continue their talk. "Not fun having to face that question, or the insinuation of it, now, is it?"

Aster's eyes were still wide. "We haven't even had sex."

Paisley lowered her mouth to Aster's ear. "You don't have to have sex to fall in love." Aster's face was as red as a cherry tomato. Paisley figured she need not torture her with talk of demon sex anymore. "When you're not walking, what do you do to keep yourself occupied?"

Aster shot Paisley a look.

Smiling, Paisley bumped her hip playfully into

Aster's. "I'm not talking about Thatch."

"Well, Case let me plant a garden on his property."

Aster couldn't have surprised Paisley more if she'd said Case was teaching her kickboxing. "Really?"

"Yeah, do you want to see it?"

"Lead the way."

Aster led Paisley to the back of the property and to a sweet garden. The first row of flowers alternated asters and violets. "Thatch helped me to plant those."

Asters and violets. *Of course, he did.*

They wandered among rows of flowers and herbs. Bees buzzed around them while sampling each bloom. Butterflies rested on petals.

Paisley was sniffing a sprig of rosemary when Aster knelt beside her.

"I have to tell you something," she whispered.

"Go for it."

Aster laid a finger against a rosemary stem. A ladybug crawled onto her fingertip. "Thatch and I...we haven't had sex-sex, but we've done...things. Incredible things."

"Uh-huh."

"I...I showed him my lady bits."

Paisley fought not to show any amusement on her face. "Uh-huh," was all she said.

"He said it looks like a butterfly."

Probably the best thing you could ever say about a fairy's vulva. That or call it a flower. Thatch may not be part fairy, but he understood them.

"Uh-huh."

"And he thanked me for showing him."

Paisley blinked. *Holy shit. He thanked her? That's*

369

hot. "Uh-huh."

"Then he kissed it."

Paisley's instinct to protect Aster reared its head right then. She shot a look over her shoulder, right at Thatch. In the way the two demons backed away, she knew her eyes were red. "Did you want him to?"

"He asked for permission first, and I said yes."

The anger faded, and the demons glanced at each other. She had a feeling Thatch was thinking, *What the hell?* And Case was thinking, *What the fuck?*

"After a soft peck, he kissed it...a lot. He even used his tongue."

Paisley lifted a hand to fan her face. *Damn, is this what they call fairy porn?*

"And it felt amazing." The ladybug flew off Aster's finger. "I had a reaction. He called it an orgasm."

Paisley cleared her throat. "From what you're telling me, that tracks."

"Is that what happens when you're with Case?"

"Every time. Without fail."

"You feel that with sex-sex, too?"

"Yes."

Aster bit her bottom lip.

"You want to have sex with Thatch, don't you?"

Aster nodded.

"Then why haven't you?"

"He's worried about hurting me."

Paisley couldn't help but smile. Thatch was gaining massive points in her book. "Okay, so this is something that you don't know, because you haven't had a need to know until now, but it's time you learned something about your fairy dust."

"What?"

"Fairy dust heals, right?"

"Right."

"Well, sprinkle a little on your lady bits and a little on his—" She paused. Calling Thatch's cock his *manly bit* wouldn't work, because she'd wager there was nothing *bit* about it. "—penis." That was relatively safe. "And then the two of you can engage in all the coupling you want. He won't have to worry about hurting you, and you won't have to worry about feeling any pain."

Aster stared. "Fairy dust can do that?"

"It sure can. I mean, I never did it, being a fairy without fairy dust and all, but yeah, that's how fairies have sex with demons and ogres and centaurs and…well, you name it."

"Oh."

That "oh" carried so much.

Paisley chuckled. "You don't have to do anything until you're ready. I don't know Thatch at all, but from what I've heard and witnessed, he'll take care of you."

Aster smiled. "He will."

"Well, hopefully not tonight, because I'd like to have a slumber party with you. You in?"

"You mean human rom-coms, pedicures, popcorn, the whole nine yards?"

"The whole nine yards."

Aster squealed and threw her arms around Paisley. "I'm in!"

When Paisley told Case about their girls' slumber party, he said, "Are you cockblocking Thatch? Or me?"

"Not everything has to do with cocks, Case."

"Your slumber party better not have *anything* to do with cocks."

"Oh, there might be a couple."

He eyed her.

"On the big screen. Maybe a cock-shaped cake. There could even be lollipops."

A cock-shaped cake and lollipops were not part of their slumber party. Nor where there any cocks on the big screen. They watched *Never Been Kissed*, Paisley's pick and a friendly jab at Aster; *Beauty and the Beast*, Aster's pick and a friendly jab right back at Paisley; and *The Princess Bride*, a movie they both chose. While they watched the films, they gorged on popcorn, drank wine, did facials, and painted their toes. Then they stretched out on the huge bed in Aster's room that could easily fit Thatch and his large horns.

A few hours after drifting off to sleep, Paisley flinched awake, expecting her kidnappers to be standing over her, ready to torture. She lay in the dark, waiting for her heartrate to settle. Thirty minutes later, and she still lay there, unable to fall back asleep. She peeked at Aster, who was sleeping peacefully. Last night, Paisley had slept soundly. The difference between then and now was one thing—Case.

She folded the blanket back, slipped from the bed, and crept out of the room. Not wanting to wake Aster, she eased the door shut as quietly as possible. On tiptoe, she snuck down the hall and into Case's room. He didn't even open his eyes when she slithered beneath the blanket. His arm lifted, though, and he nestled her into the nook of his body.

"Is the slumber party over?" he asked.

"It is now."

"Are you okay?"

"Bad dream."

"Well, you're safe with me, love."

She closed her eyes and cuddled into him. "I know."

24

That Staircase Moment

Case

hey lay in silence for a long time. So long that Case was sure she'd fallen asleep, so he said something he'd been holding in since she'd returned. "Please stay."

He closed his eyes and repeated those two words. *Please stay*.

In the morning, though, she wasn't in bed with him.

He bolted upright. "Paisley?"

The room was empty, and so was the master bathroom.

Rising panic had him running out into the hall. "Paisley?"

The terror that yesterday and the night before had been a dream vised around his throat. He raced down the stairs. Thatch's and Aster's voices drew him to the kitchen. He shoved open the swinging door and halted as if that damn door had flung back and smacked him in the face; Paisley was there, sipping coffee. "Oh, goddamn it."

The three of them faced him.

"Since when do you curse using God's name and not Diablo's?" Thatch asked.

"Since now," he snapped.

He glanced at Paisley. She wore one of his black button-up shirts, cinched at the waist with a belt, turning it into a dress, and she looked damn beautiful. So beautiful that he couldn't take it. "Excuse me." He beelined to his private gym where he whaled his fists into a punching bag, imagining that he was plowing his fists into the motherprickers' faces who had taken her from him, made him believe she'd left him of her own free will. Killing them hadn't been enough. He would've preferred torturing them, like they had tortured her.

His knuckles bruised, but he didn't stop. His knuckles swelled, but he didn't stop. His knuckles split, but he didn't stop. He became aware he wasn't alone long after his blood spotted the punching bag.

Paisley leaned against the doorway to the gym, arms and ankles crossed. "Not that I'm not enjoying you like this—" She waved a hand. He'd removed his shirt a while ago. Sweat slithered down his back. "But what's going on?"

"Nothing."

She shook her head. "When you walked into the kitchen, you went from afraid...is it fair to say you were afraid?"

"That's fair."

"You went from afraid to surprised to relieved to pissed in five seconds flat. Then you escaped like a bat outta Hell and have been in here for thirty minutes, pounding on a punching bag and ruining your hands. Now, what is going on?"

"I thought you were gone."

"What do you mean?"

"I thought you were gone-gone, that your return had been a beautiful lie."

She stepped away from the doorframe. "I came back, Case. It was real." She closed the distance between them and slipped her arms around his waist. "I'm really here."

He tucked her closer to his body.

"I heard you last night."

He frowned. "Heard me what?"

"What you said...when you thought I was asleep. 'Please stay.'" She gazed into his eyes. "Case, I'm not going anywhere. Not against my will anyway."

"Good." He leaned down, yearning for a kiss to seal that promise, but she inched back.

"Paisley."

She pulled him over to a bench press and snapped a finger at it. "Sit."

Brow raised, he lowered onto it.

"I'll be right back." She left and returned a moment later with Aster. "Dust his hands."

Aster started toward him.

"My hands are fine," he said.

Aster paused.

"They're not fine."

Aster took a step.

"I don't need to be healed."

Aster faltered.

"You do, too."

Aster lifted onto tiptoe.

"My hands have been worse."

Aster peered between them, unsure of whether to proceed or retreat.

"Case, I swear to the Goddess that if you don't let Aster sprinkle some damn fairy dust on your hands, your hands are never going to touch me again."

Her threat had his eyes blazing with heat. He was eyeing Paisley when he said, "Cutie pie, can you bless me with a bit of that fairy dust of yours?"

"I'd be happy to." Aster sprinkled granules of fairy dust to his bruised, swollen, bleeding knuckles. It didn't take much fairy dust to heal them.

"Happy?" he asked Paisley.

"Very. Aster, can you give us some privacy?"

"Sure." Aster practically skipped out of the room.

Paisley grabbed one of his horns. "I need you to understand something."

He grinned. Yanking on his horns was definitely one of his kinks now. "What's that?"

"I care about your hands."

His hands stroked the backs of her thighs.

"No one else's hands have ever felt half as good as yours do on my body, but if your hands are beaten up, your knuckles split and bleeding, you won't be able to touch me."

"Oh no?"

"How could you if you can't even move your fingers?"

"No amount of pain could stop me." He pulled her closer until she sat sideways on his lap. "You caring about my hands…does that mean you care about me?"

"It does, you damn pain in the ass."

"Your nicknames for me never fail to turn me on."

"I'm being serious." She laid her hand over one of his. "Aster told me about the Enchanted Hierarchy Ball next week. I want to go. With you."

He blinked, not expecting her to say that.

"I want to be on your arm for all the Enchanted Hierarchy to see, and I want to dance with you. That's another reason you have healed hands."

He inclined his head. "A damn good reason."

The days leading up to the ball flew by. Now, Case stood at the bottom of the staircase, waiting for Paisley to come down. She and Aster had taken a whole day to dress shop. Thatch tagged along to guard them, but Paisley had forbidden Case from joining with the promise that seeing her in her dress would be worth the wait. He fidgeted in place, barely able to contain his excitement.

Aster had already stunned Thatch speechless in a voluminous black dress covered in large Monarch butterflies. Her violet hair was braided in loops on top of her head. Fake Monarch butterflies had settled on the ropes of her braids, making her look even more like a fairy. Her makeup was subtle—nude lips and bronze cheeks, but the effect was enchanting.

The click of heels above had Case turning away from Thatch and Aster as the two of them flirt-whispered. Paisley stood at the top of the staircase in a gold ballgown. Her purple-black hair was in an updo, too, but hers was slicked into a pretty knot. She wore a crown, but it wasn't the one she wore before. This crown sprouted from her hair in wavy, gold spires. Her lips were a seductive burgundy that would match her eyes if her vampire-wrath came out to play, and her cheeks were a dusty rose. More gold glittered on her eyelids.

Halfway down the stairs, she paused. "Is this that staircase moment in romance movies where the guy looks up at the girl in awe of her beauty?"

Case didn't even have to consider that. "Yes."

"Oh, okay, well…proceed." She continued down the steps.

At the foot of the staircase, she stood in front of him. He lifted a hand, but he stopped himself before touching her hair and ruining the neat strands, or her face and smudging the pretty makeup. "You look gorgeous."

"Thank you."

He lowered his hand. "You're wearing gold."

"I am."

"Gold is my color."

"No, your color is black."

He smirked. "Gold is the daemon faction's color."

"Yes, it is."

"Is this dress a statement?"

"It sure is."

"And what is it saying?"

"That *I* am aligned with the demon lord, and I don't give a damn how anyone feels about that." She stepped closer to run her hands down his vest. "You're wearing purple."

"I am," he said, mimicking her tone.

"Purple is my color."

"Mm-hm."

"What statement are *you* making?"

He slipped his arms around her waist. "That I will gladly bow down to the faye and vampyre queen."

"Well, you don't have to get your pants dirty. Standing by my side is enough."

"I will do that and more." He shifted to the side and held out an arm. "Ready to give the entire Enchanted Hierarchy something to talk about?"

"Born ready."

Everyone gawked when they entered the ballroom. Not only was it scandalous to see a demon and a vampire arm-in-arm, but faction leaders at that? They may have heard the rumors, but seeing it firsthand was another thing altogether. Then there was the fact that a demon and fairy couple entered behind them.

"Can you believe this?" a werewolf shifted whispered as they passed.

"What is she going to do? Pair off every fairy with a demon?"

"It's sickening."

"I'm glad I'm not a fairy."

"Could you imagine that tiny fairy with that huge demon?"

"He'd tear her in two."

Laughter.

Fucking assholes. Case glanced back at Thatch and Aster. No one had the fucking right to stand judgement over two creatures finding mutual love with each other. If they only knew how sweet and protective Thatch was with Aster. Or how he adored her. Or how he talked flowerology, watched rom-coms, and went on picnics with her. Thatch was so devoted to her, so head-over-heels. And she blossomed in his presence like the flowers she planted.

Case angled toward the two female werewolf shifters. "You have no clue what you're talking about," he growled. "The next time I hear you or anyone else talking shit about them, I will give you a world of pain. Pass that around."

He continued into the ball.

More whispers met his ears.

"I can't blame her for choosing him. He's a sex demon, after all."

"That has to be why she's still with him."

"Maybe he's brainwashing her with his cock."

Rage simmered.

"What could a sex demon see in her?"

"Her personality sucks."

"Literally."

"And her wings?"

More laughter.

Case envisioned tearing them all a new one, but Paisley fastened her arm to him and tugged him back to her side. "Don't. We knew this would happen. Let them say what they want about me. I don't care."

"*I* care."

"They're gonna talk. So, let them talk."

"You want them to talk?" He shifted in front of her. "How's this?" He cradled the back of her head with his hand and brought his mouth down on hers.

She kissed him back with no reservation, without restraint. Her body leaned into his. Positively melted. Her palms skated up his chest, and she slung her arms around his neck. Their tongues met, drawn to each other. He braced an arm across her back and hauled her flush to him. A moan slithered up her throat. The kiss was slow and all-consuming. He inched back enough to end the kiss, but their lips still brushed.

"Not yet," she whispered. "Not yet." And she consumed his mouth with a hunger that ignited him.

At the back of her head, he squeezed her skull gently with his hand. His arm constricted, tugging her even closer. Their tongues plunged, all sleek heat. They groaned into each other's mouth, unable to silence or sate their craving for the other.

Tongues tangling.

Lips locking.

Mouths moaning.

Tongues lapping.

Lips massaging.

Mouths tasting.

Tongues mating.

Lips tickling.

Mouths lavishing.

They inched apart, panting.

"Damn it, Paisley," he groaned. "I don't want to stop kissing you. I want to take you home and make out with your entire body."

She whimpered. "Don't tease me."

"I think you're the one teasing me."

She shifted back. "When the ball is over, you can take me home and make out with my body all you want."

"Now you *are* teasing me, because this damn ball is hours long."

"We don't have to stay for the whole thing. Long enough to be seen by everyone, mingle, and share a few dances."

"Can we skip to the dances? I still want to feel you against me."

"We'll dance soon."

Much to his disappointment, she stepped back.

"Oh, look there's Jude. Let's go talk to him."

"That is the weirdest segue out of that conversation."

She chuckled and pulled him toward Jude, who beamed when they joined him. He wore a black velvet jacket, and a flower blanket of black and crimson roses draped over his broad back.

"What'd you do?" Case asked. "Win the Kentucky Derby in Hell?"

Paisley backhanded him in the side. "Don't listen

to him, Jude. You look dashing." She fixed Jude's black tie. "I don't think I've ever seen you in anything but leather. You're handsome in a velvet dinner jacket."

"Thank you, goddaughter. And I'll have you know," he said while glaring at Case, "Aster made me this flower blanket."

Case smiled. "Of course she did."

Jude's head tilted toward the doors. His horse body shivered, and his mouth peeled part in a look that Case knew all too well.

Lena was entering the ballroom. She wore a shimmering, pearly-white dress that flowed like water down her body, pooling at her feet.

"Wow." Jude's single word of praise was a breath barely audible.

Case smirked at his old friend. "Why don't you ask her to dance?"

"Have you seen a centaur on a dance floor? We don't fit. And we don't dance."

"You can take her to another room or outside under the stars, and you don't have to waltz. Place your hands on her hips and sway. Surely you can manage that."

"Case." Paisley glared. "Jude, you taught me how to throw daggers and how to use a bow and arrow. It's my turn to teach you something." She laid her hands on his shoulders. "Put your hands on my waist."

Grumbling, he did as his goddaughter asked.

"Now—" She swayed to the side. "Follow me."

Jude sighed and followed her lead.

They swayed from side to side for a moment.

"You know this is called weaving?" Jude said. "Horses do this when they've been locked inside a stall for too long. This is actually degrading for centaurs."

"Dancing with your goddaughter is degrading?"

"You know that's not what I meant."

"But that's what you said." She stepped away from Jude. "Maybe dancing with Lena will be less degrading for you."

Jude held out a hand. "Sweetheart—"

"If you want to make it up to me, you'll ask Lena to dance, and you won't think it's degrading. You'll think it's beautiful, as beautiful as she is."

Jude swallowed.

Holy shit. The Centaur King was the horse version of head-over-heels for the Elf Queen. He was, what? Hooves-over-antlers?

"Jude, do what your goddaughter asks, or it's going to be *me* hurting *you*."

"Alright." Jude bent down and kissed the top of Paisley's head. "I swear I didn't mean how that came out."

She nodded. "It's okay. Try to have some fun tonight."

"You, too."

He made his way to Lena.

They couldn't hear the words he said, but the blush that colored Lena's cheeks before she accepted his hands told them all they needed to know. Centaur and elf exited through the doors and disappeared into the night.

Although Paisley smiled, she still radiated sadness at her godfather's words.

Case lifted her hand to his lips and kissed her knuckles. "I'll dance with you, love, and I'll be proud to do it." She didn't say anything as he led her to the center of the dance floor where similar creatures danced with one another.

The orchestra positioned on a stage played a waltz.

Case drew her close, placed one hand on her back, and held the other one out.

She stared. "I thought you said you don't dance."

"I don't dance at clubs, but all sex demons are taught to ballroom dance."

She snorted through her nose. "Sure, another technique to get laid."

"It's not a technique with you."

Gazing into his eyes, she laid her hand in his and settled her other hand on his shoulder. He inhaled and exhaled, and then he was carrying her across the dance floor in a smooth, effortless waltz. They fit together like two puzzle pieces. Their movements were as fluid as when they made love. Having Paisley in his arms like this made him feel light. So incredibly light.

When the waltz ended, the orchestra played a slower song.

He slowed their feet to a near standstill and lowered their hands. "Step closer to me."

She took a step, but it wasn't close enough.

"Flush against me, love."

She lifted her hand from his, wound her arms around his neck, and pressed into him.

He closed his eyes as he bolted his arms around her waist. "Just like that."

They danced, molded together, barely moving and not needing to.

"Isn't that the demon who found the dead fairy?

Talking with Thatch and Aster? Wren?"

Case opened his eyes and followed Paisley's line of sight.

Wren was with Thatch and Aster.

"That is. He's an ice demon."

"He's staring pretty intently at Seraphina."

"Who's Seraphina?"

Paisley shifted to the side and tipped her head to the opposite end of the room. "She's the flame-haired beauty standing with Queen Enya and Phoenix."

Case followed Wren's intense stare. Standing a step behind the queen was a young woman with hair exactly like a flame. Her roots were an iridescent blue that faded to white. That white gradually became yellow, and then orange, and then red down to the ends of her hair. She wore an ice-blue dress that happened to be the same color as Wren's skin.

"I met Phoenix when I went to the fier faction, but not Seraphina."

"Nor would you. She's the queen's ward. Her mother died a year ago, and Enya adopted her. Not out of love, mind you, but to keep the poor girl from flourishing. I dare say she's winning. Phoenix treats her like a sister, but Enya will never treat her like a daughter. I have no idea what the future holds for Sera, but she deserves more."

Case frowned. He peered from the girl to his young friend. The fact that he seemed taken by the flame-haired beauty was interesting. "Wren takes being honorable to an all-new level. He's not merely the most honorable among demons, or creatures, or men. He's the most honorable *person* I know. Thatch knows that if something were to ever happen to me, that I've named Wren as my successor."

"Really? Not Thatch?"

"Thatch has made it clear he never wants to take the throne. He's happy with being the right-hand to the demon lord. Whether that's me or Wren."

"There is something extraordinarily regal about him."

Case studied Wren. There really was. Wren wasn't as tall as Case, but how he carried himself made him appear as though he towered over everyone. And it wasn't because he viewed himself as being above anyone else. Rather, he was simply that graceful and noble. He didn't come by that easily, either.

"His parents died a year ago. He's the oldest of seven. All of his brothers and sisters are ten years and under. The smallest is a toddler. He's taking care of them all on his own."

Paisley laid a hand to her chest. "Goddess. He shouldn't have to bear that alone."

From across the way, Aster shivered.

Thatch embraced her and drew her close. Wren, though, lowered his head and retreated a step. "I'm sorry," Case read his lips. "That's me."

Paisley had said "poor girl" about Seraphina, and the same sentiment could be said of Wren. The poor demon knew rejection because of something he couldn't control. He knew what it meant to not be free to be himself around others, because the demon he was could make even the largest creature shiver and give them frostbite. Ice demons came few and far between. He was the only one of his generation.

Case tilted his head at Seraphina. "What kind of creature is she?"

"She's a fire elemental."

His lips tugged into a smirk. What were the odds of that? "Maybe he's found the one he wants to shoulder that burden with."

Paisley shook her head. "Unfortunately, the queen would never allow that."

"Why not?"

"Phoenix is a good friend of mine. She tells me about how her mom is forcing her to choose a male dragon shifter as her consort, despite the fact that Phoenix doesn't want a consort. Fortunately, she has a year before her mother steps down. But she knows her fate, and Sera will have the same fate. She's a princess. She'll be expected to marry a prince dragon shifter from one of the clans, and it won't matter how she feels about it, or what that prince is like."

Anger burned in his chest.

"One day, this damned Enchanted Hierarchy will change. One day, two different creatures will not be denied their love. Like Thatch and Aster. Or being with someone who gives them the freedom they've never known. Like Wren and Sera. Or finding a partner who could make dancing far from degrading. Like Jude and Lena. Or choosing their perfect sex partner."

She gazed into his eyes. "Is that one supposed to be us?"

"That one is definitely us."

"It's a nice thought. All of it."

"It's already happening, Paisley. Look at us. They may not like it, but they can't do a damn thing about it."

389

He indicated with a sideways nod of his head. "Look at Thatch and Aster." The two had joined them on the dance floor and were disgustingly cute. "They're not going to let anyone dictate whether they can or can't dance together, love each other. We're already changing things."

"I suppose we are."

"Before us, it was your parents. They paved the way."

She smiled. "And we're bulldozing the rest of it."

"Damn straight."

She laughed.

Then she jerked, and that laugh halted in her throat.

Something struck him in the chest.

He lowered his head to see the flat end of an iron bullet embedded in his jacket. His gaze jumped from it to the hole leaking blood below Paisley's collarbone. When he looked at her face, the smile she'd been wearing a moment ago was still there, but fading.

She jolted again.

A second bullet tore through her body and slammed into him.

In his arms, her body became limp.

To Thatch and all the demons there, he shouted, "Cover!" Then he wrapped his wings around Paisley. The second he did, bullets bombarded his wings in their effort to reach her. He dropped to his knees. In the cocoon of his wings, he stared at Paisley. Her eyes glowed red. Blood streamed from the two bullet holes, soaking the bodice of her dress.

"Stay with me, Paisley."

She sucked in a shuddering breath. "Tell

Zara…that I named Aster…as my successor."

"No." He shook his head, even as more bullets tried to break through the barrier of his wings. "You can tell her yourself, but that's not happening tonight."

"Case." Her voice croaked. "I enjoyed our time together."

He hitched her higher in his arms. "Don't you dare. We still have time."

She trailed a fingertip down one of his horns. "When I die, our arrangement will be over. Find someone else."

A million curses were on his lips.

The barrage of bullets ceased.

"Case!" It was Wren. "The coast is clear."

He withdrew his wings.

All around the ballroom, demons had put their bodies on the line to cover every fairy in attendance. The bullets that surrounded them revealed that had been necessary. Behind Paisley, a dam of iron bullets lay on the floor where they had fallen after bouncing off his own wings.

"Aster?" Paisley's voice was a whisper.

He searched the room. Thatch held Aster in his arms, tucked onto his lap. A sea of bullets circled him like a moat. While the attackers had targeted every fairy there, the heaviest firepower had gone to Paisley and Aster.

"She's okay." Then he shouted, "Thatch!"

Thatch twisted around.

"Get her to safety!"

Thatch was up and running to the exit.

"Case…"

He peered at Paisley. A stream of blood slithered from the corner of her mouth. Blood soaked her dress to the hips.

"Promise…you'll find…some—"

He shoved to his feet. "Shut the fuck up, Paisley."

She let out a half gasp, half groan.

He flew to his home faster than he'd ever flown before.

Demons had already gathered, creating a blockade around the mansion.

He ran through the door, shouting for Aster.

"Here! Here!" Aster already had her pouch of fairy dust in her hands and was opening it as she hurried toward him.

He dropped to his knees.

Paisley was no longer conscious. Her head lolled back.

Aster sprinkled large pinches of fairy dust onto Paisley's wounds with a shaking hand.

The bullet holes shrank before they disappeared entirely.

He lifted Paisley again, carried her into the parlor, and laid her on the couch.

"She lost a lot of blood," Aster said.

He stripped out of his jacket and rolled up his sleeve. "You know what to do."

25

A Damn Good Plan

Paisley

*P*aisley opened her eyes. Case no longer hovered over her in the safety of his wings. She stared at a ceiling that she recognized as Case's home. The pain in her chest and shoulder was gone, like a dream forgotten after waking. She peered around. First, she noticed the parlor in Case's home, and then Case. He stood at the table, with his back to her and hands braced. Tension rose off him in waves.

She sat up. "I was dying, and you told me to shut up."

He whirled around.

"That wasn't very nice."

In two strides he was in front of her. Then he was kneeling on the floor. He cupped her face in the most tenderest of embraces and consumed her lips in the most urgent of kisses. She had no choice but to grab onto his arms so as to not get knocked over from the full force of his passion. Her lips responded to his. She tried to give him the reassurance that his kiss so desperately revealed he needed.

His tongue came out. The hot, slick tip probed at the space between her lips, and she opened for him. As his tongue delved into the depths of her mouth, she moaned. His name played in her mind. She would've spoken his name if she could.

Finally, Case broke the kiss to say, "Telling me to find someone else is a pretty shitty dying wish."

"I'm sorry, but I thought about how bad it had gotten for you when I was kidnapped, and I didn't want that to happen again."

"If you had died, it would've been much worse than that, and telling me to find someone wouldn't have changed that." His gaze lowered to her blood-stained dress. "Come on. As much as I loved this dress earlier, I want to burn it now." He pulled her to her feet before picking her up.

"I can walk now."

"Will you fucking indulge me?"

She smashed her lips together. Part of her wanted to snap back, but after what had happened, she figured she owed him. Allowing him to carry her was the least she could do. In his bedroom, she didn't say a word while he peeled away her dress and wiped the dried blood off her chest with a damp towel. She couldn't look him in the eye while he did any of that.

"You have no idea how much I want to make love with you right now."

There it was again.

Make love with.

Make love.

Love.

Now she didn't dare look him in the eye.

"But there's a lot of people downstairs waiting to see you."

Finally, she met his gaze. "Who?"

"Everyone who cares about you."

He led her to the conference room, and she stepped in ahead of him.

The long table was surrounded by Thatch, Aster, Jude, Lena, Phoenix, and even Wren. They spoke in hushed tones as if they were at a wake. Silence descended upon them when they saw her. Then Aster shot out of her chair and slammed into Paisley with a fierce hug. Paisley fell backward into Case.

A whoosh of air left him. "Damn, cutie pie. You may be tiny but you can tackle like no other."

Paisley laughed softly.

Aster stepped back. "That was scary."

"I know. Are you okay? Were you hit?"

"No. The second Case shouted for cover, Thatch surrounded me with his wings."

Paisley peered over Aster's head at Thatch. "Thank you," she mouthed.

He inclined his head.

Jude came over next and embraced her, lifting her

onto tiptoe. "Don't scare us like that."

"I'm sorry," she whispered. "That wasn't my intention." She looked at each of them. "Where's Silas?"

"He's leading a group of vampires, joined with a team of demons," Case said. "They're searching for the culprits who did this."

She gaped. "Vampires and demons are working together?"

"For you, they are, but I don't think they're going to be successful."

"Which is why we're here," Jude said. "Zara called an emergency meeting tomorrow. This shit has gone on too long. We have to end it."

Wren stood. "Here in this room, there's four faction leaders. Five, really, because of you. Plus, two more demons, the fier faction's heir, and a fairy ready to fight. What can we do?"

There was only one thing that they *could* do. "Use me as bait."

Everyone resumed that startling silence.

Behind her, she sensed Case's rage building.

She closed her eyes, bracing for his response.

"Excuse me?" His voice was clipped, harsh.

"Hear me out." She opened her eyes to peer at the people in front of her. "They want me, and they want me to give up my thrones. We can use this as a tipping point, as the thing that breaks me." She felt Case moving slowly like a lion on the hunt. He made his way around her. His eyes were searing gold when she dared to look at him. "We stage a falling out. At the meeting tomorrow. In front of everyone, we have a blow up. We make it good. If we succeed in convincing the faction leaders that we're over, then all the factions will know about it within an hour. I'll go home, and you'll pull back your demons. Whoever is behind this will take the bait knowing you won't be around to protect me."

"And when they come? What then?" He eyed her. "They kidnapped you once. Over my dead body will they try it again."

"Well, I won't be able to keep you away, now will I?"

His jaw clenched. "No."

"Then you really won't be far, now would you?"

"No."

"So, when they come for me, and they will, you'll know, and you'll be there. Right?"

He pulled her to him. "Right."

Paisley returned home, despite the fact that she wanted to sleep the day away beside Case and despite the fact that he tried to keep her in his bed. But she told him that she couldn't stay. In order to make their plan work, they needed to start immediately and plant the seed that something was up. He groaned, muttered something about blue balls, but relented.

Now she was heading to her throne, ignoring the stares. They all knew why they were there. They all knew someone had attempted to assassinate her during the ball. They all knew the attackers had only targeted fairies, and here she was, unharmed and ready to take names. She sat, and her gaze connected with Case's. She let the rage for the people who kidnapped her, shot her, and tried to shoot Aster come to a boil; her vampirism came to the surface.

Case lifted a brow.

It's all a part of the game.

Out of the corner of her eye, she caught Jude watching. She met his eye, letting everyone see that her eyes were red.

Jude peered from her to Case and back. "What's going on?" he mouthed, although he knew.

She gave him a slight shake of the head, as if to tell him, "Not now."

The enchantress rose from her throne. "Thank you all for coming on such short notice. We were all there last night when an attack on Paisley and the faye faction unfolded—"

"Zara," Paisley said, "I have something to say."

Zara nodded for her to continue.

"I know that your agenda for today's emergency meeting is to discuss the attack at the ball, but none of that is necessary anymore."

"Why not?"

"Because I'm done."

Zara frowned as everyone murmured under their breaths. "What do you mean?" she asked.

"I'm done waiting to find out if I'm going to die like my father or like my mother. I'm done trying to convince anyone that I'm worthy of my damn thrones. And I'm done with people caring who I have sex with." She eyed Case. "So, I'm done. With it all."

Case's hands gripped the armrests. "You're done with me?"

"Yes."

"*I'm* not done with *you*."

His words clenched her stomach with longing. "Too bad," she snapped.

He pushed to a stand, because of course he would, and stalked toward her. "You want to do this here? In front of them?"

"Why not? They all know about us anyway. They all have an opinion."

"You think I give a damn what they think?" He stepped closer. "I don't, and you hadn't cared, either."

"I hadn't, and then I took two bullets last night."

"And I took dozens more. For you." He was closing in now.

She launched to her feet. "I didn't ask you to!"

"You didn't have to. I vowed to protect you."

"I don't fucking need you, Case! Get it through your thick, demon skull. I don't want you anymore!"

The look he gave her was dangerous. "You don't want me anymore?"

"It was just sex, Case. That's *literally* what you are."

His jaw clenched, and his spine lengthened.

She hated herself for throwing being a sex demon at him, but they had to make it convincing. Still, doing that was a real bitch move. "I don't want you, us, nothing. I don't want *any* of this." She lifted her hands in emphasis. "I don't want these thrones. I don't want to be queen. I don't want to die like my parents." She sent her glare to everyone there. "You all won. You didn't want me here, so I'm not going to be here. Tell your people that the hybrid queen is finished, because I am. I'm out."

She shouldered past Case and headed for the door.

"Go ahead," Case shouted after her. "Leave. At least this time I know it's real."

She continued to the door.

"It won't take me long to find someone to replace you and your stupid fucking wings."

She flinched to a stop.

Stupid. Fucking. Wings.

Those three words cut her a million times over.

Tears sprang to her eyes.

Case knew what would get the strongest reaction out of her, and he succeeded. At that point, it was impossible to tell herself that this was all a game. Not when the shame she'd harbored over her wings her entire life returned like a flash flood. The progress she'd made, the way Case had made her feel as though her wings were precious, were obliterated with three words.

Stupid. Fucking. Wings.

A tear zipped down her cheek. As it left behind a wet trail, anger stole her breath and resided in her chest. Fuck him for knowing the three words that'd knock her down, and fuck all of them for staring while those three words unraveled her.

She whirled around, and her wings erupted from her back. For the first time in her life, she didn't give a damn who saw them. She wanted them to see. No more would she hide them or herself. No more would she shrink herself to fit their standards. She was one of a kind and a motherfucking queen of two factions. If they didn't like her wings, they could line up single file and go straight to Hell.

Case's shoulders jerked back, and his hands fisted at his sides. She ignored his reaction to seeing her wings, because his words were replaying in her head.

Stupid.

Fucking.

Wings.

Looking him in the eye, while her own eyes blurred with tears, she said, "Fuck you." She glared at the other faction leaders. "And if anyone else thinks my wings are stupid or weird or freakish, you can go fuck yourselves, too. Have an orgy." She spun on her feet, giving them all a good view of her wings as she left.

Outside, she launched into the air and flew home. She slammed the front door of her house behind her and didn't bother locking it. Why lock it when the goal was to have killers waltzing through it? She tucked her wings away, changed into jeans and a T-shirt, and plopped onto her bed.

Not five minutes later did her cell phone ring. Case's name showed up on the screen. Exhaling, she answered the call. "You had to go there? You had to bring my wings into it?"

"I'm sorry, baby, but I did. That parting was what clenched it. No one could dispute your rage when you left. It convinced them."

She gazed at the ceiling. "I convinced myself."

"Paisley, you have to know I didn't mean a word of that. I adore your wings."

A clenching sensation in her chest.

"If my words made you doubt that, once this is all over, I'll prove myself again." He didn't give her a chance to respond. "My demons are pulling back as we speak. Thatch is moving into position. I'll be in position once we hang up."

"Where's Aster?"

"Promising to stay inside with Wren."

"Good. We should hang up. We don't know when they're going to make their move." For all they knew, her would-be assassins could be there already. Or they could let her sit and wait for days. Even weeks. They had no idea what the bastards planned to do now.

"Alright. Be careful."

"You, too."

She made a show out of being home alone. Every window that she could, she passed in front of. Even the kitchen window that she'd been avoiding. Fortunately for them, the fuckers who wanted her dead didn't wait. She didn't hear the door open, but she sensed them. All those days in that cell, she'd gotten good at sensing her kidnappers before they even opened the door at the end of the hall, in the tunnel of darkness that swallowed her cell. They were in her house now. Closing in.

That didn't take long.

After all, who could resist bait when it was setting itself up so easily as prey?

Stepping out of the kitchen, ready to face the three bastards who'd taken her from her home, from Case, from Aster, she came face to face with someone she did not expect. Her feet cemented to the floor. She never thought. She never had a damn clue. Still, she forced a smile.

"Uncle Silas, what are you doing here?"

"You know why we're here."

"We?" She sensed them behind her and peered over her shoulder at three of her four male cousins. Seeing them standing like that, she had a flashback to her time in the cell, eyeing her three kidnappers. Side by side like that, she was foolish to not have noticed it before. Gaze ticking from them to her uncle, she sidled away, seeking a position in which her back wasn't to a wall or to any of them. She needed to get to the middle of the hallway, where her uncle stood.

"It was you? This whole time?"

He only sneered.

"We're family."

He scoffed. "Family."

"Yes, family! You're my goddess-damned uncle."

"We don't share blood, and thank God for that."

She continued to back away. "It was all a lie, then? You pretending to care about me?" And that fucking hurt. She already didn't know whom to trust, but she thought the people she called family could be trusted. Turned out she had been wrong.

"What do you want, Paisley? A villain monologue?"

"I want fucking answers! If you want to kill me, you at least owe me that." And so she could delay him to give Case and his demons time to realize something was wrong.

"Fine. The truth is, I tolerated you because I thought there'd be no way your father would leave the throne to a hybrid. Then he told me he named you as his successor, so I did what I had to do to keep the vampyre faction in the hands of a full-blooded vampire. You were supposed to be there when he died."

"I *was* there."

"No, you were supposed to be there beside him. That dragon's breath was supposed to take you both out, and then the throne would've gone to me."

"Sorry to derail your evil plan." She made it to the perfect position to attack. Her gaze flicked around the space, wondering how she could tip Case off that her would-be killers were there. "Why didn't you kill me while you had me?"

"Because your murder would've ramped up the investigations even more."

"My murder will do that now."

"But who would look at me, the grieving uncle who had shown so much concern over his niece when she went missing? Especially when you so conveniently broke up with Case in front of the other faction leaders, painting him as the pissed-off jilted lover?"

So, the word about their so-called falling out had already reached the other factions. That was good, because it had worked in their favor to get her uncle to act, but they failed to realize that it would paint Case as a suspect.

"This is all on you, Paisley. Your death and Case being blamed for it will be all your fault. If you had just renounced your thrones willingly, like a good girl, the vampyre faction would've gone to me, and then you wouldn't have been much of a threat. I would've made you less than nothing."

Rage burned through her veins. "I am not nor will I ever be NOTHING!" She rushed at Silas and slammed him into the wall. Her cousins came for her, too, and she evaded them. From room to room, the five of them blurred. She fled and attacked, rammed them into walls, did everything she could not to give them an advantage.

Furniture smashed beneath them when she tackled one after the other. She didn't dare slow or pause or hesitate. If she did, they'd capture her and kill her. Glass shattered as they attempted to catch her, but she was too fast. The flash of metal caught her attention a millisecond before a blade sliced across the rose tattoo on her chest.

She bit back a cry.

In each of their hands, they gripped iron daggers. Their intended target: her heart. The tip of a dagger seared as it fileted the side of her shoulder when she twisted out of its path. Still, she didn't give them the satisfaction of hearing her yell in pain. Not after all the screams she'd given them.

She grabbed one of her cousins by the collar, whipped him around, and sent him flying. His body broke through the banister of her staircase, leaving behind a giant hole, sending wood flying.

A dagger came down on her lightning fast. She jerked her head to the side and raised her arms. The tip of the blade skimmed down her cheek like a scalpel. She caught her cousin's hands, halting the point of the dagger at her collarbone. Battling for strength and dominance would be a waste of time and open her up for attack, so she thrust her knee into his groan. As he crumpled, she pried the dagger from his fingers.

Room to room they fought.

Daggers swishing.

Blood spraying.

Blood dripping.

She backflipped to avoid a dagger, and its blade cut a long line down her leg.

Before her feet could touch the tile, a force bowled into her. Her back collided into the floor. One after the other, her cousins trapped her beneath their bodies. Mateo, in the middle, had his hands around her throat, squeezing, squeezing, squeezing. Bruno, with an eye patch over the eye she'd impaled, crouched to her right, holding down her shoulders. Diego, to her left, was trying to impale her with a dagger. She held his wrist back with her right hand while reaching for a splintered chunk of wood to her left. Her fingertips skimmed over the smooth wood, causing it to roll closer by a smidge.

Mateo's fingers dug into her neck. His palms compressed her trachea.

Bruno jerked her over the tile, away from the piece of wood.

Diego shoved all his weight down.

Her hand shook as she struggled to maintain her strength.

Baring her teeth, she stretched, desperate to grab the only weapon she had.

The front windows blew inward when Case came spiraling through them. He plowed into the vampires on top of her, scattering Bruno and Diego. Then his hands came around Mateo's skull. Bone popped as he wrenched Mateo's head around.

Once Mateo was dead, Case bent over her, staring at her with glowing eyes. "Are you alive?"

"Yeah," she wheezed.

"Good."

He jerked forward, and a low rumble came from the back of his throat.

"What is it?"

Crouched, he rotated.

A dagger stuck out of his back, impaling him to the hilt.

Paisley's eyes widened. "Goddess!"

He jumped to his feet as if he hadn't just been stabbed.

At that moment, Thatch shot through the shattered

window to join the fight.

Paisley wrapped her fingers around the dagger Diego had dropped. Scrambling to her knees, she caught sight of Bruno blurring up behind Thatch with an identical dagger raised. She threw hers. It flipped, hilt over blade, inches from Case as he wrestled with Diego, and punched Bruno in the heart.

Thatch was looking at her when an iron blade met the underside of her throat, and he lifted his hands as if in surrender.

The sharp edge of the blade coaxed her to her feet.

Case rammed a stump of wood from the staircase into Diego's chest.

Diego fell limp to the floor.

"Case." Thatch's voice was a cautious whisper.

Case spun to Thatch, who jutted his chin at Paisley. When Case whirled toward her and Silas, he froze. "You don't want to do that," he ground out.

"Oh, I think I do." Silas applied pressure to the blade.

Paisley winced as the sharp edge cut through the first layer of skin.

"If you do, I'll kill you a second later. You know I will. And you'll go straight to Hell. I'm friends with Hell demons. Rumor is my father's Diablo himself. I'll make sure you're tortured in the most excruciating ways for all eternity."

"Is that a promise?"

Case advanced. "That's a fucking vow."

Silas tugged her back.

The blade shifted.

Warm blood leaked down her neck.

"Watch it or her head is going to roll off her pretty

little shoulders."

Case's jaw clenched.

"I never would've guessed it…a demon and a vampire. Well, vampire-fairy." Silas scoffed. "You shouldn't be queen," he hissed in her ear. "You never should've been born."

Case advanced.

Silas tugged her back again.

More blood flowed.

"I told you to watch it, lover demon."

Case seethed.

Silas clamped a hand onto her shoulder. "On your knees."

She lowered into a small puddle of blood from her lacerated leg.

"Bring out your wings."

"No."

"Bring out your fucking wings!"

The blade sliced deeper into her throat.

In reaction, her wings sprang forth.

Silas laid the iron blade to her left wing, the one she'd tried to cut off when she was thirteen.

Thatch held Case back.

"Do you have any last words for each other?"

Paisley met Case's eye. "Remember that vampire-demon war I threatened you with when we first met?"

He dipped his chin in a nod.

"You better win it."

The blade seared into her skin.

Closing her eyes, she said a silent goodbye to the wings she had finally begun to accept.

Suddenly, she flew backward.

Her wings hid away, seeking safety, and a moment later, her back hit the floor. When she opened her eyes, Aster hovered above her.

"I never liked your uncle." Aster ripped open her satchel, grabbed a fistful of fairy dust, and generously covered Paisley's body with it from head to foot.

The moment her cuts were healed, she sat up to see silver spikes impaling Silas's eyes. "Holy Goddess, Aster."

Before Aster could respond, violet hands swallowed her shoulders, and she was lifted into the air. Thatch held her against his chest. "You were supposed to stay home!"

Home.

Not Case's mansion.

Not Case's place.

Not your room.

Home.

Paisley smiled.

"I wasn't going to stay home when everyone I care about is here. All three of you should've realized that."

They probably should have.

"And I love you, too."

Thatch stilled. "What?"

Aster laid a hand to his cheek. "I love you, too, you big dummy."

They sank into a kiss that had Paisley's eyelids widening.

Aster wiggled in Thatch's arms, and her thighs clenched his waist. He lifted her higher, and Aster gasped.

"Okay, whoa," Case said. "I don't want to see that."

Thatch removed an arm from around Aster and flipped Case off. To Case's laugher, Thatch's wings unfurled, and he headed for the door, not even breaking the kiss.

Case shifted to watch them go, revealing the dagger still sticking out of his back.

"Wait," Paisley shouted. "Case has a dagger in his back!"

A plop on the tile drew her gaze down. Aster's pouch of fairy dust sat there.

Case's laughter echoed.

Paisley retrieved the bag as Thatch tugged the front door shut behind him.

Case knelt on the floor, and she squatted behind him. "How should I—"

"Just pull the damn thing out."

So, she did. Then she tossed a couple pinches of fairy dust at the gushing wound. It sealed instantly. When she finished, Case yanked her into a kiss. She expected it to be intense, full of emotions from what had transpired, but it was achingly sweet.

He leaned back. "Remember how I said I want to make love to you?"

She nodded.

"Well, as soon as we deal with all this"—he rotated his finger in a circle to indicate the destruction of her home and her dead vampire family—"that's exactly what we're going to do."

"Sounds like a damn good plan."

Epilogue

You Coward

Case

One month later…

Case and Paisley continued to spend time together, at her house and at his. He'd been afraid that without the threat that had started their relationship, that things between them were going to change. Would she become distant? Would she stop needing him? Would she end their arrangement because no point in it existed anymore? Every night, he held her in his arms while she slept, and he wanted to believe that he'd have this every night for the rest of his life.

They ate most meals together.

They had plenty of sex and countless eye-crossing, on-the-verge-of-blacking-out orgasms. Their stamina hadn't taken a ding. Their desire for each other hadn't diminished.

They talked about everything and nothing.

They sparred for fun.

They had even watched the elf and orc *Pride & Prejudice* together.

Now, they were preparing to go to the Enchanted Hierarchy Council meeting. The sight of her in a black lace and sequin dress with a high slit stole his breath. A lace halter connected to one side of the dress. The other side was strapless, showing off the beautiful curve of her breast and her rose tattoo. Half the dress from bodice to mid-thigh was see-through, teasing him with her skin beneath that sexy lace.

"You have the most intriguing dresses."

"And you know how to pull off a vest like no other."

He chuckled softly, but the vision of her in that dress had stayed his feet and made his heart race with nerves. Diablo, he was actually nervous. *What kind of bullshit is this?*

She frowned. "Are you okay?"

"Fine? Are you ready?"

"I am."

He held out his arm to her, and she threaded her arm through his. Then he led her toward the door, but his feet came to a stop, and he couldn't get them to move again.

"Case?"

Fucking ask her, you coward.

He shifted to stand in front of her and caressed her arms. To get the words out, he actually had to take a deep breath. "I have a proposition for you."

"A proposition?" She tilted her head. "Okay…I'm listening."

"Marry me."

About the Author...

Love Fey is author Chrys Fey's pen name for all the smutty romance stories her muse insists she needs to write. And who is she to go against her muse?

Each story is a spicy love letter to readers looking for book boyfriends and girlfriends of all kinds.

Fey's characters all have a bit of herself in them, whether that's her Arian fire or chronic pain. And every story includes something she loves—nutcrackers, Halloween, references to *Pride & Prejudice* and *Pretty Woman*, witches, gargoyles, and more.

She's a proud cat mama, a nail polish junkie, and will always write and publish romance no matter who may be against it. In fact, if a story idea may get close-minded individuals mad, that story moves to the top of her list.

Website:
LoveFey.com